DRAGON FIRE . . .

From the blackness leaped a hatchling dragon colored the slick red of fresh blood. Its head reared back on a furious shriek, wings spread wide, gleaming claws ripping at the air. It doubled in size as it surged into the room, roaring a challenge.

The creature was every nightmare of dragons that ever was, down to the flames that spewed toward the ceiling beams from jaws powerful enough to snap a man in two. The throat pulsed as another gout of fire hissed forth. Another hideous roar, a flexing of the massive muscles in the wings—and blazing ruby eyes fixed on Rohan.

He had looked into dragon eyes before. None had been like this. Will drained from him like water into sand. He was nothing. The flames would burn him to nothing, crisp his flesh and bones to ash on the blackened stones. . . .

DRAGON PRINCE: BOOK III

SUN-RUNNER'S FIRE

MELANIE RAWN

DAW BOOKS, INC.
DONALD A. WOLLHEIM, FOUNDER
375 Hudson Street, New York, NY 10014

ELIZABETH R. WOLLHEIM
SHEILA E. GILBERT
PUBLISHERS

DAW TRADEMARK REGISTERED
U.S. PAT. OFF. AND FOREIGN COUNTRIES
—MARCA REGISTRADA.
HECHO EN U.S.A.

PRINTED IN THE U.S.A.

for my uncle
Gordon Alderson Fisk

SUN-RUNNER'S FIRE

PART ONE

Chapter One

719: Stronghold

The immense emerald caught and concentrated the fire of the setting sun into a fierce glow alive with green-gold light. Sunrunner though High Princess Sioned was, and skilled in the arts of the *faradh'im*, the other rings that would signify her rank among them were missing from her hands. For many years she had worn only her husband's ring, the emerald he had given her half their lifetimes ago. But tonight she could feel the rest still on her hands, as she'd told Lady Andrade: like scars.

There were others with her in the evening hush who wore *faradhi* rings. The three circling the fingers of her sister-by-marriage, Princess Tobin, were honorary; nonetheless they betokened considerable if informally trained power. Tobin's eldest son Maarken and his wife Hollis each wore six rings; Riyan, only son of Sioned's old friend Ostvel, had four. Had Sioned still worn hers, they would have numbered seven—but she knew quite honestly that her talents and her powers would have merited eighth and ninth rings by now. That she chose not to claim them was indication enough of where her loyalties lay.

She lifted her head and met her husband's solemn expression. He knelt directly across from her on a broad blue carpet flung over dry grass. A golden brazier rested in the center of the rug. Its wide, empty dish, supported by four carved dragon claws, was polished to a mirror's gleam. Before Sioned was a golden pitcher and a small matching wine cup. She did not look at the latter very long; she gazed into Rohan's face and, as always, drew strength from what she saw there.

Rohan was flanked by Maarken and Riyan; Hollis and

11

Ostvel sat on Sioned's right, Tobin and her husband Chaynal to her left. She thought of the absent others, and the reasons why they were not here. Her son, Pol, was back at Graypearl, safe on Prince Lleyn's island under the watchful guardianship of another Sunrunner and old friend, Meath. Alasen, Sioned's kinswoman and Ostvel's young wife, was at Stronghold, but she would have nothing to do with *faradhi* ways. Although she possessed gifts in generous measure, Sunrunner workings terrified her. Sorin, Chay and Tobin's third son, was far away, the only family witness to ceremonies that would tonight create his twin brother Lord of Goddess Keep in Andrade's place.

The gardens of Stronghold were silent. Princess Milar's fountain ran dry in autumn. Servants and retainers were within the great keep or the courtyards, making ready for departures on the morrow. Tobin and Chay were going home to Radzyn, Maarken and Hollis to their manor at Whitecliff. Ostvel and Alasen would stay the winter with Riyan at Skybowl to the north before traveling to Castle Crag, where Ostvel would assume his duties as new regent of Princemarch. By tomorrow evening Rohan and Sioned would again be alone at Stronghold, linked to family and friends only by her weavings of light.

A glance at the shadows told her it was time. She rested her open hands on her knees, staring down at the emerald. "According to ritual, Andry will call Fire in front of the senior Sunrunners, and Urival will give him the first ring. Then Air, and the second ring. They'll pause while Water and Earth are honored, and then he'll have to prove that he can conjure in Fire. At that point he'll receive the third ring. Just before dusk he'll weave sunlight to summon the *faradh'im* resident at Goddess Keep who wear fewer than seven rings. Once he's done that, the fourth and fifth will be given. With moonrise he'll demonstrate his ability to weave moonlight, and that will be the sixth ring. Up until that time, the ritual will be as it has always been."

Chay shifted and frowned, knowing what she was about to say and unable to hide his disapproval of his son's plans. Sioned gave him a sympathetic look. They had gotten over the initial shock of Andry's departure from tradition, but acceptance was something else again. It had been several days since Urival had spoken with Sioned on sunlight, his colors flaring with outrage at Andry's presumption. Certain other important Sunrunners, who would also be watching tonight from great distances, had been similarly informed so their startlement would not disrupt the proceedings. But Sioned wondered what the reaction would be at Goddess Keep itself when the resident *faradh'im* actually participated in the new ceremony.

"It won't be sunset there for a little while," Rohan said. "Chay, you've obviously got something on your mind. Say it."

The Lord of Radzyn shrugged, an attempt at casualness. "Maybe I'm just getting conservative in my old age. Change isn't necessarily a bad thing. And he seems to have his reasons."

"But why couldn't he have waited?" Tobin burst out. "He's moving too fast. The tradition of hundreds of years can't be wiped out in a single night!"

Rohan looked pensive. "You're both right, of course. But consider Andry's motives. He needs to do something to indicate how different his rule will be from Andrade's."

"She's been dead forty days," Sioned murmured. "Why does it seem so much longer?"

Ostvel used one finger to smooth a ripple in the carpet. "You've told me she was uneasy about Andry. But Urival is there, and knows him well. Urival will guide him."

"But not control him," Sioned replied.

"And did Andrade ever really control you?" Ostvel smiled faintly. "Andry's not a fool, Sioned, nor is he venal or grasping. He's a very young man thrust into a position of great power before being prepared for it. I think there are those among us who can understand his feelings and his needs."

Rohan nodded. "Oh, yes. I understand him very well. I've been the architect of a few departures from tradition myself, many of them in my first year as a ruling prince. And this is Andry we're talking about here—a boy you and I played dragons with, Ostvel. Nephew, son, and brother." His gaze moved around the circle.

Sioned cleared her throat and looked down at the wine cup. Slowly she filled it from the golden pitcher. Then she reached into a pocket and took out a small cloth pouch.

"Sioned—is that truly needed?" Tobin asked worriedly.

"I don't like the idea any more than you do. But Urival was quite specific. And it will only be a little bit. Not enough to do me any harm." Loosening the drawstrings, she took out a pinch of powdery gray-green substance. "Enough to fit inside a thumb ring," she murmured, quoting Urival. "The Star Scroll advises caution, but this amount is safe enough."

"According to a half-translated book hundreds of years old!" Maarken shook his head and glanced at his wife. Hollis did not shrink back from the sight of the *dranath* in Sioned's fingers, but her eyes were haunted. She had spent the journey from Waes to Stronghold freeing herself of addiction to the drug; even though she no longer craved it, the anguish of withdrawal was still evident in her pale lips and bruised eyelids.

"The conjure I'm working tonight is difficult enough to sustain under ordinary circumstances," Sioned reminded them. "This one will take all night. Urival says *dranath* can increase powers. And he sanctioned its use."

Before anyone could say anything else, she sifted *dranath* into the wine and swirled the cup to mix it in before drinking off half the contents.

"I remember how it felt," she murmured into the silence. "Dizziness for a moment, then warmth. . . ." Her cheeks flushed. There was another effect of *dranath*: sexual desire. Or perhaps, she thought suddenly as she sensed her gifts expand within her, perhaps the power was all-inclusive, and every aspect of body and mind was touched by the drug. She began to sway gently back and forth in response to the humming sensuality compounded of physical and *faradhi* power. There was a hunger in her, not only for the touch of her husband's flesh but for the unleashing of her talents. She understood the seduction of the drug. She had always been too afraid of it to analyze its effect, but this time she was going to work with the *dranath*, not against it—glorious and terrifying and impossible to resist. The demands of her body slowly faded, subsumed into an urge to ride the last sunlight and dare the shadows, to summon a torrent of Air, to call down Fire and in it conjure fateful visions.

Sioned told herself she chose to succumb.

Her disciplined Sunrunner mind brought forth a gout

of Fire into the empty brazier. The polished bowl seemed to ignite. And in cool flames half the height of a man there formed clear, detailed pictures.

Andry, too, had just called Fire. He stood in the courtyard of Goddess Keep, hands bare of rings. All the senior Sunrunners in residence stood in a circle around the bonfire he had just lit. Urival came forward and gave him the first ring. An instant later a whirlwind circled the courtyard, plucking at clothes and hair, blowing Andry's white cloak taut against his slim body. Urival bestowed the second ring.

Sioned's view of her old friend and teacher's face cleared as he faced the Fire. She frowned. Urival's stern features were set in flinty impassivity, all light gone from his golden-brown eyes. Duty and position compelled him to preside over this ritual; obedience to Andrade forced him to adhere to her choice for Lord of Goddess Keep. He was not happy with Andry's departure from that ritual. Sioned wished she could reassure him as those around her tonight had reassured themselves. But of them all—including Andry who stood apart—Urival was the most alone.

Sioned heard Hollis catch her breath as Andry made his first change in the proceedings, one that no one had been warned about. As Air continued to spin around him, he upended a pouch of loose, dry soil onto the stones. From his belt he took a glass flask full of Water. He unstoppered it and tossed it high into the air. A few glistening droplets escaped on its upward flight; as it fell it revolved and a stream of liquid raced the glass toward the ground.

Andry spread his arms wide. The spilled Earth was caught by a new whirlwind and rose in tightening spirals. Not a drop of Water reached the stones; the Air seized it, too. Shards of shattered glass glittered like small knives within the vortex as it narrowed. The bonfire swirled in wild patterns, and Earth, Air, and Water were consumed into its red-gold heart.

Andry had brought all Elements into play in a demonstration of power meant to dazzle. Or, Sioned thought, to warn.

He gestured at the flames and within them a conjuring appeared, a vision of Goddess Keep itself, sheathed in light. But it was not the golden glow of sunshine that danced over the walls and towers, nor the cool silvery gleam of the three moons. Icy white starfire frosted the conjured stones in sharp shadows and angles, making of the great castle a citadel of silent power.

Urival stepped forward, his face still expressionless, and slid the third ring onto Andry's finger. The young man allowed the conjuring to fade, and in his fine blue eyes was a sudden flare of anticipation.

Sunset light gilded the courtyard. Andry used it to weave a summons to the less-senior *faradh'im* waiting for his call. Dozens of them filed into the courtyard, bowing to Andry and nodding confirmation when Urival asked if they had felt his colors on the sunlight. The fourth ring was given.

At Stronghold, Sioned lifted her face from her Fire-conjuring to the last rays seeping over the western walls. As the fragile, rosy warmth touched her brow, she abruptly knew what Andry would do next, who he would speak to in proving his ability to ride the sunlight at great distances.

So. You're watching.

How could I not? Sioned replied, not allowing Andry's colors to drench hers in brilliant light. *Goddess greeting to you, my Lord.*

And to you, my lady. I see Mother there, and Hollis, and Riyan.

It was a very odd thing to be seeing Andry's face in the brazier Fire while hearing his voice at the same time in her thoughts. *Yes. And Rohan, Ostvel, and your father. All very proud of you, Andry.*

And very worried. Just look at Maarken's face! Don't be afraid of this, Sioned. I know what I'm doing. Andry hesitated. *Is—is Alasen—*

No. I'm sorry, Andry. She saw his face change slightly.

I should have expected it. Sioned, please help her to not be so afraid of what she is. She'll never find any peace otherwise.

She chose her life, Sioned reminded him gently, *and you chose yours.*

Yes. Of course. A brief pause. A line furrowed his smooth forehead and something close to suspicion vibrated through his colors. *Sioned—what is it about your colors tonight? I sense something, I can feel—*

The sunlight fades here, my Lord, she replied. *You'd best return.*

You—dranath! Sioned, are you insane?

With a mannered fillip she disengaged from the contact and nudged him back down the weakening rays of light. She sensed his anger at her use of the drug, and a deeper resentment that she could rid herself of him so effortlessly. She caught a glimpse of Pol in his thoughts and the unguarded hope that the son would not be as powerful as the mother. With the drug singing in her blood she could have followed him while maintaining the Fire-conjure simultaneously. It was an intriguing thought, not the least bit frightening. But she had the distinct impression that she *ought* to be frightened.

Andry had moved closer to the bonfire. No voices or other sounds carried through Sioned's Fire, but she knew Urival had asked him to tell what he had done, who he had spoken with. As the sun went down and they waited for the moons to rise—early tonight, which was the reason for holding the ritual now—Andry replied, then went round the circle of *faradh'im* and touched hands with each.

Sioned remembered the day she had done the same. With Camigwen at her side, joined in this achievement as they had been in almost all other aspects of their training, she had stood before each Sunrunner to receive greetings and smiles as she became one of them.

"Sioned. . . ." Ostvel's half-strangled voice brought her back to Stronghold.

She looked in bewilderment at his pain-clouded gray eyes, then at the Fire in the brazier. Within, called forth from her memory by her *dranath*-enhanced senses, stood not the present circle of *faradh'im* at Goddess Keep but a group of people in full sunlight, herself and Camigwen clasping hands with each. Amazed and fascinated, she let the conjured memory last a while longer, feeling not a bit of strain at maintaining it. She looked for the first time in eighteen winters at her beloved friend's face, the exquisite dark eyes and the delicate features, watched Camigwen complete the circle and stand waiting with her, practically dancing with excitement as Andrade came forward to give them their fifth rings.

"Sioned—please," Ostvel whispered, the words raw with emotion.

She gave a start and the Fire vanished. "Ostvel—I'm so sorry, I didn't think—"

Riyan was biting his lip, as heart-caught as his father but for a different reason: he had few memories of the mother who had died before he was two winters old.

"Forgive me," Sioned murmured, ashamed.

Ostvel shook his head. "It's all right. Just—a shock. Seeing her again."

Sioned thanked the Goddess that Alasen was not present, and returned her attention to what she was supposed to be doing. The Fire leaped up again in response to her call, just in time for those watching to see Andry finish the circle and rejoin Urival by the bonfire.

She felt the latter's colors as she had known she would, his moonlight weaving necessary to confirm Andry's Sunrunning. Again it was eerie to see his face as his voice spoke on skeins of moonrays.

He's a little miffed at you for using dranath, *you know. He'll get over it.*

Why did he go to you, I wonder?

A rhetorical question, I assume. Ah, dear old friend, I feel your sadness tonight. It grieves me.

Don't worry. I have a very large flask of your brother's best wine waiting for me in my rooms. I intend to get good and drunk tonight in Andrade's memory.

To blot out the memories, Sioned corrected gently. *I wish I could be there with you.*

No, you don't. You have quite enough to occupy you, High Princess. Well, on with the festivities.

And he was too suddenly gone. Sioned ached for him, watching his face in the Fire as he announced that Andry had indeed completed a Sunrunning to Stronghold. The fifth ring went onto his right thumb, a circle of the special reddish-gold used only by *faradh'im.*

It was a ring Andry had never before worn. Up until that moment, he had only been reconfirming skills already betokened by the four rings he had earned before this night. But now he was a full Sunrunner, with all the rings, the honors, and the responsibilities this implied.

And there would be more to come, too quickly.

The scene in the brazier continued, showing Andry as

he proved his skills at weaving moonlight, attested to shortly thereafter by Urival. Sioned did not know to whom Andry spoke; she suspected it would be someone approximately as far away from Goddess Keep as she herself was at Stronghold. The *faradhi* at Balarat in Firon, perhaps, or Meath at Graypearl. The idea was for Andry to prove his strength; from the expressions of respect on Sunrunner faces as confirmation came from Urival, he had succeeded admirably.

And here came the next departure from tradition. Instead of the silver ring, the sixth, given for the right little finger, Andry had directed Urival to present him with that plus another silver for his left middle finger. This reflected the change Andry had made in the order of things: now, the sixth would be for an apprentice, and the seventh for full abilities as a Moonrunner. Formerly, the seventh had been for the ability to conjure without Fire. Andry had not yet learned that skill from Urival. Rather than show himself lacking, he had altered the rules.

Sioned tensed as she stared into the flames. She knew what was to come next. The eighth had always been for the teachers, those skilled and subtle enough to instruct others in the *faradhi* arts. Andry conformed to ritual by calling forward a student of one ring and showing the boy, only a little younger than he, how to call Air. But rather than silver for the left thumb, Urival placed there another gold and pronounced Andry a Master—a distinction formerly reserved for the ninth ring.

Andry had other plans for that ninth ring.

As for the fifth, the Sunrunner's ring, Andry as a Master was now required to make the circuit of *faradh'im*. Sioned's apprehensions betrayed her. As she watched, the Fire flickered and she felt Hollis' hand on her arm to steady her. But the flames died out, leaving them all in the silvery darkness of moonlight.

"Sioned?" Rohan asked in a low voice, concerned.

"It's nothing." She reached for the cup of wine.

Hollis put her fingers over it, frowning. "You must rest. Please, Sioned. I know what *dranath* can do."

"I'm not tired. Not exactly, anyway." She smiled at her nephew's wife. "I'm all right, I promise."

"Hollis is right," Rohan said briskly. "We've seen enough. And you've certainly *had* enough."

"We have to see what he'll do," Sioned replied stubbornly. "I'll take a few moments to rest, but I've got to renew the conjure."

Maarken, leaning around Ostvel and Hollis, plucked up the wine. "I'll do it."

"No!" Hollis exclaimed.

"Don't be a fool!" Chay rasped.

"I want to know," Maarken said simply, and drained the cup to the dregs.

Sioned tightened her lips over a furious protest. She met Rohan's gaze. He said, " 'I want to know.' That's probably the most dangerous sentence in any language. More than one of us here tonight has succumbed to it."

She shifted uneasily. "Including you," she pointed out.

"Of course." *And you, my Sunrunner witch of a High Princess,* his eyes said.

Turning to Maarken, she asked, "Well? What's it like for you?"

"Just as Hollis described it. Dizziness, and spreading warmth. . . ." He looked startled, then smiled slightly. "And the most amazing need to be alone with my wife—and *not* just because we're so short a time married."

Hollis blushed in the dimness. "That will pass," she told him.

"Goddess, I hope not!" But his laugh was strained. "This is the damnedest feeling! Like I could use my thoughts to change the tides!"

"Don't try it," Sioned warned. "Maarken, be careful."

"I'm not saying I *want* to. I just feel as if I could." He rubbed one hand over his face; the other was immobilized in layers of bandages, wrist broken in his battle against the pretender. "So this is what it's like to be a sorcerer."

"Partly, I suppose. But you haven't the gift for it." She glanced at Riyan, who did. "Don't *you* go getting any ideas."

"Not if the moons fell out of the sky." The young man eyed the empty wine cup warily, his right hand worrying at the rings on his left. Then he shook himself and looked across the carpet at Ostvel. "Father . . . I'm glad I got to see Mother tonight. I didn't know she was so beautiful."

Ostvel stared down at his hands. "Her face *and* her spirit."

Chay's eyes were fixed on his eldest son and heir, dark brows shading his gray eyes nearly black. When the young man's gaze lost focus and he turned pale, Chay demanded, "Maarken—what is it? Tell me!"

Rohan gripped Maarken's elbow. "What are you watching?"

He gave a start at the touch, gulping in a great lungful of air. "I—I think somebody's watching *us!*"

Riyan held both hands out before him. They were trembling. His eyes—Camigwen's eyes, dark velvet brown with bronze glints—were glazed with pain. "My rings," he whispered, staring at Maarken. "Just like when you were fighting Masul and sorcery was used—"

Ostvel jumped to his feet and hauled his son up. They stumbled toward the silent fountain, where Ostvel plunged Riyan's hands into the shallow pool of brackish water. Maarken was gasping for breath, supported by Rohan and Hollis. Sioned wove moonlight with desperate speed, but could sense nothing and no one along it.

Then she looked straight up at the stars.

Beautiful, aren't they? a voice said in her mind, rich with mocking laughter. *And you know how to use them, High Princess. Why not use them now to find me? You've already made an excellent start by drinking that wine. You're beginning to understand power—the kind your son will have once he's grown. Oh, yes, we know all about him, your Sunrunner child who also has the Old Blood flowing through his veins. Someday I'll figure out whether he got it from you or his princely father.*

Wh—who are you? Sioned didn't dare think. She drew into herself, knowing that to accept the invitation and weave starlight was to court disaster.

Who? You'll have to wait some years before you find that out. Or perhaps you meant "what." That's something you know very well, Sunrunner.

What do you want?

I'll let you puzzle that one out too for some little while. We're not quite ready yet, you see. Masul was an interesting beginning, but only a feint. The real battle is before you, High Princess. Do you think you're up to it? Do you honestly think you can prevail against the ones you call sorcerers?

And the last thing she heard was gleeful laughter on a breath of starlit wind.

***

Morning sunlight spilled across the floor as Ostvel gratefully accepted a winecup from Alasen, who settled uneasily on a chair near him. "Can you tell me about it now?"

"As much as I know." He took a long swallow and closed his eyes. "Which isn't much."

"But everyone's all right."

"Yes. Still stunned, I think, but not from anything Andry did." He looked at Alasen, touched her free-flowing hair. It was an unusual shade of gold-lit brown, straight and fine as silk thread. Her cheeks were pallid with worry and her green eyes, the same shape and color as Sioned's, were strained. He made himself smile at her. "Don't look so grim. There's plenty of power among us to use against these sorcerers, you know."

"Riyan doesn't much like the idea of being of their blood."

"But we learned something very useful last night." He explained his son's experience with his rings. "So at least we can know when they're working their spells."

Alasen shivered. "I can understand why they'd be watching tonight, with Andry's ritual taking place. But why here? Why not Goddess Keep?"

"Perhaps they consider what happens here more important. I don't know. Sioned says there was no contact, no communication. Besides, can we be sure they weren't watching Goddess Keep as well?" He drank again and set the cup aside. "We missed the last part of it," he added idly. "I would have liked to see him conjure with light from the stars."

"With knowledge gained from the Star Scroll?" Alasen shook her head. "He's doing dangerous things, Ostvel. And there will be more." She rose and went to the windows, where dawnlight seeped across the Desert far below Stronghold.

Ostvel gazed at her for a long, silent time. It would be difficult to find a woman more different from his first wife in either looks or character; where Camigwen's personality had been all angles and bright light, Alasen was made of intriguing spirals and a more subdued glow hinting at shadows. In Camigwen there had been no fear, but Alasen had that summer discovered absolute terror. What for Cami had been joyous and exhilarating gifts were to Alasen things to flee from as fast as she could. Both Sunrunners, one trained and one who would never be trained. That he loved both women was no surprise. That both loved him was a blessing from the Goddess. And he knew that Alasen's love for Andry had nothing and everything to do with the fact that she had Chosen him instead.

He rose and stretched, then went to slip an arm around her slender waist. "I do love you, you know," he murmured.

She tilted her head back and smiled up at him. "And I love you. So no more chatter about how scandalous it is that I'm half your age, hmm?"

He laughed. "Well, it *is* a scandal. A little one, anyway. But I'm feeling younger all the time."

Alasen pressed closer to him. "Rohan left orders that no one was to be disturbed until noon at the earliest. Are you feeling *that* young, my lord?"

"My lady, by the time we get to Skybowl for the winter, you'll have made me eighteen years old again." The sunlight rippled along her hair and he buried his lips in its silken thickness. Alasen's hands skimmed up and down his back, lingering over the muscles of his shoulder. Ostvel smiled into her hair and bent his head to take her mouth with his own.

All at once she broke away from him and cried out. Sun flooded her white face and sank its light deep into her green eyes. "No," she whispered. "Andry, please—no!"

Ostvel caught her up in his arms and carried her to the bed. Once out of the direct glare of the morning sun, she stopped trembling. He smoothed back her hair and waited for the terror to fade from her eyes.

"I'm sorry," she breathed. "It was Andry—he—"

Ostvel cursed himself. He ought to have remembered, and kept Alasen out of the sunlight. At dawn after the ritual, the new ruler of Goddess Keep wove the colors of all *faradh'im* present into one vast fabric of light, spreading it across the continent and as far away as the islands of Kierst-Isel and Dorval. With Andry dominant, directing the flow, every Sunrunner everywhere was touched. Through the weaving it was announced that a new Lord of Goddess Keep had been accepted, having demonstrated his worthiness to wear the ten rings. Ostvel ought to have realized that of all *faradhi*-gifted people, Andry would have singled out Alasen in particular for his touch.

"I should have known," he told her now. "He loves you. And it's the only way he can touch you."

"Sioned must tell him never to do it again." She raked her hair back from her brow and sat up. "Ostvel, I don't want him intruding in our lives!"

Ostvel spoke very softly. "He'll always love you, my dear. And I know that you'll always love him—just as you know I'll always love Cami." He took both her hands in his. "Both of us must undertake not to be jealous."

"I Chose you, not him. He'll have to accept that."

Ostvel pressed a kiss into the warm hollow of each palm, and smiled.

***

Sioned did not tell Rohan about the words exchanged on starlight. She told no one but Urival. And he promised that as soon as he could, he would come to Stronghold —with a translated copy of the Star Scroll.

Chapter Two

721: Castle Crag

On taking possession of Castle Crag in the spring of
720, Ostvel had set about several formidable tasks—
the most immediate of which was to learn his way around
the labyrinthine keep.

After spending much of his youth at Goddess Keep, an
imposing and logical structure, he had become chief steward of Stronghold, a castle built for defense with a correspondingly efficient design. Skybowl, his holding for
fourteen winters, was a small place without need or opportunity for eccentricities. But his new home was something else again.

Cut into the side of cliffs above the Faolain River and
built out from those cliffs in cantilevered overhangs, Castle Crag was a maze of rooms, halls, suites, staircases,
and the most exquisite oratory in all thirteen princedoms.
Ostvel had taken his first tour of the place guided by a
small battalion of functionaries, all eager to point out the
wonders of his or her own domain within the keep. Their
chatter had prevented him from gaining any reliable knowledge of where he was, let alone where he was being led.

That night he had frowned over his problem, knowing
that the next day would show him as ignorant of the
castle's environs as he had been at the moment he'd
arrived. The servants, he knew, would be watching for
mistakes; that afternoon Alasen had lost her way after
what she suspected was purposeful misdirection on the
part of a page. At midnight therefore he had enlisted her
and their Sunrunner, an old friend of his named Donato,
in a secret expedition through the twisting corridors.
Each of them chose an essential location. Armed with a
collection of trinkets—bronze, gold, silver, copper, blue

25

ceramic—privately color-coded to each destination, they spent the rest of the night seeking out the best routes and at all important junctures left behind a vase, a candlestick, a figurine, a dish on convenient tables and shelves.

"Copper to the kitchens," Alasen had recited as they finally fell into bed, exhausted but well-pleased with their trick. "Gold to your library, silver to mine, bronze to the great hall, blue to the gardens. But, Ostvel, what if somebody moves everything tomorrow morning?"

"You forget, my princess, that when you began rearranging our suite you ordered that anything we changed or added be touched only to clean it."

"Did I?" She chuckled. "That *was* clever of me."

The next morning all their signposts were still in position. With supreme confidence they strode through their new home. The servants were astounded. Donato even waited three whole days before rearranging the entire system. But the joke had been on the Sunrunner; *he* was the one who had forgotten the direct route to the back gardens.

Now, a year and a half later, Ostvel rarely needed a glance at the trinkets to remind him where he was. Still, every so often he found himself in an unfamiliar corridor without the faintest idea which hallway led where. On one of these confused wanderings, too embarrassed to ask directions from servants, he had discovered the archives.

He never ceased being grateful to the impulse from the Goddesss that had made him go through the archives himself rather than send them untouched to Stronghold or Dragon's Rest. The records of five High Princes—Roelstra and his ancestors—and a Regent of Princemarch were stored at Castle Crag, enough parchment to fill a square measure of bookshelves. He had been working methodically back through them since finding the locked door that led into a series of dark, dry chambers. Into history. At first he had thought to have Alasen help him, but one of his first discoveries had quashed that notion immediately. For in the archives he had found Pandsala's precise, logical, oh-so-secret list of her murders.

Rohan had told him the bare minimum of facts: that during her regency Pandsala had removed several persons she considered detrimental to Pol's future as High

Prince. The disclosure had been brief and bitter. Ostvel had not pursued the matter despite horrified curiosity about what Pandsala had done and how. But he had at last understood why she was a forbidden topic around Rohan and Sioned, and why they had not gone to Castle Crag for her ritual burning.

Roelstra's daughters, he told himself, shaking his head as he locked his library door and sat down at the huge slate-topped desk. One of a score of keys unlocked yet another coffer of most-secret records. The lesser archives were being sorted by trusted scribes. Treaties, trade agreements, marriage contracts, the everyday effluvia of running a large and powerful princedom; none that held any dangers. But all that was in the locked coffers Ostvel read himself. *Roelstra's daughters*, he thought again; the labeled dates told him that within would be Roelstra's concealed records about Ianthe, Feruche, and Rohan.

And perhaps what he feared to find: record of Pol's true ancestry.

He flinched when rusted hinges squealed a protest as he raised the lid. At least it had obviously not been opened in years, probably not since Pandsala received the keys he himself now possessed. He wondered what she had felt on reading this parchment giving Feruche to her hated sister, or this copy of a letter from Roelstra congratulating Ianthe on the birth of her first son, Ruval. Ostvel stared at the name, remembering with terrible clarity the first time he had seen it: on Pandsala's list of murders.

He had decided to investigate the most recent records first after finding the archives, and chose a coffer bearing Pandsala's seal and the date 719. The top layer had been her private diary, sporadic entries regarding politics and their implications for Princemarch and the Desert; internal difficulties, how she had dealt with them, and what she suspected motivated them; and, dated in the summer of that year, a heartbreaking series of jotted notes regarding Pol.

I am blessed by the Goddess with the presence of the only two I have ever loved. Pol is all I hoped he would be, and more besides. I love him more than I would have loved the flesh of my own flesh. His mother could not love him more. He ought to have been mine! Rohan is as I remember him: as perfect and golden as his son. They both should have been mine. Instead they belong to Sioned. Why does she have everything and I nothing?

But those words had not given him the shock of the other parchments, drawn up as if formal Acts of her Regency. He had found them at the bottom of the coffer, neatly folded, each penned in her elegant script. Sentences of death. And at last he had learned the how of her murders, and the why.

He could see the documents as clearly as if they were spread out before him, could feel again the horror of first reading and realizing what she had done to her own blood on behalf of a boy she did not know was her own blood.

An induced miscarriage for Naydra, depriving her and her lord of an heir for Port Adni, which would become a Kierstian crown holding after Lord Narat's death. Slow poison lanced through the parchment of various letters sent to Cipris, before the latter could marry Halian of Meadowlord and produce a legitimate princely heir of Roelstra's blood who might one day challenge Pol. A hunting accident to dispose of Rusalka before her marriage could produce an heir. The same reasoning applied to Pavla; the method, the gift of a necklace whose prongs were tipped with a slow poison. Rabia, wedded to Lord Patwin of Catha Heights, had borne three daughters and died in childbed of the third, who survived her—but there had never been a breath of rumor that the death had been anything other than natural. Yet she was on Pandsala's lethal list, too, the means of her death delineated in bold pen strokes. Hired assassins in Waes had rid Pandsala of Nayati before she, too, could marry and produce offspring. Of Roelstra's eighteen daughters, the Plague had taken five; Pandsala had eliminated five more; five still lived. Of the other three, Kiele had been executed for the murder of a Sunrunner and Pandsala was dead of sorcery. Ostvel himself had killed Ianthe.

But Pandsala's crimes had not been limited to her sisters. An arranged accident for Obram of Isel, Saumer's only son, had left Arlis, grandson of both Saumer and Volog, heir to both princedoms. Thus the island would eventually be united under Sioned's kinsman. Reading this, Ostvel had thanked the Goddess he had not asked

Alasen to help with the archives; her adored elder sister Birani was Obram's widow.

There were similar cold-blooded horrors to be found in Pandsala's records, all of them with justifications that were perfectly reasonable by her standards. None of her murders had ever been suspected, and some had been positively brilliant in their cunning. For example, she had marked Tibayan of Lower Pyrme for death because of his intransigence regarding certain issues. He had been one of those rare people to whom a simple bee sting was poisonous. Pandsala's notes showed that in the summer of 714, she had arranged for a whole swarm of the insects to be set loose in his private chambers. This was her most creative kill, and even through his nausea at her logical reasoning and matter-of-fact death sentences, Ostvel was compelled to admire the woman's ingenuity.

Success in another murder had not brought the desired result. Ajit of Firon's death—a seizure of the heart caused by poison, according to Pandsala's record—had left that land without a prince. But Firon had not gone to Pol, despite his superior blood claim. Ostvel now understood the reason Rohan had given it instead to Prince Lleyn's younger grandson. Though he had unwittingly profited by Pandsala's other political executions, on discovering the reason for Ajit's death Rohan had refused to take the princedom Pandsala wished to give him and Pol.

Pandsala's final murders, however, had produced exactly her intended result. The deaths of Prince Inoat and his son Jos had left Chale of Ossetia without a direct heir. His niece, Gemma of Syr, married Sioned's nephew Tilal, and when the old man died they would become Prince and Princess of Ossetia. Pandsala had thought Gemma would wed Tilal's brother Kostas, heir of Syr, and thus merge the two princedoms; but her major aim had been to bring yet another princedom under the control of Pol's kinsmen. Through her efforts, Sioned's kin would rule Ossetia, Syr, and Kierst-Isel; allies would possess Dorval and Firon; Pol himself would hold the Desert and Princemarch. Eight out of thirteen princedoms: not a bad return for a mere eleven murders, Ostvel thought acidly.

Pandsala had had four more deaths in mind. But Kiele had destroyed herself without any assistance. Ostvel wondered if an earlier attempt had failed—which led him to speculate about other murders she might have attempted that were not listed. But whatever her other vices, stupidity had not been among them. Eleven deaths in fifteen years were enough to fulfill most of her ambitions for Pol. More might have attracted suspicion.

It was the last entry that had given him the most worry. *Ruval, Marron, and Segev, bastard sons of Princess Ianthe: locations unknown. They must not be allowed to challenge Pol for possession of Princemarch.*

Ostvel had stared long and hard at the names, as if ink on parchment could give him sight of their faces. He knew what everyone else knew: all three had different fathers, young lords of surpassing physical beauty; all three had been born at Feruche—Ruval in 700, Marron in 701, Segev in 703; all three were thought long dead. What he and only a few others knew was that they had escaped the destruction of their mother's castle in 704, carried off by loyal guards on horses he and Sioned and Tobin had ridden to Feruche, stolen from them in the chaos of Fire and panic that night. And he shared the knowledge with even fewer people that they were Pol's half-brothers.

These three, of all persons living, Pandsala would have killed if she could.

He glanced over to the carved wood paneling where a secret hiding place kept that parchment and certain other dangerous documents safe. Old Myrdal, long-retired commander of Stronghold's guard, had found that niche and many other interesting things when she'd paid him a visit during the first year of his residence here. She had gone through Castle Crag stone by stone and her expert eye had found not only the sliding panel in Ostvel's library, but hitherto unknown doors, passages, and stairs.

"I doubt Roelstra knew about any of this," she had remarked as they explored a concealed corridor one afternoon, her limping steps assisted by a dragon-headed cane. "He killed his father, you know, when he was barely ten. Poison, it's said. If he'd waited for a natural death, he might have learned Castle Crag's secrets. But you can see by the dirt and the mess that these haven't been used in a very long time. Probably over fifty winters."

Ostvel had personally overseen the walling-up of every

concealed passage, staircase, and chamber. The servants followed his orders, agape at the revelation of a world within the world they had known all their lives. But certain things he had left as they were, known only to himself and Alasen. The hiding place in his library was one of them; a similar secret compartment in the walls of her office was another—the reason she had chosen the room, in fact. And he left one passage clear, leading from their private chambers to those reserved for Pol when he was in residence, and thence to a concealed exit from Castle Crag. Myrdal had insisted on the latter. "You never know," she had reminded him, "when you might need to get in or out in a hurry with no one the wiser."

Not that Castle Crag had been even remotely threatened in centuries. Ostvel hoped that as he went deeper into the archives he would learn who had built it, when, and why. But for now he was more concerned with recent events, and thus returned his attention to the coffer containing documents from the years just before Pol's birth.

Roelstra and Ianthe's alliance with the Merida was nothing new to him, nor was the record of their difficulties keeping those descendants of ancient assassins in line. He smiled a little as Roelstra's anger spilled over onto parchment in venomous written accounts of the negotiations. Another congratulatory letter to Ianthe on news that she was pregnant again—with Marron, Ostvel deduced—was followed by a return note from her asking about rumors of Plague.

Ostvel set that page aside, unwilling to relive a spring and summer twenty years past, when he had helplessly watched Camigwen's agonizing death. The next parchment was a copy of an agreement drawn up by Rohan and Roelstra setting the price for the *dranath* that had cured the Plague. Through his merchants, Roelstra had demanded and received a colossal sum for the herb that grew only in the Veresch. His following letter to Ianthe had been full of amazement and fury that Rohan had produced the required amount of gold. Neither had ever guessed that it had not come from emptying his treasury, but by using dragon gold.

But the cure had come too late for his Camigwen,

Rohan's mother Princess Milar, Maarken's twin Jahni, thousands of others—and Sioned's unborn child. Ostvel's jaw muscles tightened. Rohan had always suspected but never been able to prove that Roelstra had withheld the drug until certain of his enemies were dead of Plague. It was the Goddess' blessing that Rohan had not been among them.

He dug deeper, finding a letter in which Ianthe exulted at the birth of her second son, another asking her father to arrange an attack on a trade caravan—and a copy of his testy reply suggesting she get her pet Merida to do it. He wondered at that, then realized that such an attack would bring out the garrison of Desert troops which had been stationed below Feruche at that time. Anything Ianthe wished Rohan to know could be told to the commander, who would tell his prince. There had been just such a gambit when dragons had flown over Feruche in 704; nothing was more calculated to bring Rohan to a place than the chance to see dragons. And when he had ridden up to Feruche, Ianthe had captured him.

Another several layers of parchment dealt with Segev's birth, Ianthe's subsequent ostentatious celibacy, her plan for getting Rohan out of Stronghold to view the dragons. Ostvel nodded; his guess had been correct, then. She obviously intended all at Feruche to know that the child she carried that year was Rohan's; her smug letters to her father gloated on that very subject. But did anyone know this child was Pol? He held his breath when he came upon her last letter.

It's rumored that Sioned is pregnant—although I saw no signs of it when she was my guest here. I hope one of my guardsmen fathered the child—did I send you details of how often they entertained her? If I forgot, remind me to tell you in person. You desired her at one time, I believe? So it should be highly satisfying to watch her public disgrace. Whatever she whelps, it will be my son and not hers who is Rohan's acknowledged heir. Soon I will hold the next High Prince in my arms, and all will know him as your grandson. He'll rule the Desert after we've disposed of Rohan, Maarken, Andry, and Sorin—and anybody else who might claim either land or stand in his way. I'll write again after delivery of our little shining star. And who knows—he might even inherit the Sunrunner gift that appears in Rohan's family!

How odd, he mused, that Ianthe had used the word Sioned had chosen as the boy's name. "Pol" meant "star." Ostvel reached into the coffer once more. Its final contents consisted of a bit of torn parchment bearing words in Roelstra's hand: *Born to my daughter Ianthe, a son, my grandson, heir to Princemarch and the Desert, the next High Prince. May he live a hundred winters and destroy an enemy during each of them—especially his elder brothers.*

Ostvel shivered. What a legacy to leave a child. A legacy Pandsala had sought to fulfill, even to planning the murder of her own nephews, Pol's half-brothers.

But they still lived. They would have to be found and their threat eliminated. They were too dangerous. With a few exceptions—gentle Danladi, quiet Naydra, cowed Moria and Moswen—Roelstra's offspring were uniformly ambitious, arrogant, and scheming. Thirteen of the sisters were dead, but one still lived who was definitely her father's daughter.

Chiana was at last a princess in fact. Her marriage to Halian of Meadowlord had given this formerly powerless (therefore relatively harmless) woman a taste of ruling a whole princedom. Chiana had in two brief years grasped as much of her husband's power as she could. When Clutha died, she would rule, not Halian. Ostvel suspected she would never rest until her son, born this past spring, was High Prince. Though all Roelstra's daughters had renounced any claim to Princemarch for themselves and their heirs, Chiana had been only a child at the time and could always say she had not understood what she had signed.

Goddess help them all if she or anyone else ever found out that Pol's right came from Roelstra's blood in his veins, not just Rohan's conquest. Ostvel mentally listed those who knew: himself, Rohan, Sioned, Chay, Tobin, Myrdal, and one servant at Stronghold. Not even Andrade had known. If Sioned had her way, no one would ever know, especially not Pol. He doubted the wisdom of never telling the boy the truth, but it was not his decision to make.

He closed and locked the coffer, storing it with the other dangerous one in the secret space. Sioned might

just get away with it, he mused. Nothing in the archives
even hinted that Ianthe's fourth son had not died at
Feruche. Everyone knew she had been pregnant; many
believed the child had indeed been Rohan's. Ostvel had
been at Stronghold that summer and autumn, when Sioned
had emptied the keep of all but three servants and spread
word that she was pregnant again. Two of those servants
had since died, their knowledge of the secret blown away
with their ashes on Desert winds. The one who remained—
Tibalia, a young girl at the time and now in charge of all
maidservants at Stronghold—was trusted implicitly. At
Skybowl, where Sioned and Ostvel and Tobin had fled
from Feruche and where Pol had been Named, the story
was that Sioned, furious beyond reason at knowing Ianthe
carried Rohan's child, had gone to destroy her rival—and
that the strain of the journey had brought Pol's prema-
ture birth. No one had ever questioned this tale, though
Ostvel was never able to decide whether it was really
believed or not. Still, Skybowl's people had kept the
secret of dragon gold. Whatever they truly believed, they
could be trusted. And surely any rumors would have
surfaced long ere this.

So Sioned was probably safe in her deception. Goddess
knew, she had paid dearly for it. Ianthe's sniggering
reference to multiple rapes had knifed through his heart,
and with more than the anguish of knowing proud Sioned
had been used thus. For to her, none of it had ever
happened. She had never said a word about what had
been done to her at Feruche; Ostvel had learned of it
from Rohan. Neither did she ever speak of that summer
and autumn of waiting, or of the night Feruche had
burned. None of it existed for her. Sometimes he wondered if she even had a clear memory of that time. He
truly believed she had gone a little mad that year. He
knew from experience that agony and terror and grief
must be cleansed from the heart. Sioned's wounds were
still open and bleeding. Ostvel had known her since
childhood; she could hide very little from him.

He twisted the small carving of gilded elk-hoof that fit
cunningly into the wood paneling. Myrdal had noted that
other secret rooms, doors, and passages were opened
with a similar carving that depicted a rising star. Ostvel
found it intriguing that Pol's name was the key to Castle

Crag's secrets, and eerie that Ianthe had written words calling him what Sioned had Named him. And, strangest of all, the same stars provided the light used by *diarmadh'im*.

The word meant "Stoneburners" and came from the manner in which rock cairns glowed during certain ritual sorceries. Urival shared odd bits of Star Scroll knowledge with Sioned on sunlight, and she passed on some of them to Donato, Ostvel's court Sunrunner and a friend of their youth. Stars were everywhere these days, it seemed: used in sorcery, Pol's name, indicating Castle Crag's secrets—could the place have been built by these *diarmadh'im*?

Ostvel stretched the weariness from his shoulders, reminded by various impudent aches that this would be his forty-eighth winter. A smile formed as he reflected on where those winters had taken him—from obscure retainer at Goddess Keep to Regent of Princemarch. He had a grown son who was *faradhi* and lord of his own keep, and an infant daughter whose mother was a princess, and—

He gasped. It was two years ago today that he had married that princess. He barely remembered to lock the library door before sprinting to his suite. A frantic search in his wardrobe had him cursing. He'd had the ring made, he *knew* he had. Alasen had given him his ring last year; by Kierstian tradition, the partner superior in rank had a second year to decide about continuing the marriage. But this year he could claim her and—*where* was that damned ring?

Finding it at last, he sat back on his heels and sighed his relief—and toppled over in startlement as he heard Alasen laughing softly behind him.

"I was beginning to wonder," she said, smiling, "if you were expecting me to divorce you. After all, that ring is the only one I ever really wanted."

Chapter Three

722: Skybowl

"**S**o you'll be off to Feruche in the morning?" Riyan asked as he and Sorin mounted the steps to the central hall.

"Why don't you come with me for a few days? I could use your advice. My little army of architects have battled each other until I've forgotten what I originally wanted to do with the place!" Sorin winced. "It took a whole year to clean out the ruins and make sure what was left wouldn't collapse. Then we had to sort out the usable stone and set it aside for when we needed it. And then another year before the new foundation was set."

"But you *have* started to build?"

"At last—and if you can call it that. Miyon hasn't been exactly eager to pay up his bet to Aunt Sioned."

Riyan sighed involuntarily with relief as they entered the cool dimness of the foyer. A mere fifteen measures away in the Veresch Mountains, autumn had already brought crisp days and chilly nights. But here in the Desert it was still stiflingly hot, even at nearly sunset.

Sorin continued his good-natured complaints. "He stalled on delivering the iron last winter and again in spring. And all this time we've been living in excruciatingly close quarters in the old barracks below the castle. I've lost track of how many fights I've broken up over what tower goes where, which windows should face what direction, and how many rooms there should be. Do you know we're still arguing over whether it's to be a defensive keep or not?"

"Considering the proximity of Cunaxa, the thicker the walls, the better."

"Granted. But building a warrior's castle isn't my idea

of fun, and it would be a direct challenge to Miyon and his Merida allies to come and try to tear it down."

"What does Rohan say about it?"

"He grins and tells me to let the Cunaxans watch and fume while my new keep is built with their iron. But they're more likely to be laughing. Goddess! You don't know the half of it. Bracing up the old dungeons was a nightmare."

Riyan chuckled at his friend's tribulations. "I heard that out of the kindness of his heart, Miyon sent down his best smiths to work the iron."

"And I packed them all back to Cunaxa," Sorin replied vigorously. "It seems their mission was to build me a castle whose underpinnings would make it tilt like a drunken merchant. Before it fell down altogether, that is!"

The two young men washed their hands and faces in a large stone bowl set into a wall embrasure and accepted towels from a waiting servant. Then they checked their relative tidiness in a mirror on a nearby wall. Sorin paused to run careful fingers over the delicate frame, carved with intertwined leaves and apples.

"It's beautiful. As if dark liquid gold was washed over it."

"It was my mother's," Riyan said. "She never lived at Skybowl, but lots of her things are here. Father brought them from Stronghold when Rohan gave him this castle."

"I remember her a little, I think."

"I wish I remembered her more." Then, more easily, he continued, "Well, we're as clean as we'll get without baths. Can't do anything about the horse-stink, but I trust we won't offend the ladies."

"Alasen won't mind and Feylin never notices—and Sionell's probably as dirty as we are."

"Now, now! She's growing up!" Riyan grinned as he gestured to a guard to open the doors to the main hall.

"Mmm. Pol's doing the same at Graypearl, I'm told. Your father had a long talk with Chadric at the *Rialla*, and Sionell's not been shy about demanding every detail!"

Riyan spotted Sionell immediately. She sat by Alasen at the high table, playing with his half-sister, Camigwen. Small Jeni was two years old, with Ostvel's dark hair and gray eyes, but in feature was exactly like her mother.

That Alasen had Named her first child after Riyan's mother was an indication of the serenity of her marriage; Riyan didn't know many women who would pay gentle tribute to a beloved first wife.

During the winter of 719, when they had lived at Skybowl while Castle Crag was being readied for them, Riyan had had ample opportunity to talk with his father's new wife. Alasen had never insulted him by sitting him down to an oh-so-sincere little chat; neither had she made the mistake of trying too hard to take on the role of stepmother. That would have been ludicrous, as she was only three winters older than he. Instead, she had merely been herself: witty, intelligent, kind, and very much in love with his father.

Any awkwardness had been Ostvel's. Riyan smiled as he took his chair at the high table, remembering his father's bemused happiness—and the inevitable embarrassment that came to a man who, after eighteen years, took a second wife fully half his age. Alasen's one comment to Riyan about it had been, "I do wish he'd stop being so silly. It's as if he expects to descend into doddering decrepitude any moment." Impending fatherhood, casually mentioned by Alasen early that winter, had reduced Ostvel to stunned speechlessness and a foolish grin that had not left his face for days.

"The horses you bought from Chay must be coming along well," Alasen observed as Riyan sat beside her. "You're looking very happy."

"They are, and I am. But I was thinking about the night you told us you were carrying Jeni."

She took the baby from Sionell and laughed.

"Why?" Sionell asked. "What happened?"

Riyan glanced down the table. His father, Walvis, and Feylin were deep in discussion with Sorin about Feruche; they would not overhear. "Well, he—"

"Riyan!" Alasen scolded, and held her daughter high in the air to make her giggle. "Consider your father's dignity."

"*He* didn't have any mind for it that night!" Riyan reached over and tickled Jeni's chin. "Someday I'll tell you the story, little one. When you can appreciate it."

"But what *happened?*" Sionell insisted.

"He was pouring wine for Alasen when she just up and

announced it, and he kept on pouring, and pouring, and—"

"All over my best dress!" Alasen finished. "Not to mention Skybowl's best table silk, and the best Giladan rug, and—"

"And himself, I'll bet," Sionell supplied, grinning. "How did he react when he found out about *you*, Riyan?"

Alasen winked at her. "I'm reliably informed that his knees collapsed and he fell into one of Princess Milar's little chairs so hard he splintered the poor thing. Sioned's been trying to get him to pay for it for years."

"So *that's* why she teases him about it!" Riyan hadn't known that story.

"I wonder what happened when Prince Rohan learned about Pol," Sionell mused.

Alasen winked again, this time at Riyan so Sionell couldn't see. "You'll have to ask Sioned. Is Jahnavi going to serve us our dinner, or is he still primping in his new Skybowl tunic?"

Sionell jumped to her feet. "I'll go see what's keeping him."

"Take Jeni with you. Her nurse will be waiting for her."

When Sionell had hoisted the child into her arms and left them, Riyan shook his head. "She's not subtle, is she?"

"About Pol? No. But then, she's only fourteen. Wait a few more years and she'll have acquired all the arts. She's going to be pretty enough to get plenty of chances to use them, too!"

"I hope she doesn't. There's something very charming about her directness. I'd hate to see her become one of those simpering idiots who plague the *Rialla*."

She nodded, green eyes dancing. "A plague I notice you avoided quite nicely this year by not attending."

He groaned softly. "Alasen, *please* don't try to marry me off!"

"Not at all. Your father and I are much too young to be grandparents."

Jahnavi appeared then from the side door to the kitchens, trying not to stagger under the weight of a huge white tureen made of Kierstian ceramic. The boy presented the dish for approval, bowed when Riyan nodded permission to serve, and hefted it onto the table. Silver ladle and blue ceramic bowls were waiting; Riyan watched critically as Jahnavi portioned out the soup without spilling a drop. Sionell had returned to her seat next to Alasen, holding her breath as her little brother performed his first duties as Riyan's new squire. She sighed her relief when he finished without incident, bowed, and returned to the kitchen for bread.

"Very nice," Riyan commented so Sionell could hear. "A little lacking in polish, but done very smoothly just the same."

"Thank you, my lord," the girl replied formally. But then her irrepressible spirits made her grin. "He was so nervous! You were a squire at Swalekeep, and everybody knows what a stickler old Prince Clutha is for decorum!"

"A stick across my backside once when I spilled a tray of pastries," Riyan reminisced. "But I doubt any such remedies will be necessary with Jahnavi. I was such a clumsy little mess!"

He did not mention that at eleven years old, Jahnavi had not yet entered into the tortures of puberty, with all its insecurities of abruptly long limbs, distressingly large feet, and humiliatingly uncertain voice. It was foolish to punish an adolescent for what he could not help. Riyan was determined to be more understanding than Clutha, who had been of the old school when it came to training his squires. Jahnavi was Riyan's first foray into such training. Walvis and Feylin had entrusted him with their only son, and he resolved to justify their faith in him. He knew there would not be many young highborn boys given into his care; Skybowl was a small, remote keep, and he was only a minor *athri*. Both he and his holding were insignificant as far as the rest of the princedoms were concerned. But others' perceptions troubled him not at all, for Skybowl was vital to the Desert in a way no one had ever guessed.

There was nothing here that would indicate Skybowl's importance. The hall was a third the size of the one at Stronghold, and much less grandly decorated. The people were well-dressed and well-fed, but sat at trestle tables on benches instead of in individual chairs. Early evening sun shone through windows paned in clear glass, not the colored Fironese crystal of more fashionable keeps.

High on the walls were torch sconces rather than the branches of white candles Rohan had made popular at Stronghold, and the sconces were made of plain bronze, not silver or gold. Those at Skybowl lived in comfort but not luxury, and nowhere was there any indication of the wealth of dragon gold taken from nearby caves and cached in the lowest levels of the keep.

Jahnavi made swift, efficient work of the bread, then poured out wine and stood at the end of the high table, alert to the needs of those seated there. His parents treated him as they would any other squire; no one teased him or attempted to engage him in conversation. Everyone knew how important this first duty at table was to him. But not even his solemn dedication to his new status could survive when Alasen made her announcement.

It came about when Sionell leaned slightly forward and asked, "Lord Ostvel, we've been talking about how men react when their wives tell them they're going to be fathers. How did Prince Rohan take the news about Pol?"

To Riyan's astonishment, his father's face went stone still. The smile that appeared soon thereafter was a trifle strained around the edges for a moment, as if it was a bad fit.

"I don't really know, Sionell. I was at Stronghold, and they were all down in Syr with the army, fighting High Prince Roelstra."

The girl looked disappointed. Alasen set down her goblet and smiled. "My dear, listen and watch carefully. You're about to witness a man making a fool of himself." To her husband she said, "My lord, I have the honor to inform you that you will become a father once more before the New Year Holiday."

Ostvel performed according to expectation: his soup spoon clattered from his fingers into his bowl, overbalanced, and flipped onto the table, sending a splash onto his tunic. Jahnavi forgot himself and gave a whoop, quickly silenced by Walvis' attempt at a stern glare. But the Lord of Remagev was soon grinning along with the rest of them as Ostvel struggled valiantly to recover his dignity, forfeit to a soup stain on his clothes.

"Alasen!" he finally bellowed, and silence erupted into laughing congratulations.

Riyan signaled to Jahnavi to refill all the wine cups. The castle folk down the hall, seeing the merriment at the high table, were attentively quiet as Riyan got to his feet and raised his goblet.

"The Princess Alasen!" he announced. "And my father the Lord Regent, who's to be a father again!"

The echo rang out from more than seventy throats, and cups were emptied down those throats an instant later. Skybowl's people had been, until three years ago, Ostvel's people; Riyan knew that in many ways they still were. He saluted his father with his goblet and grinned.

Wearing a *You'll pay for this, boy* look, Ostvel cleared his throat, blotted ineffectually at his tunic with his napkin, and rose to make the required response to his son's toast.

But he had barely drawn breath when a rush of wings filled the hall and the sky trembled with a hundred trumpeting calls. A stunned instant later, everyone scurried for the windows or to get outdoors. The dragons had come to Skybowl.

Sionell and Jahnavi's mother, Feylin, was the first of those at the high table to escape the hall. Riyan saw her dark red head in the crowded foyer, but she did not join the rush out into the courtyard. She nudged her way clear of the surging throng and turned for the stairs, bounding up them three at a time.

Sionell grabbed Riyan's hand. Her round cheeks were flushed, her blue eyes brilliant with excitement. "Hurry!" she cried, and pulled him forward.

They found Feylin where Riyan had suspected, in the uppermost chamber of the main tower. She was leaning precariously out an open window. Sionell let go of Riyan's fingers and joined her mother. He shook his head, smiling, and put an arm around each to keep them from falling.

"Mother, just *look* at them all!"

"Hush! I'm counting!" Feylin responded almost frantically.

The dragons were swooping in over the lake for a drink. Some plunged directly into the water for playful baths, while others landed almost daintily on shore. Still more flew lazy circles over the bowl of liquid sky from which the keep had taken its name. A few dragonsires drank their fill, then perched on the rocky heights of the ancient crater to guard their flight of hatchlings, females, and dozens of three-year-old immature dragons.

Riyan watched, enchanted. He told himself that even if not for the honor of holding Skybowl and mining dragon gold for his prince, with all the trust this implied, he would gladly have taken the keep for the sheer delight of watching dragons. As bathers left the water, green-bronze and gold and black and russet hides glistening in the sunlight, wings were spread to flick showers of droplets and reveal contrasting underwings. No, Skybowl could have been as barren and rough as those who had never seen it believed it to be, and Riyan would still have counted it a privilege to live here.

The dragons seemed inclined to linger, and Feylin gradually relaxed as she was given time to do a second count and a third. Sionell and Riyan faithfully repeated the numbers she gave them.

"Three memories are better than one," she said, "especially when one of them is a Sunrunner memory trained by Lady Andrade." Stepping back from the window, she sighed. "Just the population I expected from prior statistics. But unless they find more caves, the extra females will die at the next mating the way they did this year, and three years ago, and—damn it, we need more caves!"

"There's Rivenrock," Sionell said.

"Which they won't go near, after so many of them died of Plague there. Oh, they fly over it, it's on their path through the Desert. But if they'd only use the caves, their numbers would increase to a safe level. I won't feel confident until we see upwards of eight hundred after hatching." She paused, then pointed and exclaimed, "See that one over there, the russet one with gold underwings? That's Sioned's dragon, Elisel!"

"The one she can speak to?" Sionell almost lost her balance and Riyan held on more tightly to her waist.

"Careful!" he said. "She doesn't really talk to her—more like shares feelings and pictures with her. Although Sioned says Elisel knows her name."

"You don't believe she does?" The girl turned her head, brows raised. "You're a Sunrunner, too—have you ever tried it?"

"Never."

"Don't you want to?"

"Of course!" Riyan answered. "But Sioned isn't really sure how *she* does it, and she's cautioned the rest of us not to attempt it until she understands what really happens between her and the dragon."

"A wise precaution," Feylin added, eyeing her daughter. "It's a good thing *you're* not a Sunrunner, my pest, or you'd be wild to find a dragon of your own!"

"It'd be wonderful," Sionell murmured, gazing wistfully at the dragons. "It doesn't seem fair—I know *I* can't ever touch one, but the *faradh'im* can, and Sioned won't even let them try! Think of all the things we could learn from them, and what we could tell them!"

Riyan blinked and nearly lost his hold on Sionell. There was one thing that dragons needed desperately to know if their population was to increase to a level Feylin considered safe. Could Sioned communicate it to her dragon?

He asked; Feylin shrugged. "She tried. She conjures a picture of hatchlings coming out of the caves—and Elisel whines and trembles, and shows her dragon corpses. Even though she's not old enough to have seen it for herself. Which indicates," she added with a pleased glint in her eyes, "that they communicate information to each other from one generation to the next rather neatly."

The sires keeping watch on the crater's lip bellowed suddenly, and the hatchlings reacted with a flurry of splashing water and flapping wings. Soon the evening sky was thick with dragons, circling over the lake until all were airborne. The sires trumpeted once more and the group set off for the south, where they would winter in the hidden canyons and valleys of the Catha Hills. Several of the females lingered behind, including Sioned's russet dragon, to chase the slower hatchlings along. Riyan wondered if Sioned would be waiting at Stronghold for Elisel to fly past, waiting to greet her dragon on the last of the autumn sunlight.

Dinner being perforce over, Riyan ordered Jahnavi to have small cakes and hot taze sent up to each bedchamber, and dismissed his new squire for the evening. He then went to help Camigwen's nurse put her to bed—not an easy task, for the child had seen the dragons, too, and wanted an instant repeat of the morning's game with her big brother. To the nurse's dismay, he obliged. Wearing wings made of a blanket, he swooped around the room while Jeni squealed with laughter and tried to "slay" him with a wooden spoon. At last Alasen came in, calmed the uproar, and had her daughter smartly in bed with the promise of one more game of dragons tomorrow before they left for Stronghold.

"But I thought you were going to stay for a little while," Riyan protested as they left Jeni to sleep under her nurse's watchful eyes. "I know Sorin wants Father's advice about Feruche. I was thinking of riding up there with him and Walvis tomorrow."

"Oh, don't worry about that. You three can go while I visit Sioned." She gestured him to a chair and seated herself on a couch, leaning forward to pour cups of steaming taze from the pitcher which had been placed on a low table. "Rohan wants us to look in on the work at Dragon's Rest, so we'll return to Princemarch through Dragon Gap. Just us and the horses, no baggage wains or anything. Although your father will probably spout some nonsense about having me carried in a litter the whole way. Sioned says he was absurd when your mother was pregnant with you and he was certainly that way before Jeni's birth."

Riyan chuckled. "From what I know about my mother, I can't see her paying any attention!"

"From what *I* know about her, she probably laughed in his face! I can tell it's in his head to stay here until spring. But if this child is a boy, he should be born at Castle Crag."

"Of course," Riyan agreed.

She shifted and looked down at her elegantly slippered feet. "I wanted to talk to you about that, actually."

He held up a staying hand and smiled. "I know what you're going to say. Skybowl is all I want, Alasen. I'd be a disaster in a place as grand as Castle Crag. You're a Princess of Kierst, born to that kind of life, and you'll teach it to your children. Your son can have Castle Crag with my profound gratitude."

"Are you sure?" she worried. "It's the most important keep in Princemarch until Dragon's Rest is finished. And even after, the whole of the north will be governed from there. *And* it's the major trading center in the Veresch.

Your talents could be put to excellent use at a busy castle like that. And it *is* your right as Ostvel's eldest son."

Riyan shook his head. "He had absolutely nothing to give me until I was six winters old and Rohan gave him Skybowl. I don't want anything else, truly. I'm Desert-born and bred. I've seen enough of other places to know that this is where I belong."

"As long as you're certain. . . ."

"I am."

"This is going to sound awfully sentimental," she murmured. "But if this baby *is* a boy, I want him to grow up just like his elder brother."

Ostvel said from the doorway, "I'm sure he will, though it'll be none of my doing. My children have remarkable mothers." He crossed the room and bent to kiss the crown of her braids. "And here I thought you were simply getting fat!"

She assumed a cloyingly sweet expression, her voice all honey-wine as she replied, "At least I have a good excuse." She prodded him in the stomach.

"My belt's been in exactly the same notch since I was your age!"

Riyan grinned. Ostvel, realizing he was being teased, growled playfully down at his wife and then kissed her again. He then took the chair beside Riyan's. "Sorin's got a little expedition going up to Feruche tomorrow, Alasen. Would you mind traveling down to Stronghold without me?"

"It's already settled," Alasen replied, pouring a cup of taze for him. "I'll have more time with Arlis this way. I wanted to give him a while to settle in before I went to see him." She sighed and shook her head. "I can't believe my little nephew is old enough to be Rohan's squire! And I'm so relieved that Saumer agreed with Father about his fostering."

Ostvel shrugged. "A mutual grandson is no guarantee of mutual agreement on his training."

"How old is Arlis now?" Riyan asked. "Nearly eleven?"

"Yes." She poured a cup of taze for Ostvel, then leaned back and sighed. "Father thought that maybe he'd have *faradhi* gifts like me, but he didn't so much as bat an eyelash on the sail from Kierst-Isel." She gave an exaggerated shudder. "I only experienced it once, but

Sunrunner seasickness isn't something I ever want to go through again."

Riyan noted with interest that, for the first time in his hearing, she had admitted what she was. She must be feeling easier about it. Three years had passed since the terrifying events of the 719 *Rialla*, memories that could still give Riyan nightmares of death and sorceries and unspeakable pain.

"That's why she married me," Ostvel said. "To avoid another crossing."

"So Arlis isn't *faradhi*," Riyan mused. "That'll be a relief to the other princes."

"The stupid, prejudiced ones," Alasen said in disgust.

He shrugged. "Look at it from their point of view. I'm no bother to them. They hardly know I exist. But Maarken's going to inherit Radzyn one day and all his father's power in the Desert. As for Pol—he makes them so nervous they practically flinch whenever he's mentioned."

Ostvel sipped at the hot drink. "There was plenty of hostility three years ago. And he wasn't even fifteen then, still only a child, completely untrained in the arts. By rights he should have gone to Goddess Keep last year."

"Sioned won't ever send him, will she?" Riyan glanced at his father.

"I'd be astounded if she did," came the frank reply.

Alasen was silent for a moment, then said softly, "How horrible it must be for Andry—Lord of Goddess Keep and not trusted by his own family to train the next High Prince as a Sunrunner."

Riyan frowned. "You saw him at the *Rialla*. What was he like?"

"Polite and proper and regal, just as he should be in his position and with his ancestry. And there was no trace of youth about him, Riyan. It hurt Tobin terribly to see it. So many responsibilities—and so many plans kept secret! That's what they don't trust. His innovations."

"I don't hear much about that, being in the wrong camp for it." Shaking his head, he added, "I hear myself dividing us up into factions and it scares me."

Ostvel sat back, sprawling his long legs in a casual posture belied by the tension in his face. "But that's where we're all headed, isn't it? Andry on one side, Pol on another, and suspicious princes on the third. Andrade wanted to unite the continent under a Sunrunner High Prince. Instead, we're splitting apart. And it's going to get worse as Pol gets older."

Gesturing her annoyance, Alasen said, "When Lady Andrade had control over the *faradh'im*, the princes could at least be assured of her discipline. But the break between Andry and the Desert is obvious, now that Pol is old enough but isn't at Goddess Keep."

"You've forgotten a fourth faction," Riyan reminded her. "Sorcerers."

She got to her feet, pacing, her hands wrapped around the steaming cup. "That's the worst of all! After hundreds of years they appear out of nowhere, then vanish again. Who can say where they are, what they think, what they're planning? How will they next challenge Pol and Andry? Because it will be both of them, Riyan. They'll have to stand together as *faradh'im* against the threat. And I'm so afraid their pride won't allow it."

"Surely it won't get as bad as all that," he said, trying to soothe her. "After all, these sorcerers may not emerge again at all."

Alasen's lips curled bitterly. "No? You felt their power, Riyan, just as I did, at Lady Andrade's death and at the combat. Do you think something like that will be content to stay in hiding another few hundred years? If Pol and Andry can't oppose them together, these sorcerers might win."

"Yes, I felt their power," he said quietly. "More so than almost anyone. I'm of their blood, Alasen."

"And no more like them than your father is," she emphasized.

"Ah, but do we really know what they want?" Ostvel mused.

Alasen leaned against the arm of a chair. "*Faradh'im* defeated them. They'll want their revenge. But why now? What is it about now that makes them think they can succeed?"

"They failed with Masul," Riyan pointed out.

"They weren't half trying," she scoffed. "I think he was a means of getting Andrade out of the way."

"Well, if it ever comes down to finding out who is and who isn't of the Old Blood, then quite frankly I trust Pol's protection more than Andry's."

"Riyan!" Alasen stared at him. "You're shadow-fearing, Sunrunner," she said more calmly.

"Am I? What about it, Father? What's the easiest way to unite various factions? Give them a mutual enemy—or someone they *perceive* as an enemy."

"Alasen's right," Ostvel snapped. "You're starting at shadows."

"Andry would never even *think* anything like that!" she added. "Riyan, you've known him all your life!"

He had heard things recently to make him wonder if he had ever known Andry at all. He forced an apologetic smile and hid what was in his heart. "Sorry. I'm no politician, and all this playing one side against another confuses me."

Ostvel's brows arched in eloquent doubt at this avowal of incomprehension, but he said nothing. While Alasen made a calming little ritual of refilling their cups, Riyan deliberately turned the conversation to Sorin's plans for Feruche.

But alone in his own chambers that night, he looked pensively at his rings. One way to tell *faradhi* from *diarmadhi* was miserable sickness when crossing water. Riyan, like purebred Sunrunners, had that problem—and knew that he also had the Old Blood in his veins, part of his mother's legacy. His protection was her other heritage as a Sunrunner that gave him the reaction. But what about trained *faradh'im* whose power came solely from their sorcerer blood? Pandsala had been one of them. Crossing water had never troubled her.

The only sure method of discerning one from the other was response to sorcery, when *faradhi* rings became fiery circles of pain around the fingers of anyone with *diarmadhi* blood. He wondered if Andry knew about that—and, if so, whether he would ever use that knowledge in ways that would make Pol's protection necessary. Riyan thanked the Goddess that Pol was not of the Old Blood. At least Andry would never be able to threaten him on that score.

Chapter Four

723: Stronghold

The sound of the dragon horn announcing visitors startled Rohan from concentration on his correspondence. A quick mental review of expected guests made him frown. No one was due here until winter. Sioned's nephew Tilal and his wife Gemma were coming from Ossetia with their children to spend the last half of the season and the New Year Holiday; Maarken and Hollis had promised to bring their year-old twins from Whitecliff. But Rohan had counted on a peaceful autumn in which to catch up on work, and now there were visitors. Sioned was not even in residence, having ridden up to Feruche to see how construction progressed. She had not asked him to accompany her. They both knew he would never set foot near that place again as long as he lived.

A knock sounded at the library door and Rohan called permission to enter. Arlis hovered there, wide-eyed and breathless. "My lord! I ran all the way up from the guardhouse—"

"To tell me who's here," Rohan supplied, giving the squire a chance to catch up on his breathing. Arlis nodded, sun-lightened brown hair rumpled by one careless hand. "Someone important, from that blast on the horn. Who?"

"Lord Urival!"

Rohan could not help a start of surprise. No wonder the boy looked impressed. "Well, then, we'd better go greet him, hadn't we?" He capped the inkwell and put away his pens, glancing once over the parchments littering the huge double desk. There was nothing on the tables that could not have been read by anyone. He trusted his servants down to the last scullery maid, and

50

no one would have dreamed of entering the private office without explicit permission. But Sioned had insisted on extreme caution the last few years. Sunrunners were not the only ones who could weave light and look upon things that perhaps needed to be kept secret.

"Lord Urival isn't alone, my lord," Arlis told him, holding out a damp cloth so Rohan could clean his ink-stained fingers. "There's another Sunrunner with him, a woman, and they have two packhorses loaded from ears to tails."

"It seems he's planning a long stay. How many rings has this other Sunrunner?" Rohan scrubbed at a stubborn mark, scowled, and tossed the cloth onto his empty chair.

"Eight." The squire hesitated. "May I ask a question, my lord?"

"Asking questions is largely what you're here for, Arlis. Both your grandsires would be very disappointed if you did not. And they'd be even more unhappy with me if I didn't try to answer." He smiled and flicked a lock of unruly hair away from the boy's deep-set eyes.

"Lord Urival and this other *faradhi* are here with everything they own, it looks like. She's too old to be of Lord Andry's new training. Could they have come because Lord Andry threw them out?"

Rohan considered his wife's kinsman, this princeling who was all earnest face and troubled green eyes and child-soft features. Arlis would one day rule a united Kierst and Isel, a fact he had known almost before he'd learned to walk. Right now he was trying to think like a prince—admirable, but depressing to Rohan, who wanted the boy to stay a boy for at least a few more years.

"Do you think that could be it, my lord?" Arlis said anxiously.

"He's probably just come for a visit, and has brought someone with him for company." Or so Rohan devoutly hoped.

Arlis looked relieved. Rohan sent him down to the kitchens to bring refreshment up to the Summer Room, where Rohan then repaired to receive his exalted guests. He had just seated himself in a comfortable chair when a servant scratched on the door, opened it, and announced Lord Urival and Lady Morwenna of Goddess Keep.

Rohan went forward to greet them, hiding his curiosity as best he could. "A most welcome surprise, my lord," he said. "My lady, please sit down. Something cold to drink will be here shortly."

"Amenities are so soothing, aren't they?" Urival observed cynically as he sank wearily into a chair. "Essentially useless, but soothing."

"Pay him no mind, your grace," Morwenna said. "He's saddle sore."

Arlis hurried in with chilled wine. "I've ordered the Tapestry Suite readied, my lord," he said to Rohan as he served. "Is that all right?"

"As long as it has a bed and a bathtub," Morwenna sighed, then grinned. "Actually, I'd settle for just the tub!"

"Three rooms and a beautiful bath, my lady," Arlis told her shyly.

"Sounds perfect." She inspected him as he gave her a goblet of wine. "You'd be Latham's boy, wouldn't you? Volog and Saumer's grandson."

"I have that honor, my lady."

"Prince Arlis, I'm very pleased to meet you. My mother served as your grandfather Saumer's court *faradhi* at Zaldivar for many years."

"I hope she was happy there, my lady."

"Very."

Rohan noticed Urival's restless frown, and gestured the squire out. "That will be all, Arlis. Make sure the Tapestry Suite is ready quickly, please."

"Yes, my lord." He bowed his way out and closed the door.

"A fine lad, your grace," Morwenna said. "I recognize the Kierstian green eyes."

"Sioned's eyes," Urival said. "Where is she, Rohan?"

"With Sorin at Feruche. What brings you to Stronghold?" he asked, too bluntly, he knew, but Urival had never been one for indirection.

The old man shrugged. "Tapestry Suite, eh? I don't remember that one from my stay here in 698."

"My mother's old rooms," Rohan explained. "Sioned chose the hangings at the last *Rialla* and we renamed it. I assume your business is with her."

"It would be, if she were here. Since she's not, I'll

burden you." Urival's smile was more of a grimace. "One of the privileges of your position, High Prince."

Morwenna, several years Rohan's junior and with the dark skin, black hair, and tip-tilted brown eyes that marked her as Fironese, gave a derisive snort. "What he means to say, your grace, is that neither of us could bear to stay at Goddess Keep anymore and have come to burden you with superfluous Sunrunners. I knew the High Princess slightly when she was a young girl earning rings faster than Andrade could keep up with. In herself she's more Sunrunner than you'll ever need."

"She'd be pleased to hear you say that. But we're informal here—if you don't feel comfortable calling me by my name, then at least deliver me from being 'my grace.' " He smiled, all the while fretting inwardly at Urival's uncharacteristic slowness in divulging the reason for his presence at Stronghold.

"Charm," the old Sunrunner mused. "The whole family has it to one degree or another. Andry's worse—he gets it from Chay as well as Tobin. Charmed all of us into accepting things we'd never have considered in a hundred generations. And by the time we realized where he was going with it. . . ."

"Oh, for the love of the Goddess and all her works, *tell* him!" Morwenna snapped.

Urival eyed her. "It's the privilege of my seventy winters and nine rings to speak when and as I please." He set down his untasted wine and sank back in his chair, looking every one of those seventy winters. His golden-brown eyes, remarkably beautiful in an otherwise unhandsome craggy face, were dark and lackluster. But not from mere tiredness, Rohan thought. There was an older and deeper weariness in him, one of the spirit.

"Andry was never what you'd call biddable," Urival began. "Brilliant, intelligent, mind-hungry, yes. But as ungovernable as Sioned in his own way. A more dangerous way, it turns out. Had you heard he's to be a father next spring?"

"Andry's married? Who to?" Rohan didn't bother to hide his astonishment. Tobin and Chay, as uninformed on the subject as he, were going to be furious.

"Did I say he'd Chosen a wife?"

Rohan looked at Morwenna, who nodded grimly.

"That's why we left. Not because he didn't marry the girl, or even because he'd gotten her with child. But it was the *way* he did it and the future which it implied that shattered all for us."

"For me," Urival corrected. "You wanted to stay and try to talk him out of it. Perhaps that would have been the right way. I don't know. But I couldn't stay there any longer. Not when he's using the first-ring night to sire a son on a girl no older than sixteen!"

Rohan's wine cup nearly dropped out of his hand. He stared at the *faradh'im*, too stunned to speak.

"You know about that night, of course," Urival went on. "The boy or girl calls Fire formally for the first time in front of the Lord or Lady of Goddess Keep. That night they're virgins no longer." He glanced briefly at Morwenna. "*She* has been one of the more enthusiastic initiators of boys into the delights of being men."

Morwenna tossed her black braid from her shoulder. "And, of course, they had to drag *you* kicking and screaming to the same duty for more than a few girls!"

A smile flitted across his face. "That's many, many years ago."

"But I'll bet you still remember!" Her manner was sharp, but her dark eyes danced.

"Memories to warm an old man's long, cold nights," he riposted easily. Then he turned to Rohan again. "The guise of the Goddess is used to hide identity from the virgin."

Rohan nodded. "Sioned . . . spoke of it once or twice, a long time ago. She never knew." He recalled his own disgraceful behavior of—could it really be twenty-five years ago?—when he'd found out that his Chosen lady would not come virgin to their marriage bed. He looked on the memory from a bemused distance now, amazed to think that it had meant so much to him at the time. Of course, at the time he had been barely twenty-one, unsure of himself both as a prince and as a man, and desperately in love.

"She never knew," Urival echoed softly, holding Rohan's gaze with his own.

And the High Prince suddenly realized that one of the sweetest memories to warm the old man's nights was the initiation of Sioned. He felt blood heat his face, and told himself sternly that at his age he should be long past the curse of a fair complexion. Urival gave another fleeting half-smile.

"Of course she didn't," Morwenna said briskly. "None of them do. The point here is that Andry's changed tradition. At least as far as the girls are concerned. We've always been very careful to time that night so no child comes of it. And the duty is parceled out among several men. But Andry's reserved the right to himself and two others. When I questioned him about Othanel's pregnancy, he flat out admitted he arranged it so she'd conceive!"

"And then declined to marry her." Urival was grim-faced again. "Told me that she had agreed to bear his child—was honored, in fact. As what ambitious woman wouldn't be, to have the child of so powerful a Lord of Goddess Keep, and a close kinsman of the High Prince into the bargain?"

Rohan thought this over for a time. Then he asked, "How many others feel as you do?"

"Quite a few. They stayed." Morwenna shrugged uncomfortably. "We're here because of your son—Urival to train him, me to be Urival's company."

The old man added, "Ostensibly I'm in retirement. Morwenna's along to keep an eye on me, as she said. At least *she's* not had to lie."

"Then Andry doesn't know—"

"He suspects." Urival shrugged. "His suspicion may be a certainty by now. But officially he can't take any notice. I go where I like and do as I please. I gave over my keys as Chief Steward to one of his friends. Trained the boy myself, so he knows his work. Sorin met him in 719."

"The Fironese? The one who had so many fine ideas for rebuilding Feruche?"

"Torien's his name. And now that I've left, he can do to the Keep what Andry's doing to the Sunrunners themselves—remaking the entire structure of both." Urival shook his head. "I'm too old for this, Rohan. I don't like so many changes."

"And yet," Morwenna pointed out, "you're going to change the way the most important Sunrunner alive will be trained."

Rohan stared at her long and hard. "You're not here merely for Urival's sake, are you?"

Her dark skin acquired two blossoms of dusky color across the cheekbones. Then she laughed heartily. "Ah, my lord, you have me there! But from what I hear from Graypearl, I won't be Pol's first by any means!" She paused and sighed her regret. "Wish I could be. But I'll take care of the first-ring night for him, yes. He'll know it's me, but that can't be helped. It's something he has to experience if his training is to approximate that at Goddess Keep."

"But it won't," Urival said. "That's the whole point."

Rohan poured himself a much-needed second cup of wine. "Meath and Eolie have been training him at Graypearl. They keep in close contact with Sioned and she's pleased with his progress. Andry knows about it."

"And doesn't dare say anything," Morwenna added. "He has to behave as if it's perfectly all right with him, or people will realize that he doesn't have the power he claims to have. A good deal of his influence rests in his relationship to you and Pol, my lord."

"Exactly the way Andrade engineered it when she married her sister to your father," Urival said, nodding. "She envisioned a Sunrunner Prince connected to her by blood, trained by her to rule with both kinds of power, princely and *faradhi*."

Andrade had been disappointed in the first generation, for Rohan's sister Tobin had the Sunrunner gifts, not he. So she had arranged for him to marry Sioned, reasoning that *their* children would be her tools. What she had not known—what only seven people now living knew—was that Pol was not Sioned's son.

"There's a third kind of power," he said in level tones.

Urival met his gaze unblinking. "Which is why I'm here."

"The Star Scroll has been fully translated, then," he guessed. "And you have a copy Andry doesn't know about."

Morwenna shifted uneasily in her chair. "He's not afraid of it," she burst out. "The Star Scroll is only another means of power to him. More knowledge. But it scares me half to death. I'm the one who copied most of it in secret for Urival. Who knows better than I what it contains?"

"Calm yourself," the old man advised. "If you don't feel comfortable discussing it, perhaps you'd better go have your bath now."

"Treat me like a child and I'll use what I learned from it," she threatened.

"I do have a small demonstration in mind, actually," he replied. "Will you do the honors, or shall I?"

Rohan noted with interest that she immediately shook her head. Were the spells so very dangerous? he wondered. Or was it only that they came from ancient enemies of the *faradh'im*?

Urival gestured, and Morwenna went to lock the door. She drew the window shutters, closing out daylight. Going to the side table, she poured water into a polished bronze bowl and brought it to Urival. He had pulled up another chair to his knees. When the bowl was placed on it, he hunched forward over the water.

"We use Fire as a focus for such things," he said matter-of-factly, and it startled Rohan to hear his voice so casual when he was about to—to do what? "But they had a technique for working with Water, an element we usually avoid, as you know. Rohan, have you something of Sioned's? Something small enough to fit into the bowl, preferably a thing she wears or uses frequently."

"What are you going to do?" he asked, unable to keep suspicion from his voice.

Urival glanced over at him, laughing sardonically. "I presume you miss your wife and would like to see her?"

After a moment's thought, Rohan got up and crossed to a glass-fronted bookcase. Opening it, he extracted one of a pair of tiny carved cups. "The Isulk'im sent us these a few years back, for rattling dice in. Sioned uses this one when playing Sandsteps."

"Isulk'im?" Morwenna repeated blankly, then nodded. "Oh—those crazy people who live out on the Long Sand."

"Go gently with your descriptions," Urival smiled. "They're Rohan's distant kin."

"But I'm crazy, too. Hadn't you noticed?" He gave the old man the sand-jade cup. "Will this do?"

"Perfectly." It disappeared into his palm for a moment, and then he slid it into the water. "Stand close, so you can see."

He did so. Morwenna stepped back warily. Her skittishness would have been catching had Rohan allowed himself to react to it. Urival cradled the bowl in his long, knotted hands, holding it but not lifting it from the chair. After a moment Rohan heard soft metallic vibrations and realized the Sunrunner's nine rings were quivering delicately against the bronze.

"Mark this," Urival breathed. "When others do sorcery while I am nearby, the rings burn. The stronger the magic, the more heat. But when I myself perform a spell, my rings merely tremble. I am of the Old Blood."

"And so am I," Morwenna whispered. Rohan stared at her. She was chafing the rings on her hands and the muscles of her face had tightened with pain. "Get on with it, won't you? This hurts."

"It's the one sure way to tell," Urival said. "I never understood one particular part of fashioning our rings, but now I do. A . . . warning . . . is set into them. Last year I taught young Torien that part of the Chief Steward's duty, but I didn't know what it was for, any more than the rest of us do. Our devious Lady Merisel didn't mention the why of it in her scrolls—only that it was essential."

"Urival, please!" Morwenna's hands had curled into fists. Rohan brought the pitcher of water from the sideboard and she gratefully dipped first one hand and then the other into it. "That helps a little," she said, but he read no easing of the pain in her eyes.

Rohan's attention was snatched by the bowl, where the cup had begun to glow softly. His eyes widened as the golden light spread, permeated the water, swirled slowly and coalesced not unlike the way *faradh'im* used Fire. Water was not the Goddess' element; Sunrunners were all violently ill when they attempted to cross it. Fire and Earth, these were the children of the Goddess. As for Air and Water—the Father of Storms obviously had dominion over them. Destruction and life were in each, balancing the world, and all four were used in the most somber and powerful of *faradhi* conjurings.

He saw Sioned, slim and vigorous in pale riding leathers, thick fire gold hair braided around her head. She was speaking to Sorin, who nodded and unrolled a parchment on which architects had sketched and resketched plans for rebuilding Feruche. Beyond them the castle itself rose, fleshed out in stone for its first two floors, a skeleton of steel supports above that. Rohan saw girders for two towers, a balcony running the length of the Desert side of the keep, and a watchspire reaching skyward with steel fingers.

Old Myrdal, long-retired commander of Stronghold's guard, limped into the vision, leaning heavily on her cane. She pointed to the design parchment, then to the keep, and laughed. Sorin looked startled; Sioned, thoughtful. Myrdal drew patterns in the dirt with her cane, speaking rapidly, then wiped out the sketch with her boot.

Rohan knew what the old woman had proposed—in principle if not detail. She knew every secret of every castle in the Desert—including the gutted ruin that had stood where a new keep was now being built. She had frankly admitted that her reason for accompanying Sioned to Feruche was to remind Sorin to sneak secrets into a design where no one suspected them. Beauty had won over preparedness for war in most of the final plans for the new keep, but Myrdal's adamant face told Rohan she would insist on precautions just the same. There were ways in and out of Stronghold, Remagev, Radzyn, Tiglath, and Tuath that no one but Myrdal knew of, ways she had imparted to him and Sioned but not, in most cases, to the owners of the keeps. By just such a secret passage, Sioned had entered the old Feruche and taken Pol from his mother, Princess Ianthe.

Urival drew in a shuddering breath and his hands fell away from the bowl. The vision faded as he sagged back in his chair. Rohan forced him to drink some wine, and color gradually returned to the old man's face.

"It would be easier to sustain if I'd taken *dranath* first, of course," he said. "But I assume you understand."

"I understand that you now can do certain things—which Andry also knows how to do from his copy of the Star Scroll," Rohan said slowly. "And you propose to teach these things to Pol."

"And to Sioned. I may not last long enough to teach

the boy everything myself. When does he return from Graypearl?"

"He'll be knighted at the next *Rialla*, when he's almost twenty-one. When Sioned feels he knows what he should of *faradhi* arts, he'll take over Princemarch from Ostvel and rule from Dragon's Rest."

Urival nodded. "How close to completion is the new keep?"

"It's coming along slowly," Rohan admitted. "I hope to have one large building and two smaller ones finished by the *Rialla*."

Morwenna was startled. "Five years you've been working on it, and only three parts done?"

The basics of a small defensive keep could be finished in a year. Upper stories and embellishments—what Sorin was doing now—could take up to two more. The fancy work of towers, spires, and so forth could go on forever, depending on the ambitions, tastes, and funding of the builder. Feruche was taking a long time because it was something of an experiment; techniques used there would be applied to Dragon's Rest. But the latter was not a keep; it was to be a palace.

Rohan said, "We're not creating a castle, but an impression. It must be perfect for the first *Rialla* held there."

"What you're saying is that your three parts of Dragon's Rest will be *completely* finished, down to the rugs and doorknobs," Urival mused.

"Yes." He rose and opened the shutters, letting in light and air.

"I'll wager Princess Gennadi is relieved not to have the responsibility of the *Rialla* at Waes anymore," said Morwenna.

"But young Geir is not," Rohan reminded her. "He's sixteen, and that's a proud age. Gennadi allowed him to preside with her at the Lastday banqueting, when the move to Dragon's Rest was formally announced. If looks were daggers. . . ." He shrugged.

"Taking the *Rialla* from Waes wasn't perhaps the smartest thing you ever did," Urival remarked. "But I can see the necessity. Bring the princes to Pol once every three years and make your—impression. Be that as it may, we will need more than that, his status as your heir, and the Princemarch title to fulfill Andrade's scheme."

"And that's what it's about for you in the end, isn't it?" Rohan asked softly. "She chose Andry to succeed her because she could choose none other—and was just as trapped into accepting Pol as her *faradhi* prince."

The old Sunrunner got to his feet and said with dignity, "Your own schemes mesh with hers, my lord High Prince."

"Not necessarily."

"Lying to yourself was never one of your vices."

"I have others more interesting," Rohan said smoothly, "but this is hardly the time to discuss them. I tell you now, my lord, that what Pol learns he will use as he sees fit. Sunrunner arts or sorcery, neither you nor Andrade's memory nor anything else will rule him in their use."

"Just like Andry," Urival snapped.

"With a subtle difference." He gave the old man a hard smile. "You *trust* Pol."

Chapter Five

725: Dragon's Rest

The roses had not performed to expectations. Everything and everyone else had, this first *Rialla* at the new palace, but not the roses. Pol had been extremely irritated. *How dare flowers not bloom precisely when and as he wishes them to?* Sionell asked herself acidly as she paced the water garden. Ruler of Princemarch, High Prince's heir, Sunrunner—thwarted by uncooperative roses. *Serves him right—arrogant swine.*

Reaching a little hillock at the garden's edge, she sat with her back to a sapling and began shredding the leaves of an inoffensive bush. It needed a trim anyway, she thought—just like Pol's conceit. Newly knighted, awash in compliments for the beauty of the Princes Hall—and hip-deep in pretty girls—he'd had a lovely *Rialla*. Just lovely.

She had seen him at least once a day for the past twenty days. He positively oozed self-confidence for all that this was his first year as a ruling prince, mingling with his highborn guests or striding purposefully to yet another meeting (where he was undoubtedly brilliant, tactful, and wise, she told herself snidely). Everyone's model of perfection, was Pol of Princemarch.

Who had come to greet his parents riding on the back of a cow.

Sionell felt her mouth defy her mood by twitching upward at the corners, remembering her first sight of him after six years. Any romantic notions about his riding back into her life (or, more accurately, her into his, through the narrow gorge that protected the valley of Dragon's Rest) on one of those golden horses had crumpled like old parchment. Rohan had blinked in astonish-

ment, Sioned had sighed and rolled her gaze skyward,
and Pol had smiled innocently.

"You caught me in the middle of trying her paces!
Actually, she's quite comfortable, once you get seated
right. I may start a new fashion. No, really, I'm trying to
teach her to take a path that doesn't involve trampling
the crops. Where she goes, the others follow. I thought if
we nudged her in the right direction, we wouldn't have to
replant every few days."

Chay snorted. "One of my best studs and three of my
best mares I gave you last year, and you greet us riding a
cow."

" 'Gave'?" Pol laughed. "Sold!"

Sioned fixed her green eyes on her son. "Where's this
glorious set of chambers you've been promising?"

He pointed to a fretwork of girders and chimneys.
"See that?"

Rohan squinted down the valley to the palace complex. "What happened? I thought the crafters had orders
to finish by now."

"It was a choice between living quarters and the Princes
Hall," Pol said cheerfully. "Mine are up there somewhere, too. Or so my architects tell me."

Rohan peered at the empty air divided off by stone
and steel. "Sleep well at night, do you?"

"Sorry, Father. For now you'll have to make do with
the Guard Tower."

Sionell knew the plans for Dragon's Rest as well as she
knew the ancient walls of her home castle, Remagev.
Her brother Jahnavi was Riyan's squire at Skybowl; Riyan
often visited Sorin at Feruche; Sorin had helped with the
design for Dragon's Rest; Jahnavi had made a copy of
the plans for Sionell. She knew what the finished palace
would look like down to the last gravel pathway and
fountain. Most of it she approved; some of it she would
have altered for the sake of comfort, convenience, or
charm. As if she had any right to say a single word about
Dragon's Rest, or share in it as anything more than a
guest. She'd known that while riding down the valley to
the Princes Hall, and the days that followed had made it
even more painfully clear.

Well, so what, she thought, digging her bootheels into
the soft, damp soil. Who needed him, anyway? She'd

been surrounded by young men of wealth and position all during the *Rialla*, men eager to claim her attention and, if possible, her heart. *Not to mention my dowry*, she added cynically.

One thing was certain: Pol would never Choose a wife for her wealth. He needed more money the way dragons needed more teeth. Dragon's Rest was ample proof—built, in fact, to impress within a hair of overawing.

Two buildings had been completed in time for the *Rialla*. The Guard Tower, five floors high and perfectly round, was constructed of pale silvery-gray stone, its roof of gray-blue Kierstian tiles. It would be matched on the other side of the Princes Hall by a similar tower for the masters of horses and hawks and vines and harvests, with all their assistants and gear. For now, the Masters Tower was only a circle of flagged stakes in the ground, making the whole place look lopsided.

The Princes Hall was a masterpiece of dazzling Fironese crystal windows and graceful proportions, round on the approach side and flat where it faced the water gardens. In time, two more buildings would face each other across the fountains, hollow and curving like halves of a Sunrunner's ring. One was the iron-and-stone skeleton Pol had pointed out to his parents, and would become his private domain. The other was for servants, guests, reception chambers, and the machinery of Princemarch's government. Of course the palace would be beautiful; it wouldn't dare be anything else. It was Pol's.

Sionell got to her feet, pacing restlessly toward the central fountain. The pool was quiet now. Water had blossomed there during the Lastday banqueting, but she supposed that since there was nobody left here to impress, Pol had ordered it stilled. That night, he'd called and extinguished Fire to racks of torches in sequence, constantly changing the direction of light thrown onto the water. It had been a spectacular show as seen from the dining chamber of the Princes Hall, culminating in his casual gesture that had illuminated hundreds of white candles around the pool at the same time all the torches went out. The glow had spread from candles outward to ignite the torches once more, until the whole of the water garden was ablaze in Sunrunner's Fire.

And Pol had reveled in it. A season away from his

twenty-first winter, he was taller than Rohan by a hand's span, his hair a darker blond, his eyes green and then blue and then both as he smiled with a not-quite-innocent pleasure in his own skills. Wearing a shirt of Desert blue and a tunic of Princemarch's violet, his shoulders beginning to broaden toward maturity, he had been a prince to his fingertips.

But no *faradhi* rings sparkled on his fingers. Nor had Lord Andry offered them. Only the moonstone that had been Lady Andrade's, reset into a ring sized to his hand, told of his Sunrunner gifts. The unspoken, unacknowledged antagonism between Pol and Andry had not been allowed to spoil the work or the festivities of the *Rialla*, but everyone knew it was there. Only a matter of time before they clashed, Sionell's father had muttered one evening, shaking his head. She hoped it wouldn't happen. But she also knew who would win.

Seating herself on the blue tiles at the fountain's rim, she trailed her hand through the water to wash leaf-stains from it and smiled grimly at her own unadorned fingers. Like Pol, she would never wear *faradhi* rings. But, unlike him, she had no choice in the matter.

"What are you doing out here all alone, Ell?"

She glanced around. Pol strode lithely toward her from the shell of his future home, long legs encased in tan riding leathers and tall black boots, white shirt open at his throat. His waist was circled by a belt dyed blue and violet, decorated with the gold buckle of his new knighthood and by a dagger set with amethysts that had been Chay and Tobin's gift. Energy and power rippled from him; sunlight crowned his sun-bleached head with bright gold.

How can I want him and hate him at the same time? Then, chiding herself disgustedly, *Oh, grow up! You've always known it was hopeless—*

"It's quiet here," she said aloud. "After all the fuss, I was enjoying the silence."

"If it's quiet you want, why are you staying to watch the dragons? Goddess, the racket they make! You *will* stay until they get here, won't you?"

"Of course. My mother wouldn't miss them."

Pol chuckled and propped one boot on the fountain rim. "Feylin's almost as scared of dragons as she is fascinated by them. But they don't frighten you, do they? Remember years ago at Skybowl, when you nearly fell out a window trying to fly after them?"

Sionell laughed easily. "As if you never wanted to do the same thing!"

Grinning wry agreement, he gestured to the Princes Hall. "I haven't had the chance to ask you how you like my two-fifths of a palace."

"It's magnificent—as you don't need me to tell you. Now that everybody's gone, I suppose you can get back to work on the rest of it."

"Only until the rains. That was our big mistake—we never considered how much time we lose to winter. But no snow, thank the Goddess."

"Better to thank the Storm God. But I'd like to see it snow someday. I'm told it's beautiful."

"I've ridden through it, walked on it, and even slept on top of it, but I've never seen it fall, either."

"From what Princess Iliena says, it's rather like a freezing sandstorm—only it blows down, not across."

"Down, if you're lucky," Pol corrected. "Across, with a vengeance if you get stuck in a blizzard."

Such polite, social conversation; they might have been friendly strangers. "Iliena must find Graypearl a nice change after Snowcoves."

"Strange, isn't it? That she and her sister married brothers." He hesitated, then shrugged and went on, "And that Ludhil and Laric visited Snowcoves and fell in love at exactly the same time."

He sounded wistful. Perhaps his parents were hinting that with Dragon's Rest livable, if not finished, he ought to start looking for a wife. If she steered the talk away from love, he might suspect—no, he had never suspected a damned thing. Arrogant, insufferable, and *blind*.

"I think Iliena got the better geographical bargain by marrying Chadric's heir," she replied lightly. "Lisiel may be Princess of Firon now as Laric's wife, but she's still in blizzard country."

"Do you know what Firon means in the old language? 'Silent hoof.' A tribute to the snow, no doubt." He paused again. "I'm supposed to go find myself a princess, you know," he finished irritably.

So he wasn't ready yet. Interesting. "In your position, *they'll* come looking for *you*."

"Don't I know it. In a way, I'd like it to happen quickly—it'd save me years of nonsense. Trying to find the right person must be awful. I haven't even started yet."

"But *they* have," she said before thinking, remembering all the highborn maidens who had clustered around him during the *Rialla*. Sionell had removed herself from the vicinity as often as possible, accompanied by her own clutch of admirers—who for some reason only annoyed her.

"I just hope she'll be somebody I can talk to the way I can to you. It's wonderful, Ell, finding out you've grown up sensible!"

She smiled wryly at the backhanded compliment.

"I mean it. The girls here, the ones at Graypearl—gigglers and gawkers, all of them. I can talk to you like I'd talk to Riyan or Maarken or Sorin. It's a relief to find there's at least one intelligent woman my own age in the world."

How nice of him to categorize her as one of the boys.

He had fixed his gaze on the delinquent flowers nearby. "Damned roses," he muttered.

Sionell laughed at him. "As if all you had to do was wave your hand for them to appear! Prince and Sunrunner you may be, but not magician."

"But I wanted them to be spectacular. My grandmother Milar loved messing about with gardens, too, you know. I think I inherited it from her." Glancing down at her and then away, he asked, "Ell, what do you think of Tallain?"

"I think very highly of him," she responded. "He's very capable, as he's shown since his father died last winter."

"He's determined to keep the Cunaxans and the Merida pent up in the north so we won't have to worry about them ever again."

Sionell nodded, wondering why he'd mentioned the young lord of Tiglath. An additional honor for him, perhaps? Tuath Castle had no direct male heir; perhaps Pol and Rohan were considering a union of the two holdings.

"Tallain's a fine man—he was my father's squire for years," Pol went on.

"I know."

"I like him a lot. A prince is only as good as the people who support him, the *athr'im* who're loyal to him. Tallain's one of the best."

"I like him, too," she said, a trifle impatiently, wishing he'd either tell her why he wanted to discuss Tallain of Tiglath or go away and leave her alone.

Pol did not enlighten her. She did, however, receive her second wish. From the Princes Hall came a young maidservant, black-haired and slender; she paused just long enough in the sunshine to make sure Pol had seen her, then stretched her arms wide, as if she'd just slipped out for some fresh air. Pol excused himself a few moments later—not even having the grace to enter the Hall by a different door.

Sionell watched him disappear, stunned. *Right in front of my face, too! All the subtlety of a rutting dragonsire!*

Then: *Fool! Idiot! He's the High Prince's heir, the great Sunrunner Prince—he can do as he likes and—damn him! I am not going to cry!*

And, finally: *Very well, then. If that's the way the wind sets, so be it. I'm not twelve anymore. If he doesn't want me, lots of others do. He can find a convenient Hell and rot in it for all I care.*

***

The next afternoon the High Princess enlisted her namesake's help in packing presents for Andry's son and daughter. He had not brought them to the *Rialla*. Rumor had it that this neglect earned him an interview with his parents that acquainted him intimately with their blistering views on the subject. Their anger was not that the children existed; they were furious and hurt that Andry had left them behind at Goddess Keep. Sionell and everyone else knew why. He intended little Andrev and Tobren to be raised as *faradh'im* only, with no ties and thus no second loyalties to the Desert. She could just imagine what Lord Chaynal—not to mention Princess Tobin—had said to that.

The latter had indulged her thwarted grandmotherly instincts with a buying spree at the *Rialla* Fair. It was this collection of toys, clothes, and trinkets that Sionell helped wrap and label for the children—while Tobin fretted at not having had them ready for Andry's departure two days earlier.

"He *would* ride out in a hurry, wanting to make good time back to Goddess Keep, when he *knew* I had things for the babies! I swear that one of these days I'm going to skin that boy alive."

Surveying the piles of packages—and the things yet to be wrapped—Sioned laughed. "Smart of him to escape while he had the chance. Honestly, Tobin, it's going to take two wagons and four pack horses to get all this to Goddess Keep."

Sionell said innocently, "The pony cart she bought them ought to hold quite a bit."

"Goddess in glory, don't remind her!" Sioned begged. "She'll go after the departing merchants and load that up, too!"

"Go on, tease me," Tobin invited, making a face. "You just wait until *you* become a grandmother, High Princess!"

Sionell prudently did not comment that if Pol kept putting off marriage while doing what he was doing with the maidservants, Sioned would have grandchildren long before she had a daughter-by-marriage. His bedchamber exploits were no one's business but his—not even his mother's. *And certainly not any of my concern—the graceless swine—*

She glanced up from folding a stack of shirts to find that both Tobin and Sioned had run to the windows. An instant later the whole tower seemed to shake as an arrogant roar shattered the morning stillness.

Dragons.

Sionell was first down the stairs. She arrived breathless outside the tower and stared up at the flight of dragons heading for the lake. Training her mother had given her in the intellectual study of the beasts warred briefly with the sheer delight of watching them. Emotion won, as ever. The day it didn't, she'd order up her funeral pyre—for surely she would be near death.

"I never get over it," Sioned murmured at her side, as if she'd heard Sionell's thoughts. "All these years, watching them everywhere from Remagev to Waes, and I've never gotten used to their beauty."

Others joined them on the grassy slope in front of the Princes Hall—Sionell's parents, Maarken, Hollis, Arlis, and the High Prince himself. He was shirtless and barefoot, his damp fair hair indicating he'd leaped from a bath and barely remembered to pull on trousers. He looked his son's age as he turned his face skyward, rapt and ecstatic.

"Sionell!"

Turning, she saw Pol ride up on one of his golden horses. He reined in, eyes brilliant, and gestured. She grabbed his hand and used his booted foot as a stirrup to swing up behind his saddle.

"Faster!" she urged as he kicked the mare to a gallop, and laughed into the wind.

Some of the dragons were already at play along the lakeshore. Others, hungry after a long flight, pounced on the terrified sheep kept penned for their refreshment. A three-year-old gray female with gorgeous black underwings swept down in a controlled glide, plucked up a woolly lump with one hind foot, snapped its neck with a twist of front talons, and landed neatly on the opposite shore. She snarled at a sibling who attempted to steal her lunch and settled down to devour the sheep with dainty greed. The entire operation took less than twenty heartbeats.

Sionell slid to the ground before Pol brought the mare to a full halt. He was right beside her after slapping the horse back toward the stables—having no wish to see one of his prizes become dragon fodder.

"Start counting!" Sionell cried. "My mother will kill us if we don't!"

"Five russet hatchlings, seven green-bronze, ten black—Ell, just look at them! As alike as if they'd shared the same egg!"

"Four grays, three more black—I don't see the gray-blue sire who was at Skybowl. He must've died in mating battle—but there's the black one, and the worse for wear! How does he fly with that scab on his wing?"

"Where's Elisel? Can you see her?"

They searched the lake and the skies, but could find no trace of Sioned's russet dragon.

"She has to be here," Sionell fretted.

"Maybe she went to Skybowl." Pol tried to be soothing, but his face betrayed his worry.

Sioned ran up, winded. In silence she scanned the shore, biting her lip. At last she whispered, "She's not here."

If anything had happened to Elisel—the only dragon any of the Sunrunners had been able to talk to. . . . But Elisel might have been one of the females who died each mating year. There were insufficient caves for all the she-dragons; if they did not mate and lay their eggs, they died.

Sionell glanced up at Pol, seeing the same worry in his eyes. He muttered, "We have to coax them back to Rivenrock. We have to tell them it's safe there."

"How?" she asked bleakly. "If we've lost Elisel, then—" She broke off, mindful of Sioned nearby.

"Maybe Maarken and Hollis just chose the wrong dragons to touch," he mused.

"Trying it had them unconscious for a whole afternoon," she reminded him. His lips twisted as he gnawed on the inside of his cheek, his eyes narrowing as he focused on a single dragon. She knew what he was going to do as surely as if they'd thought it at the same time—and didn't say a word to stop him.

The others had arrived at the lake by now, occupied with the count or speculating on Elisel's absence or simply staring awestruck at the dragons. Only Sionell saw Pol take a deep breath to steady himself, fix his gaze on a large blue-gray three-year-old with silvery underwings, and close his eyes.

The young dragon stood with wings spread out to dry after his swim. Well-grown for his age, as an adult he would be a sire of formidable size. His head with its long face and huge eyes turned toward Pol, then away, then shook as if insects irritated him. Shuffling to one side, he bumped into another youngling who growled at him.

Sionell held her breath, willing Pol to succeed. How could he not? Nothing had ever been denied him; the world and all its dragons were his by right.

But not today.

The dragon shrieked, head lashing toward the sky. Pol cried out at the same time, a terrible groan that shuddered his whole frame. Sionell flung her arms around him to keep him upright, calling his name.

"Pol! You idiot!" Rohan gathered him from her and

lowered him to the grass. His eyes were open and he mumbled incoherently, the muscles of his legs and arms quivering. Sionell knelt, shifting Pol's head to her lap. Rohan framed his son's face with his hands and called his name.

The dragon howled again and took wing, circling the lake in panicked flight. All at once Pol's eyes opened startled and wide. He gave a great sigh and went bonelessly unconscious.

"Idiot," Rohan said again, but in a relieved tone this time. "Maarken, Tallain, get him out of here and put him to bed."

The young Lord of Tiglath gently assisted Sionell to her feet. "He'll be all right now, my lady. Let us take care of him."

She nodded numbly, grateful for his strong supporting arm as he gave her over to Arlis. Pol was slung between the two young men and carried away, utterly oblivious.

"Whatever possessed him to try such a thing?" Hollis asked. "He knows how difficult it is—"

"You just answered your own question," said the High Princess. "If he'd gotten tangled in that dragon's colors—"

"He wanted to ask about Elisel," Sionell murmured.

"Perhaps," Sioned conceded. "But what he really wanted, what he's *always* wanted, is to touch a dragon himself."

Rohan rubbed a hand over his face. "If he wasn't already to be punished by a sore brain for the next two days, I'd take him over my knee."

"*I'd* take him by the ears and shake some sense into him—if I could reach up that far," Sioned countered. "Has that poor dragon settled down yet?"

"Sunning himself and having a snack," Arlis reported. "Are you all right now, my lady?"

Sionell managed a shaky smile for the future Prince of Kierst-Isel. "Thank you, my lord."

Pol woke in time for dinner, sat up, moaned, clutched his aching skull, and collapsed back into the pillows. Tallain came downstairs to inform them that the prince had wisely decided to stay in his room.

"How long did it take you to bully him into it?" Rohan asked curiously.

Tallain grinned. "Two tries at standing, one at getting

his pants on, and some very creative cursing, my lord. I hardly had to say anything at all."

"Good man. Let him convince himself. Walvis, I assume Feylin is lost in her statistics again, and won't be joining us for dinner?"

They were a small group that night, seated around a table in what would one day be the guards mess. Sioned had chosen to stay upstairs and wait for first moonlight to contact Riyan at Skybowl; he would know about Elisel. Chay, Tobin, and Maarken were at the stables tending a mare suspected of colic. So Arlis served Rohan, Walvis, Sionell, Tallain, and Hollis from a cauldron of stew made of leftovers from the Lastday banquet. When sweets and taze were presented at the end of the meal, the young prince was dismissed to his own dinner.

Despite the day's events, conversation was not of dragons or Sunrunning. Rohan plied Tallain with questions about an agreement signed only days ago with Miyon of Cunaxa regarding the border between princedoms. The gist of the matter was, could Tallain live with the terms?

"Kabil of Tuath and I had a long talk this spring. With Sunrunners at our holdings able to contact Riyan at any time, we both feel fairly secure. And glad to give our people something better to do than patrol."

"Trust my son to need more iron than even Sioned was able to trick Miyon out of," Rohan sighed. "And trust Miyon that the only way to get it was a reduction of troops along the border."

"That's not quite fair," Walvis observed. "Sorin learned so much from building Feruche that more iron had to come to Dragon's Rest—plus it's so much bigger."

"And whose fault is that? Again, my son." The High Prince shrugged. "Ah, well. Reduction of patrols reduces the chance of any little 'accidents' like last winter."

Sionell sipped hot taze, remembering how close they had come to war with Cunaxa. An encounter along the border had led to a disagreement about who had encroached on whose land, ending with several dead on each side before both backed off. A courier had galloped into Tiglath that night; Tallain rode out at once with an escort. His quiet diplomacy—aided by a map drawn by Goddess Keep's Sunrunners in 705 that strictly defined boundaries—had convinced the Cunaxans that the matter wasn't worth further bloodshed.

"Yes," Tallain was saying in response to Rohan's comment. "But if they'd been led by a Merida, I wouldn't have let them away so lightly."

Sionell turned to him with interest. "How did you know it wasn't?"

"Northerners can smell a Merida at ten measures, my lady," he answered with a tight little smile. "Ask your mother. She's from our part of the Desert." His brown eyes, startling contrast to the sungold hair swept back from his brow, lingered on her. She realized abruptly that he liked looking at her. She fought a blush as his attention returned to the High Prince. "Miyon's impudent lately, though, which must mean he has a new ally. I suspect Meadowlord."

"Chiana and her Parchment Prince," Walvis said sourly. "They've a natural affinity with Miyon. I can't believe Chiana's insolence in Naming her son after her grandfather —and her daughter for her whore of a mother."

Hollis blinked large, innocent eyes. "I'm surprised she didn't Name him Roelstra."

Rohan grinned and rapped his knuckles on the table. "Now, now, children. We can't encourage such disrespect for other princes—next, you'll be insulting us! Tallain, will incidents increase or decrease along the border?"

The thin smile crossed Tallain's face again. "I couldn't say, my lord—but for one factor. There's an advantage to dealing with Prince Miyon. His merchants and crafters. They've got him by the throat, as ever. And they constantly try to sneak their shipments into Tiglath. Sometimes I let them."

"Reaping a substantial profit thereby?" Sionell asked, amused.

"Of course, my lady. I let enough through to keep them trying. The rest I confiscate. You'd be astonished what they're willing to pay to get their goods back and legally shipped. My father built two schools and a new infirmary on the proceeds. I'm planning to refurbish the market square next year."

"Oh, I do enjoy the law," Rohan sighed. "Especially the ones my *athr'im* ignore to our mutual advantage. But I never heard any of this, Tallain."

"I never mentioned it, my lord." The young man was unable to keep a twinkle from his dark eyes.

"It's not civilized of me, of course," Rohan went on. "And I really shouldn't condone this sort of thing, even unofficially."

Walvis was grinning openly. "But so much fun," he urged. "And such a comfort to the rest of us to know you're not perfect after all."

The High Prince pretended horror. "Sweet Goddess, don't tell anyone!"

Sionell laughed. Rohan really was so much *nicer* than Pol. "Your secret is safe with us!"

"My eternal gratitude, my lady," he responded with an elegant bow. "To return to the matter of the Cunaxans— Sorin feels they may start to use the trade route over the Veresch again, now that Feruche is there for protection. I hope you'll forgive me, Tallain, if I make the passage fees low enough to encourage them."

Sionell answered, "He can hardly object, can he?"

Tallain gave her a long look, then grinned. "Hardly," he said in dry tones.

"You'll still make a profit," Rohan added. "But if Miyon feels too bottled up, he'll get nervous and start thinking about war again."

"I don't think he's fond of you, Rohan," Walvis said blandly.

Hollis was frowning. "He asked a lot of questions about Pol this year. And he was usually close by wherever Pol was. He might simply have been taking his measure, of course. . . ." She trailed off doubtfully.

"Did you get that impression?" Sionell asked. "His half-sister sat next to me at the races, being subtle." She snorted. "She practically asked which boot Pol puts on first. As if I'd know anything, not having seen him for so long."

"Audrite and I got the same treatment," Hollis said, nodding. "And she knows him much better, his having been a squire at Graypearl."

"None of you ladies said anything to the point," said Tallain. Reverting in Arlis' absence to the squire's role he had held at Stronghold for many years, he rose to refill everyone's cups.

"No, but—thank you, Tallain—but why would Miyon's

sister ask such questions?" Hollis dipped a spoonful of honey into her taze. "Not political, personal. Private things."

"She's only a few years older than Pol," Walvis offered. "Maybe his grace of Cunaxa sees a match?"

Sionell stared. "With a bow-legged, thick-ankled, witless shatter-skull?"

"I agree, Ell. Pol has better taste," Rohan said. "But maybe you've got something, Walvis. Which of Miyon's allies have daughters, sisters, or cousins around Pol's age? Pretty ones, I mean. An interesting idea." Rising, he stretched and yawned. "That's all for this evening's meeting of the informal High Prince's Council," he smiled. "Hollis, with your permission I'll join you in tucking Chayla and Rohannon into bed—*again*."

"You're welcome to try." She grimaced. "Thank the Goddess dragons don't fly over Whitecliff more often. It took both their nurses plus Pol's poor steward to catch my twin terrors today."

Sionell went upstairs to her room, escorted partway by Tallain. She had finished unplaiting her hair and was brushing it out for the night when her father came in, looking very thoughtful. After asking permission to be seated—even in a room he himself inhabited, the good manners learned as Rohan's squire stayed with him—he settled in a chair and meditatively stroked his beard.

"What is it, Papa?" she asked at last.

"I don't quite know how to begin," he said with a bemused smile. His blue eyes narrowed slightly as he watched her tease tangles with the brush. He had given her those eyes, but she more closely resembled her mother and had Feylin's dark red hair. "You've spent more time at Radzyn and Stronghold than at home these last couple of years. I suppose I haven't really noticed that you've grown up."

"Surprise," she smiled.

"Rather! I like the way you've turned out—though I miss my pudgy little pest," he added, his smile becoming a grin.

Until last winter, Sionell had despaired of ever acquiring a waistline. Desert dwellers tended to be vain about their slim figures. In Gilad, a comfortably rounded woman was much preferred over a slender one—but Sionell no longer had to wish she lived in Gilad.

"I suppose there's no way to get around it," her father sighed. "I wanted to talk to you about Pol."

She felt her cheeks burn. "A childish habit I've grown out of."

"Are you sure?"

"Yes." She'd have to, sooner or later.

"You're very young, darling. I thought this might be the case. It would hurt your mother and me to see you dream after a man who can marry whom he chooses—as long as his Choice is highborn and *faradhi*."

"I know."

"I needed to be sure because of something that happened tonight."

He was watching her in a way that made her want to squirm. Thinking over the conversation at dinner and afterward, she remembered her outburst regarding Miyon's half-sister and blushed again.

Walvis was quick to see it. "So you have an idea about it already. I'm glad. He's a worthy man, and a good friend. He quite rightly asked permission to begin a formal courtship. But I told him I'd have to consult you first. As fine a man as he is, and as good a husband as he'd make you, I wouldn't give my consent even to Tallain if you were still—"

The brush dropped to the rug.

"So you *didn't* know."

Her wits reeled like hatchling dragons darting through the sky. *Tallain?*

"He admires you and would like to know you better. Give you the chance to know him. If you both like what you see, and can love each other, then your mother and I would be very happy with the Choice."

Humiliating that her first coherent thought was: *I could have him if I wanted—that'd show Pol!*

"He wants to spend part of the winter at Stronghold so he can visit Remagev every so often. He won't rush you, love. He knows you're only seventeen, and certainly by next *Rialla* you'll have an even wider choice of young men than you did this year."

And there had been plenty—but Tallain had not been among them. He had danced with her only once. Shyness? She doubted it. Fear of competition? Not with those eyes and that hair and that face—not to mention all that money. Abruptly his words about the riches to be obtained from Cunaxan merchants took on new meaning, and she almost giggled. Subtle of him, to indicate he didn't need her dowry. More seriously, she realized that he didn't need her family's connection to the High Prince, either. If he Chose her, it would be for herself alone. Sionell was forced to admire his tactics. And his wits. And his sense of humor. And his looks.

He wasn't Pol—but no man could be. And Pol would never be hers.

With a suddenness that stopped her breath for a moment she recalled the previous afternoon's conversation with Pol. *He knows—that's why he said all those things about Tallain—trying to get me married off!*

Her father was talking again, a bit nervously as she stayed silent. "Think it over for now, Ell. You don't have to decide yet. There's plenty of time."

"I don't need any time," she heard herself say. "Tallain can come visit me if he likes." After a brief pause, her lips curving slightly, she added, "But we don't need to tell *him* that just yet."

Walvis blinked, then burst out laughing. "You'd keep him guessing until the moment you accept him, wouldn't you?"

Sionell answered only with a shrug, but she was thinking, *Yes, and if he thinks he has to work harder to win me, we'll probably both fall in love. Nothing so interesting as someone unattainable, as I well know. But if I do marry Tallain, it'll be because I can make a life with him.* She had a brief vision of Pol hurrying to join the flirtatious maidservant. He'd look at every woman in the world but her. She'd known that since childhood. But now she believed it.

Walvis rose and ruffled her hair as if she were still ten, saying she was too clever for her own good. Then he went back downstairs to persuade Feylin to leave her musings about the dragon population and come up to bed.

Sionell smoothed and rebraided her hair with automatic movements. If not Tallain, then someone else. But she did like him. And it was soothing to be admired by a handsome, wealthy young lord.

"Lady Sionell of Tiglath," she whispered. Then, even more softly: "High Princess Sionell."

No decisions tonight, except the one allowing Tallain to try. But if he was as she believed him to be, then it wouldn't be difficult to love him. Not as she loved—*had* loved—Pol, of course. Tallain would know that. But he would never say anything about it, no more than Ostvel ever said anything to Alasen about Andry.

And it was very nice to be wanted. Very nice indeed.

Chapter Six

726: Swalekeep

Autumn was breathlessly hot in Meadowlord. Nothing moved. Swollen gray clouds neither blew away nor rained nor seemed able to do anything but loiter. Even the mighty Faolain River lay sluggish just outside the city walls, as if reluctant to flow. The stillness would break soon. But until it did, even walking through the stifling air was an effort.

If autumn affected Swalekeep's population, who were used to it this way, it was even worse for visitors. Two such, longing for the Veresch Mountains where they made their home, dragged themselves from their beds at the Green Feather Inn, hoping for some vague coolness in the dawn.

"Hideous climate," the old woman muttered. "How do these people bear it?"

Her companion, a tall young man with copper-threaded brown hair and intensely blue eyes, bent a sardonic glance on her and made no comment.

"And so many of them," she went on. "All jammed together—it's not natural to live like this, Ruval."

Still he said nothing, knowing as well as she the history of Swalekeep. The warrior who had originally set himself up as lord of the general vicinity had built the first part of a defensive castle, to which his heirs had added as need or whimsy prompted. Swalekeep's population had swelled periodically as Meadowlord's powerful neighbors treated the princedom as their private battlefield and refugees swarmed in. Eventually a Prince of Meadowlord, weary and impoverished by the sporadic influx of mouths to feed, decreed that enough was enough and built a wall higher than a dragon's wingspan around his holding. During High Prince Roelstra's last war with Prince Zehava, that wall had kept Swalekeep safe.

During the twenty-one years since Rohan had taken Roelstra's princedom and title, the wall had been unnecessary. When bits of it were spirited away to become foundation stones for new homes and shops, no one did anything but shrug. Swalekeep's inhabitants had eventually knocked down whole sections of wall, and all over the city blocks of gray-veined granite did duty as everything from mounting blocks to entire first floors. And the words of Eltanin of Tiglath, that Rohan would build walls stronger than any stone to keep peace among the princedoms, were in Swalekeep attributed to their late prince, Clutha.

The old man had never had half so abstract a thought in his life. But it made a good story—except in Princess Chiana's hearing.

"I wonder how Marron likes it here," the old woman asked suddenly.

"Servitude is hardly his style—but he'll have to get used to it. Only one of us is going to be the next High Prince, after all. And it won't be him."

She chuckled low in her throat. They paced off the neat cobbled streets, past shops with living quarters above, the elegant homes of rich merchants and court functionaries, and finally neared the old castle itself. Of the more than five thousand who lived in Swalekeep, perhaps a hundred were out and about in the muggy morning heat.

"He's probably become quite civilized these last two winters. Let him rub some polish onto you, Ruval." She stopped outside a shop where a fine Cunaxan rug was displayed. A *rathiv*—"carpet of flowers"—done in brilliant colors, it was perfect for her purposes. "I want that. Come back later and acquire it for me."

"With money or persuasion, Mireva?"

As she glanced up to return his grin, by the soft light she suddenly seemed half her nearly sixty-seven winters. The fine lines raying out from her fierce gray-green eyes vanished, as did the slight fleshiness along her jaw as her lifted head tightened the skin.

"None of that," she chided, though she shared his glee at the possibilities open to them in placid Swalekeep, where *diarmadh'im* were unknown and *faradh'im* barely tolerated by proud Chiana of the long and grudge-filled memory.

They continued down the street to the appointed meeting place just outside the low brick wall surrounding the castle gardens. They lingered for some time, pretending to admire the late roses.

"I can't help wondering how much he's changed," Ruval said as they waited for his half-brother.

"Do you really think he has? He'll be just the same as ever: stubborn, jealous, and ambitious."

"But he's bound to have picked up a few ideas of his own. Like Segev."

They both paused to recall the youngest of Ianthe's brood, dead these seven summers by a *faradhi* hand. Segev's failure to steal the Star Scroll had been a setback; his scheming to take its power for himself had been a shock; his death had been a blessing. But the manner of his death—stabbed by Lady Hollis—earned Mireva's vow to avenge him. Killing her—and her husband and children —would be almost as satisfying as killing Pol and Rohan.

And Sioned, who had captured Rohan before Ianthe had even met him, thus fouling one path back to power for Mireva's people. Sioned had protected Rohan from Roelstra's treachery during their single combat by constructing a dome of glistening starfire at an impossible distance—stars forbidden to Sunrunners by Lady Merisel of abhorrent memory—after she had ordered Feruche razed and Ianthe slaughtered in her bed.

But only one of Ianthe's sons had died with his mother: the boy who was Rohan's get. Ruval, Marron, and Segev had escaped on Sioned's own Radzyn-bred horses and been brought to Mireva. Ruval wanted the High Princess dead in payment for his mother; Marron, always more direct, simply wanted her dead. Mireva's reasons were more complex. She had, after all, touched the woman's powerful mind.

Addressing Ruval's last remark, she said, "Segev was a fool as only a sixteen-year-old boy can be a fool. Marron is older, and one hopes he's wise enough to know that you two can't fight it out until there's something to fight over. Until we have the Desert and Princemarch, he'll go where he's reined."

"I'll be riding him with a pronged bit and spurs just the same."

Mireva paced a little way down the low wall, pausing to inhale the heavy spice of a flowering bush. Ruval followed, and together they gazed up at the castle. An eccentric structure, befitting its long history and the varying tastes of its owners, it exuded towers, extra wings, and additional floors with no regard for any architectural grace. Vines climbed thick and close up gray stone, softening some of the more awkward angles, but taken as a whole it was a rather ugly place. Dragon's Rest, on the other hand, was reported to be an exquisite blend of beauty, strength, and power. How nice of Pol, Mireva thought with a sudden almost girlish smile, to make a palace fit for the Sorcerer High Prince who stood at her side.

She must be sure to thank Pol before she killed him.

"At last," Ruval muttered. Mireva turned and saw a familiar young man dressed in the light green of service to Meadowlord's rulers. Similar in feature and build to his eldest brother, Marron's coloring was ruddier; even in the muted gray light his hair was a dark red mane. His eyes were brown, like Ianthe's. Ruval was the taller by two fingers' width, but Marron was the heavier and more physically imposing. They were unmistakable as brothers, especially when they smiled—sly, mocking, and shrewd.

Marron nodded pleasantly as he approached, as he had done to the one or two others he passed along the wall. When he was abreast of them, he whispered, "The Crown and Castle." And walked on.

Mireva was irritated, but understood his need for caution. Had there been more people about, they could have met with complete unconcern right outside Chiana's windows. But the sultry heat kept most of Swalekeep indoors. Thus they had to meet there, too.

The inn was situated at the end of a street that itself ended at the lofty outer wall. This was one of those places where the granite had been stolen away for more prosaic uses; the gap was big enough to ride through without ducking. Not that Ruval would have cared to try it—those upper stones looked a little tentative, deprived of their underpinnings.

One side of the Crown and Castle abutted on an iron-monger's. The other was Swalekeep's main wall itself. Over the hearth fire hung a cauldron from which patrons dipped their own stew. A smaller pot held mulled wine, also on a self-serve basis. Ruval showed a gold coin to a girl who sat near the hearth and ordered chilled wine. She left off petting the fat orange cat in her lap long enough to point to a nearby table—and to take the coin from his fingers.

Mireva joined him in a corner and they made slow drinking of the wine, trying to ignore the incessant hammering of the smith next door. How anyone could find the energy to work in this weather—let alone over a furnace—was utterly beyond him. Eventually, full but not particularly refreshed, Ruval got up, stretched, and made his way out the back door as if to relieve himself. Marron was waiting for him, fuming.

"You knew where I'd be! Why did you make me wait?"

"Because I was thirsty. Because it amused me." He assessed his brother with a scathing glance. "You've fed well, these last few winters."

"And you still look like a half-starved wolf who doesn't know how to hunt for himself," Marron shot back.

"Why should I, when I have a little brother to do my hunting for me?" Ruval grinned and walked toward the watering trough, seating himself casually on its edge. "Well? What news of our darling Aunt Chiana?"

"Keep your voice down!" Marron hissed.

"Are your senses grown as soft as your belly? There's no one in hearing distance but those cats." He gestured to the gray striped cat and kittens nearby. "And I doubt they're interested."

Marron sighed and shook his head. "I hate being closed in like this. You don't know what it's been like. The Veresch forests are walls you can walk through."

Ruval felt unwilling sympathy. He hadn't considered until arriving in Swalekeep how difficult it must be to adapt to life inside stone. "Come sit down, brother."

Marron perched on the far rim of the trough. "You know my position in Swalekeep. It's taken me two years to get into the chamberlain's confidence, even using bits of power here and there. Chiana's a bitch up one side and down the other—our grandfather's daughter, no doubt about that! She wants all done to perfection, then finds fault and makes you do it again."

"I'm looking forward to meeting her."

Dark eyes widened. "You can't!"

"No?" Ruval laughed. "Go on."

Marron looked as if he might argue, then subsided with a glower. "Mireva was right about Chiana's ambition. She wants Rinhoel to have Princemarch as well as Meadowlord, even though all the sisters renounced it for themselves and their heirs—"

"All the sisters except Mother. Dead—at Sioned's order." A fragrance, a silken rustle, a throaty laugh, a sharp scowl when he played too rough—the meager memories darted through his mind, always escaping too quickly.

"I saw Sioned at last year's *Rialla*. Toured Dragon's Rest, too, but we'll talk of that another time. She's fifty next year, and looks thirty-five. Rohan's the same." Marron hesitated. "He's not even a Sunrunner, Ruval—yet I could almost see the *aleva* around him. Sioned's is almost painful to look at. And as for Pol—!"

Ruval frowned. The *aleva* was literally a "circle of fire" that the truly sensitive, especially among *diarmadh'im*, could glimpse around the highly powerful. That Sioned possessed such an aura was taken for granted; that Pol's would also be visible was expected, too. But Rohan, whose Sunrunner blood was so thin—

Still, it was the Dragon's Son and not the Dragon Prince who concerned him now. "Tell me about Pol."

"I didn't catch more than a few glimpses of him. I had to spell Chiana to get her to take me at all. And she's not easy to work on, believe me. They're building Dragon's Rest out of stone and steel—she's made just the same, only of ambition and hate."

"My, how poetic."

Marron looked as though he wanted to take a swing at him. "If you want to try getting through all that, go right ahead."

"Pol," Ruval said.

"No Sunrunner's rings, but he's been well-trained, wager on it. Tall, blond, good-looking—the women were all after him. He's got an eye for the prettier ones."

"Hmm." Ruval smiled. "That's interesting news for a

little project of Mireva's. But never mind that now." He glanced at the inn's back door, where a boy had just thrown scraps to the cats. "You must have more to tell, and Mireva wants to talk at length. And in private."

"There's a musical evening tonight—Chiana likes to present herself as cultured and sophisticated," he added sourly. "Another thing about Pol, he's got an absolute passion for music. I'll meet you in the garden near the Pearlfisher Inn after dusk."

"I'll find it. But why not here? The wine's good."

"The wine is terrible. You've a lot to learn about the finer things available to a prince," Marron jeered. Before Ruval could put him in his place with a sharp answer, he strode off.

***

Mireva hissed with annoyance when Ruval entered their small chamber at the Green Feather. She intended the precious *rathiv* to be part of her performance for Chiana, and he had lumped it together as if it was a horse blanket.

"Wait," he grinned, correctly interpreting her angry look. Unfolding the rug, he revealed a torso-sized gleam of silver and glass that took her breath away. "I thought you might like this."

"By the Nameless One—!" she breathed, taking the mirror from him. Kneeling with it set before her on the wooden planks, she ran reverent fingers over decorative wires that swirled and twisted in a pattern as old as her people. "What is *this* doing out of the Veresch?"

"The shopkeeper didn't know what he had, of course. I actually paid money for it—though not for the *rathiv*—the price was that low." Ruval crouched beside her. "Do you have any idea what to do with it?"

"See this?" She pointed to an intricate knot woven in silver wire at the top of the frame. "Recognize it?"

"I'm not blind," he replied impatiently. "Can you get it to work?"

"Yes. Oh, *yes!*" She laughed and threw her arms around him. "My clever High Prince!" His hands ran eagerly over her back and hips, but she pushed him away. "Later. Leave me alone with it for now. Come back when it's time to meet Marron. I need to set the spell within it."

"And you won't let me watch." His handsome face

with its cruel, curling mouth went dark. "After all these years, you still don't trust me."

"If you knew what I do about this mirror, you wouldn't trust your own mother."

"Considering who my mother was, you're quite naturally right." Rising, he cast one last hungry glance at the mirror and left her.

Mireva rocked back and forth, hugging her breasts. The mirror rested in mute impotence on the floor, its strange dusky gold surface like a stormy sky at sunset. The silver frame was old and tarnished, the wires broken in some places and missing in others. But she knew it for what it was—and gave thanks that Ruval had seen and identified the crowning knotwork.

Her old, gnarled fingers caressed the flat face as a maiden might her lover's cheek. The small hand mirror she'd planned to give Chiana had been a risk. This was a certainty.

It took her some time to find the right words—she initially misjudged the age of the mirror, and had to restructure her accent and phrasing to awaken it. But when it finally brightened in the gloom of her chamber, it was with a sure and steady glow.

***

Marron opened all his windows to the evening rain. The heat had finally broken with a sweep of icy air that from its feel had come all the way from Firon's early snows. The trees outside bent in the wind and he nodded in satisfaction. It was plenty cold enough to justify the heavy hooded cloak he wore to disguise his distinctive hair.

Descending the stairs, he heard the faint echoes of strings and drums from the hall where Chiana was perpetuating her "great lady" image. Several times a season she invited influential merchants and their wives to spend the evening in her presence. She did not go so far as to give them dinner; she broke bread with no one under the rank of *athr'im*. But a summons to the castle was a social distinction no one refused, no matter how deeply Chiana was loathed.

On his way out he encountered the chamberlain in a back corridor. A doddering holdover from Clutha's time, the old man drank himself stuporous most nights and

whined about the good old days to anyone who would
listen. Marron found himself caught by a wizened claw,
unable to escape without being rude. The role of humble
servant did not sit easily on a man descended from High
Princes and *diarmadh'im*, but Marron had little choice.
At last he claimed a pressing appointment with a young
lady who did not like to be kept waiting, and slipped
away while the chamberlain mumbled about ancient loves
of his own.

Swalekeep was patchworked by little public parks, islands of trees and bushes and flowering plants connected
by meandering streets. Chiana had appropriated the larg-
est of them for one of her oddest self-indulgences: an
animal garden. In it roamed several deer and elk, and an
eagle with its flight feathers regularly plucked to keep it
earthbound. In large cages were a wolf pair that had
produced nothing but dead pups in the five years of their
captivity, and a female mountain cat, her claws torn out.
Chiana had offered a substantial reward for anyone who
could bring her a mate for the cat; it was said she would
have paid half Meadowlord's yearly income for a dragon,
but no one had taken her up on that, either.

Marron paused outside this sad little place, watching
the wolves pace endlessly behind steel mesh. A strong
kinship welled up in him for his fellow captive exiles. But
he could afford no weakening sentiment right now. He
was about to meet Mireva for the first time in two long
winters.

Chafing his cold hands beneath the cloak, he hurried
to the enclosure opposite the Pearlfisher and entered,
snicking the gate shut behind him. The hand on his arm
startled him into a curse.

"Your senses *have* dulled," she murmured. "But they're
lost in a good cause."

Ruval's cause, he wanted to say, but held his tongue.
Time enough to deal with his brother and leave Mireva
with only one of Ianthe's sons to work with.

"I've missed you," she said abruptly. "I didn't think I
would."

The words surprised him, but he was still wary. "Where's
Ruval?"

"Standing watch. Come and sit with me."

It was fully dark now. The rain had eased to a fine mist

that veiled her graying hair as she pushed back her hood.
He could see every line on her face in the lamplight
across the narrow street; she had aged with the tension of
waiting. He knew how that felt.

"It is time to prove your brother's legitimacy," Mireva
began without preamble.

Marron had known this was coming. Bastardy was not
a stigma as such—illegitimate offspring shared inheri-
tances with trueborn—but Roelstra had sired such an
embarrassing number of bastard daughters that the custom of fathering children outside marriage had gone out
of fashion. In practice these days, legitimate heirs had
the edge. Rohan's father had in many ways begun the
trend by being scandalously faithful to his adored wife. It
was a foolish practice, for most women bore only three
or four children. Those who conceived five times and
lived to tell of it were uncommon; no one had ever heard
of any who had borne more than six. Prolific bloodlines
were sought after, and those who produced twins, like
Princess Tobin, were most desirable of all. It was only
sensible to get as many heirs as possible—possession of a
single son was dangerous, as Prince Chale of Ossetia had
learned years ago when his had died.

"Chiana's son is legitimate, a prince," Mireva went on.
"But she was quite spectacularly born a bastard." A
smile gleamed around her lips for a moment. "Imagine
it—being utterly frantic to *prove* herself a bastard! Ianthe,
on the other hand, was the daughter of Roelstra's wife. If
we can provide evidence from Lord Chelan's own mouth
that he and Ianthe were wed—"

"I made inquiries when you asked last winter," he
interrupted. "He lived at a manor on the Syrene border."

Her eyes lit with silvery sparks. " 'Lived'?"

"And died, and burned there this summer. A wasting
sickness, it's said."

"Damn him! Damn him for dying!"

Before she could get what she wanted and then kill
him herself, Marron thought. But he said nothing.

Mireva inhaled deeply, struggling for calm. "It's my
own fault for not taking care of this sooner."

"If you had, attention would have fallen on him—and
he would have been around our necks."

"That's true." She sighed.

"Ruval will just have to do without," he said, a trifle more acidly than intended. She fixed an icy gaze on him. "I know, I should've told you on starlight. But you've both been traveling so much—Cunaxa and all over Princemarch—it was impossible to find you."

"And you've never been very good at that sort of thing," she snapped. "Are you sufficiently good at palace politics to get me in to see Chiana? Tonight?"

"Tonight—" He swallowed hard. "What do you plan to do to her?"

"What do you think?" she countered.

"You don't understand about Chiana. She's—*hard*." He explained how he'd been able to nudge her in directions she already favored—such as removing Halian's sister Gennadi as regent of Waes and reinstating Lord Geir. Though the young man hated Halian's father for the execution of his parents, he was alive to the advantages of working with Chiana. This had become one more thread of power in his aunt's grasping little hands. "But she has to think things are all her own idea. Even a hint that you're trying to influence her, and—"

"Give me credit for being subtle, boy."

"Well, *she's* not," he said frankly. "She covets Castle Crag the way some covet wine. She's the only one of Roelstra's daughters not born there, and she's never set foot in the place. Pandsala forbade it and Ostvel won't let her within a hundred measures. But she wants it and would die to possess it even for a day. It's the symbol of royalty to her."

Mireva nodded slowly. "After six winters at Goddess Keep, and fifteen more living with whichever half-sister would tolerate her for a while, and finally having her birth publicly doubted—I can understand her. That's helpful, Marron. But she can't be allowed to interfere with our right to Princemarch."

"We need her. We'll have to give her something."

"Miyon alone is not enough," she mused. "He sits atop the Desert, but I need Chiana's armies to take Princemarch."

"You mean you've allied with that Cunaxan snake?" he gasped.

"Remind me one day to tell you about it." She grinned at him, then sobered. "So Castle Crag is the key to opening Chiana. Thank you for that, Marron." Rising, she smoothed her skirts. "I'll meet you outside the gates later. I'm anxious to meet this Princess of Meadowlord."

"I'm not sure I can arrange it—"

Her gaze and her fingers grasped at him. "If you wish to live long enough to battle your brother for Princemarch and the Desert, I suggest you find a way. I only need Ruval, you know."

"And he needs *me*," he stated, trying to hide his fright.

She only laughed.

Marron kept his steps firm and even as he left the enclosed garden. But he was shaking by the time he got back to his chamber at the castle. Even in privacy he dared not weaken, however—it was as if he could feel two pairs of eyes, one piercing gray-green and the other fiercely blue, watching him, could hear laughter aimed at him.

A large cup of wine and a memory calmed him. The *dranath* was less responsible for his renewed confidence than the recollection that Mireva had not caught him in his almost-lie. It was true enough that Ruval's father was dead, but not of a wasting sickness—unless one included slow poison in that category. Marron might not know the complete range of *diarmadhi* spells, but he knew very well how to create death in a bottle of wine.

***

"It's late. I'm tired."

"I thought her prattle might amuse your grace," Marron said diffidently. Chiana shrugged. "There are many such women in the Veresch where I grew up. Harmless, of course, or I would never have brought this one to your grace's attention. But sometimes one is entertained by their tricks."

The scowling princess tapped her fingers on the arm of her chair. It had not been an entirely successful evening, Marron had heard. Strings repeatedly snapped in the chill night air, putting an early end to the music, and Chiana had been forced to converse with her lowborn guests.

He waited for her decision, playing humble and anxious servitor. At last she shrugged again and nodded.

"Oh, very well, Mirris. Send her to me. Wait—is she clean?"

"I took the liberty, your grace. . . ." He trailed off delicately.

"Fetch her, then. If she amuses me, have her fed and paid afterward."

"Very good, your grace."

He stepped out of the chamber, soothing his eyes with the cool length of white-and-gold corridor. A relief after the hundreds of different greens in the private reception room, colors Chiana surrounded herself with in the belief that any and all shades of green suited her auburn looks. *Diarmadh'im* were as sensitive to color as any Sunrunner; the juxtaposition of hues no forest or meadow would ever know was as acutely painful as a score of lutes playing different tunes, all off-key.

Mireva waited at a back door. She had dressed her part as mountain witch in a many-patched rag of a gown, an old black shawl, and thin wool gloves missing three fingers and a thumb. Stooped, bedraggled, with quivering hands and aimless gestures, if he had not known her, he would not have known her. He hid a grin on recalling Chiana's fastidious query about her cleanliness, and ordered her to follow him.

"And no begging for money, mind," he snapped as they paused outside Chiana's suite. "Amuse her grace and you may see a few coins. Displease her, and you'll be lucky to leave with your tongue still between your teeth."

The gray-green gaze twisted up at him, sardonically acknowledging his enjoyment of the role played for the benefit of the young servant who carried the *rathiv*-wrapped mirror.

Marron scratched at the door, opened it, and announced, "The . . . person, your grace."

Chiana, magnificent in a yellow-green gown that clashed with the pillows of her chair, waved a languid hand. "A witch, eh?" she said as Mireva approached and bowed several times. "The only witch whom I *know* to be a witch is the High Princess Sioned."

"I've heard it said that Lady Andrade was, too, Your Splendor."

"And who would know it better than I?" Chiana laughed mirthlessly. "Very well. Mirris, bring a chair."

Mireva shook her head and bowed again. "No need, Your Radiance. The floor is good enough for me, especially in such a presence."

The rug was spread across polished stone, the mirror set on it almost as an afterthought. As the servant bowed and left, Chiana began to look interested.

"If Your Graciousness would be so kind as to show me her pretty hands, perhaps I can read something of her future."

"Perhaps?" But Chiana stuck out both slim, white, beringed hands. Her lip curled as Mireva touched her fingertips. "Well?"

"If I might look into those lovely eyes?"

Marron bit back a grin, wondering if Mireva intended to inspect Chiana's teeth. Hazel eyes stared unblinking into gray-green. Mireva made a few noises low in her throat, then settled back on her heels, nodding sagely.

"Speak!" Chiana ordered.

"I am overwhelmed by the brilliance of your future. To be sure, I must look into a flame lit by Your Grandeur's own hand."

"Mirris, bring a candle."

Chiana struck steel to flint and the wick sprang to life. Mireva peered into the flame—giving it all she had, Marron thought, greatly amused—muttering to herself while the princess fidgeted. At length a wide smile broke across her face, revealing artfully blackened teeth.

"Your Greatness will be granted her dearest wish: to enter Castle Crag as a princess."

Chiana sat forward, snared. "Have you seen it? What else? Will I rule there? Will my son?"

"Slowly, gently! I have seen many things. Deaths. . . ."

"Whose?"

"Two men. Fair-haired, much alike, from a land that burns."

"Rohan and Pol!" Chiana laughed. "But what of Sioned? Does she die, too?"

Mireva's face twitched slightly. "Her death . . . is written."

Marron kept his face smooth—not that either paid him any mind. Sioned frightened Mireva. She would have denied it if asked, but he knew the High Princess was her target even more than Pol.

Chiana burbled with glee. "Wonderful! When? Tell me when!"

"Before the next *Rialla*. Your Worshipfulness must prepare herself for a long, difficult fight—I see soldiers, horses—"

"What?" the princess exclaimed angrily, the candle flame almost guttering with her breath. "There won't be any war. The Desert and Pricemarch have us on two sides, and Syr is on a third. Kostas would come to his Aunt Sioned's aid in an instant."

"It will be difficult, Your Mightiness. But there is no other way to win Castle Crag."

The words had the desired effect. Chiana's eyes sharpened with the look of a starving woman shown a banquet through a window.

"I *will* have it. Rinhoel will rule all Princemarch from Castle Crag—"

"No." Mireva let the word fall like a stone. "I see a name, but it is not that of your son. A kinsman. Close. Very close to you."

"I have no brother and my father is dead. Who else could claim Princemarch, once Pol is—" She paled suddenly. "No! Not Kostas' son by Danladi! *My* son will inherit! *My* son!"

"No," the old woman repeated. "The one who will rule Princemarch is Ruval."

Only for as long as it takes me to kill him, Marron thought.

"Ianthe's son," Mireva whispered.

Chiana's delicate knuckles whitened around the candle. "Ianthe—!"

"Ruval, Your Wisdom's nephew, will reclaim—"

"Not if I can help it," was the grim reply.

"If Your Magnificence will indulge an old woman— please, look into this mirror. It will help me see more clearly."

Marron reminded himself to ask how long it had taken to think up all the honorifics—and then lost all impulse toward humor as the mirror was turned, angled at the princess. Chiana slid to the floor on her knees with the candle barely secure in lax fingers, lost.

Shaken, he locked his own knees and clenched his jaw shut. He knew about the mirror hidden in the back room of Mireva's hillside dwelling; this one looked older still and was undoubtedly even more powerful. They had really known how to make mirrors back then, had his *diarmadhi* ancestors. . . .

The reflected candlelight illumined Chiana's face in smoky gold. Mireva's voice crooned to her, soft and unthreatening.

"Your son will never rule Princemarch. That is reserved for those of the oldest blood. But there is a way to gain Castle Crag. Support Prince Ruval in all he does. If you wish to see Sioned burn in her own Fire, obey me. If you wish vengeance on the Sunrunners who jailed you in childhood, you will obey. If you wish to enter Castle Crag as a princess. . . ."

"I—will obey," Chiana whispered, her voice like death.

"And when you do, you will be strong. I will give you this mirror to remind you. Keep it with you always. Look into it by starshine every evening. If you wish to live. . . ."

"I will obey."

"Leave us," Mireva said over her shoulder in a completely different voice. Marron gave a start. "Now," she added sharply. And he fled.

Chapter Seven

727: Goddess Keep

Andry came from a family whose members had no difficulty expressing themselves. In fact, Chay had observed more than once that Tobin never shut up, even in her sleep. But it was a long time since Andry had spoken to any of his relations with complete honesty, saying precisely what was on his mind—or in his heart—without hesitation. Time and titles had come between them and him. But today he would change that. He had to, if they were to survive.

Everything was ready in the long room above the gates—the goblets, the Sunrunner at his side, even the clothes Andry wore—all of it exactly as Andry had planned, and as Lady Merisel mentioned in her writings. Though she warned against symbols rather than endorsing them. *"Symbols stand for power. But don't mistake one for the other—as my enemies often did, poor things. And don't allow the symbols to make you forget what they should help you remember. The rings are only as strong as the hands wearing them."*

Two of his chosen symbols—the goblets—waited to be filled with wine and *dranath*. Actually, he'd taken a lesson from Rohan in this: Rohan who knew how to use expensive things to impress and, if he wished, to awe. Look at Dragon's Rest, Andry thought, or even Stronghold's Great Hall. Or even the High Prince himself when he wanted to remind certain people of exactly who he was—clad in rich silk and gleaming gems and that ultimate symbol of his authority, his coronet. But Rohan could show up bareheaded, barefoot, in peasant woolens, and still dominate everyone—with the living symbol that was Sioned at his side.

Andry had not yet reached a time when he could dispense with the props. But he could wait. The goblets were for himself and Nialdan, the clothes for the Sunrunners assembling now in the courtyard. Nialdan himself was a symbol of sorts, though the young man would have gaped at the very notion. Though Andry was a tall man, well-made and muscular, Nialdan was built like a tree. He topped Andry by a head and outspanned him in the shoulders by two hands. Brown eyes regarded the world patiently from a brown face below reddish-brown hair. Nialdan wore six rings that had not come from the coffer Andry inherited with his position here—the Waesian's smallest finger was as thick as any other man's thumb. He didn't just knock on a door; he dealt it a mortal blow, and his rings had to be specially made.

For him, too, a special goblet had been fashioned, shaded with the browns and russets and greens of his mind. Colors were symbols, too, and the gems that Sunrunners used to define them. The Star Scroll was rife with jewel symbology. A faint prickling of irritation stung Andry when he thought of the scroll.

He'd invited Maarken to look at the illuminated final copy just that morning. His brother had more comments for the delicate drawings than for the text—because he had seen the copy Urival had made in secret and taken with him to Stronghold three years ago. The copy Andry wasn't supposed to know about.

Maarken inspected the painted capitals, the tiny marginal sketches of various plants mentioned in recipes, and the star clusters that headed each division of topics. That he did not read more than a few words here and there was indication enough that he had no need to. Andry wondered if his brother knew how completely he had given himself away.

Not that reading would have done anyone any good. This was a direct translation, exactly as Lady Merisel had dictated it—but lacking the little markers that indicated lies. Anyone attempting to cast a spell or concoct a potion using this version of the Star Scroll would be sadly disappointed.

The accurate copy resided in Andry's chambers. He supposed Maarken knew about that one, as well. Today Andry would show him the uses to which he had put it.

He knew how Urival had used the other copy—an accurate one, Goddess damn the old man. When he'd died late last winter, Andry had almost asked for its return along with the few things of Andrade's sent back to the archives after Urival's death.

What he'd really wanted, though, were the rest of her rings—or what remained of them. Maarken had reset the chunk of amber into his wedding necklet; Sioned sometimes wore the emerald on a chain around her neck; the ruby now graced Tobin's coronet. Chadric had inherited the sapphire, given to old Prince Lleyn who had been Andrade's friend. Chay, Rohan, and Pol had the other stones—the last being the most irksome to Andry. Pol wore the moonstone as unsubtle reminder that he was a Sunrunner, even though he hadn't been trained at Goddess Keep.

Andry sometimes took out the garnet Urival had given him after Andrade's death, but had never quite been able to bring himself to wear it. The old man had left the tenth ring on Andrade's finger, token of the wedding ring he would have put there himself if they had been ordinary folk. But the chains that had connected all the rings to bracelets on Andrade's wrists had been fashioned into a delicate, unobtrusive necklet worn for the rest of Urival's life, and burned with him in the Desert.

Andry wanted those rings back. Years of studying the Star Scroll and the histories unearthed with it on Dorval had convinced him that there was more to the symbolism of gemstones than pretty tradition. But to ask for them would alert Pol to their possible significance, and this he refused to do.

And then there were the mirrors, the most frustrating of all Merisel's enigmatic little hints. *"If you find a sorcerer who possesses a mirror, exile the sorcerer—but shatter the mirror."* Just that one sentence. No explanation, no elaboration. Andry, who had fallen a little in love with Merisel through her vivid writings, had long since decided that at several hundred years' remove, she was fascinating—but that face-to-face she must have been several hundred different kinds of Hell to deal with.

Nialdan waited placidly beside him for Torien to come up and announce that everyone was assembled and all was in readiness. Anyone else would have been fidgeting by now; Nialdan merely planted both big feet on the floor and stood as motionless and patient as a pine. Andry found the man's solidity soothing, especially after the long night behind him and in view of the tough work ahead.

Valeda had given him a daughter just before dawn. Hollis, here with Maarken on a visit all hoped would help heal the troubles no one ever talked about, had assisted in the birthing room. Andry had seen her holding the new baby earlier today, and his heart filled with compassion. One of her reasons for coming to Goddess Keep was to consult the Mother Tree. Her twins, Chayla and Rohannon, were five winters old and there were no signs of more children. But, judging by her determinedly cheerful expression after a brief disappearance the other day, the tree circle had not shown her what she wished to see.

Andry still remembered being shown what he wished to forget.

He shut his eyes and let the visions form behind his lids, dyed red with the sunlight streaming onto his face, awash in the color of blood.

The day of the ceremony that would make him Lord of Goddess Keep (Oh, Sweet Lady, let me be strong and worthy—), he went to the tree circle. Naked, shivering a little in the crisp autumn air, he knelt before the pool below the rock cairn and plucked a hair from his head to float on the Water, symbol of the Earth of which he was made. He'd always considered this a gentle, harmless ritual—a minor use of power, a quaint little ceremony reminding him of his origins in and kinship with the Elements. He called Air and the Water ruffled; he summoned a fingerflame and set it dancing atop the rocks. Lovely in the morning sun, warm and bright—

First the children—faces in rapid succession, vanishing too quickly for him to receive more than the vague impression that they all had his blue eyes.

Then the chaos. Swords, steel-tipped arrows, horses gutted and dying, men and women warriors scythed down like harvested wheat. Battle. Blood. Radzyn demolished, Stronghold in ruins. His parents and brothers and all his family destroyed. Goddess Keep a smoldering wreck of shattered stone clinging to the sea cliffs, Sunrunners never to ride the light again.

And finally the stars. Uncounted pinpricks of blinding light, like daggers thrusting straight up from the bottom of a deadfall. He hurtled toward them in an endless plunge into darkness punctuated by stars. The sorcerers' stars.

It was Sorin who woke him, running headlong into the circle where no one not faradhi *was allowed. "Andry! Andry, wake up!" He was shaken roughly, opened his eyes, and saw his brother's fear-paled face. He clung to Sorin, grateful for the warm strong arms around him and the presence that, but for the one vital gift, was twin to his own.*

How Sorin had felt it was a mystery to them both. They had heard of how Maarken, after his own twin died of Plague, wandered Radzyn lost and haunted, calling for the second self always there and now gone. But what they shared was stronger—perhaps because they were older, or because Andry was a Sunrunner even more powerful than Maarken.

Since then, Andry dreamed occasionally of what the Goddess had shown him. Once it happened while Sorin was at Goddess Keep, on a quick visit before sailing for Kierst to supervise the making of tiles for Feruche. Andry had been shaken from the dream as he'd been from the vision, his brother's hands frantic on his shoulders and his brother's voice crying out his name.

"What does it feel like?" Andry had asked as they waited for dawn beside the hearth, wrapped in blankets and gulping mulled wine.

"Like when we were little, and one of us had a bad dream." Sorin's brows arched speculatively. "You never told me the details then—"

"Neither did you. We were a prideful little pair, weren't we? Never could admit to being that scared." Andry smiled.

"—and I don't suppose you're going to talk about it now, are you?" Sorin finished as if he hadn't been interrupted.

"No. Sorry. It's bad enough that *I* see—what I see. If I told you, you might start dreaming the same thing. And it might bounce between us all the way to Feruche and back—and neither of us would ever get any sleep."

Andrade had always emphasized that the Goddess showed what *might* come to pass. "Nothing is written in stone—and even if it were, stones can be broken." He wondered sometimes what she had seen of the future. *Did the Goddess tell her to marry her sister off to Zehava? Or was that to change a future she didn't happen to like? Did she ever see Pol? Or me? Did she realize what work I have in front of me? Is that why she chose me as her successor? Or did she see someone else, and pick me by default?*

Not what he ought to be thinking right now. As for what everyone else would think—he couldn't bring himself to care about any of them but Maarken and Hollis. They had to understand. The Sunrunners here could be frightened, horrified, shocked, or awestruck. It didn't much matter which. His brother had to understand and explain it to Rohan and Sioned and Pol.

But he admitted to himself that he didn't much care what *they* thought, either. If Rohan considered him power-hungry, and Sioned was affronted by his uses of power, and Pol felt threatened—too bad. *They can look on this as they like, so long as they don't hinder me. I can keep that vision from becoming real. This is my work to do, my warning from the Goddess. Only—please, Gentle Lady, let Maarken understand.*

He gave a violent start when Nialdan cleared his throat. The big man shrugged an apology. "Sorry, my Lord."

Andry smiled thinly. "Uproot yourself from the floor and go see what's keeping Torien."

"Yes, my Lord."

With Nialdan gone, Andry could give in to nerves and pace. He was used to circling a room; the gatehouse was long and narrow, and the change in pattern unsettled him even more. He stopped by the table again and poured wine into the goblets for something to do with his hands. The *dranath* sifted down from his rubbing palms, fine powder vanishing instantly into the green-gold wine.

"My Lord?" Nialdan came back in, leaving the staircase door open behind him. "Torien says they're about ready. He'll be up in a moment. Oclel's making doubly sure about the swords and arrows."

Oclel was Nialdan's good friend and the only man at Goddess Keep big enough to give him a decent workout with a sword. Born in Princemarch of a huntsman's daughter and a soldier who had fought for Roelstra in 704,

Oclel had married the mother of Andry's elder daughter. Andry preferred it so. Rusina had not wanted the child he'd given her on her first-ring night. Already in love with Oclel, she bore Tobren grudgingly and had wanted nothing to do with her from the day of her birth. Another woman had nursed the child, and Valeda took care of Tobren's need for affection.

Othanel, mother of his only son, was another matter entirely. Triumphant in her pregnancy, she kept little Andrev close and barely allowed him to play with other children, as if fearing contamination. She was possessive and jealous, barely able to hide her fury when first Rusina and then Valeda bore Andry's children, and not bothering to hide her glee when both women birthed daughters.

Contemplation of Rusina's anger and Othanel's ambition brought an uncomfortable memory of his mother's stinging rebuke at the last *Rialla*. When he'd tried to explain that both babies were too young to travel, Tobin had exploded like heat lightning across the Desert sky.

"What are you afraid we'll see? Children conceived not because you care a damn about their mothers—which you don't—but because you want your own little brood of Sunrunners? Not even Andrade went that far!"

"Didn't she? What are you and Rohan but her experiments in *faradhi* royalty? Not to mention Pol!"

Maarken had come by later that night. Man-to-man reasoning left Andry unmoved, but when Maarken's temper flared he capitulated. He had never gone against his adored eldest brother's wishes in his life.

And, truthfully, he didn't regret the meeting last summer in Syr. Time spent with Andrev and Tobren had softened his mother's wrath. Sorin made the journey from Feruche to High Kirat, Maarken came with his family from Whitecliff, and Tilal from Athmyr. Kostas, a father now himself, presided over the whole noisy crowd with a sardonic grin. The eight children—Andry's, Maarken's, Kostas', and Tilal's—had seemed bent on demolishing anything that got within reach of their fists, including, on occasion, each other. For ten days it was almost as if they were any ordinary big family.

Rohan, Sioned, and Pol had sent their regrets. Andry understood perfectly. They would let the others make the initial moves toward peace. Thus this current visit by Maarken and Hollis.

It fit in perfectly with Andry's own plans. He knew now the method by which he would change that future of horror and blood.

Maarken had to understand.

Torien appeared at last, visibly annoyed by the delay. "But everything's ready now, my Lord. They're waiting for you to begin."

He nodded and gestured to Nialdan, who emptied his goblet in two large gulps. Andry took a little longer at it, savoring the slow pulse of the drug in his body. He had been careful to use only enough for an increase of power—he'd heard from Maarken how Hollis had suffered after her addiction to *dranath*. He didn't want that for any of his people, and certainly not for himself. But the augmentation of gifts was too important to reject *dranath* completely.

When he could feel its effects—soft heat in his cheeks, a tingling in his groin, a flush of energy through his body—he straightened his clothing and went to the balcony that overlooked the courtyard. Taking another lesson from Rohan, he had chosen his clothes carefully: wool trousers dyed red, white shirt and short white tunic. Radzyn's colors, meant to remind Maarken that whatever he might witness today, they were of the same place, the same heritage.

"Your cloak, my Lord?" Torien murmured behind him, and he shook his head. A breeze off the sea quickened the air, but he wasn't cold. He never was, except in the depths of winter. The joke around Goddess Keep was that he'd soaked up so much Desert sun in childhood that he'd never feel anything but the worst blizzard the Father of Storms exhaled from the icy heart of the Veresch.

Many of those below him were in warm woolen gowns and tunics, with cloaks against the wind. Several wore the hoods pulled up—perhaps to keep their ears warm, and perhaps to hide their reaction to whatever shocking innovation Andry was about to present. He shrugged, but made mental note of them anyway. They could be sent elsewhere for duty and cease to trouble him. Again he thought of Urival, whose removal from Goddess Keep had been no guarantee of lack of trouble. Whatever Pol now knew of *faradhi* arts, it was too much—because Andry had not been the one to teach him.

This wasn't the time to think about *that*, either. He rested his hands lightly on the smooth balcony rail and surveyed the assembly with justifiable pride. The Sunrunners, students, and servants of Goddess Keep numbered over four hundred—two-thirds of them *faradh'im* at various levels of expertise.

In Andrade's time there had been as many non-gifteds here as Sunrunners. The reason was not talent, but money. Prior to Andry's rule here, students were required to give to Goddess Keep that share of their parents' wealth that would have dowered them. No prejudice was attached to the gift's size; the price of a few sheep, all Nialdan had brought, weighed equally with the substantial slice of Radzyn's wealth that had been Andry's portion. Indeed, it was this princely sum that had allowed him to cancel the dowry custom. Parents loath to sell off goods for the stipulated cash were now perfectly happy to send gifted sons and daughters to become Sunrunners; the other children benefited through increased dowries. Andry had brought with him more than enough to make up for any loss of income. It afforded him a certain grim amusement to wonder how Rohan would have worked it out if Pol had come here; *he* was dowered with all Princemarch.

They probably would have done what Chay and Tobin did with Maarken—told Andrade that if she wanted Whitecliff (his dowry while his father lived), she could come collect it lock, stock, and paddock.

But Andry had insisted on giving the whole of his fortune to Goddess Keep. He could have had almost any place he wanted in the Desert, a manor or castle and honors befitting the son of the Battle Commander and the grandson of a prince. But this keep was all he had ever wanted. Now it was his. And, thanks to him, wealthier and more populous than Andrade had ever dared hope.

And all of them looked to him for guidance. No one, not even those chosen for this demonstration, knew of his terrible vision and the dreams that haunted his sleep. Caution told him they must trust him for himself, not out of fright of a dreaded future. They must follow him because they believed in him, give him loyalty, dedicate themselves to him so that when he finally revealed his reasons, faith would conquer fear. They must be certain to their bones that he would teach them how to use their gifts against the coming battle and blood.

He could not glimpse his brother's head in the crowd, and so looked for Hollis' distinctive tawny hair. Where she was, Maarken would be. At last he located them by the well. He murmured to Torien, "Take my brother and his lady closer to the gates. I want them to have an unobstructed view."

"Yes, my Lord."

Andry drew in a deep breath and addressed his people. "Since *faradh'im* left Dorval to end the sorcerers' control of the princedoms, we have been forbidden to use our gifts to kill. This is a wise law. Without it, we might have become hired assassins like the Merida, our honor the price of a wineskin—or worse.

"But in reading the scrolls left by Lady Merisel, who led the Sunrunners with her husband Lord Gerik and their friend Lord Rosseyn, I discovered something. They and their *faradh'im* went into battle alongside their allies— *and they used their gifts to protect.*"

He waited for this to sink in, then continued. "The concept of warrior *faradh'im* was as astonishing to me as I know it is to you. But the fact remains that they were. And it was only *after* the so-called Stoneburners had been defeated that the law was made forbidding us to kill with our gifts."

Torien had reached Maarken by now, and was urging him politely toward the main gate. Andry ignored the little rustling they made through the crowd. He also did himself the favor of ignoring the many faces eloquent with suspicion that he was about to unmake that particular law.

"Lady Merisel was wise," he said quietly. "We are so made as Sunrunners that we cannot conceive of causing death with our art. This is as it should be. We are here to work with and for the princedoms, not to terrorize them with our power as the *diarmadh'im* did.

"But I have come to believe that we must learn to do what our ancestors did. Not to kill in battle, but to protect. Many of you were at Goddess Keep in 704, when Lyell of Waes camped outside our gates—ostensibly to protect us against the war between Roelstra and Prince Rohan. You who were here remember how helpless you were against only fifty or sixty armed soldiers.

"You may rightly say that times are peaceful now, with no need for learning what I propose we learn. But consider the possible results of a single death: that of Prince Pol."

Hollis' dark golden head jerked up at that. He met her gaze calmly, knowing he need not spell it out in words of one syllable or less. But he explained it anyway. They had to understand. This was a thing dire enough to convince them, while leaving the real threat unrevealed. The prospect he detailed was real enough in any case, and frankly made him sick to his stomach.

"My cousin is heir to two princedoms, and to the High Prince. He is the *only* heir. He is a strong young man in excellent health—but so was Inoat of Ossetia, who died very suddenly with his only son, leaving Chale without an heir. Had there been no Princess Gemma to inherit Ossetia, war would have come—and in the very princedom Goddess Keep inhabits.

"My cousin's life has been threatened before, by the Merida. I don't need to number Roelstra's grandchildren for you—enough to make life interesting, certainly, should the Merida or mere accident claim Pol's life, Goddess keep it from happening. Which of Roelstra's get have parents powerful enough to back a claim to Princemarch? Don't remind me that their mothers signed away all right—what would that signify, with a princedom at stake?

"My brother Maarken would inherit the Desert, of course." He nodded at the tall, composed man in their midst—Sunrunner, able warrior, Radzyn's heir—and his heart gave a skip of sheer pride. There was no finer man alive. "But there would be war over Princemarch. We all know it."

He paused again, gathering all his determination. "I don't believe any of this will happen. But it could. And who can say what else might occur that none of us could ever d–dream of?" The stumble was almost unnoticeable; he had a sudden vision of Sorin's worried eyes. "One day we may be called upon to defend ourselves. Quite frankly, I don't intend to be trapped within Goddess Keep as Lady Andrade was. Beside this, it is unfortunate but true that my kinships excite the suspicions of certain princes. If war comes, for whatever reason, Goddess Keep is the first place they would attempt to capture. And how easy it would be to do it!"

Andry gestured to Nialdan. The tall Sunrunner stepped forward and with one lifted hand called a flame to a torch pole set just outside the open gates. A moment later the crowd was startled by the quiet thunder of hoofbeats. All eyes fixed on the forty riders, led by Oclel, galloping across the fallow fields. Andry knew what they were imagining: not men and women they knew, wielding blunted swords and cloth-wrapped arrows, but soldiers under enemy banners. He slipped down the inner stair, deliberately unobtrusive, but few marked his passage in any case. He nodded his satisfaction. Let them see danger, he thought; let them see their own helplessness.

Oclel raised his sword, and arrows thickened the sky. They thudded to the ground, hopelessly out of range. But the next volley hit the walls—away from the open gates, yet close enough to emphasize the threat. There were gasps, and a few cries of protest or outrage. Andry repressed a smile.

"What in all Hells do you think you're doing?" demanded a familiar voice at his side, anger echoed in the strong grip on his arm.

"Hush," Hollis murmured to her husband. "We're about to find out, I think. Let him work, Maarken."

Andry gave her a sharp glance, surprised that she knew his mind better than his own brother. He shook Maarken off and strode to the gates. Standing in the center of the wide gap, he lifted both arms. Jeweled rings and wristbands flared in the sunlight—and in the glow of a wall of Fire that sprang up fifty paces from the castle.

Nialdan was nearby, arms similarly raised, rugged features clenched with the strain of calling another barrier of Fire just this side of Andry's. What no one but the two men knew was that whereas Nialdan worked with the sun, Andry had mastered the *diarmadhi* technique of constructing the wall without it.

The riders slowed when Fire appeared. Oclel bellowed an order and they abandoned their frenzied horses to approach on foot. Andry whispered a silent apology to his friend; Oclel had no idea what he was letting himself and his people in for.

Sunrunners approached Fire—and began to scream.

Andry silently counted to twenty, then lowered his arms. He spoke Nialdan's name into the horrified stillness of the courtyard and the smaller Fire sputtered out. Oclel led his weak-kneed troop through the gates, pausing only to fling an order to the grooms to gather the horses.

"Sorry," Nialdan muttered to Oclel, who gulped and shook his head.

Andry said nothing. The testimony of those who had felt the spell would be enough. He watched solemn-faced as furtive glances slid to him and then away.

The shaken "attackers" had recovered their voices. Andry listened to scraps of conversation and once more had to keep his lips from curving in a grim smile.

"—dragon-sized wolf with eyes of flame and claws bigger than my fingers—"

"—came right at me, I tell you—"

"—one of those rock lizards like the ones on Dorval, only with teeth—"

"Wolf? Lizard? *I* saw dragons, all black and breathing fire—"

"Dragons I'll grant you, but blood-red, and dripping it from talons and jaws—"

"My Lord?"

Andry looked around. Oclel stood there, expressionless. A wave of sympathy nearly swamped Andry's glee over how well his ploy had worked. "Rough, hmm?"

"Indescribable."

"It had to be done this way the first time."

"I understand, my Lord. May I tell the others that?"

"It should be common knowledge by dinner tonight."

Oclel nodded. "As you wish. I think—"

What he thought would have to wait. Maarken strode up, coldly furious.

"Andry," was all he said.

"In a moment, Maarken—"

"*Now.*"

Oclel bristled; no one spoke to the Lord of Goddess Keep in that tone, not even the Lord's own brother. Andry gave brief consideration to asserting rank over a

man who was, after all, a Sunrunner, then discarded the
notion. He wanted understanding and cooperation, not
resentment. And Maarken, though in general even-
tempered and gently-spoken, was proud as a dragon—
and the son of their fiery mother.

"Very well. Let's go upstairs to the gatehouse. We can
be private there." He sent a caustic message with his eyes
that acknowledged Maarken's need to express his rage.
A gaze like gray winter ice met his, and for the first time
he wondered if he'd miscalculated.

Hollis followed them. She shut the door and leaned on
it, trembling a little. Before Maarken could say anything
she gave a choked gasp. "Andry! The wine—you didn't—"

He went to the table and picked up the piece of folded
parchment Sioned had given Andrade eight years earlier.
"I did. And I'd like you to ask Pol if he'd send some
more. This is the last."

She flattened her spine against the door, eyes wide.
"Don't you understand? Don't you know the risk?"

"Calm yourself," he said, biting back impatience.
"There's no danger in small amounts, rarely taken. Besides, it's necessary."

Maarken's voice was silk-soft now. "You can't work a
diarmadhi spell without it?"

"It works better with the added power. We're not here
to discuss *dranath*."

"No."

The brothers squared off with the table between them.
Andry knew he should stay silent until he could judge
what form Maarken's fury would take, but he had to
make him see, had to convince him.

"Everything I said was true. You know how helpless
we'd be here if it came to war. I'm kin to the High Prince
and his heir—and I'm the Lord of Radzyn's son. Somebody like Miyon or Chiana or even Pimantal of Fessenden
would know exactly how to paralyze you in the field with
a threat to Goddess Keep."

"Go on."

Andry realized abruptly that he'd been wrong about
Maarken's anger. It wasn't Tobin's—volatile, incandes-
cent. This was Chay at his cold, hard, implacable worst.

"We must be able to defend ourselves. Not just against
the threats we can anticipate, but—" He broke off and

eased his stance, taking his hands from the table and extending them palms up to his brother. "I've seen things, Maarken—"

"Oh, yes." Dismissively. "Sorin says you have odd dreams."

Andry felt his own temper begin to ignite. "Not just dreams—visions. Of a future that terrifies me. Maarken, you don't have any idea of the blood—"

"I saw none today," the older man said quietly. "What I saw was terror. And what I would have seen was madness, if that wall hadn't collapsed."

"That was the damned idea!" Andry exclaimed, frustrated. "The *ros'salath* doesn't kill—not in this form, anyway—"

Hollis caught her breath. " *'In this form'*? Andry, what have you done?"

"Broken more rules," Maarken snapped. "Taken the traditions and laws of Goddess Keep and thrown them into the middens!"

He made a last try. "Andrade saw things. Sweet Goddess, Maarken, you and I *exist* because of what she saw—and what she did about it! I'm telling you that what I've seen is destruction you can't imagine! I can't let it happen—and the only weapon I have against it—"

"Is Sunrunners learning the ways of sorcerers! Why haven't you said anything about these visions before, Andry? Why keep them such a secret? You have an uncle and a cousin who are princes with armies to command—why do you need an army of your own?"

"You mean the uncle who trusts me so much he sent his *faradhi* son to me for training? The cousin who sees me as a threat to his own Sunrunner powers? Is that who you're talking about, Maarken?"

"Andry—" Hollis came forward, still trembling. "Andry, please, you don't see what you're doing. Will they trust you more when they learn of this?"

"I've seen death," he snapped. "What's more important, Hollis? Pol's conceit or hundreds and hundreds of people? Rohan's trust or R—" He choked off the name of his birthplace, the ravaged waste of it swirling in his mind.

Maarken slammed his hands flat on the table. "What's

more important, Andry—your might-be vision or the reality of Sunrunners learning how to kill?"

There would be no understanding. He had been a fool to expect it. His brother belonged to Rohan. To Pol.

Andry pulled his clenched fists in to his sides. "I ought to have known. You're a Sunrunner, trained at Goddess Keep, owing duty to Goddess Keep—and to me. But you're also an *athri*, loyal to your prince. One day they might not live so comfortably together within you. One day you might have to choose."

The skin around those gray eyes tightened just a little, and he knew he'd struck home.

"But not today," Andry finished softly. "Not today, my brother. Go back to the Desert. Tell Rohan what you like. It won't make any difference. If war comes—any war—then it will come. But I'll be ready for it, Maarken. Tell Rohan that, too."

"Andry, wait—"

He left the room feeling incredibly old, incredibly tired. Not even the lingering *dranath* could warm his blood.

Torien waited for him outside near the well, dark Fironese face creased with worry. Andry summoned up a tiny smile.

"Order my brother's horses made ready for him tomorrow morning."

The Chief Steward was rubbing his fingers absently, as if a chill had seeped into them. "I thought they'd be staying another eight or ten days."

"No. And I don't think they'll be staying here again."

PART TWO

Year 728

Chapter Eight

Near Elktrap Manor: 3 Spring

The dragon was dying.

He lay on his belly, wings nailed to enormous trees felled for the purpose, spread like a skin left to dry in the sun. Spikes of the kind used for mountain climbing in the Veresch had been driven through the bones of his wings. Blood had crusted around these wounds and where his talons had been gouged out. There were a few sword slashes on his blue-gray hide, but not deep enough to let him bleed his life out quickly. Whoever was responsible for this intended a slow, slow death: the great amber eyes were dulled with long agony.

The sword dropped from Sorin's shaking hand. He gulped back nausea and glanced at Riyan's stricken face. A short time ago their horses had refused to go any farther, shying and rearing when the two young men urged them on. So they had left their mounts tied in the forest, unsheathed their swords, and warily proceeded. To find this.

"Sweet Goddess," Sorin whispered, or tried to. His mouth was dry and tasted of the foulness of this deed; his throat was too tight for speech. Who had done this? Through his shock he felt a savage anger beginning, an incoherent vow to give the murderer a death that matched the cruelty done to this dragon.

Riyan put a hand on his arm. He had to clear his throat several times before he managed, "Sorin, we have to do something—"

He nodded. But he knew how helpless they were. "Water. That's all we can do for him."

Riyan let his own sword fall to the grass. "I'll get the extra from my pack."

115

While he was gone, Sorin moved a little closer to the dying dragon. Amber eyes saw him, sparked faintly with rage, then glazed over again. A man had done this to him, but he lacked the strength even to glare his hatred for long. Sorin circled the huge, pain-rigid body, fists clenched. The spikes were new steel, shining in the morning sun above the bloody wounds they had inflicted; they marched in a perfectly straight line down the felled trees, stretching the dragon's broken wings to their full span. Sorin fought back mind-numbing fury and took careful note of the circumstances of the dragon's agony. Whoever had done this had taken all the time in the world to make his crime a grisly work of art.

Riyan came back as Sorin knelt beside the dragon's head. "Careful," he warned as neck muscles rippled and the head shifted sluggishly.

"He's got strength to swallow, and that's all," Sorin replied. He shifted the great head onto his knees and stroked the smooth hide between the eyes. "I'll hold his head. Try to get some water down him."

The dragon proved angry enough still to take a feeble snap at Riyan. But when cool water slid down his throat from the goatskin carrier, his eyes closed and tension seeped from some of his muscles. Sorin went on rubbing the dragon's face and neck. Riyan gave him as much water as he would take, then stoppered the skin and sat back on his heels.

"This can't be the one that brought us up here," he said slowly. "Word came twenty days ago. Not even a dragon could survive this for twenty days. This must be the whoreson's second kill."

"And his last," Sorin answered grimly.

"We'll catch him." Riyan settled onto the grass, kneeling by the dragon's head. "Sorin, I've never tried this, but I know how it's supposed to work. Sioned let me watch when her Elisel came flying by Stronghold last year. But I've never actually done it." He gave a brief grimace of a smile. "Catch me if I fall over, all right?"

Before Sorin had time to protest, Riyan had closed his eyes and begun the mysterious—to Sorin—work that would allow him to touch the dragon's colors. Even though his twin brother had explained the feeling and a little of the technique many times, Sorin despaired of ever understanding what happened when a Sunrunner used light. Andry had likened it to master weavers gathering threads for a multicolored tapestry, master glasscrafters selecting stained glass for a window. But to touch sunlight or moonlight, or to perceive a person in terms of the hues of the mind—it was like asking Sorin to imagine drinking music.

Riyan's spine snapped straight as a sword blade and a groan escaped him. His eyes opened, the dark brown lit by strange bronze and gold and greenish flecks, the pupils pinpoints like black stars. He dug his fingers into the ground as if they were talons, shock and fury swirling in his eyes. Sorin held his breath as an expression of mortal anguish twisted his friend's face. Then Riyan cried out and slumped.

Sorin placed the dragon's heavy head onto the grass, sparing a look at the amber eyes. They glowed faintly, then faded once more.

"Riyan!" He shook a shoulder. "Come on, wake up!"

It seemed to take forever. Finally a long shudder coursed through him and he braced himself on one arm, head raising slowly. "Sorin?"

"Have some water." He unhooked the water skin from his belt and made Riyan drink. A few moments later he steadied and sucked in a deep breath. "What happened?" Sorin asked.

"I—I touched him. Goddess, the colors! But all lit in black. I can't describe it." He shook himself and reached for the water skin. More firmly, he went on, "He's furious enough to have nearly killed me with his emotions. Sioned explained that. They don't communicate in words, but in pictures and feelings. And this one, if he had any strength, would be feeding off our entrails right now. The only reason he *didn't* kill me is because we gave him water—and you were soothing him by rubbing his face."

Sorin glanced over his shoulder at the dragon. Could dragons kill with a thought? In the half-closed eyes was only pain, none of the fierce intelligence he had so often seen in the creatures. "What else?" Sorin asked.

"I tried to ask who did this to him. That's when he remembered and—I felt it," he ended in a whisper.

Sorin took him by the shoulders. "What did you feel?"

A shake of the dark head. "It was—something grabbed

hold of him, something he couldn't see, only sense. Then he crashed to the ground from full flight, as if he'd been slammed in the head with a club. But nothing touched him! Nothing! Just this—something—pulling him down out of the sky."

"Grandfather Zehava killed quite a few dragons in his day," Sorin mused. "But not even he could pull them down out of the sky."

"That's what happened to this one." Riyan stared at the dragon, whose breathing was shallow but regular now. "Somebody more powerful than he got to him, and he couldn't even struggle. It wasn't a battle at all."

Sorin pointed out what he had noticed earlier. "Riyan, look at the spikes. They're new and made of fine steel. Like rock-climbing spikes, but thicker. As if they'd been made for this. And they're hammered in as if at leisure, straight as nails in the floorboards of Feruche." He rose and began trying to prize one out of the dragon's wing. A low, keening moan quivered the creature's throat; Sorin stopped.

"Evidence?" Riyan asked.

"Exactly. We're going to find the filth who did this, and use his own spikes on him."

"We'll have to track him down first. Sorin, I want to talk to Sioned. She may know how to get the image from the dragon. And there has to be something we can do to ease his pain."

"Are you strong enough for a Sunrunning? The dragon's colors must've hit you pretty hard."

"I'm all right."

Sorin eyed him, then shrugged. "I'll see what I can do for the dragon."

While Riyan wove sunlight in the direction of Stronghold, Sorin used the rest of the water to cool the worst wounds. By the time Riyan spoke again, the dragon's breathing was stronger and some of the pain had left his eyes.

"She says I can do it, if the dragon trusts me." He rubbed his palms on his thighs.

Sorin saw reluctance in the dark face. "Riyan . . . all we really have to do is ask around for someone who's been flaunting a dragon kill. No one does this kind of thing unless he wants it found. He'll be *bragging* about it," he added bitterly.

"No. I mean, yes, I agree with you about that. But it might take all spring to find him in these mountains. Whatever he meant by this, I doubt he wants to be caught for punishment." He eyed the dragon. "If I can get a picture, it'll be that much easier to find him." He gave a quick smile. "Besides, Sioned's a good teacher, even at a distance. She showed me how to weave sleep, too."

Sorin glanced at Riyan's six rings. Four had been given by Lady Andrade; he had made a special journey to Goddess Keep last year to request that the fifth and sixth be given. But the skills he had demonstrated to earn them had been taught by Urival and Sioned, not Andry. And sleep-weaving was known only by those with eight or more rings. "You're not supposed to know things like that."

"Andry wouldn't approve," Riyan agreed somewhat sharply. "But then, I don't entirely approve of him, either." An instant later he shrugged an apology. "I'm sorry."

Sorin shifted his shoulders uncomfortably. "Do what you have to."

Riyan gestured him back and pulled in a deep breath. A moment later the dragon quivered delicately. Riyan gasped, fists clenching, tension again making a ramrod of his spine. One hand came up as if to ward off a blow; the dragon's right wing trembled at the same time. Both throats growled simultaneously—deep, threatening, raising the hairs on Sorin's nape. All at once the dragon hummed, and Riyan's drawn face responded with a smile at once feral and triumphant. As if, Sorin thought suddenly, as if he had the murderer pinioned by his sword—or his talons.

Dragon and Sunrunner continued their bewildering communion for some moments longer. At last Riyan's eyes opened and he sighed his satisfaction.

"Got it," he said, the strange smile still on his face.

Sorin wordlessly handed over the water skin again, and after a long drink Riyan looked more like himself. The dragon had totally relaxed. Sorin thought the sleep-weave must be responsible until he saw that the amber eyes were open, lucid, and gleaming through the pain.

Riyan spoke before he could ask. "He's tall, dark-haired, blue-eyed, very good-looking if one favors arrogance. Dressed expensively, silk and good Cunaxan wool, that light stuff that slips through the fingers like velvet. But what's really interesting is the color he wore." That fierce smile flickered across his face again. "Violet."

Sorin's brows shot up toward his hairline. "Princemarch? Pol's color? But why?"

"I couldn't say. But the dragon was most emphatic—they think in colors even more than *faradh'im* do."

"So we know who to look for." Sorin crouched beside the dragon's head again. "We'll get him for you," he promised, stroking the soft hide around the eyes and forehead. "Riyan, can't you put him to sleep now? He's in terrible pain."

"Move away from him. I don't want to catch you up in it, too."

A few moments later lids drifted shut over sleep-hazed eyes. A long sigh coursed through the dragon's body, and then he lay still. When he was certain the dragon was oblivious to all physical sensation, Sorin began removing one of the spikes from the wings. Riyan helped. It took all their strength to work the steel from the wood. At last it was free, stained with blood that superstition said was poisonous to the touch. Untrue, of course, just as the legends about dragons having a taste for virgin girls or being able to kill with a glance were untrue. Dragons were dangerous only when their food supply was threatened or when they were directly attacked. The wolves of the Veresch were the same—but wolves did not inspire the same fear dragons did. Wolves were, like men, creatures of the ground and could be fought more or less as equals. But wings made dragons terrifying.

Then again, Sorin thought suddenly, Riyan had said that the dragon had been capable of killing him while in contact with his colors. Perhaps there was some truth in the legends after all. He didn't much want to consider it.

Still, what creature would not use any means at its disposal to kill an enemy? They were men; a man had done this to the dragon, a man powerful enough to bring him down out of the sky like a falling arrow. He examined the fine, elegant structure of the wings, the sweep of strong bone and muscle covered in blue-gray hide. The contasting underwings were black, the skin almost silky to the touch. He had never seen a dragon this close. And he wished for this dragon's sake that he had not had this opportunity.

He considered the tall, blue-eyed, arrogantly handsome man responsible for this horror. And abruptly the connection was made between what Riyan had said about the method and the dragon's ability to kill. No Sunrunner could have done this—but a sorcerer, a *diarmadhi*, might.

"Will he wake up again?" he asked Riyan, who shook his head.

"He'll only last until sunset at most. Sioned tells me the sleep-weaving is good for a whole night." He ran one hand down the dragon's neck. "Poor beast. Sorin, when we find the man who did this—"

"Rohan will want him brought to Stronghold for trial." He met his friend's eyes. "Somehow I don't think he'll live that long, do you?"

"Funny you should put it that way."

In perfect agreement, they hiked back through the hills to their horses.

***

Late afternoon found them in the congenial comforts of Elktrap Manor, and in the more than congenial company of Lord Garic and Lady Ruala. The former had reached the colossal age of eighty-six; the latter, his granddaughter and only surviving relative, had just seen her twenty-seventh winter. Ruala's parents had died of Plague the year after she was born, and her only sister had succumbed to injuries suffered in a climbing accident four summers ago. It was just the old man and the young woman now in the sprawling manor house, supervising a few servants, the herds of sheep harvested for their wool, and the elk harvested for meat and the tough, beautiful black hooves that were carved into anything from drinking vessels to jewel boxes. The dinner service they brought out to honor their lordly guests was a gorgeous collection of plates, bowls, and goblets inlaid with elk-hoof that Lord Garic himself had made over the course of his long life. The food was simple but good, and wine fermented from honey-pine resin was served in very old Fironese crystal stemware. Sorin and Riyan were made happily welcome, and it was not until they sat with the *athri* and his granddaughter in her private antechamber that they got around to explaining their presence.

Word of a slain dragon had brought them into the Veresch. Decreed with uncharacteristic imperiousness twenty-three years ago on assuming his title, High Prince Rohan's strict law severely punished anyone who killed a dragon. Most thought the law sentimental nonsense, if not actually threatening; Rohan was known to have a ridiculous love for the frightening creatures who decimated herds and crops when food supplies in their habitual ranges grew low. It was true that he wished to protect dragons because of his feeling for them—but also because their melted shells yielded gold. Riyan, Lord of Skybowl where abandoned dragon caves were mined for their gold-bearing shells, knew this; Sorin did not. That the law was Rohan's law was enough for Sorin, who shared his uncle's love of dragons.

But the law had been broken, and they had come to investigate. Lord Garic told them that he had heard of a dead dragon several measures to the north, confirming their guess that the dragon they had found that morning was a second kill. Lady Ruala paled as Riyan described the scene. He apologized for the graphic description.

"Forgive me, my lady, but I had to make clear the horror of the crime."

She nodded silently and gestured for him to continue.

But he hesitated a moment, glancing at Sorin, before deciding he might as well tell it straight out. "I was able to get a description of the man. From the dragon."

Lord Garic's unfaded blue eyes narrowed in a direct look at Riyan's *faradhi* rings. "Ah," was all he said. His granddaughter, whose eyes were so dark a green that in shadow they seemed nearly black, merely nodded again, as unsurprised as the old man. Riyan found this disconcerting. He hadn't thought Sioned's trick of communicating with a dragon to be common knowledge.

But he let their lack of reaction pass. "He's tall, with dark hair and blue eyes, very handsome, arrogant, strongly made. I suppose it's too much to hope that you've heard anything about such a person."

Midway through his description Lady Ruala's gaze twisted around to Lord Garic. "Grandsir—it's not possible!"

He fixed a grim stare on the two young men. "Not only have we heard of such a person, we gave him shelter not two nights ago."

Sorin leaned forward eagerly. "What did he say? Did he tell you his name? Did he give any clues about who he is, where he's from, where he's bound?"

Ruala shook her head. "None. He gave the name Aliadim, but after what you've said we can deduce that it was false. He told us he was of independent means, traveling through the Veresch for pleasure. He was alone and he only smiled when we cautioned him against wandering too far from the main roads." She frowned, her eyes darkening. "He rode a very fine horse, I remember— not one of our mountain ponies, but feather-hoofed."

"Kadar Water," Sorin supplied. "Lord Kolya's breed. What about the saddle, my lady? The bridle? Anything at all you can remember."

"Grandsir? You were in the stables when he arrived."

The old man rocked gently back and forth, gnarled fingers laced together over his lean chest. "Plain saddle, nothing special. Bridle the same. But the blanket—deep violet. Like his tunic."

That settled it for Riyan. He had deliberately not mentioned that detail of color, hoping that Sorin's questions would elicit the information and confirm the man's identity. "Which direction did he ride out?"

"North, but that means nothing," Ruala explained. "There's a crossroad a measure up the north road. He could be anywhere."

"We know where he was today," Sorin said tightly.

"Not today, my lord. Three days ago." Ruala set down her cup. "I remember now. There was a strangeness to his horse's eyes, calm enough to ride but still skittish from some recent fright. And the first thing he asked for was a bath to wash the road from him. But dirt isn't red-brown the way dried blood is—and that was the color I saw beneath his nails."

Riyan felt his stomach lurch. "You're saying it took that dragon *three days* to die?" he whispered. "Sweet Goddess."

"This 'Aliadim' killed the dragon on purpose, you know," Garic mused. "He deliberately broke the law."

"But why, Grandsir?" Ruala pleaded. "Why would anyone want to kill anything as miraculous as a dragon? The wisest thing the High Prince ever did was decree their protection!"

Riyan glanced at her with interest; most people were terrified of dragons and thought Rohan's law the stupidest thing he had ever done.

"The dragon was killed in challenge, to flout the law," the old *athri* replied. "To bring investigating Desert lords into the Veresch, as has happened. But—no disrespect intended, my lords—I believe this man was hoping not for those of Skybowl and Feruche but Stronghold and Dragon's Rest."

***

"You have to tell them," Sorin said some time later, when they were alone in the pleasant, well-lit chamber allotted to them.

Riyan came out of the bathroom, rubbing his face with a towel. Elktrap Manor was a well-appointed place with many modern conveniences. Lord Garic had kept his wealth secret during Roelstra's rule for fear of its being legally confiscated, but in the years Rohan had been High Prince he had gleefully used his hoarded treasure to make improvements in his beloved holding. Unlike Roelstra, Rohan believed that as long as the contract between lord and prince for supplies in return for protection and shrewd bargaining with other princes was upheld, an *athri*'s goods and lands belonged to an *athri*. Unlike Roelstra, Rohan was not a thief—legal or otherwise.

"I suppose I *will* have to let them know," Riyan said. "But you know Rohan, you know Pol—and you know what will happen."

Sorin nodded. "They'll be here like arrows shot from a single bow. But there's a nasty section of that law saying that anyone who fails to report a dragon's killing immediately is judged as guilty as the one who did the deed."

Tossing the towel onto a chair, Riyan laughed. "Can you seriously see Rohan stripping us of half our wealth?"

Sorin did not find this particularly amusing. "There have been rumblings lately that there's one law for the highborns and Sunrunners, and another for the common folk. Frankly, I don't want to be caught in the middle of the same kind of dispute."

Riyan sobered. "I suppose you're right. Very well. At moonrise I'll contact Sioned and then Pol. But I can't help hoping that clouds will blow up so I can't work. I think Lord Garic is right. 'Aliadim' isn't interested in us. He's out to provoke Rohan and Pol."

"And knew exactly how to do it." Sorin picked up a rolled parchment borrowed from Elktrap's surprisingly fine library. "A treatise on dragons," he explained as Riyan's brows arched. "I'll try to borrow it for Lady Feylin, but right now I want to do a little reading myself. Did you get a look at the dates on some of Lord Garic's books? Right back to the year Goddess Keep was established. As old or older than the scrolls Meath found on Dorval."

"But not as dangerous, I hope," Riyan murmured to himself. He sat in a deep armchair by the windows and stared at the purple mountains, waiting for the moons to rise.

After a time he heard the rustle of parchment that meant Sorin had rerolled it. "Interesting enough to borrow for Feylin?" he asked.

"Yes." Sorin's voice was strained, and Riyan glanced around curiously. "But that's not what I want to talk about. I didn't want to mention it until you did. But you don't seem to realize how that dragon was killed."

"What do you mean?"

Sorin raked pale brown hair out of blue eyes, an impatient gesture. "Don't you see? You're a Sunrunner. Could *you* bring a dragon down from the sky? You told me that's what happened, and for all my admiration for *faradh'im*, I don't think any of you could have done it. You probably have the power—*but not the right spell.*"

Riyan felt himself go absolutely still, mind and body and spirit.

"Which means Andry should be told about this, too," Sorin continued stubbornly. "I know you don't much like what he's done the last nine years, but you would've told Lady Andrade, wouldn't you? My brother is Lord of Goddess Keep now. He needs to know this."

"The law is Rohan's," Riyan heard himself say.

"But the spell was *diarmadhi*."

"No proof."

"Oh, for the love of—Riyan, you were the one who communicated with that dragon! And by the way, Pol's going to be crazy once he hears. He still hasn't managed it and neither has anybody else. But did the man who killed that dragon wear Sunrunner's rings? Yet he yanked the creature right out of the sky! Andry has to be told."

"I'll mention it to Sioned," was as far as Riyan was willing to go, and with that Sorin had to be content.

Chapter Nine

Dragon's Rest: 4 Spring

Pol hung on as best he could, but the effort was in vain. Daylight opened up between him and the saddle. The next instant he was flat on his back in the lush spring grass with the wind knocked out of him. The filly, with fine regard for his comfort now that it no longer depended on her, sidled over and poked her delicate nose into his ribs. Propping himself on his elbows after he'd caught his breath, he frowned up at her in disgust. "I'm fine, thanks for asking," he growled.

A young man leaning on the paddock rails had been laughing uproariously all this time. "I don't see what's so damned funny," Pol complained as he regained his feet.

"Don't you? From where I'm standing, it was hilarious."

"You have no respect for your prince's dignity, Rialt— let alone his sore backside."

"If your dignity *depended* on your backside, you'd have a problem," Rialt replied as grooms loosened the filly's saddle girth. She was perfectly reasonable now without a man's weight on her back. "I just hope the mount you bring to your marriage bed is easier to ride than this lady here," he teased.

"And no respect for your prince's privacy, either," Pol snapped.

"Temper, my lord," Rialt grinned. Marriage was an increasingly irritating subject for Pol, who had just finished his twenty-third winter and was being delicately pressured by almost everyone but his parents to find a wife. "Come, a nice hot bath will—"

"Don't try to manage me the way you manage my palace, Chamberlain," came the sharp reply, and Rialt shut up. Pol's bad humor righted itself by the time the filly had been led away, and as he closed the paddock gate behind him he apologized with a rueful smile. "Sorry. But it seems that everything, including my own horses, gets the better of me these days."

"Cheer up. There's excellent news that I came down here to tell you. We lost only half the sheep we originally thought in the winter floods, and saved most of the vines and young trees."

Rialt chattered on about their domestic state as they walked the long road from paddock to palace, and Pol's mood improved. Livestock and crops were doing better than initial word had indicated. Torrential rains that winter had endangered Dragon's Rest; other holdings had been all but ruined. Pol hoped to use some of his own stock to replenish herds drowned in floods or dead of resulting disease, and the information heartened him. It had the added benefit of taking his mind off the tedious business of preparing to Choose a bride.

He hoped he would have as much luck in finding a wife as he had had in finding a chamberlain. Rialt, encountered by chance many years ago at an inn below Graypearl, was the youngest son of an important Dorvali silk merchant. He had often appeared at Prince Chadric's court during Pol's last years there as a squire, representing his father and a small group of other merchants. Pol had gotten to know him, liking what he saw. But an invitation to visit Stronghold and further his education in the economics of trade was reluctantly declined; Rialt was married by that time, with one daughter born and another on the way. Two summers ago his wife had died in childbed and a son with her, and Rialt had written a respectful letter asking if the offer still held. By then, though only three winters Pol's senior, he had a successful trade of his own in both silk and pearls. But he found home insupportable with its memories of his beloved wife.

Leaving his daughters behind with their grandparents, he had come to Dragon's Rest to set up the books. Within a season he was running the whole palace, from the horse-breeding farm to the purchase of ornaments for Pol's own chambers. Rialt was a fiendishly capable administrator whose talents, unbound by the strictures and the relatively minor scope of trade, had found their true calling in the completion and governance of a palace. It had taken several years to build the first three sections of Dragon's Rest—the Princes Hall and the two towers flanking it—but the great semicircular structures that finished the palace had gone up in an astonishingly short time. The *Rialla* would be held here again this year, and the princes and lords would find every arrangement for their comfort. Pol wasn't sure quite how Rialt had managed it, but was grateful that he had done so.

"Your Ostvel," Rohan had told him once, smiling. "He, too, took all the everyday worries of running a castle from me, so I could sit back and think great thoughts!"

And as Ostvel had become Rohan's friend, so Rialt was Pol's. This year Prince Chadric and Princess Audrite were bringing Rialt's two daughters from Graypearl to live with their father. Pol looked forward to having more little ones running rampant around the palace—but he knew that what he really wanted were children of his own.

Finding their mother, however. . . . He frowned again at the inevitable return to the inevitable Choice awaiting him. Noting the expression, Rialt sighed.

"If you're determined to be aggravated, my lord, please do everyone a service and do it elsewhere! The older servants know better by now, but the new ones still walk in terror of their Sunrunner prince—and your expression is anything but reassuring."

Pol was startled out of his mood. "Are they really frightened of me?"

Rialt grinned at him. "It doesn't help when you light every candle in your suite all at once, you know. *Plus* the hearth fire."

A smile twitched one corner of his mouth. "Mother scolds me for being a bit of an exhibitionist. Very well, I'll take my temper into the gardens and terrorize the roses. And try to remember to resist my more startling impulses."

Rialt chuckled. "I recall very well my own startlement in Giamo's inn that day nine years ago."

Their first meeting teased Pol's mind: himself and Meath, peacefully eating a meal; a Merida posing as a Gribain soldier starting a fight meant to cover the assassination of the High Prince's heir; Pol's instinctive call of Fire that had given Meath a precious moment of surprise; Rialt's competence with his fists during the brawl. Pol clapped his friend on the back. "I startled *myself*, too. But we both seem to have gotten over it. I'll be in the gardens if you need me."

The roses ruled serenely in the soft spring sunlight. Pol had arranged the plantings so that some part of the gardens was in bloom all year long; winter flowers lingered now, and spring blossoms were on the verge of opening. Summer and early autumn were the spectacular seasons, with a profusion of color such as made *faradhi* senses drunk.

The water garden was laid out in the central court between the two identical buildings Rialt irreverently called twin barns. Rose trees were growing large enough to coax into shapes like torches; when in full bloom, gradations of color from yellow to crimson would make them appear like rows of flames. Herbs and hardy little rainflowers bordering the paths were the only color now. By summer the air would be alive with the scent of roses and the music of fountains.

Beyond was the informal garden, a teeming riot of botany barely contained by hedges that separated plants and walkway. Audrite had helped Pol plan this area for shape and texture as well as color. Delicate ferns nestled near substantial flowering shrubbery; round-leafed plants alternated with tall blooms and sprays of ornamental grasses; rising banks of strange, spiraling Desert succulents supported graceful trees whose lacy canopies offered summer shade. Other princes thought him utterly mad, he knew, to discourage elaborate gifts and ask instead for cuttings from their lands. But the result was a garden unlike anything ever seen before. Pol never walked through it in any season without feeling lighter of heart.

Now, with winter only days over and spring making its first few tentative responses to the warming sun, the garden was scant of flowers but full of beauty just the same. Pol wandered along a path covered in coarse dark sand from Skybowl's slopes, pausing to admire the juxtaposition of dark green vines winding up a pale golden bunchberry tree, fluted red winterbells snuggled close to a broad-leafed fern. Desert-born and Desert-bred though he was, he had taken Princemarch to him and made it part of his heart. The land and its people had done the same to him; he belonged to them now as surely as he belonged to the Desert. The odd thing was that he felt no conflict. Different as the two were, they were both his as much as he was theirs. He'd begun to feel in the last few years that he was the living link between them. His children would strengthen that bond.

Pol swore in exasperation. He wanted to avoid thinking about that aspect of the future, yet everything brought him back to it. Very well, he *would* think about it. It appeared he had little choice.

Little choice, either, in the manner of woman he must wed. He had always known she must be *faradhi*-gifted. One Sunrunner parent was no guarantee of continuing the heritage, certain only if both possessed the talent; at the very least there should be Sunrunners in her family. But what if he fell in love with a girl who had not the slightest hint of the gift? Well, he simply would not allow it, that was all. At times he felt a wistful desire to have it all done for him the way Lady Andrade had arranged his parents' marriage. But he rebelled at the notion of Andry's doing such a thing for him, which led him to consider his wariness of all trained *faradhi* women. It was a terrible thing to admit, but he wasn't sure he could entirely trust a wife who had been Andry's student. His father had never had the slightest doubt of his mother's loyalty—but then, Sioned had glimpsed Rohan's face in Fire and Water when she was only sixteen. She had always been committed to him because she had always known.

While still under Meath and Eolie's tutelage on Dorval, before his return to Stronghold to become Urival and Morwenna's student—with substantial lessons from his mother—Pol had once looked into Fire and Water. The summer after his sixteenth birthday he had been allowed formally to demonstrate his ability to call Fire and was given his first ring. It was not a true Sunrunner's ring, just as Maarken's first had been given by Rohan and not Andrade. But silver crowned with a tiny moonstone from one of Andrade's own rings had been placed on his right middle finger. And that afternoon Meath had ridden with him to the ruins of a *faradhi* castle, shown him a tree circle much like the one near Goddess Keep, and left him there alone.

Pol had scooped moss and dead leaves from a stone basin sunk into the ground. Enough water remained for the simple conjuring. He was well aware that he was not following the ritual as specified for many hundreds of years. He had not spent the previous night with a *faradhi* woman wearing the guise of the Goddess for his man-making night—that initiation having been rendered unnecessary by a lovely and enthusiastic kitchen maid at Graypearl. But he obeyed Meath's directions and called Fire across the shallow water. And in it he had seen only himself: a face fully matured, proud, serious but with ready laughter hovering around the curve of the mouth, and the circlet of royalty crossing his brow. His mother had seen her future husband's face as well as her own, and Pol had hoped for a similar vision. But there was only the one face, his face. He studied it with surprise and shy approval. He would enjoy being that man, old enough to make his own decisions and run his own life.

He grinned ruefully now at the memory. If he'd thought his life would be easier once he had control over it, he had been even more innocent than most boys. He enjoyed ruling his own palace while learning from Ostvel how to rule a princedom, and pleasing himself in the matter of his guests, his gardens, his everyday activities, and—truth be told—his bedmates. But if he'd caught a glimpse of his destined wife in the flames dancing gently across the Water, at least he would have known who to look for. And that part of his life would have been settled.

Suddenly he could hear Sionell laughing at him. "Poor prince!" she would say. "More wealth than he knows what to do with, the most beautiful palace ever built, fine horses racing through his paddocks, and *two* princedoms to rule one day—feeling sorry for himself because he can't find a woman to complete this portrait of perfection! Poor, poor prince!"

Imagination provided memory of her bracing mockery, fond and nettled all at once, and the teasing glint in blue eyes below coils of dark red hair. If only he could find someone with Ell's wit and understanding, someone he could talk to and depend on. Tallain was a lucky man.

A glance at the sun reminded him that he had a late afternoon appointment with an emissary from Gilad. He was not looking forward to it, but it would at least be a distraction. He ran up to his own chambers and washed away the stink and dirt of horse—and abrupt contact with the ground. He was about to go back downstairs when his scandalized squire hurried in with one of the casually elegant outfits Aunt Tobin regularly sent him. She despaired of his ever developing the right instincts about his appearance, something that came naturally to his father. Pol was oblivious when it came to clothes, and tended to greet important persons in dusty riding rig or with half the rosebeds on his trousers rather than the silk and velvet decreed by his position. Tobin's gifts were compromise, being cut as comfortably and casually as everyday clothes, but made of gorgeous fabrics she chose herself when the silk ships came to port at Radzyn. Pol wrinkled his nose at the green shirt, dark blue tunic, and gray trousers presented for his inspection, then laughed as the boy's face turned stubborn.

"Stop glowering at me, Edrel," he chided. "I know I have to look pretty for the Giladans."

"Very good, my lord." Thirteen years old, nearly as dark as a Fironese, Edrel was the younger son of Pol's vassal Lord Cladon of River Ussh. He had been a year at Dragon's Rest, was the very first of Pol's squires, and took his duties with absolute seriousness. Pol had been trying to teach him a sense of humor, but thus far had had little luck.

As he donned clothes, Edrel gave brief descriptions of the guests without being asked. It was a little trick Pol had developed, and not entirely for his own amusement. Edrel escorted visitors to an audience chamber, then came to Pol with verbal sketches of any unknowns in the group. It flattered guests to be identified on sight by their host—but it also amazed them that somehow Pol instantly knew who was whom without introductions. A nice bonus was the training Edrel received in powers of observation and judgment. It was a task at which the solemn little boy excelled.

Prince Cabar had sent his cousin Lord Barig and two experts on Giladan law. His lordship was characterized as short, gray, bearing little resemblance to his grace of Gilad, of an age with Pol's father but looking many

winters older and, "Rather sour, my lord. The lawyers
are worse."

"Lawyers usually are."

"My lord!" Edrel's own studies at Dragon's Rest included law.

He fastened his shirtsleeves. "I admire my father with
all my heart for instilling such respect for the law in
everyone—but people who study it are thunderously dull.
I anticipate an excruciating afternoon. Perhaps I'll cancel
it and go out riding instead. I'd cut quite a figure in these
clothes on horseback, don't you think?" He grinned at
the boy.

It took Edrel several moments to realize he was being
teased. He reacted with a tentative smile. Pol clapped
him approvingly on the shoulder and gave himself a swift
glance in a mirror before leaving his dressing chamber for
the corridor outside.

Edrel scampered ahead of him to be the first at the
door of the reception room. The boy straightened his
own clothes, gave his prince's outfit a critical look that
made Pol grin, and nodded importantly to the page who
opened the great wooden doors inlaid with bronze. Edrel
stepped through, bowed slightly to the three men within,
and announced, "His Grace of Princemarch."

Pol distributed a polite smile all around as they inclined their heads to him. "Lord Barig," he said, "we
hope you had a pleasant journey from Medawari, and
that his grace our cousin is well."

Use of the plural was cue enough to any courtier. His
lordship bowed again, murmuring affirmatives, and did
not introduce the socially inferior lawyers. Pol gestured
to chairs and they were all seated. Edrel hovered at the
door, waiting for word about refreshment. Pol gave none.
This was a formal audience, not a private chat.

Barig took some time to get to the point. Pol could
have set to music the standard progression of topics. First
the civil inquiries about his parents' health, then the
compliments on the beauties of Dragon's Rest, then the
remarks about the weather, made interesting this year
only because of the winter downpours that had half-
drowned the continent. A digression was made when he
mentioned a visit to Swalekeep on the way here. Finally
the usual wishes for a fine and profitable *Rialla* were

expressed. That done, Pol wondered how Barig would work his way around to Sunrunners.

He did it with a strategic return to the weather. Sour-faced he certainly was, and gray from his hair and eyes to his goat's wool tunic, but Pol gave him credit for a nice degree of subtlety.

"I trust this long season of rain has not interfered too much with *faradhi* communication, your grace. It must be frustrating for Sunrunners to be trapped by the weather like the rest of us."

"Clouds are a *faradhi*'s natural enemy," Pol responded. "But we manage."

"Then your grace will have been apprised of certain unhappy events in Gilad. Specifically, this matter of a Sunrunner's involvement with the death of one of our most distinguished citizens."

"Yes. We have heard something of it." He had, in fact, heard a great deal. Thacri, a master weaver who lived near the Giladan seat of Medawari, had contracted a severe fever at winter's end. *Faradh'im* had knowledge of medicine, though not as extensive as trained physicians; in the absence of the latter, Sunrunners offered their services. Despite the best efforts of a young *faradhi* traveling through the area, the man died on the first night of the ten-day New Year Holiday. Afterward it was discovered that one of the potions tried against the fever had been concocted wrongly. And therein lay the difficulty.

Barig presented his case. "The position of His Grace of Gilad is that this Sunrunner, acting beyond her capacity as a physician, is responsible for the death of Master Thacri."

One of the lawyers, as brown in coloring, clothing, and countenance as Barig was gray, shuffled his lanky bones and said, "Your grace, it is only by the strenuous efforts of myself and my colleague that the widow was persuaded to abandon her plan of charging the Sunrunner with murder."

"We understand," Pol murmured, privately shocked. The penalty for murder was death; although the Sunrunner must indeed pay for her mistake, it should not be with her life. But had she been anything other than a Sunrunner, he would not be listening to this at all.

Barig went on, "As it stands, your grace, the charge is

misrepresentation of skills, which led to criminal negligence and Master Thacri's death. The punishment for this in Gilad is a fine, the amount to be determined by his grace on review of the victim's probable earnings over the course of his remaining natural lifespan. Master Thacri," he added, "left behind a wife and many dependents."

Pol had a sudden strong suspicion that Master Thacri had probably lost several years off his age and that the number of his dependents had at least doubled in hopes of wringing that much more in fines. But the real difficulty had yet to be stated. Weary of flying in circles, Pol broached the subject himself.

"The Sunrunner, of course, owns nothing. All that she originally possessed is now the property of Goddess Keep."

"I am pleased to discover that your grace is conversant with the facts." Barig inclined his head. "The Sunrunner in question was accepted for training at Goddess Keep in 717, before Lord Andry canceled the practice of dowries."

So Andry was in for it, Pol thought. Cabar, doubtless supported by Velden and Miyon, would assess a staggering fine that Andry would in honor have to pay. And wouldn't appreciate at all.

But it appeared from Barig's next words that Andry had no intention of paying a single gold piece.

"The case has, of course, been presented to Lord Andry. He has replied, your grace, that a Sunrunner's transgression is a matter for Sunrunners to deal with, not princes or lords or anyone else."

This time he could not keep reaction from his face or his voice. "He *what*?"

Barig and the lawyers looked indecently pleased with themselves for a fraction of an instant before the courtiers' masks settled back in place. The second lawyer spoke for them.

"It is my very great regret to inform your grace that the Lord of Goddess Keep appears to consider that there is one law for Sunrunners and another for the rest of us. Once can only hope that your grace and your grace's father, the High Prince, can persuade him differently."

"Let me get this straight," Pol said, abandoning the royal plural in his worry. "The Sunrunner made a mistake, and a man died. Now there's disagreement about who has jurisdiction over punishment. Tell me, is it Lord Andry's position that the Sunrunner was acting *as* a Sunrunner, and thus should be disciplined by Sunrunners?"

Barig nodded. "Precisely, your grace."

"And Prince Cabar says that she was acting as a physician, not using her *faradhi* gifts but instead skills available to anyone who cares to do some reading?"

"Your grace has summarized the essentials."

My grace is madder than hell at Andry for this! How dare he make a mockery of Father's laws? He had control of his expression again, however, and merely nodded. Life would be interesting indeed at the *Rialla* this year.

"Where is the Sunrunner now?" he asked.

"She is being held in close but comfortable confinement, your grace," the first lawyer replied. "And treated with every courtesy."

Pol had a sudden insight. "Except that of the sun."

Barig stiffened. "Prince Cabar felt that—"

"I'm sure he did," Pol interrupted, not wishing to hear excuses for the deliberate cruelty of shutting a Sunrunner away from the light. "But I believe it to be unnecessary. I will speak to your court *faradhi* and ask that this woman be placed in a room where she can feel the sun." As Barig opened his mouth to protest, Pol snapped, "Her punishment will be decided, but until that time it would not be in keeping with his grace's reputation for mercy to—sweet Goddess, my lord, do you think she could weave herself gone?"

"As your grace wishes. May I assume that your grace will also consult with the High Prince on this matter?"

Pol correctly interpreted this to mean, *Take our side and we'll take the wretched woman out of the dungeon.* He did not respond well to being coerced. "We will certainly communicate with his grace through our mother the High Princess at the proper time."

But his lordship was not so easily put off. "This matter has naturally been of great interest at other courts, all of which desire a clarification and speedy resolution as much as your grace does."

Now Pol knew why he had mentioned Swalekeep. Chiana must have chortled all afternoon. Fixing Barig with a cool stare, he said, "No doubt. And the High Prince will be most interested to hear of that, too."

Barig got the message, even if the lawyers did not. One of them started to speak, only to receive a quelling look from his lordship.

Pol stood. The other three rose also and Edrel, still hovering at the door, took his cue and opened it. "We thank you for making the long and difficult journey from Medawari. Please make yourselves comfortable while we consider the matter brought to our attention."

"Your grace," Barig said, bowing again.

The outer wall of the corridor was a gentle inward curve, following the line of the building, its windows overlooking the water garden. Sunlight spilled across the hall and into the chamber in irregular rectangles bordered by dark lines of wood frames. Rainbows danced here and there on the white stone floor, flung by the beveled edges of glass windows open to the warm afternoon breeze. Pol had taken but three steps into the light when he felt his mother's brilliant colors swirl all around him. He smiled and concentrated on the familiar tender touch.

Goddess greeting, my son! What have you been up to all this time?

Goddess greeting, Mama, he replied, giving her the childhood name he never used aloud anymore. *I was just about to weave my way to Stronghold. But how did you know where I'd be within the palace?*

If I said it was a lucky guess, you'd never believe me. I tried earlier and couldn't locate you, but then I saw the pennant on the roof indicating a Giladan presence. You always receive emissaries in that particular chamber, so it was only a matter of waiting for you to finish. Child's play.

He was aware of the Giladans behind him, struck dumb at the sight of a Sunrunner at work. The complete stillness of total concentration while standing in sunlight was unmistakable. But they had almost surely seen it before, he thought. His mother's quiet laughter rippled through his mind.

Of course they've seen Sunrunners at work. But never a Sunrunner who is also a prince. No wonder they're startled. But it won't do them any harm to be reminded exactly who you are. What news from them, Pol?

It can wait while you tell me what brings you here. He

sensed her colors darken subtly, and frowned. When she had finished telling him about Sorin and Riyan's discovery of a dying dragon, he was seething with fury.

That's two dragons slain, Pol. And your father says it's undoubtedly a deliberate provocation.

But why? Who'd kill a dragon to flout the law, or even for sport? The stipulated penalty—

—is severe. But whoever has done this doesn't care. He probably wants to be found. Sorin and Riyan will search for him. I expect to hear more tonight, and if I don't, then I'm going to contact Riyan myself.

I've been discussing penalties, too. He gave her a brief summary of the talk just concluded, finishing with, *Andry's arrogance is beyond belief!*

Yes, his mother responded thoughtfully. *But it's exactly what Andrade would have done. Tell the Giladans that your father will consider the matter very carefully—and get that Sunrunner out of the dark if you possibly can.* There was a quiver of emotion along his mother's shining colors, a thrill of fear that he did not understand. Before he could ask any anxious questions, it was gone.

They want to make it a bargaining point, he told her bitterly. *My instinct is to tell Cabar that Andry will pay the fine if I have to skin him alive to get him to do it. But this way, it looks as if I'm agreeing with Cabar just to get that poor woman back into the sunlight where she belongs.*

Andry has a lot of explaining to do, she observed. *I've kept you long enough, my son. Send to me tomorrow at noon, and we'll talk further.*

And her elegant pattern of colors faded down the sunlight.

Pol raked his hair from his forehead and swung around to face the stunned Giladans. The entire conversation had taken no more than a few moments. But during them Pol had made several decisions.

"Lord Barig," he said, "the High Princess agrees with us that the Sunrunner must be given other quarters. We have explained the situation to her, and she also agrees with our analysis. Nothing can be done until we have spoken with Lord Andry. But we remind you that he will probably be more disposed to an amicable settlement if he knows his *faradhi* has been taken out of the dark." Using his mother's phrase, he recalled her mental shiver and wondered if it was from more than a *faradhi*'s understandable fear of being shut away from the sunlight.

Andry's attitude had evidently not occurred to Lord Barig. He nodded slowly. "I understand, your grace."

"Good. We will be leaving tonight for one of our northern holdings. Please feel free to remain at Dragon's Rest and refresh yourselves for the journey back to Gilad."

"I thank your grace."

Pol left them, Edrel at his heels. When they were far down the curving corridor, sun through the open windows striking bright glints off silver and copper candlemounts on the walls, Pol said, "Tell Rialt to come to my chambers. Then order the grooms to have five good horses ready by sunset. And I'll want to see the underchamberlain and the commander of the guard as well."

"Where are we going, my lord?"

Pol glanced down at the boy. "*We* are not going anywhere. *I* am going to Elktrap Manor. *You* are staying here to make sure those damned Giladans don't linger more than a day or two. Let them go plague Chiana for a while."

"My lord, as your squire it's my duty to be at your side—"

"Edrel, just do as I ask. We can argue about it later."

Dark eyes rounded in shock. "My lord! I would never presume to argue about anything with—"

He stopped, took the boy's shoulders, and smiled. "Forgive me. I know you wouldn't. I should have said we'll *discuss* it later. All right?"

Edrel nodded. "Very good, my lord." His tentative responding smile suddenly widened into a grin. "You should have seen their faces when you were Sunrunning!"

Pol choked on laughter, but not over the astonishment of the Giladans. "Edrel! If you're not careful, you're going to develop a sense of humor."

"Oh, I hope not, my lord." The young face raised to his was the portrait of earnest gravity—but the eyes held a dancing glint that made Pol laugh anew.

The household organized by Rialt for Pol's comfort and convenience went into smooth, efficient action as his orders were made known. By sunset six horses carrying Pol, Rialt, three guards, and Edrel—who had won his point—were cantering toward the narrow northern pass out of the valley. At moonrise, when a confused and then horrified Riyan located Pol, the group was twenty measures from Dragon's Rest.

But you can't come to Elktrap! That's exactly what this dragon killer wants!

Will you relax? And don't you dare go looking for him without me. Tell Sorin it's my order that he stay put. You can leave if you want, of course—you're my father's vassal, not mine. But Feruche—

—is technically part of Princemarch, and you know damned well I won't leave without Sorin. That's a nasty trick to play on a friend, Pol.

But necessary. I know both of you too well.

He smiled as Riyan slid along skeins of moonlight back to Elktrap without more than a mental grunt in reply. And it occurred to him as he rode through a spring night bright with moons and stars that he was, like his father and grandfather before him, finally going to go dragon hunting. Because where a dragon was, this slayer of dragons would be.

Chapter Ten

Elktrap Manor: 5 Spring

The trail to Elktrap was a fairly direct one, and they made good time. But after several steep climbs and nerve-shredding descents through the Veresch, Pol was looking forward to a rest. He didn't even have to enter Elktrap to receive welcome; a lovely young woman was waiting outside the gates with a wine cup of a size that sent a flush of relaxation through his muscles just looking at it. Reining in, he smiled gratefully down at her as she bowed low. Straightening, she lifted the cup.

"Be you welcome to Elktrap Manor, and rest within," she said in the ritual formula of mountain folk.

"Lady Ruala," he said, identifying her by the black braids and green eyes that her grandfather, proud of her beauty, had described in great detail at a vassals' conclave last year. "How did you know this is just what I need?"

She smiled back. "I know these mountains, your grace. Every traveler who comes through here is in need of a strong draught of wine."

He took a long swallow, sighed with pleasure at the fine vintage, and gave the cup back to her. "With this and your smile to refresh me, my lady, I've almost forgotten that last pass. Whoever named it Tumblewall knew exactly what he was talking about."

Ruala chuckled and went to offer wine to Rialt, Edrel, and the three guards, repeating the traditional words of welcome to each. Pol hid a grin as Rialt's gaze widened slightly; she was indeed very beautiful, with the slim, quick figure of a girl and the graceful poise of a woman. The combination of black hair, white skin, and lustrous dark green eyes was enough to make any man look

142

thrice. Add a tip-tilted nose, a charming smile, and that indefinable *something* about a woman of breeding and intelligence who knows her worth, and Lady Ruala of Elktrap was a formidable creature.

Once inside the gates, their horses were taken by grooms. Riyan, Sorin, and Lord Garic descended the short steps of the manor house, the latter giving him warm welcome. The former two still looked slighty disgruntled. Pol grinned at his friends.

"Oh, stop glowering. I'm here and you're stuck with me. And I've been thinking about how best to trap this dragon killer. Riyan, you and I can weave sunlight and go looking from here, after you give me the picture of him you got from the dragon."

"As you wish, my lord."

"And stop being so formal—I already know you disapprove of my being here." He turned to Garic as they entered the wide downstairs hall that seemed entirely carved of dark-stained pine. "And that reminds me, I'd be honored if you and your granddaughter would call me by my name."

"The honor is ours. Although I'm afraid our folk will bow and stare quite devotedly." The old man chuckled. "They've never served a prince before."

Rialt laughed as they started up the stairs. "The easiest way to rattle his grace here is to bow to him fifty times a day. It keeps him humble."

Ruala sent him a gentle frown of puzzlement. "I don't understand."

For a moment the chamberlain looked as if he'd wink at her. "He's just like his father, my lady—treating him like a prince is the best way to remind him he's only a man like the rest of us."

Pol made a face. "Thank you for sharing that piece of wisdom with us, Rialt. My lady, you see what I have to endure in my own palace." He hesitated on a landing, catching sight of the group in a magnificent old mirror. It wasn't himself he stared at, but Ruala—the dark-gold sheen cast onto her skin, the misted secrets in her eyes. Goddess, she was beautiful—

She smiled at him in the mirror. "Startling, isn't it?"

He nodded helplessly, and with an effort shifted his eyes to the frame. "Exquisite work."

"The craft is a lost one, more's the pity," Garic said. "They used some combination of metals we don't know how to make anymore. The glass seems to be special, too."

"Isn't there one at Skybowl like this, Riyan?" Pol asked.

"It belonged to my mother. I've no idea where she got it or how old it is."

"Very, if it's similar to this one." Garic asked casually, "I believe your mother was Fironese?"

"Mm-hmm." The young man traced a section of knotwork with a careful finger. "When I was little, I had the feeling sometimes that somebody was watching me from inside the mirror." He looked around, embarrassed, and shrugged.

"They're all like that," Ruala said, exchanging a quick glance with her grandfather that Riyan missed and Pol did not. "My sister and I used to try to sneak past this one so it wouldn't see us!"

"All?" Sorin inquired. "How many more are there?"

"We have this one, and four small hand mirrors. And another one almost this size, but the glass cracked about ten winters ago and the replacement doesn't feel the same at all." She started up the next series of steps.

"Andry's interested in mirrors," Sorin remarked as the men followed her. "The way Rohan is fascinated by things like water clocks."

"Is he?" said Lord Garic politely, then let the subject drop by saying, "I think you'll find this a pleasant chamber, my lord. Ruala, did you have them bring up the mossberry wine?"

"Allow me, my lady," Rialt said, going to the table to serve the highborns.

Pol relaxed in a soft chair and nodded thanks to his chamberlain for the wine. "Beautiful tapestries. Giladan, aren't they? Riyan, I want to hear all about touching that dragon—later. For now, tell me everything that happened from the time you found him."

Between them they made quick work of the tale, and Riyan finished with, "I've already tried to find him on sunlight. No luck. But now that you're here, there'll be two of us working. He can't be more than three or four days' ride in any direction, but that's still a lot of territory to cover."

"Our people have been instructed to keep their eyes open," Ruala offered.

Pol nodded his thanks. "Excellent. But I don't think it will take very long to discover this man's whereabouts. All we have to do is look for dragons."

Sorin made an annoyed gesture. "Father's always telling me not to be more stupid than the Goddess intended! Why didn't I think of that? Of *course* he'll go after another dragon!"

"Of course," Riyan echoed. "I just hope that when he does, we won't be too far behind him. I don't want to see another one dead, Pol. You can't imagine the horror of what he did to the poor beast."

"Show me," Pol said simply.

Riyan hesitated, then rose from his chair and fetched a fat white candle from the sideboard. Wrapping the fingers of both hands around it, he called Fire to the wick. Ruala blinked; Garic showed no reaction at all. The little flame flickered, steadied, rose to five times the height of a normal flame, and expanded to encompass the conjuring Riyan created within it.

Some moments later Pol was aware that there was blood in his mouth; he had bitten the inside of his upper lip. He forced himself to think clearly, to calm his sick fury at what had been done to the dragon. "Show me the man's face as the dragon saw it."

The arrogant, clever, handsome face appeared, blue eyes laughing above the violet clothes. Pol felt hate twist his vitals. He banished that emotion, too, and tried to read that face while committing it to memory. There was something familiar about it, but nothing he recognized as coming from a particular region or a specific highborn lineage.

Fironese heritage like Riyan's—dark eyes, dark skin, dark hair—was easy to identify. Pol's light hair and eyes came from his grandmother Milar, a blonde like most natives of the Catha Hills. In one remote area of Dorval, everyone had the same short-fingered hands; the shepherds on the south coast of Kierst were substantially taller than most people. Even in the more diverse populations, such as that of Einar, certain characteristics regularly appeared. Pol knew all the regional distinctions and none of them applied to "Aliadim."

Of course, with every generation such telltale signs blurred a little more. In the families of princes and *athr'im,* who habitually married outsiders, definitive traits were only accidents by now. Tobin was obviously of Desert stock with her black hair and black eyes, but Rohan was as blond as their mother. Pol's squire, Edrel, lacked the thin streak of white in his hair that had been characteristic in his family for generations. And in the Kierstian and Syrene royal lines, of which Pol was a part through Sioned, the green eyes and the gifts of a Sunrunner from Goddess Keep who had married a Prince of Kierst showed up sporadically.

He didn't notice that Riyan's candleflame had guttered out. He stared into empty space, Fire still burning his eyes and searing the face into his mind. Something was itching at his perceptions, like a half-heard insect whine or a barely felt twitch in a muscle. If not identifiable by region or family trait, then possibly—

No. He knew the bloodlines, legitimate and otherwise, of every noble family in all the thirteen princedoms. Audrite had drilled him in genealogy as part of his training at Graypearl. That this man did not have specific signposts as to his origins did not mean he was a mixed-breed highborn.

Still, there was something tauntingly familiar about that face. He looked forward to seeing it in person—and would take great pleasure in altering it with his fists.

Aware that the others were trying not to stare at him for his long silence, he roused himself and spoke. "Very well. Now that I know who to look for—"

He broke off, knowing suddenly why he had been jumpy a few moments earlier. He ran for the sunlit windows, Sorin a half-step behind him. He had felt it, too; it was said that their grandfather had had this particular talent to burn. Pol had come into the perceptions late, but at last that oddest of family traits in all the princedoms had awakened in him. Proof that he possessed it flew over the towering pines: a dragon.

He gripped his cousin's arm and felt Sorin's muscles shiver just like his own with the awe-filled joy of seeing a dragon. No matter how many times he saw the great

beasts, the tingle along his nerves that heralded their
arrival and the transcendent wonder of watching them in
flight moved him to his marrow. This one was a fine,
full-grown female, green-bronze in color with black underwings. She flew a lazy series of spirals perhaps half a
measure from them, as if she knew she was being watched
and wanted to show off her beauty and her skill. She
rode the wind like some fantastic twin-sailed ship, soaring, drifting, beating her wings to take her upward again.
On or about the fortieth day of spring she would fly with
her kind to the Desert, there to choose her mate and wall
up her eggs in caves to bake through the long summer.
Fifteen or so of her hatchlings would die in the cave, too
weak to struggle out of the shell, to break down the wall,
or to avoid becoming a sibling's first meal. Perhaps three
would live to fly—a far greater number than in olden
times, when men had slaughtered the survivors as they
emerged into the sunshine. Rohan had outlawed the Hatching Hunt long ago. Killing a dragon had been forbidden
for the length of Pol's life.

But someone was trying to kill this one. She faltered in
mid-wingbeat and a cry that was half fury and half terror
thundered through the mountains. Her head lashed back
on her neck, her tail whipping from side to side in frantic
rhythm. The balance of flight lost, she plummeted to the
ground like a falling stone.

Ruala found her voice first. "He'll kill her if we don't
hurry!"

Riyan's head jerked around. "What makes you think
you're coming along?"

She opened her mouth to protest as the three young
lords and Rialt hurried to the door, Pol shouting for
Edrel. Her grandfather clamped both strong hands around
her shoulders from behind to keep her from following.
She twisted to glare up at him.

"Don't even think of it," he told her.

Ruala shook him off. She went to the windows that
overlooked the courtyard, where nearly every servant at
Elktrap had joined in the frantic scramble to saddle and
bridle fresh horses. Pol was mounted first, then Riyan
and Sorin, and finally Rialt. They clattered out the gates,
the squire and three guards galloping behind.

"I'll be going with them soon, though, Grandsir," she

said thoughtfully. "After all, one of those young men is going to be my husband."

"Ruala!" He grasped her shoulders again and turned her to face him. "Which one?"

Her answer was an innocent smile and absolutely nothing else.

"Hmph," he replied.

***

Controlling a fast horse in a headlong race up a mountainside while at the same time weaving sunlight to find a downed dragon were not recommended for the easily distracted. Pol shifted precariously between his body's consciousnesss of the mare moving beneath him and his mind's consciousness of the terrain moving beneath his fabric of plaited light far above. The doubled sensation should have made him as motion sick as crossing water, but all he felt was a vague dizziness. Thanking the Goddess for her mercies, he split his concentration in two neat, separate parts and didn't have time to think about anything else.

But Riyan did, and as they began the descent down into a ravine he deliberately slammed his horse into Pol's to gain the prince's attention. Reining in, Pol shook himself free of the weaving and glowered at Riyan. "What in all Hells did you do that for?" he shouted. "I nearly fell!"

"You would've been worse off than that if you'd kept on Sunrunning. Have a look." As the others pulled up, he gestured to the trail ahead which led into shadowy trees.

Pol felt his stomach turn over. If his body had left the sunlight while his mind and gifts were tangled in it—Urival's lectures on the Star Scroll gave him the ancient word for the most hideous death a Sunrunner could imagine: *daltiya*. Shadow-lost. An empty mind in a body that functioned for a few days and then died.

"I'm sorry. It was careless of me," Pol murmured. "Thank you, Riyan."

"Did you catch sight of the dragon?"

"Not yet. Anybody hear anything?" Heads were shaken in the negative all around. "She can't be that far from us. Riyan, will you take the south for about a measure? I'll range north."

Only a few moments later Riyan gave a guttural cry. Instantly Pol was back on the slope, shocked by his friend's expression of horror.

"Can't fly—afraid—kill him! Kill them! Can't *fly*, wing broken—hurts hurts hurts—"

Sorin kicked his horse over to Riyan's. Shaking his friend hard with one hand, he shouted his name several times. At last sense returned to Riyan's dark eyes. "Are you all right?" Sorin asked worriedly.

A gulp, a curt nod. "Her pain . . . reached out to me. We must hurry, Pol. Just over that rise is a little box canyon with a waterfall at the east end. That's where she is."

Pol frowned. "You said 'them.' "

"I did?" Riyan seemed to review memory of what he'd said—or seen, or felt, Pol wasn't sure. "Yes. Another man—red hair is the only impression I got, along with her fear and pain. Pol, how did she do that? Catch me up in her feelings that way? For an instant, she and I almost . . . it was as if we touched *minds*, not just colors on sunlight. As if we were almost one being."

"We'll get Feylin and my mother to speculate about it some other time. Though it's killing me that you can do this and I can't." He turned to Rialt. "A box canyon presents interesting possibilities. You and Damayan ride up this ridge. If they try to escape this way—"

"They shall be strongly discouraged, my lord," Rialt replied at once. "But I hope you remember that whereas you taught me how to look as if I know how to use a sword, I'm really rather hopeless at it."

"I'm sure only the appearance will be needed," Pol soothed. "Besides, Damayan has given *me* lessons in swordsmanship. If it comes to it, just protect yourself and don't worry about attack. He'll take care of that part of it."

"Of course, my lord," Damayan said, never one for false modesty, glowing at his prince's praise.

"Anto, Zel," he said to the remaining guards, "you'll swing around to the other side and cut off any possible escape over those hills. Riyan and Sorin will come with me. If you see us getting in trouble, you have my full permission to come to our rescue." He grinned tightly.

"And me, my lord?" Edrel piped up. "Shall I come with you?"

Pol was responsible to Lord Cladon for the boy's safety. He also remembered what it was like to be thirteen. "You shall. A squire's place is with his prince, as you so often point out to me." As the boy's face lit, Pol flicked a glance at Riyan, then at Anto. Both gave almost imperceptible nods. Edrel would be whisked out of danger by whoever was closest to him when and if danger threatened. Even if Anto had to gallop headlong down from the hilltop, or Riyan had to leave off battling the dragon killer, Edrel would be looked after. Pol had the distinct feeling that his companions had all made a similar and equally silent pact regarding Pol's own safety. Yes, he remembered very well what it was like to be thirteen. It was very much like being twenty-four. "Off with you now. We'll wait for you to get in position. And keep your eyes open. We don't know if there's anyone else waiting for us."

"For you," Rialt corrected grimly. He and Damayan galloped away, followed by Anto and Zel. Pol turned to Sorin.

"Sorcery is undoubtedly being used on this dragon, too, just like the one you found the other day. Sunrunners can't work more than one spell at a time. And I've never read or heard anything to indicate that the *diarmadh'im* are capable of it. If he looses his hold on the dragon to deal with us, I want you to free the poor beast if she's in the same state as the other one. Riyan, you and I will probably be rather busy." The other Sunrunner arched his brows at the understatement. "But don't kill him. My father will want him alive."

"I trust you won't object if I singe him a little," Riyan said.

"Lightly browned around the edges and blood-rare in the middle. Let's go."

***

Pol had been thinking up something princely and righteously wrathful to say on confronting "Aliadim." But the words flew right out of his mind when he left the trees bunched at the canyon mouth and saw the dragon. She was still standing, hind claws dug into the grassy soil, one wind unfurled like a gleaming bronze-and-black sail.

But the other wing hung limp. Awkward angles at the shoulder and halfway down the main wingbone confirmed what Riyan had said earlier: broken in two places, rendering not only the wing but the forearm useless. She hissed her fury of pain and fear, but did not move. She couldn't; the tall, dark-haired man who stood within easy reach of her talons held her in terrible thrall. And he was laughing.

The horses had flatly refused to go farther than the trees, and so Pol, Riyan, Sorin, and Edrel approached on foot. Unnoticed by the dark-haired man and his red-headed companion, whose backs were turned, they paused only long enough to make sure of their reinforcements' positions on the hillsides. Then they advanced, and Pol's glance at the others showed him rage to match his own.

The dark-haired man taunted the dragon, striding up to poke the tip of his sword into her useless wing, drawing more pinpricks of blood. He could just reach her limp, wounded forearm, and abandoned sword for dagger in slicing out one talon. The other man, a bit shorter and built more heavily, kept a respectful distance, obviously not trusting even in *diarmadhi* spells. His companion turned to laugh derisively—and found Pol's sword point an arm's length from his throat.

The dragon shuddered, her eyes like onyx shot through with silver, glittering suddenly as she looked down at Pol. He hoped the reaction was in response to an easing of the spell's hold on her, but didn't count on it. He saw out of the corner of his eye that Riyan was in charge of the red-haired man, who swore luridly and glared at them. Sorin had snatched up the sackful of spikes and looked as though he was contemplating using them on the dragon killer.

"Your grace," the man said, still smiling, laughter hovering around his eyes and mouth as if this really was too funny, "I assume you've come to forbid me, or arrest me, or some other nonsense."

Pol smiled back, a stretching of his lips from his teeth. "I'd rather kill you."

"Of course. But you won't." He tossed dagger, sword, and bloodied talon to the ground, his movements casually elegant and reeking of insolence. "I think I ought to tell you that once I'm occupied with you, the dragon will be released from certain . . . restrictions. She's not at all happy right now. In fact, she's likely to rip any or all of us to shreds."

"Unquestionably," Pol replied with perfect calm.

"So rather than play other and, I'll admit, equally interesting, games, why don't you put up your sword and ride away like a good little prince? It'll save everyone a great deal of bother."

"You understand that I can't do that," Pol said as if to a particularly slow child. "But while we're discussing things, I'd like to know who you are and why you're doing this. Neither my father nor I take kindly to persons who murder our dragons."

"As if they belong to you!" He laughed.

"They are mine as Princemarch is mine—which is to say, they are under my protection as prince and Sunrunner."

"Ah, yes. Credentials must be presented, like good ambassadors. You already know mine, I gather. But I thought you'd puzzled this out by now. I wanted to meet you, and this seemed an invitation you couldn't ignore."

"And my palace at Dragon's Rest would have been a little too . . . confining." Pol nodded. "Well, you've met me. What now?"

"Nothing so crude as killing you. Not yet, anyway. I require a larger audience for that." A short pause and a mocking smile. "Cousin."

"I thought you'd make some claim to that effect," Pol mused. "And since it's on the soil of Princemarch that you've chosen to perpetrate this outrage, it must be Princemarch you want." He sighed tolerantly. "Another bastard son of Roelstra's, no doubt, wearing a color you have no right to. That's been tried before. Try to think up something more original."

"So you have reasonably quick wits. I'm glad—it will make this more interesting. I don't like things made too easy. But as to originality. . . ." He grinned into Pol's eyes. They were much of a height, Pol perhaps a finger-span shorter; the prince was as broad in the shoulders, but slimmer through waist, hip, and thigh. A trained warrior's physical instinct had sized up his opponent earlier; a trained statesman's cunning had given him the man's intellectual measure; but more than either, the sensitivities of a *faradhi* fully trained in Sunrunner arts and conversant with the secret, dangerous Star Scroll chimed clear, shrill warning. When he met this man in battle, it would not be with swords, as his father had fought Roelstra, nor would it be with words, as he had confronted the pretender Masul nine years ago.

The man gave Pol a slight, impertinent bow. "My name is Ruval, I was born at Feruche, and I have the honor to be the firstborn of Ianthe of Princemarch." He grinned then. "Not Roelstra's' son, you see, but his grandson."

Pol felt himself go very still. He should have laughed in the man's face, told him that Ianthe's sons had died with her the night Feruche had burned to the ground. But he could not, because he knew the truth. Urival, just before his death, had called him to his bedside in private.

"No one knows what I'm about to tell you. Not Andry, not even your mother. Ostvel may suspect—he has access to Roelstra's archives, remember. But you must tell no one until you believe the right time has come. You recall the boy who died at the Rialla, the sorcerer? I kept him anonymous, threw his body into the Faolain so no one could identify him as I had done. What I saw in his face was Ianthe. He was her son, Pol—the youngest, Segev. He called himself 'Sejast' but he was Ianthe's son. The other two must also be alive. Ruval and Marron are their names. I don't know where they are, though I've searched whenever I had the chance. I believe they're in the Veresch somewhere, but—who can say? If they're anything like her, and judging from Segev you can bet that they are, they are the greatest danger you could face. They are diarmadh'im, Pol. Princes, just as you are, but sorcerers as well. I've taught you all I know, all I safely could, of the Star Scroll, anticipating them. Now it appears I won't be there, my prince, to help you face them. For they will come, Pol, never doubt that. Ianthe's sons. When you find them, kill them. They must die. They deserve to die. Segev killed Andrade."

Pol stared at Ianthe's eldest son, recognizing at last the distinctive shape of nose and chin. Urival had once conjured for him a representation of Roelstra's face in Fire; two generations had altered the face subtly, changed the coloring a bit, added a narrower jaw and wider cheekbones —enough changes to foil identification unless one was looking for it. He knew that this man was who he said he was. And his companion must be Marron. But he could not admit it. Must not.

"You're no more Roelstra's grandson than I am," he snapped.

"Then perhaps you truly are my cousin in fact, and not merely in courtesy between princes." Ruval's blue eyes were laughing again. "Which of my mother's esteemed sisters could have spawned you?"

"I've heard it said that of all the sisters, Ianthe was the most like Roelstra in her bedroom habits," Pol riposted smoothly. "Which servant, squire, or groom do you claim as your father?"

At last Ruval reacted with something other than amusement. His eyes lost their taunting glitter and narrowed dangerously. "My father was Lord Chelan, a highborn with bloodlines—"

"—suitable for standing at stud," Pol interrupted, beginning to enjoy himself.

Ruval's jaw clenched. But he swiftly regained control of himself. "In any case, you have many things that belong to me, but restoring to me my mother's castle of Feruche will make a good start."

Pol smiled. "When dragons spend winters in Snowcoves," he said.

"There'll be hatchlings riding icebergs next summer," Ruval snarled.

This time Pol was the one who laughed. "Sorin!"

"My prince?" His cousin was beside him immediately.

"I see a tree felled over there—obviously intended for securing the dragon. Slice off two branches an arm's span long, if you would."

Sorin grinned, understanding Pol's intention. "We already have the spikes, my prince."

"So I noticed."

Ruval had recovered his poise again. "You wouldn't dare," he commented easily.

Pol eyed him. "No? Oh, go ahead, release the dragon. Do you think I don't see that in your face? Let her go—and see what good it does you."

He hoped Riyan had heard and comprehended the challenge. The possibilities of sorcery worried him, but he was counting on timing. To work against Pol, Ruval would have to release the dragon—but the instant she was free, she would go wild with rage and the only thing on anyone's mind would be getting out of her way. Riyan could, he hoped, subdue her before Ruval or Marron could either work any magic or use more conventional forms of attack. Besides, the brothers were outnumbered and Pol's other allies were watching from the hilltops. Pol felt confident in his gamble; it was a wager Sioned would have taken at once, being inordinately fond of a good, dirty bet when almost all the odds were in her favor. It just might work, Pol told himself.

And it would have, too, if not for the dragon. Dangerous enough at any other time, she was crazed by pain, terror, and her frantic consciousness of the eggs forming within her body. Increasingly through the spring and up until her chosen cave was walled up, she would focus more and more on the new lives slowly swelling her belly. Once she flew from her cave, she would forget all about them, and treat her own surviving hatchlings just as she would any others. Dragon parenting was a communal effort, shared by all females and sires. But until that wall was secured, she was concerned only with her instinct to protect her eggs—and right now that meant protecting herself.

Thus when Ruval abruptly released her, she went mad. With a terrifying roar she threw her head back, then came down with her good foreleg clawing for Ruval. He made the mistake of grabbing for his sword; talons ripped through his tunic and shirt, tearing long slashes in his back. He cried out with the pain and fell, rolling onto his back with the sword raised to hack at her if she went for him again.

But she turned her attention to Pol, raising up once more in preparation for disembowelment. It was how his grandfather Zehava had died. He thought this in the same instant he wove sunlight into a strong, tough fabric, not even lifting his sword. The dragon's jaws opened wide and she bellowed her fury down at him, her massive body drawn to full height now and ready to descend on him.

He heard a harsh scream nearby; wondered in anguish if it was Sorin or Riyan or Edrel; hoped it was Marron. Ruval was near him on the ground, his sword pointed up at the dragon, frozen in horrified fascination as she reared up. Her tail lashed, the uninjured wing folded to her back, the broken one dangling at her side. Pol stared up at her, protected by nothing more than the offered sunlight. She was magnificent and beautiful and lethal, and he knew he ought to be terrified of her.

What felled him was not her talons or her dagger-sized teeth. He staggered as the full force of her sunwoven colors smashed into his. He went to his knees hard on the grass, gasping, using every bit of his strength to keep sane and whole. *I won't hurt you, I'd never harm any dragon—I'll kill this other for you, I swear I will—* The emotions flooded through him, undammed by contact with the pain-maddened dragon. Savage hatred, unspeakable agony, furious terror for her hatchlings' safety—he tried to counter with his love for dragons, his fierce joy in their beauty, his determination to protect them—and to kill Ruval, who had done this hideous thing to her. He looked up, senses reeling, his mind close to shattering like fine Fironese crystal, expecting that at any instant those talons would gouge out his guts.

The dragon never touched him.

The contact gentled despite her terrible pain. Pol caught his breath as wordless questions tumbled over and over each other, pictures and feelings and demands all mixed up until he felt his grip on sanity weaken dangerously. She seemed to realize it and drew back a little. In the air between them his *faradhi* senses touched the brilliant pattern of her, more complex than anything he had ever felt before. His attempt at Dragon's Rest had resulted in a shock that had well and truly scared him. Now he understood that there simply had not been enough time—or enough need.

Lost to all else in the intensity of the encounter, he never saw the battle that raged around him for a few brief moments. He showed her an image of the lake at Dragon's Rest, the sheep kept there for the exclusive use of her kind. A low hum reached his ears and he smiled when she painted light in the form of his palace, the blue-gray stone all aglow in the dawn. He was aware of her agony, but as a remote thing now, not the shrieking fire in her wing and foreleg. But when he tried to convey help—a splint, salves, tender care for as long as it took

for her to heal—tears ran down his cheeks at her reply:
an image of her own lifeless corpse. She would never fly
again, even with a mended wing. And a dragon without
flight was as a *faradhi* shut away from the sun.

"My lord! My lord, please! Come back!"

He whimpered with pain as someone shook his injured
wing. It passed, and his own arm was gripped in Edrel's
trembling hands. He looked up at the boy.

He said thickly, "Get Riyan—tell him to send the dragon
into sleep, spare her any more pain—" All at once he
remembered why he was on his knees in the grass, and
twisted his body around. "Sweet Goddess," he whispered.

Rialt and the guards had come, but not in time. Ruval
and Marron were gone. There was blood on Riyan's
tunic, more on his hands; he rubbed his ringed fingers
convulsively, as if he would chafe the skin raw. He stood
over Pol with a stricken, desperate look in his eyes.

"Sorin—" he began, and choked.

"No," Pol breathed. He hauled himself up with Edrel's
help and stumbled to where his cousin lay. The blood on
Riyan's hands had come from the gaping wound in Sorin's
thigh, the urgent pulse weakening. A frantically applied
tourniquet was useless; the deep artery had been severed.

Pol sank to his knees and brushed the sun-streaked
brown hair from his cousin's eyes, and tried to swallow
his sick fear.

Sorin met his gaze. "My prince," he said softly, his
voice steady. "Lost them—I'm sorry."

"No. Sorin—"

"Let me speak, Pol." The corners of his mouth turned
up in a slight smile. "They're a threat to you and need
killing. Do that for me."

He nodded helplessly, then flung a look at Rialt and
Riyan. The latter had unashamed tears in his eyes that
terrified Pol; the former merely shook his head and glanced
away.

"Doesn't hurt, really," Sorin whispered. "Tell Mother
that." A sudden gasp negated his denial of pain.

"Easy, easy," Pol soothed, taking the water skin from
his belt. "We'll get you back to Elktrap and—"

"No. To Feruche." His eyes lost focus for a moment,
then sharpened. "I know you can't trust Andry as I

do—but at least try to . . . understand him. For my sake, Pol. Please. And for your own."

"Sorin—"

"Promise. Never asked . . . anything of you, my prince . . . I'm asking now."

Pol cleared his throat. "Yes—anything, Sorin. Please—I need you."

He smiled vaguely and his eyes closed.

"Sorin!"

The hand on his arm made him look around. Riyan was white with shock. He held out both shaking hands, the shining rings dark with Sorin's blood. "Pol, there was sorcery at work here."

"They'll die for it," Pol heard himself say. Then he wrapped his arms around Riyan's trembling shoulders, and they both wept.

Chapter Eleven

Castle Pine: 7 Spring

"**Y**our grace!"
"My lord!"

A swift, wary embrace like that of two dangerous animals in an unnatural mating, and Miyon of Cunaxa stepped back. He was tall, leanly made, with deceptively lazy eyes and a mouth too wide for his narrow face. During the seventh winter of his reign and the nineteenth of his age, he had personally executed the greedy advisers who had thought to rule Cunaxa forever through him. For the last twenty years he had ruled with an authority that had challenged the considerable power of his fractious merchant class. He desired two things in life: safe, inexpensive trade routes, and the Merida out of his princedom. His lips parted in a smile over sharp white teeth as Ruval bowed to him, for here was the means to acquire both.

"Forgive the necessary secrecy of your reception," Miyon said, waving the younger man to a chair. "I am not yet in a position to welcome you openly. But accept my congratulations on your recent accomplishments."

Ruval laughed. "If you mean the dragons, thank you. But if you mean Sorin of Feruche's death—my brother Marron was responsible. I wouldn't insult my sword with the blood of anyone under the rank of prince."

"By which *you* mean Pol. I see. Well, I'm grateful to your brother, then, for leaving Feruche without a lord. I'm considering giving it to my eternal pests, the Merida."

Ruval's face froze in a pleasant smile. "Your grace understands that it is the castle of my birth."

"Of course," Miyon agreed blithely. "And belongs to Princemarch. But that's why you're here, is it not? To find out what I want in exchange for my help in getting what you want."

"Your grace is very direct."

"It saves time," Miyon acknowledged. "Where is your brother, by the way?"

"Enjoying the hospitality of the guards mess, the better to fit in with your suite when you go to Stronghold."

The prince could not disguise his astonishment. "What?"

Ruval, having betrayed Miyon into an honest reaction, smiled again as he followed up the advantage. It would not last long; he had made a study of the Cunaxan prince. He shifted his shoulders gingerely against the talon wounds on his back and said, "It would be entirely natural for you to wish a pre-*Rialla* discussion with Rohan, Pol, and Tallain of Tiglath—who speaks for Tuath Castle as well these days, since Kabil has no sons to follow him and his holding will undoubtedly go to Tallain on his death. Working out a trade agreement prior to the *Rialla* at Dragon's Rest will put all three princedoms in a position of strength when it comes to further negotiations with Dorval, Grib, and so on."

"How very clever of me," Miyon drawled, angry that he had been outthought but too pragmatic to argue. Then his dark eyes began to sparkle with genuine glee. "And in my party at Stronghold will be you, your brother— and my daughter, Meiglan."

"Exactly, your grace. I knew you'd find it an interesting proposal."

Miyon leaned back in his chair, long legs sprawled in front of him. "Well, well. Now I understand. You'll be disguised, of course. Members of the guard, I suppose. I hope you're able to hide yourselves well. Pol has already seen you."

Ruval waved away his worries. "You needn't be concerned, your grace. Only get us to Stronghold, and we'll do the rest."

"Stronghold."

Hate and envy lurked beneath the rich tones of Miyon's voice, but the emotion in his eyes was covetousness. Ruval had never understood why the prince so desired that pile of rock on the Desert's edge; perhaps it was a symbol for him, the way Castle Crag was to Chiana.

"You may have Feruche with my goodwill," Miyon

was saying. "But Stronghold is mine. And Tiglath." He paused. "And Skybowl as well. That's my price."

"Done," Ruval said, relieved that help was coming with so cheap a promise. "I've always thought draining the lake at Skybowl would make an intriguing agricultural project." He smiled. "Tiglath is obvious, of course. Profits should increase tenfold once your merchants don't have to triple the price of their goods because of transportation costs."

Miyon's brows rose. "I cannot describe to you how relieved I am that you comprehend trade objectives."

"I should have thought they'd be clear to anyone with eyes to look. No one could visit Swalekeep, for instance, as I have, and not see the difference between its level of prosperity and your own."

"The Desert strangles us," Miyon agreed. "Tricks us, extorts money—" He broke off with a frown. "Perhaps you have some thoughts on a matter that has vexed me for some years now. Why is it that Rohan is so damnably rich?"

Ruval blinked. It was not a question that had occurred to him before. His grandfather Roelstra had been extremely wealthy, so he had assumed Rohan's revenues from Princemarch had swollen Desert coffers all these years. He said as much to Miyon.

"Perhaps," the prince admitted. "But consider what's been spent in the last eight or nine years. Feruche appears to have been built out of Sorin's share of Chaynal's obscene wealth—and the iron that bitch Sioned tricked me out of in 719. Yet there's been no discernible decrease in Sorin's reserves—not that he's around anymore to enjoy them, for which I must remember to thank your brother. And then there's Dragon's Rest. Total up the cost of the buildings, furnishings, carpets, fixtures—everything down to the silk napkins. It's a colossal amount, probably equal to five years of revenue from Princemarch."

Ruval leaned forward, intrigued. "Yet it doesn't seem that he's beggared my princedom."

"No. And the sum I estimate is not even the whole. I am immediately informed whenever a caravan makes its way to Dragon's Rest." The prince grinned suddenly, as if daring Ruval to discover his sources of information. "They come from Castle Crag, from Syr, from Ossetia, from Radzyn—"

"Supplying still more items that *look* as if they were purchased by other courts!" Ruval made an incautious move and hid a wince as his shoulder twinged.

"Precisely. The money involved is staggering. Where is it coming from? Your grandfather was rich, but not *that* rich. And Rohan is fool enough not to take advantage of his position as High Prince to accept gifts in exchange for his favor."

"Do you know where he's getting the money, your grace?" Ruval asked, not bothering to disguise his eagerness.

Miyon shrugged irritably. "If I did, would I be sitting here trying to puzzle it out? There's something else, too. The Desert took much less time to recover from the Plague than other princedoms—especially considering the amount of gold Rohan paid Roelstra for the drug that cured the disease. He didn't demand money when he distributed it elsewhere. He didn't bleed his vassals dry to pay for it. Where does his wealth come from?"

"When we capture Stronghold, we're likely to find out."

"Possibly. But I would rather find out before that, so we don't have to go looking for it. I don't trust Rohan, he's too clever. He wouldn't keep his treasury at his own castle. Perhaps it's at Remagev."

"Or Radzyn or Feruche—or Skybowl," Ruval murmured.

Miyon grinned. "Second thoughts about your bargain, my lord?"

"Not at all, your grace. Princemarch's wealth will be quite enough for me."

"And your brother?" Miyon asked shrewdly.

Ruval only smiled.

The prince snorted his amusement. "I see. Well, then, shall I take you to meet my daughter? Or would you prefer anonymity as far as she's concerned?"

"The latter. She should be as innocent as the first snow."

"Stupidity is a great guarantee of innocence."

Smile fading, Ruval asked sharply, "Has she brains enough to do as told?"

"She'll ride where she's reined," Miyon said with a curt shrug.

They left the private suite for the antechamber where

other petitioners waited. Ruval had come as a merchant pleading for patronage; it was a trifle unusual to gain an audience alone, but the court chamberlain was notoriously addicted to bribes. Those who had no money to buy their way in and must wait their turn cast sidelong glances of loathing at Ruval.

He ignored them, but could not ignore his brother. Marron lounged in the doorway, where he was not supposed to be. He had been ordered to the mess to learn what he could so he and Ruval could fit in easily when the time came. Ruval could have strangled him as he ambled forward to greet Miyon.

Marron gave the prince a smile that clearly said, *I, too, am Roelstra's grandson—and you will understand that, cousin.* Before he reached them, however, a young girl, perhaps seventeen and perhaps not, came into the antechamber from a side door. She was delicately slender and had a glory of golden hair and very dark brown eyes that glowed with excitement, and she was incredibly beautiful if one appreciated the type.

"Father?" she ventured. "Oh, Father, please let me thank you for—"

"Meiglan!" The prince glowered down at her and she stopped dead in her tracks, all the pretty flush of enthusiasm dying from her face.

So this was the girl, Ruval mused.

"I–I'm sorry—" she stammered.

Miyon made a visible effort and smiled at her. "No matter, my little treasure. Run along now. You may thank me later for your gifts."

Marron had paused a few paces away from them. The girl backed away from her father and Marron advanced once more, smiling as if to an equal.

"Your grace," he said with a bow. "You favor me with your notice."

"We are pleased to entertain the proposals of clever merchants in our princedom," Miyon responded. "But we have many others to listen to this day."

Ruval took the hint and escorted his brother out.

They made their way by a back staircase to the doorway of the mess. All Ruval said, between his teeth in fury, was, "Get in there and do as you were told!"

Marron chuckled. "As you command, brother dear."

Ruval watched for a moment as Marron used the charm perfected in Chiana's court to ingratiate himself. But beneath the affable grin was a profound distaste for the company of common soldiers. Neither did Ruval look forward to submerging his identity in that of a hired swordsman. But it was necessary in order to get within Stronghold's walls. Marron, taken on as escort, would bring along a "friend." And they would walk right into Rohan's castle, unsuspected.

Suspicions roiled in his own mind, though, as he left the castle and walked through town. Where *did* Rohan's wealth come from? Miyon's reasoning appeared sound, but exacerbated curiosity rather than satisfying it. Reaching the precincts of the merchant district with its shops and public houses, he glanced at the sun and decided he had time for a contemplative wine cup before meeting Mireva at their lodgings in the poorest section of town. He chose a tavern and sat in a corner with a crudely made glass container of sweet, potent wine made from pine cone resin, ignoring all around him as he thought the matter through.

One of his few really clear childhood memories—other than the horror of the night Feruche had burned—was of gold. Ianthe had taken him to the deepest level of the keep one night to show him their wealth: square, palm-sized gold ingots stacked on shelves in a locked room. He remembered touching one with almost superstitious awe, taking as many as he could into his hands, feeling their heaviness, flinging them up into the air to make a glittering rain by torchlight. He could still hear echoes of his mother's delighted laughter.

But should it not have been minted coin in sacks, rather than ingots?

He scowled into the golden-brown wine. Sediment had gathered at the bottom, leaving the liquid almost clear. A swift glance told him that the few patrons were paying him no attention. He spun the necessary mental threads and plunged his thoughts into the wine, cupping his hands around the glass.

He never looked at her without a thrill of pride that this magnificent woman was his mother. He didn't understand why her body was growing so thick, but the extra flesh dimmed her beauty as little as the darkness of the stair-

case. He clung to her hand as they descended, his breath rasping in his throat with the dampness and the chill and the excitement of sharing a secret. When she unlocked the door of the storeroom, he flinched back as torchlight struck a flare of gold brighter than the Desert sun. He looked up at her face in wonderment and she laughed, setting the torch in a holder and flinging her arms wide as if to embrace the wealth stacked neatly on the shelves.

It was real; he touched it, took up handfuls of it and flung it toward the ceiling to watch its enchanting glitter as it fell. And he was laughing, too. He plucked up one of the leather sacks from the pile near the door to pretend he was robbing the treasure room. His mother laughed and told him he didn't need to steal it, it was all his, just as the Desert and Princemarch would be.

Ruval pulled in a deep breath and looked up. No one gave him so much as a glance. He poured the wine down his throat and left a coin in the cup to pay for the drink.

After a long, aimless walk through the streets to clear his head, he allowed himself to remember what he'd seen. Peripherally he was aware that the question of paying for rebuilding Feruche was answered; Sorin must have found the treasury in the rubble. He also knew that his mother's increasing bulk had meant she was pregnant with her last child, Rohan's son who had died with her that terrible night. But something else concerned him now, something a little boy had seen but not recognized.

The ingots had been carried to Feruche in leather sacks left tidily folded in case of future need. By law all raw materials and finished goods indicated place of origin. Crafters had their various hallmarks, holdings and princedoms their colors or ciphers. Cattle and goats were branded; pottery, furniture, ironwork, and other manufactured items were stamped. Foodstuffs were labeled on packing crates, wine on bottles. The gold ingots at Feruche had been no exception: on those sacks had been the image of Skybowl.

But it was *silver* they took from the ground near Skybowl. Ruval kept walking, distracted by his thoughts, and annoyed honest citizens by pushing peremptorily past them in the crowded residential section of Castle Pine. Threadsilver Canyon was named for the metal mined there for a hundred years—yet the leather sacks of gold had been stamped with an outline of Skybowl. Not Stronghold, not Radzyn, not Tiglath, not any of the other important keeps of the Desert. Had Rohan been clever enough to arrange this bit of misdirection if anyone noticed the sacks rather than the gold? Or had this been an oversight?

Ruval left the gates of the town and walked out beyond the first fields. Torrential winter rains had washed away topsoil in buckets, and farmers were trying to encourage the crippled land into its yearly yield of grain. He walked past their ponies and wains and anxious conferences, up a hill and in among the trees. Over the rise was a ravine likewise stripped bare by the rains, where not even enough grass grew to sustain sheep. The place was deserted, and it was from this privacy that he worked a hated but useful Sunrunner spell.

Skybowl crouched like a brooding dragon on the shores of its perfectly round lake. The crater had filled way past its usual level, and a trench had been dug to drain the water. Ruval paused, noting that bags had been filled with sand to guide the course of the runoff; these bags bore the outline of Skybowl. With Lord Riyan absent, his blue-and-brown pennant did not fly over the keep. But there was plenty of activity and a line of pack horses just disappearing over the crater rim on the route to Threadsilver Canyon. Ruval followed on sunlight to where perhaps thirty men and women went about the business of hacking silver from the walls of long-abandoned dragon caves. At the bottom of the canyon light flickered from within a large cavern; the smelter, Ruval guessed. But no evidence of gold.

Frustration gnawed at him. Returning to Cunaxa, he reached into his pocket and pulled out a small, thin, hexagonal gold coin. He turned it in his fingers for a moment. Mireva had given him this coin. It depicted an outline of Castle Crag on the obverse, his grandsire's profile on the reverse: both proud, regal, commanding. Rohan had recalled all money minted by Roelstra, replacing it with coins stamped with his own crowned dragon. But Mireva had kept this one and when he had become adept enough had presented it to him. But it was more than a souvenir.

This coin was dated 703, the year before Roelstra's and

Ianthe's deaths had splintered Ruval's world, and it had been struck from some of the gold Rohan had paid for *dranath*. And if he was fortunate, contact with Fire would release a vision of where it had been minted and, earlier even than that, where it had been forged.

He conjured a gout of pallid Fire in the dirt and knelt beside it, glad he had imbibed enough *dranath* that morning to facilitate the spell. Dropping the coin in the flames, he spared a moment for appreciation of his own disciplined mind, working with Fire he'd created to gain a picture of fire many years dead. The primal attraction of each element for itself functioned with smooth swiftness; he was soon looking at the thin, sweat-streaked face of the artisan who had made coins of liquid gold. Ruval squinted at the sudden brightness, his eyes tearing. But he forced the spell back further, seeking the flames from which the ingot had sprung.

His vision was limited by the dazzle that stung his eyes. But there, just beyond the glowing run of molten metal into molds, he saw them. Faces—a man and woman, wearing Skybowl's colors. Harsh fire-thrown shadows behind them on cave walls. And stacks of finished ingots— not silver, but gold.

Smelted at Skybowl after all—

An excruciating blaze made him cry out. He was drawn farther back, to another fire.

Dragon fire.

Seared by a hatchling's breath that dried his wings, shining flecks trapped in broken shells melded together in another elemental bonding.

Dragon gold.

Ruval cried out again as he wrenched himself from the spell. The Fire vanished, leaving a blackened patch of earth. The coin was still hot when he picked it up.

With shaking hands he scooped dirt to hide the scar. It was a long time before he could stand. But when he did, he began to laugh very softly.

Skybowl. Dragon caves. Dragon gold. How sweetly, perfectly logical. That he had promised Skybowl to Prince Miyon bothered him not at all. It had never been planned that his grace of Cunaxa would live long enough to take possession.

***

Mireva stepped out the kitchen door into the squalid back court. Towns, even one as small as Castle Pine, offended her. The dirt, the stench, the crowds, the closeness—all were poisonous to her senses and exhausting to her mind. She hated the tiny, cramped upstairs room she had slept in for two nights now, hated it almost as much as she hated the greasy-haired slattern who ran this place. They had just concluded a stormy passage featuring Mireva's opinion of the slop the woman had the gall to term "dinner." Only her own prohibition against use of power and the fact that she, Ruval, and Marron had nowhere else to go prevented her from blasting the woman to quivering jelly. The foray into the back court-yard was an attempt to calm her nerves. It did not succeed.

The first stars had appeared in the dusk, barely visible over the eastern wall. Mireva gazed at them longingly, their light burning into her eyes. So clean, so beautiful and diamondlike, so welcome after a long, irksome day of bright sun outside and dim corridors within.

She heard Ruval's soft footstep a few moments before he spoke. "If not for the prize to be won, I'd say let's get out of this swine-wallow and go home."

She kept her gaze fixed on the emerging stars. "If not for the prize to be won, I would agree with you."

"You haven't said what you thought of Meiglan."

"She'll do."

"But what's she like?"

"Small, frail, spineless, and fascinatingly beautiful. She accepts me as Thanys' friend."

"Not as her relative?"

Her jaw clenched at the biting mockery in his voice. He knew how she prided herself on her pure *diarmadhi* blood and how she hated admitting that any of her family had polluted that blood by marrying common folk. Thanys was indeed related to her, and not as distantly as Mireva would have liked. The woman was her grandniece. But this was not the time to renew her anger, useless at this late date anyway, over the stupidity of her family. Besides, Ruval and Marron were talented enough, even though only quarter-breeds like Thanys.

She ignored his question. "It will be easy enough to go with her when her father takes her to Stronghold. I assume you've presented the idea to Miyon?"

"Of course. I'm more interested in the girl, though. Can she be trusted?"

Mireva gave a snort. "She only knows how to be afraid, and her fear cancels any wits she may otherwise have. She'll be useful only as long as she's afraid of her father." Ruval knew as well as she did the inevitable fate for those who were no longer of any use. This reminded her of someone else. "Marron has many soothing things to say about Chiana. *She* can be trusted only so long as her imagination stays within limits. But I fear that when military maneuvers begin, she'll start scheming again."

"Not even you can be in two places at once. We'll keep an eye on what goes on at the Princemarch-Meadowlord border."

"So will Rohan, through Sioned. It should make him good and nervous." She chuckled, bad humor easing at the thought of Rohan's discomfort. "He'll recognize the tactic, of course—'training exercises' was the excuse used by Roelstra in 704. I must remember to ask Marron to tell me how he got her to think of it on her own."

"It's so obvious a copy of grandfather's ploy that Rohan won't suspect our interference. But Chiana still has ambitions for Rinhoel. They may be more or less submerged, thanks to your time with her in Swalekeep, but she still has them."

Mireva shrugged and walked the broken cobbles over to the well. The water level was only a few handspans below the stone rim, its underground source saturated over the winter. She reached down and trailed her fingers through the water. "I don't like having to use her. But Miyon is even more unreliable. They each have their own grudges and their own ambitions which could be dangerous if indulged. There are limits even to what *we* can do, Ruval. We have no army of our own, and so we must make it seem as though we have the resources of others to draw on. But it's such a risk."

Ruval stared down at her in the gathering dark. "What need do I have of an army? Or are you losing faith in me?"

"Listen to me, you fool!" She swung around, her words low and vicious. "You may know almost—and I stress *almost*—everything I do about the ways of our ancestors. And with those ways you will defeat Pol and take us back to our rightful place. But Rohan and Pol are different from us. They think like princes, of armies and politics. So we will use those things to distract them. Chiana will provide the army, Miyon the politics. We've already given them knowledge of your identity—and that at the back of their minds all spring will make them ever more anxious about Chiana and Miyon. We've presented things they understand and will try to counter in their usual ways. But when you appear with your *unusual* challenge, on *our* terms, they won't know how to deal with it. They'll try to use their accustomed methods—which won't work."

Ruval nodded slowly. "I understand. But there's another factor here: Andry. If rumor and our observations are correct, then *he's* the one thinking like us."

"Dangerously so. But this business of the Sunrunner in Gilad is a wonderful stroke of luck. Rohan will have no choice but to support Prince Cabar's right to punishment—and thoughts of you and the *diarmadhi* threat you represent will be on his mind in this, too. He'll be thinking of the support of the other princes against us. But his problem is to give the appearance that there's not one law for Sunrunners and another for ungifted folk. He must come down on the side of general law, consistent with his policies and mindful of the other princes—and your presence. Idiot!" she spat suddenly. "He entertains the conceit that we who are gifted with power are subject to the same legality and morality as the common herd!"

"Andry will be furious," Ruval mused. "He won't give Pol any substantial support. Not that he would have, anyway. They're jealous of each other's power."

"And this will only make it worse. After we're finished with Pol, Andry will be next. And he does *not* think like a prince," she warned.

"Leave Andry to me, just as I'll take care of Pol. Besides, we're providing other distractions, too." Ruval smiled. "And I'm assuming you have one or two more in reserve."

"One, certainly." She smiled back.

"I can almost feel sorry for Pol. But at least he'll be well-educated before he dies."

Chapter Twelve

Feruche: 9–10 Spring

"Tell me."

Pol sent a pleading glance at his mother, unable to deal with Tobin's quiet, desolate command. Sioned met his gaze solemnly, said nothing, and from the compassion in her eyes he realized that this was one of the terrible times, when being a prince meant taking responsibility even when one was helpless. He nodded slightly and touched his aunt's shoulder, drawing her from the tapestry room that had been Sorin's pride out to the broad balcony overlooking the Desert. The others remained indoors—Sioned, Chay, Hollis, Tallain. Rohan, true to a vow Pol neither understood nor dared ask about, had not and would not set foot in Feruche itself, and was staying in the refurbished garrison quarters below the cliffs. Sionell and Ruala were with Hollis' son and daughter and Sionell's own little girl in the hastily arranged nursery, away from the grief that children could not understand. And Maarken and Riyan were readying the ritual that would take place that night.

The dunes spread out in heaped gold before them. Pol stared out at the endless Desert, wondering how he should begin. Tobin had said very little since arriving yesterday evening. She had spent the night beside her son's body, and though all preparations had been made by Ruala, she had insisted on washing Sorin once more and dressing him herself in the colors of his holding and his heritage. The blue and black of Feruche in his tunic; the red and white of Radzyn around his waist; the fierce blue of the Desert in the cloak covering his body—silk and velvet she placed on her son, her eyes dry and her face set in stone.

"Tell me," she said again, and for the first time he

171

heard her pain, like a low moan of thunder in the distance. He faced her, took both her hands, and made himself look down into her lusterless black eyes.

He told it slowly, completely, leaving out nothing but Sorin's dying agony. He spared himself not at all, filled with bitter self-hatred for losing himself in communion with the dragon while Marron attacked. He let her see the scene as Riyan had described it to him. Ruval scrambling to his feet, lifting his blade to take Pol's life. Sorin's desperate intervention. Marron seizing Edrel's slight form, throwing the squire bodily at Riyan. Ruval's defenses weakening, the talon slashes across his back crippling his sword arm. Marron plunging his sword into Sorin's leg, shattering the bone as well as severing the large artery. And the burning of Riyan's rings that meant sorcery had been used somehow.

"Riyan . . . Riyan says he and Edrel had to pull the sword with all their strength to get it out of the wound. He thinks it was some binding spell, something—oh, Goddess, and all the while—it's my fault. He saved my life and I was—if I hadn't been caught up in the dragon—"

"Hush."

"But it's true." He forced his gaze to meet hers. "Andry was right. If I'd been able to help, Sorin would still be—"

She pulled her hands from his and he flinched. But the next instant she reached up, framed his face with small, delicate fingers. "Andry had no right to say such a thing to you. He was hurt and grieving, Pol. He needed someone to blame. When a twin loses his second self. . . ." She paused, shaking her head. "I saw it in Maarken when Jahni died of Plague. Andrade felt the same thing when my mother died. Don't blame him for what he said on moonlight. And don't blame yourself. It wasn't your fault."

"Wasn't it?" he asked bleakly. "Sorin said that I should try to understand Andry."

"And you promised that you would." Tobin stroked his forehead, and then her hands dropped to her sides. She turned from him, folding her arms atop the carved stone balustrade. Her voice was soft, tired, wistful. "I bore my husband four sons. Four strong, proud, beautiful boys, grandsons of a prince. I watched them grow and learn and play at dragons. I saw one of them dead and burned before he was nine winters old. Now I've lost another of my sons." She was silent for a long time. Pol watched her head slowly bend, her shoulders rounding as if grief would crush even her indomitable spirit. At last she straightened again and glanced up at him. There were tears in her eyes, unshed. "Thank you for telling me, Pol. It can't have been easy for you."

"For *me*—?" he began incautiously, then gulped back the rest. She didn't need his guilt and sorrow added to her burden.

"You're Sorin's cousin, his friend, and his prince. And I think losing him is teaching you things you'd rather not learn about the pain of your position."

How had she known? He stared at her in awe, knowing he would never have her wisdom. Her compassion. Her understanding of what it was to be a prince.

She looked back out at the Desert. "Something astonishing is going to happen this spring," she mused. "Something that happens only once in a hundred years. My father heard of rains like these from his father, who saw them once in his youth. I can already feel it beginning, Pol. The land is still in shock, I think, from so much water after so long a drought. But I feel the restlessness. It'll happen soon."

Pol looked down at her, puzzled. She glanced up, smiling slightly.

"Those not of the Desert marvel that we can find our empty sands so beautiful. So compelling to the spirit. They think that because it doesn't bloom or bear fruit it's a dead land, a place the Goddess forgot to give life. But what she gave us is so much more miraculous than the bounty that comes to others every year. They take their riches for granted. But we of the Desert understand how precious life really is, how it blesses us and seems to vanish, but always returns, always lives anew."

He struggled to understand. "Like—like the sun each day, or the dragons every three years."

"I hadn't thought of it that way, but yes, like the sun and the dragons. Always returning." She stared blankly at the dunes. "Jahni and Sorin will never stand before me again. Never smile at me again, never—but they are alive in this land, just as my father and mother live here still. Earth and Air, Fire and Water, all of what they were lives in this Desert that seems so lifeless to those who cannot understand." She sighed quietly. "Go back inside now, please. I want to be alone for a little while."

He nodded, feeling more helpless than ever, and hesitated a moment before bending down to kiss her cheek. Her arms went around him and he was startled as always by the strength in her tiny frame. When she released him, the tears had spilled over and he had enough wisdom to leave at once.

Sionell had come downstairs from the nursery, and was helping Edrel pour wine. She glanced over as Pol entered, nodded slightly, and continued speaking.

"—so we finally got them to sleep. Ruala's going to sit with them for a time and make sure they *stay* asleep, and a little later their nurses will take over the watch. Hollis, I can't tell you how lovely Chayla has grown since I last saw her."

Pol was impatient with the ensuing talk of children, and only gradually realized that Sionell had deliberately introduced the topic as a soothing counterpoint to grief. Hers was another form of wisdom, he thought: she was wise in the ways of people and their needs. But he could not enter into the give-and-take of anecdotes and tales of baby tricks. He was as restless as Tobin had said the Desert was, like an itching deep in his blood and bones that demanded—something. He made an excuse to his mother and left the room to prowl the halls and towers of Feruche until nearly dusk.

Sorin's corpse was burned that night in the sands below Feruche. Oils and piles of sweet herbs and spices thickened the air, borne upward with the smoke of the pyre. Pol stood alone in the silence, waiting for dawn when he and the other Sunrunners of his family would call up a breath of wind to scatter the ashes across the dunes. As the moons made their stately way across the star-stewn sky he knew he should be thinking of Sorin: the friendly squabbles they'd had as children, his pride in his cousin's elevation to knight and *athri*, the affection and respect they'd shared as young men. But with every scene that came to him, Ruval's face intruded. His might not have been the sword that killed Sorin, but his was the responsibility. *He wants my princedom—and my death. What he'll get instead is—*

Brave words, cousin. Did you think the same while you let my brother die?

Andry! The swift assault of angry color, only slightly paled from being woven with moonlight, startled him. Andry's fine control, his sleek subtlety, were things Pol only aspired to. But the Lord of Goddess Keep, daily practitioner of skills Pol used only occasionally, already possessed an easy grace in the use of power that Pol both admired and resented. He riposted quickly, keeping his emotions hidden, telling himself he should have been prepared for this. *I thought you might be here tonight.*

The only way I could be, considering your haste to see my brother burned. Andry's grief and fury were almost palpable. *You couldn't wait for me to be there, could you? I've been in the saddle since I felt him die—*

You're too many days from Feruche. With deliberate and slightly guilty cruelty he added, *Would you have your brother's flesh corrupted by days of waiting, rather than cleanly burned by fire?*

There was a vast silence for some moments. *I felt it when he died. Like half my soul had been ripped from me. You can never understand.*

I share your grief, Andry. You can't blame me any more bitterly than I blame myself. But I'll promise you what I promised him. Ruval will die for this. Ruval and Marron both.

Tell me about them, Andry said—and before Pol could form words he felt his memories fingered, examined, and discarded as casually as he might have picked through a pile of fruit. *So. I see.*

Pol shook with anger at the invasion. *How dare you! Sorin asked me to go gently with you, try to understand you—Tobin asked me to forgive you for blaming me. But now I'll be damned if I'll—*

Forgive me? Don't make me laugh, cousin! How could you possibly understand me? You've never even set foot in Goddess Keep, you don't know the first thing about it or our traditions or being a real Sunrunner! Urival may have been fool enough to teach you a few tricks and give you one of Andrade's jewels, but as for real power—stick to political nitpicking and prettying up your palace. You're simply not in my class.

No?

He knew he should not do this. He did it anyway. Using an obscure spell learned from the Star Scroll, he closed his eyes and flicked a knife of thin, bright Fire toward Andry—not strong enough or sharp enough to sever the moonweaving but sufficient to give fair warning. He sensed Andry's gasp of startlement, his angry suspicion, sudden certainty—and hasty retreat.

Pol glanced at his mother where she stood beside Tobin, knowing she would not relish the mistake he'd just made. He was ashamed of himself for giving in to the taunting. He should be above such things. He must be, in order to function as a prince.

Or a Sunrunner. Andry's words had lanced his pride. He was as much a *faradhi* as Maarken or Hollis or Riyan. Urival himself had trained him, Morwenna continued to give him lessons when he was at Stronghold. But unlike the others, he had never been to Goddess Keep, never lived there in the Sunrunner community, absorbing its atmosphere of long tradition and ancient honor. The rest of the *faradh'im* in his immediate circle had known that union, discipline, fellowship. Not even Sioned had entirely rejected it, though she had long ago removed her rings and chosen to be a princess first and a Sunrunner second. Pol knew that Maarken feared having to make the same choice one day, rendered even worse by the fact that his brother was Lord of Goddess Keep. What if Andry one day asked something of Maarken as a *faradhi* that conflicted with his duties as a vassal?

And that was bound to happen very soon, Pol realized. This business of the Sunrunner in Gilad was sure to have Andry claiming Maarken's support—and that of Hollis and Riyan as well. He would not bother with Sioned; challenging the Sunrunner loyalties of the High Princess was something not even Andrade had dared do. But because Pol was not officially *faradhi*, Andry would use the matter to delineate even more sharply the rift between Princemarch and the Desert on one side and Goddess Keep on the other. Pol hated to think what the other princes would make of this, especially Miyon, Cabar, Velden, and Halian.

He couldn't win. If he supported Andry, he would be untrue to laws he believed in. If he supported Cabar as he intended, the princes would be reassured about his commitment to the law—and worry even more about his refusal to come under traditional *faradhi* discipline. Few

approved of Andry's power. Which would be the stronger
—satisfaction that Andry could not influence him, or fear
of a Sunrunner prince without loyalty to Goddess Keep?

It had been wisdom on the part of Lady Merisel and
the other long-ago *faradh'im* to discourage the mating of
Sunrunners with princes; the potential conflict was a terrible one. Andrade had taken the chance with Sioned—
and, by her lights, failed. Pol had been trained without
ties to Goddess Keep except the powerful one of blood-
kin. He wondered suddenly if Andrade had planned that,
too, chosen Andry to succeed her for just that reason.

Pol and Maarken both would be caught up in this. And
both of them would lose. The only thing Pol could put his
hopes on was Andry's abiding love and respect for his
eldest and now only brother. But that was placing the
entire burden on Maarken—and as a prince, Pol knew
the responsibility must be his.

And his father's. Relief swept through him, swiftly
followed by guilt. He had no right to dump all this on his
father. Rohan was High Prince, and the matter of the
Sunrunner would be taken to him for judgment. To wish
he could leave everything to his father was a coward's
way, and he was ashamed of himself for even thinking it.
Nearly as ashamed as he was that while he had been
caught up in the dragon's colors, Sorin had died by
Marron's hand.

He felt knowledge run through him like a spark down
his spine. That was the answer: the *diarmadhi* threat
would be his leverage with Andry. For if Pol was defeated, Andry would be next.

*Join with me in destroying Roelstra's grandsons, cousin,
or fear for your own power. You can have Marron, since
he was the one who killed your brother. But Ruval is
mine.* But he despaired that he should have to bargain
from Andry's cooperation with promises of vengeance
and death.

Sorin had been wrong. Pol *did* understand Andry, and
he wasn't sure this was to his credit. His promise to be
tender of Andry's feelings and position would be difficult
to keep. As he watched the flames consume the flesh and
bone that had been his cousin, he knew that perhaps the
most important link between Andry and himself would
soon be ashes.

***

"Father. . . ."

Rohan glanced around from the windows. It was early morning, and he had been watching Feruche by sunrise. It was a lovely castle, very different from the one that had clung to the cliffs twenty-four years ago. But he would not enter its precincts. Ever. Not even if his life depended on it. Looking now at the life that had resulted from time spent at Feruche, he turned away from the castle and his memories. "What is it, Pol?"

They were alone in the commander's rooms at the garrison built by Rohan's great-grandfather, Prince Zagroy. A squat, functional, inelegant barracks, it had guarded the pass through the mountains to Princemarch for more than a hundred years. Sioned, Chay, Tobin, and the others had returned to the comforts of Feruche, but Pol had accompanied his father back here. For some time now Rohan had been waiting to hear whatever it was Pol wanted to say, reflecting that if age had brought him nothing else, it has supplied patience.

Not a quality Pol possessed yet; he had been prowling the long, narrow room, obviously trying to find the right words. He opted for directness, as usual. "Why is it that we always have to wait for something to happen before we can do anything?"

Rohan had been expecting frustration over the escape of Sorin's murderers, grief and guilt at his cousin's death, any number of things. But not this. "Go on," he said.

"It just—it seems we always *react* to things, rather than *act.*"

"Ah. You want to hunt down this Ruval by any means at your disposal and execute him as he so richly deserves."

"Don't you?" Pol swung around from the far windows.

Rohan considered a light answer to relieve the tension that fairly crackled from his son's body. But to say that he himself was too old to go racing about the countryside would be to insult Pol's feelings and treat him as the child he had not been for many years. Still, Rohan *had* begun to feel twinges of his own age recently, though fifty-one never seemed much different from thirty-one until he was faced with Pol's youth.

But his reply was, "It's the curse of our position and our principles. We have the power to act, but we're condemned to wait until others have acted first."

It was not an answer Pol was ready to comprehend. "I won't sit around polishing my sword until Ruval decides to reappear!"

"I understand." He sat down and lifted the wine cup left for him on a table. "But consider, Pol. The greatest temptation of any kind of power is to use it."

"What good is power if you *don't* use it?"

Rohan sighed. "Think of the laws written the past seven *Riall'im*. Very few involve prohibitions of one sort or another. They simply state what will occur if a certain thing is done. People do what they wish to do, and saying it's not legal usually won't stop them. But if the consequences of a particular action are clear, they may do the thing anyway, but they also know exactly what will happen if they're caught."

"I don't see what that has to do with—"

He rapped his knuckles on the arm of his chair. "Pay attention. The old ways commanded that one must not do thus-and-so, end of law. For instance, Sunrunners were forbidden to use their gifts in battle. If I were to rewrite that one, it would be to the effect that *faradh'im* who do so would die if pierced by iron, as is very likely to happen in battle, iron being incompatible with the functioning of those gifts. Present the consequences and allow people to make the choice as adults, rather than simply forbid a thing, which treats them like children. To take a more common example, the law used to read that a person must not murder. Very precise, but punishment was arbitrary and differed from princedom to princedom. The law now is that if a person commits a willful murder, his own life is forfeit and all his possessions go to the family of the person he killed. People don't obey a law just because they're told to. But if they know the consequences of an act and do it anyway, then that's a conscious and informed choice and they have no cause to protest the punishment.

"Certainly we could go off hunting this man, and we'd be right to do so. You heard from his own lips that he knew exactly what he was doing by killing dragons and what the penalty is, and did it anyway. And Sorin. . . ." Rohan had a sudden, poignant vision of a little boy with whom he'd played at dragons. "But there's more to this than his death and the deaths of three dragons. And that's why we have to wait for the next move."

"I don't understand."

"You've got a good brain, Pol. Use it! Until he and his brother come out into the open again, we don't know who else might be using them or hiding behind them—or, what might be worse, working with them. If we use our considerable resources of princely and *faradhi* power to administer the swift justice we both want, it's entirely possible we'll miss a larger threat. And you know very well what that threat probably is."

"The *diarmadh'im*," Pol said reluctantly. "The way we would have missed—the boy who infiltrated Goddess Keep."

Rohan noted the editing of what Pol had been about to say, and frowned.

"But isn't it also possible that if we deal with this pair now, we'll be removing some very useful tools from their hands? Ruval and Marron really do have a claim to Princemarch in the strict sense. They're Roelstra's grandsons."

"Yes. But in killing Roelstra in fair combat, and by all the rules of war, I won Princemarch."

"Why did you give it to me, Father? I've always wondered."

Again he was tempted to a light answer, and could not bring himself to turn aside the young man's question. But neither could he tell Pol the truth. Not yet. And not without Sioned's agreement. "All I ever wanted was the Desert. Becoming High Prince was something necessary, if I was to make the kind of world I wanted for you. Quite frankly, I didn't want Princemarch on top of all the rest of it."

"So you gave it into Pandsala's care as regent for me."

"Under her and now under Ostvel, the people there have grown used to the idea of you as their prince. Not me. I was never theirs. You are."

"Well, *that* ploy worked, anyway."

"Your faith in my wisdom is comforting," Rohan replied wryly. "You also have to remember that at the time our family was growing more powerful—your mother's brother Davvi Prince of Syr, Volog cousin to them—it seemed wiser to keep Princemarch separate from the Desert until my death unites them under you as High Prince."

"Do me a favor and live forever, will you?"

"I'll do my best." He smiled briefly. "Actually, I only worry about it every three years."

"I don't understand."

"Didn't you ever notice? Ruling princes of the Desert are always born in a Dragon Year—back five generations. We always die in a Dragon Year, too. Take care of me until next New Year, my boy, unless you're eager to inherit."

"Thank you, no," Pol grinned. "Princemarch is quite enough to handle!"

"I'll try to expire at your convenience," Rohan responded with a slight bow, then grew serious again. "But you have to understand why we can't act until Ruval does. We must wait and find out exactly who else is involved."

"I suppose." Pol sank into a chair at last, long legs sprawled. "What I finally understand is why you waited to kill Masul. He was a threat, but you wanted to find out how serious. It was only when Maarken's life was in the balance that you acted. But, Father, if you'd killed Masul right away—"

"Andrade might still be alive."

Pol flushed. "I didn't mean—"

"Oh, it's quite true." He rolled the wine cup between his palms, staring into the cloudy red liquid. "I know it seems that I act only when I'm forced to. And I suppose that's so. And it also seems that I don't use power because I'm afraid of it—and that's true, as well, but not for the reasons most people think. It's fair to say that I don't wish to antagonize already suspicious princes and I have a horror of conflict, armed or otherwise. Everyone knows I haven't touched my sword since I hung it in the Great Hall at Stronghold just after you were born. We've all lived pretty much at peace, with no widespread wars and only a few messy private situations since I've become High Prince. That's exactly what I wanted. It gives the flowers a chance to grow—and me the chance to watch them." He smiled. "But do you see that all this has come about precisely because I *don't* use my power? It's not that I'm afraid of it. In fact, there are times when I relish it. And *that's* what really frightens me. Power is . . . an interesting feeling. Once you get accustomed to it, you go looking for chances to use it. It's the difference between an arbitrary prince in love with his own power, and a thoughtful one who understands its responsibilities."

"We can act as we please, and everyone knows it," Pol mused. "But by *not* acting—"

"We indicate that we're so powerful we don't *have* to pounce on people like a dragon on a lamb. And when we do use power, it's not just for specific punishment. It provides a really necessary demonstration of what we could do if we chose. Sweet Goddess, with the armies at my disposal I could have taken this whole continent by now. But I haven't, and everyone knows I won't. I don't have to prove my manhood or my power by making everyone feel the strength of my sword."

"Manhood? So *that's* Miyon's problem—and Halian's! Of course, with a wife like Chiana—"

"Granted." Rohan smiled suddenly. "Not everyone is blessed with a woman the caliber of your mother. Be careful when you Choose, Pol. What you want is not just a wife, but a princess."

"I know." He shifted in his chair, obviously uncomfortable with the subject of Choosing a bride, and Rohan stifled a chuckle. "But going back to Ruval and Marron—"

"They committed crimes, and will be punished. But I suspect a larger crime, Pol, against not just the law and our family, but against everyone. Andry's been very possessive of the historical scrolls Meath found on Dorval, but Urival told me quite a lot of what's in them. The oppression, the rule of fear, the suffering caused at the whim of these *diarmadh'im* simply because they had power the common folk did not—their time was all I loathe about power. Lady Merisel and her Sunrunners made a commitment never to grasp for princely power to augment their other gifts, a reassurance to the people that wasn't broken until your mother's grandmother married a Prince of Kierst."

"And now there's me. But the *diarmadhi* times are long forgotten, Father."

"Do you think so? *They* haven't forgotten. And with Roelstra's grandsons pressing a princely claim with sorcerer's power, everyone else is likely to remember very clearly and very soon."

Pol gave a grim chuckle. "Will I start to look better to the other princes, do you think?"

"Perhaps. But anybody who can do what they can't makes them uneasy."

"So we wait and see."

"Or *not* wait and *not* see. You comprehend the frustration, I take it."

"Of being a civilized man with principles, yes. It'd be a lot easier on my nerves to behave like a barbarian."

"I've given in to the impulse many times. And had to live with myself afterward."

He looked up as Pol's squire, Edrel, entered the room. Rohan smiled encouragement to no avail; although the boy had grown used to serving Pol, he still paled around the High Prince. After a bow much more formal than any of Rohan's own squires ever gave him after their first few days of service, Edrel spoke in a voice barely above a whisper. "Lord Tallain is here, your graces, asking if you have a moment to see him."

"Always. Send him in, Edrel." Turning to his son after the boy gave another deep bow and left, Rohan sighed, "*Do* something about that, will you?"

Pol only grinned and rose to welcome Tallain.

The responsibilities of the most important holding in the northern Desert suited Tallain—as did marriage and family life. Rohan saw much of the father in the son, the way Eltanin had looked for the tragically few years of his marriage to Antalya of Waes. She was evident in their son's face, as well, her sweet smile and self-possessed calm which in Tallain was a serene charm quite unlike Pol's occasional fire.

"Sorry to disturb you," Tallain said. "But there are a couple of things I think you ought to know about."

"Sit down. We've all been on our feet all night." Rohan suppressed a sigh, thinking that whatever Tallain felt couldn't wait until later was bound to be irksome in one way or another.

After pouring himself a cup of wine, Tallain seated himself and began. "Andry spoke to Tobin on sunlight just a little while ago. He'll be here in three or four days."

"And went to his mother rather than any of the other *faradh'im* present because she lacks the training to talk back to him," Rohan said, nodding. "Clever lad. Go on."

"I hadn't thought of it that way, but you must be

right," Tallain mused. "He could just as easily have spoken to Riyan."

"But not my mother," Pol put in.

"Well, no. They don't talk much, do they? At any rate, he also says there's a girl at Faolain Riverport who ought to be told about Sorin before she learns it from common talk. It seems she's owed the courtesy."

Rohan's brows shot up. "Sorin had a young lady? First I've heard of it."

"Andry's the only one he told. Not even Riyan knew about her. I suppose that until he'd made formal Choice, it wasn't something he wanted known except by his brother. There wasn't anything between them. But she ought to learn it privately."

"But who is she?" Pol asked.

"Daughter of the chief architect. It seems Sorin was hesitating because the Desert is a hell of a place to bring an unsuspecting bride."

Rohan smiled. "I remember thinking the same thing myself thirty years ago. You were wise to pick a wife who knew exactly what she was getting, Tallain."

"I was luckier than I deserved, my lord." Tallain's brown eyes sparked and softened as he glanced out a window to where Feruche and Sionell were. Rohan noted the look. Pity, he thought yet again, that Pol hadn't had the sense to make both himself and Sionell happy. But she was entirely content with Tallain, for which grace he thanked the Goddess. Sionell deserved to be loved.

"I hope I'm half as lucky," Pol said warmly. "I keep wondering how I'm going to break it to whoever I marry that she'll be spending a goodly portion of her time in the Desert!"

Tallain grinned at him. "Young ladies pale at the very thought, do they?"

"All they see is Dragon's Rest," Pol sighed. "I don't dare mention the other! But you say Sorin's lady didn't much like the idea?"

"Who knows if it even got that far? Anyway, Riyan will get word to her through the Faolain Riverport Sunrunner, and Tobin says she'll write to the girl within the next few days."

"Very good. And now the more difficult matter, Tallain?" Rohan asked.

The young man grunted. "There's no fooling you, is there? A courier rode in a little while ago with a note from Miyon of Cunaxa. He wants a conference regarding trade, and has several interesting proposals. He also wants a swift answer, so I came down here to ask what reply you want sent."

"*How* interesting?" Pol leaned forward, blue-green eyes narrowed with suspicion.

"Very. For instance, he suggests a yearly port fee for trade through Tiglath, the same for what goes past Feruche. His initial figure is fairly substantial, but it's still less than I make fining the shipments they try to slip by me."

"I see," Rohan said softly. "And what do you think?"

Tallain shrugged. "You must do what you believe is right, my lord, as always. I trust you to see to my advantage as well as your own. But there would be a benefit in setting a yearly fee for as much as they can ship from Tiglath. I wouldn't have to play this ridiculous game of spying on Cunaxan shipments. It's highly undignified. I'm willing to give up a little profit for a little peace."

Rohan flicked a glance at his son. But Pol had never had any experience of greedy, self-serving vassals who said one thing, thought another, and did a third. Pol found Tallain's words perfectly natural as well as logical.

Pol thought the look was to prompt his comments. "Relations among all three princedoms would improve, you know. We wouldn't have all this squabbling over fines on illegal trade. It is, as you say, undignified."

"Exactly. And I'd save the wages of six or eight inspectors, too." Tallain chuckled. "Ah, they call us lords and princes, when all we really are is glorified merchants!"

"Speak for yourself," Pol shot back, grinning. "*I* happen to be a glorified farmer!"

Rohan laughed with them, but as he was agreeing to the conference he was also thinking about the other factor probably involved. Ruval and Marron had escaped north from the vicinity of Elktrap Manor; Miyon was a possible ally in any attempt against himself and Pol. It was conceivable that this trade negotiation in advance of the *Rialla* was a second move in that challenge. If so, Ruval and Marron might be—no, *would* be—part of Miyon's suite.

Might be, could be, would be—so much of a prince's

life was based on conjecture and speculation. No wonder Pol accused him of not *acting*.

"However," Rohan finished, "I won't have Miyon at Stronghold. Invite him to Tiglath. And keep a sharp eye on him. Riyan can go with you and act as Sunrunner to keep us apprised of what's going on." Riyan also knew what the brothers looked like. Rohan would speak to him about his suspicions, but not to Tallain. The young lord would have enough to do without seeking spies as well.

Tallain nodded slowly, his eyes lighting. "Perhaps I can fool him into thinking we can make a private deal, and learn what's behind all this sweet friendship. I don't believe any more than you do that all he wants is an agreement prior to the *Rialla*. But I hadn't thought before of sounding him out in private at Tiglath." Turning to Pol, he added, "I was your father's squire for eight years, like Tilal and Walvis before me. And not one of us has ever been about to outthink him!"

"Neither have I," Pol grumbled, shooting a teasing glance at his father. "He does it just to annoy us, you know."

"I always suspected as much."

Rohan sipped his wine and looked innocent, unwilling to show that Tallain's interpretation was one he had not hit upon. From his aunt Andrade he had picked up the trick of taking credit for more cleverness than he possessed. And very useful it could be, too.

"Go away now, children," he said, waving them from the room. "All this thinking has worn a hole in my brain. I'm growing old, and the younger generation exhausts me."

Snorting, Pol got to his feet and accompanied Tallain to the door. "Mother said something about coming down this evening to dine with you. Shall I tell her you're too feeble to do her justice?"

"If you did," Rohan said serenely, "she wouldn't believe you."

Chapter Thirteen

Tiglath: 20 Spring

It had happened as Tobin had said it would; for the first time in a hundred years, the Desert bloomed.

Rain, soaking into the parched land all winter, had washed away the work of countless storms that constantly resculpted the dunes and piled layers of sand atop the seeds and spores that had lain dormant since the last floods. Deposited there long ago by winds and dragons and migrating birds, the sleeping life swelled with water, quivered in the sun's warmth as the sand sluiced away. More recent arrivals washed down gulleys and were caught by rocks or in little pools. These muddy cauldrons were the first to bloom.

Scrub that flowered seasonally with miniscule dry blossoms burst into luxuriance. Cacti and succulents drank in water, put forth new growth and wildly beautiful flowers. The Desert that in living memory had never worn any colors but gold and brown and sun-bleached white slowly bedecked itself in a motley of blues and reds and oranges on a background of startling green.

And it spread, gradually and then with increasing speed, up from the canyons and ravines across the dunes: veils of dusky, hesitant green that thickened into blankets of flowers. All across the Long Sand incredible color unfurled, rippling over the curves and hollows like a velvet quilt across a sleeping body, moving gently with every breath.

Always before, any flowers that appeared in the Desert withered within a few days. But roots and stalks had stored up the glut of water, and the colors not only lived, they increased with new blossoms. Scents sweet and spicy and pungent and heady obliterated the dry, thin smell of wasteland air. And with these came other movement, tiny winged creatures attracted by the fragrance of flowers. Insects by the millions came to the feast, some wearing as many colors as the flowers. Their humming underscored the usual silence, slowly overtaking it—until the birds came. And then there was not only color and scent and sound in the Desert, but music.

Sionell of Tiglath, absently working a lapful of flowers into a chain, saw her present companion as very like this brilliant spring: beautiful to begin with, but wearing unfamiliar finery. She wondered which would be the first to cast it off—the Desert, or Meiglan?

Occasionally she suspected that the girl was thinking the same thing.

Her history was simple enough. Born at Gracine Manor to the first of Miyon's several mistresses, she had spent the first fifteen winters of her life despised by the mother who had counted on a son. Miyon had ignored them both. At Lady Adilia's death two years ago, Meiglan had been brought to Castle Pine, given a personal servant, pretty clothes, and a strict education according to Miyon's idea of the perfect prince's daughter.

"Not a happy schooling, either, from what I was able to learn from her servant," Rialt had told Sionell. "Whatever she does, and however hard she tries, Miyon finds fault."

As if everyone at Tiglath hadn't guessed that by now. Yet Meiglan was part of her father's entourage on this little visit to Tiglath. Miyon no longer ignored her—but why exactly he had decided to bring her with him gnawed at Sionell's curiosity.

Meiglan was a succession of contradictions. At nearly eighteen, her face was still as sweetly wistful as a little girl's, but her body's perfect curves were those of a woman grown. She was a blonde, with delicate white skin and masses of pale hair that floated down her back like a golden cloud, but her eyes were the deep brown of fallen leaves. In that dark gaze was a watchfulness that combined an adult's shrewd calculation of the moods and whims of others—and a child's wariness of their power to hurt her.

She sat near Sionell now on a grassy knoll that last spring had been a sand dune, frail hands also weaving chains from the flowers brought by Maarken's five-year-old twins. The children raced about, Rohannon a little awkward on long legs he couldn't quite get securely under him, plucking up blossoms to dump in the ladies' laps. Sionell had suggested the outing to get Meiglan out of her room for a morning—the girl had hidden there all day, every day, for the six she had been at Tiglath, emerging only at dinner. And small wonder. Miyon no longer ignored her, but his attention was no blessing.

Sionell gave a sudden start as Chayla rained an armful of pollen-heavy goldbeard all over her. She grabbed for the child, tickling until they were breathless and had rolled halfway down the hill. When she climbed back up, retrieving scattered flowers along the way, she caught Meiglan looking at her with an expression bordering on tears.

Poor little one, Sionell thought. Her throat ached with pity for this child, growing up alone with a mother who loathed her and now trapped at Castle Pine with a father whose contempt was expressed in mocking endearments—"precious jewel," "sweetest treasure," "perfect golden rose." If he had brought Meiglan with him simply to infuriate his hostess, he had accomplished his aim.

But there must be something else, Sionell fretted. The girl wasn't stupid—there was intelligence enough behind her cowed silences. Perhaps she had some part to play in the negotiations that was so obscure only Rohan's devious mind would discern it.

Miyon, however, seemed intent on creating the impression that his daughter was a moron. Only last evening he had commented, "Her mother didn't have the wit to come in out of a sandstorm—but Meiglan doesn't have a wit in her head." Then, smiling a smile that made Sionell want to slap him, he added, "But a beautiful woman doesn't need a brain, does she, my precious flower?"

Meiglan *wasn't* stupid. And no one could be as innocent as she appeared to be. She must know many useful things about her father and his court. With a mental shrug, Sionell decided that at least she could draw her out about Miyon's other bastards, rumored to number at least three. So, gathering the blossoms Chayla had scattered, she started chatting about her own extended kin-network. Though she was related by blood to none but her parents and brother, the position of squire to the High Prince held by her father and later her husband included them and her in the vast tangle of highborns that embraced six princedoms. She spoke casually of Kostas' young son Daniv and Tilal's boy Rihani, both of whom would be ruling princes one day; Alasen's little Dannar with his head of flaming red hair, and Volog's grandson Saumer, Named for his old enemy of Isel. It was utterly lost on Meiglan that all the offspring mentioned were boys. She merely nodded and looked impressed, and volunteered nothing about any siblings she might or might not have who could one day inherit Cunaxa. Sionell couldn't decide if this was due to cunning, orders from Miyon to keep silent, or simple shyness. Perhaps, she thought, a combination of all three.

It irritated her to suspect Meiglan of anything—and the fact that she could come up with no specific reasons for her suspiciousness irked her all the more. The girl looked so utterly guileless, innocent as a raindrop in the sun. It almost made Sionell feel unclean to mistrust her.

And perhaps that was exactly how she was *meant* to feel.

Still, after seeing Meiglan turn white as ice in response to Miyon's barbed superlatives at dinner that night, Sionell had had enough.

"I've never seen a *servant* treated like this!" she fumed as she and Tallain got ready for bed. "He says he brought her along to see something of the world—but she's really here to provide an outlet for his temper!"

"Which he doesn't dare inflict on the rest of us," Tallain replied. "It sounds as if she's made a friend in you, though."

"I don't think she knows what it is to have a friend." She unbound her hair and angrily began brushing it.

Tallain smiled. Taking the brush from her fingers, he smoothed the thick, dark red waves of her hair, his touch caressing and proud. "I understand your irritation, Sionell. But don't scrape your head bald over it. Meiglan probably doesn't see him here as much as she does at Castle Pine, so he has less opportunity to devil her. That alone must be Goddess blessing to the poor girl."

She closed her eyes, sighing with the pleasure of his

hands. "I keep waiting for her to smile a little. This morning we went out picking flowers—nobody can resist Chayla and Rohannon at play. But she was all stiff and withdrawn. It's pathetic, Tallain. She's little more than a child herself."

"Mmm. When one looks at her face, yes. Perhaps."

Sionell met his gaze in the dressing table mirror. "Which means?"

"There's a woman's body on that child. Not a man here hasn't noticed it."

Her brows arched. "Yourself included?"

"Of course," he replied blithely. "But I prefer women who *are* women."

"Prettily said, my lord."

"It also has the merit of being the truth—not a thing I've heard much of these last six days."

She turned to face him. "Have you discovered Miyon's real reason for being here?"

"Nothing I can put my finger on." He shrugged, tapping the back of the brush against his palm. "It's as if he's waiting until lack of agreement makes it necessary for him to visit Stronghold for direct talks with Rohan and Pol. But what he wants from *them* isn't clear at all."

"He knows you're authorized to negotiate in their names," she mused. "So we're correct, and this business of yearly fees isn't his real aim at all. I wonder what he wants."

"What he's always wanted: Tiglath itself. We toured the warehouses the other day and his eyes were positively glowing with greed."

"Has he some scheme in mind to take the city from us?"

"To do that, he'd have to get rid of Rohan. He has no right to the Desert and everyone knows it. He hasn't the armies to concoct a military victory that would win our land by right of war. Not even Miyon is fool enough to try it."

"On his own, no. But you're forgetting his probable allies. Roelstra's grandsons."

Tallain nodded, admiration in his face that he never spoke of aloud—which was an even greater compliment than if he had congratulated her on her wits. He *expected* her to be clever; telling her she was would be insulting.

"You're right. I *had* forgotten. But that still doesn't tell me why he wants to be at Stronghold."

"Betrayal from within?" she mused. "He's got an armed escort. Some of them are probably Merida. It may be hundred of years since they started their filthy trade, but I doubt their talents for assassination have wilted."

Tallain shook his head. "Any challenge has to be public. And for that they need Pol alive. That was Rohan's reasoning in the matter of the pretender nine years ago. He wanted Masul denounced in public so Pol's right would be in no doubt." He shrugged again and resumed brushing her hair. "It didn't quite work out that way, of course. But depend on it, no son of Ianthe's could be stupid. It wouldn't be enough simply to kill Pol and seize Princemarch."

"They'd have his death and his princedom. What else could they want?"

"Revenge. There's not a vicious bone in your body, my love. You don't think that way. But consider the sons of a princess, grandsons of a High Prince, condemned to obscurity all their lives."

Sionell nodded slowly. "It's just what motivated Masul."

"But his birth was in doubt. Ruval and Marron know precisely who their mother was."

"Lucky them," she said sourly. "Well, at least we don't have to fear glass knives in our princes' throats. Whatever happens will happen out in the open. Rohan's already thought of all this, of course."

Tallain smiled. "He'd be shocked if we ever doubted it. I'm going to stall Miyon here until Rohan wants him at Stronghold. Which should make for an interesting spring, given Miyon's behavior and your fondness for Meiglan." He laughed suddenly. "Do you remember what Rohan said about him once? That rumor had it Miyon made a detailed study of human beings and learned to imitate them rather well. Not perfectly, of course, but he manages to get most of it right."

She gave him her sweetest smile. "My mother once carved up a dragon to find out how he worked. Perhaps I ought to do the same for Miyon."

***

It had been hard to arrange, but Ruval and Marron had their own chamber at Tiglath. Small, cramped for one person and nearly impossible for two, lacking window or fireplace for light and stuffy beyond toleration, still it had the one essential feature that made it perfect. It locked.

Marron slid the bolt home and secured it. Ruval's lips twisted at his brother's long, relieved sigh.

"Too much of a strain?"

"Don't pretend you're not tired," Marron replied irritably. "You may be used to the high dose of *dranath* necessary for this, but it's not easy."

"Still, rather amusing, you'll admit." Ruval stretched out on one narrow cot, arms folded behind his head, staring up at the rough-hewn ceiling. "I never realized before what scant notice highborns take of those who serve them. For instance, I rode escort with Miyon and Tallain the other day to the merchant quarter, and neither looked twice at me. Miyon's aware of the shape I've taken, but he honestly didn't see me."

"I know what you mean." The younger of the brothers leaned back against the wooden door, fists in the pockets of his trousers. "I used to get the same treatment at Swalekeep. Until I *made* Chiana notice me." Peering at Ruval by the light of a candlebranch—outrageous expense that indicated the extent of Tallain's wealth—he snorted suddenly. "You're fading."

"I'm relaxing," Ruval corrected. "And anyway, we *diarmadh'im* can more or less see through this if we're looking for it. You are. The others aren't." He laughed. "I may spend tomorrow around Riyan, if I can manage it."

"Stay away from him!" Marron warned.

"Stop fretting." Kicking off his low boots with the soft heels that were mandatory within this residence of polished floors and priceless carpets, Ruval stretched. "Maybe you're right about this being a strain. Or maybe I'm just bored. By the Nameless One, this bowing and scraping is hard on a man's nerves. I don't know how you tolerated it at Swalekeep." Yawning, he untied the top laces of his light silk shirt. "I can hardly keep my eyes open."

"Well, let go of the working, then. And get some sleep."

"Such solicitude, brother," Ruval said mockingly.

"Self-preservation, brother," Marron replied in the same

tone. "If you start to waver, that'll put an end to this. And, frankly, I intend to be a guest at Pol's burning, not the centerpiece at my own."

Marron blew out the candles one by one. Eight small puffs—but he hesitated before the ninth, glancing at his brother to confirm the slow change. Gone was the eerie impression of sharper cheekbones, cleft chin, brighter hair, and longer jaw superimposed on the familiar like the presence of a ghost. Ruval's face was again Ruval's face, not the subtly altered features of a stranger.

Marron let go of his own iron control, bolstered by huge amounts of *dranath*. He didn't need to reassure himself with the sight of his own transformation in the small mirror by the door; he had watched it before, fascinated. There was little physical sensation either in the assumption of the differences or in their fading, only a slight tingle in his head as he projected the illusion.

At first it had felt as if he was wearing someone else's clothes—a good fit but not perfect, binding here, loose there. His movements and facial expressions had been correspondingly awkward, the way one walks against one's natural rhythms, trying to compensate, when wearing another man's boots.

Only what he and Mireva had designed was a whole new skin, and it had taken time and work to adjust the fit.

The loosening of the spell relaxed him. He glanced at the scar on his wrist, souvenir of a childhood mishap, now visible again. His mouth was his own once more—wider, full-lipped, stretching in his own smile as the release of tension washed through him. He imagined sometimes that he could even feel his eye color change from pale yellowish-green back to brown.

At night even a *diarmadhi* mind must reliquish control, and anyone looking at him or Ruval would see their true forms and features. Thus the locked chamber. Mireva had no need for similar accommodations, and shared a tiny room with Thanys near the nursery. She had never been seen by any of their enemies; the only alteration in her appearance was a concerted effort to make herself seem even older than she was. *Her* illusion working would come later, at Stronghold.

Marron made sure once again that the door was locked,

then blew out the last candle and lay down on the second cot. The air was close and hot, and for the past six nights he had not slept well. But tonight he was exhausted, lack of sleep and accumulation of strain from sustaining the illusion finally catching up with him. After turning once or twice to find the least uncomfortable position, he sought and quickly found oblivion.

He did not wake when Ruval sat up, pulled on his boots, and silently left the room.

***

Mireva whirled angrily, nearly choking on a swallow of *dranath*-laced wine as the door opened and Thanys slid into their chamber.

"Don't startle me like that!" she hissed.

"You think *you* got a fright—she's gone!"

The older woman's jaw sagged for a moment before she collected herself. "Then *find* the little bitch at once! We don't have all night!"

"This isn't a cottage—she could be in any of fifty rooms," Thanys snapped. "Where do you propose I start looking?"

"I thought I told you to make sure—"

"She hasn't needed anything to help her sleep. How was I to know she'd pick tonight to go wandering around the residence?"

"Find her! And from now on keep your eyes open—and hers closed!"

Thanys' face tightened like a clenched fist. "I'll try the kitchens. She didn't eat much tonight at dinner—Miyon's doing, *again*."

Alone once more, Mireva downed the last of the wine to keep her hands from shaking. Damn the girl—and damn Thanys for not following orders. It had taken serious effort to get her kinswoman appointed Meiglan's servant two years ago, and even more work to arrange Mireva's own presence here at Tiglath. Miyon knew what his bastard daughter was being groomed to do, and played his own part with real enthusiasm. But he'd balked at the idea that Meiglan's consequence required an extra maid—especially when Ruval made the mistake of telling him Mireva would be a valuable asset in more ways than one.

Well, it was done. She kept out of Miyon's way, not

wanting to intercept any caustic glances that might arouse suspicion. Princes did not deign to notice menials.

Shrugging, Mireva slipped out of the room and padded softly down the hall, casting a brief, longing look at the nursery door. Behind it slept the children of Segev's murderer. Later, she told herself firmly. It would be done when they were all at Stronghold—and preferably right in front of Hollis.

With Miyon in his residence, Tallain had posted guards— supposedly of honor, but fooling no one as to their real purpose. Mireva smiled to herself, recalling what Miyon had said on arriving here: "By all means, Lord Tallain, put someone outside Meiglan's door to guard whatever honor she has. She certainly didn't inherit any from her mother." Yes, he was enjoying his role in their little scheme.

But there was no guard outside Meiglan's chambers right now. Mireva, prepared with a distraction, was glad she didn't have to expend the energy. Perhaps Thanys had been clever for once and enlisted the man's aid in finding their wayward charge. But how had Meiglan gotten past him in the first place?

Again she shrugged; it didn't matter. What mattered was the tall form that suddenly detached itself from the shadows and crept toward her from the staircase. She opened Meiglan's door and the two of them were swiftly inside the antechamber.

"What's going on?" Ruval demanded instantly.

"Save your breath. We'll have to hide you until she gets back and into bed again—" Her heart jumped painfully for the second time that night as she heard soft voices outside in the hallway. Flinging open the door of a huge standing wardrobe, she hissed, "In here! Quickly!"

"This is ridiculous—"

"Silence!"

She slammed the wardrobe shut just in time. Meiglan was ushered into the antechamber by a scolding Thanys, looking chastened but with a spark of defiance in her big brown eyes. Mireva made a mental note to keep the girl away from Sionell; that lady's independent spirit was influencing her.

"—in the middle of the night! Whatever were you thinking of?"

"I only wanted some taze and cakes—and the guard was kind enough to escort me downstairs so I wouldn't get lost—"

"My lady, you should have sent him to fetch me, and I would have had *Mireva* bring you something to eat," Thanys said, with a subtly sarcastic look at the older woman. She went on talking all the way to Meiglan's bed, where the girl was summarily tucked up beneath silk sheets. "—and hope you don't dream after drinking Lady Sionell's spicy taze at this time of night!"

"Dreams don't necessarily have to be bad ones," Mireva said soothingly, deciding that her kinswoman could be forgiven the disrespect; she had just provided Mireva with a lovely opening for suggestion. "And Lady Sionell's blend is a very good one, I'm told. I'm sure you'll have happy dreams, my lady."

"Candles, Mireva," Thanys ordered curtly, and when the room was in darkness the two sorcerers closed the door behind them.

Mireva started to speak, but the other woman shook her head violently and motioned to the outer door—still half open. "Stay here tonight, in case she wakes again," Thanys said, and smiled mirthlessly, and departed. This time the door closed firmly behind her.

Mireva liberated Ruval from the wardrobe. He stepped out, rubbing his nose. "Do you know how close I was to a sneeze?" he complained in a whisper. "That damned perfume of hers—my nose itches to the eyebrows!"

"You're the only man around here who *doesn't* approve," she countered. "But I may change it all the same—in case someone else has the same reaction."

"Do that. Well, I'm ready. Is she?"

"In a little while. You know what to do—and what *not* to?"

Ruval grinned. "It's tempting, you know. Are you sure I can't—"

"Not if you value what you'd like to do it with! She must remain virgin."

"Oh, all right. If she smells the way her clothes do— let's get on with it. By the way, how am I going to get out past that guard?"

Mireva merely looked at him.

"Never mind. A stupid question."

She pulled a leather pouch from her pocket and sifted some of its contents into her hand. Half she gave to him, and the rest she licked from her palm. "I know what it tastes like," she snapped. "Eat it anyway." When he had done so, grimacing, she drew in a deep, steadying breath. "Begin, Ruval. Picture him in your mind, just as you saw him in the flesh—the lines of his face, the shape of his body, the color of his hair. . . ."

***

Sionell woke at Antalya's first whimpers, alerted by that intuition born in most mothers with the births of their children. Thanks to her husband's skill and dedication in proving his preference for grown women rather than young girls, she had been deeply asleep. But when her daughter began to cry, Sionell got out of bed and went down the hall to the nursery, where Antalya had succeeded in waking Chayla and Rohannon as well.

The cause of Talya's distress was the loss onto the floor of the big green stuffed dragon her grandmother Feylin had given her. Sionell put all to rights while the twins' nursemaid quieted them down—not an easy task, as Hollis had cautioned when accepting Sionell's suggestion that the pair would enjoy a brief visit to Tiglath while their parents were at Stronghold. "They have a tendency to bounce—not just off the beds but all the way to the ceiling," Hollis had sighed. "And if there wasn't a ceiling, they'd fly."

Bouncing restrained for the night, Sionell shut the nursery door behind her and smiled. Tallain, she was morally certain, hadn't woken up—probably hadn't even moved. He'd earned his rest tonight. The smile became a grin as she reflected that she had, too. Retracing the steps to their chambers, she glanced down the long hallway to where the guard stood outside Meiglan's rooms. Tomorrow she would start a campaign to put a little spine into the girl. And if Miyon regretted losing the cringing object of his mockery, too bad for Miyon.

Sionell was about to discard her bedrobe onto a chair in the anteroom when she heard another cry. Not a child this time—an adult. Struggling back into the robe, she hurried down the hall, following a second high-pitched scream. She thought she glimpsed two shadows descending the stairs, but suddenly there were so many other people around that she forgot about them. Meiglan, her cloud of golden hair in wild tangles, was the center of attention and the source of the screams—which were abruptly silenced as her maidservant shook her. She gasped for breath, trembling from head to foot.

Riyan, whose room was two doors down from Meiglan's, got to her first. "Easy now, my lady—that's it, calm yourself. Shh. It's all right." He patted her shoulder and smiled reassuringly—and Sionell noted wryly that he couldn't quite keep his eyes off the slender curves half-visible through a misty silk nightdress. "Nothing to be afraid of, Lady Meiglan, nothing at all."

The little knot of people untied for Sionell. But before she could take charge, Rialt stepped forward and said, "If I may, my lady?" He dismissed the extraneous servants and guards with a glance, told the maid to fetch mulled wine, and shepherded Meiglan through the ante-chamber door. Sionell traded glances with Riyan, whose shoulders lifted in bewilderment.

They, and Meiglan's assigned guard, followed Rialt. "What happened?" Sionell asked.

"She flung open the door, my lady, screaming that there was someone in her room. A man."

"Impossible," Sionell stated.

The guard nodded his gratitude for her trust in him. "Exactly, my lady. Even if someone had gotten past me, her other servant, the older one, was inside. She would have called out."

"Hmm." Sionell peeked around the inner door, seeing that Rialt had gotten Meiglan propped on pillows with brisk, sympathetic efficiency and was lighting candles. Suddenly a whole branch of them sprang to life and the girl caught her breath in fright. Rialt merely glanced around, brows arching mildly.

"Riyan," Sionell chided in disgust.

"Saves time," he told her with a shrug.

And gets you a better look at her in that flimsy little scrap of silk, she thought, amused. "Go back to bed. I'll see what's troubling her."

"I'll stay if you like—"

"No, *you'd* like," she responded, unable to resist teasing him. He grinned, unrepentant. "Oh, get out of here," she added, giving him a push.

A little while later she had calmed Meiglan down enough to get some speech out of her—not that it made much sense. Sitting beside her, Sionell pressed her chilled fingers and smiled bracingly; the second time tonight she had soothed a scared child.

"It was just a dream, my dear."

"I'm sorry, my lady—I didn't mean to cause any trouble! But *please* don't tell my father!"

"Don't worry about anything. It's quite all right."

The pallid face with its huge, liquid dark eyes was nearly lost in the unruly mass of curls. "There was a man here, my lady—I swear it."

"Meiglan—"

"There was! You have to believe me!"

Sionell humored her. "Did you see him clearly enough to identify him?" A small, tense nod. "Then you must tell me, so he can be found and punished. Tell me exactly what happened and what you saw."

Meiglan nodded again like a good little girl. "I couldn't sleep—the room is beautiful, my lady, and the bed is very comfortable, it isn't that—"

"At times we all have trouble sleeping," Sionell said, hiding her impatience with the frantic apology. "Go on."

"I—I went to the kitchens, the guard showed me where, and had hot taze and cakes. Thanys found me and brought me back upstairs, and Mireva stayed in the outer room when I went back to bed. I was almost asleep but—but something woke me up and I opened my eyes and he was standing right there—"

Meiglan's eyes glazed with fear and fixed on a point at the foot of the bed. Sionell squeezed her hand reassuringly. "What did he look like?"

"He—he was tall and slim, with blond hair. I think his eyes were blue."

Most Desert dwellers were as dark as the Fironese, though without the tip-tilted eyes characteristic of that princedom. Redheads like Sionell and her mother cropped up occasionally, even in bloodlines unmixed with outsiders, but true blonds were extremely rare. There were perhaps five fair-haired men in all Tiglath besides Tallain himself—and Sionell knew that none of them had been in Meiglan's bedchamber. It had been a dream.

"He was wearing two rings," Meiglan whispered. "One

on each hand. A large ring with two stones, one golden and one dark, I think an amethyst. The other hand—it was on his middle finger and it glowed like clouds around the moons—"

Rialt made a slight sound by the doorway. Sionell kept her voice even and said, "There's no one like that here at Tiglath, my dear."

Meiglan shook again as if her fragile bones would shatter. "But I saw him! I swear I did!"

"I'm sure it seemed that way to you. Dreams can be very real at times, when we're halfway between sleeping and waking. I know you think you saw this man, Meiglan, but he wasn't here."

He could not have been. He was at Stronghold.

The girl sank back into her pillows. "Do you think it *was* just a dream?" she ventured.

"I think that's exactly what it was." Sionell made an effort, and smiled. "When I was carrying Talya, I used to dream the oddest things—and then wake up the whole residence asking for the most absurd things to eat!"

A little smile hovered around her soft mouth. "Did you really, my lady?"

"Yes, I did—and no more of this 'my lady' nonsense. I'm Sionell and I'm your friend, Meiglan. Lie back now, and close your eyes."

"I'm sorry I woke everyone. I feel such a fool—all for a silly dream."

"Don't think about it another instant."

"You're so kind, my Sionell," she corrected shyly. "And so beautiful—may I really call you my friend?"

No one could possibly be this innocent—most especially not someone with Miyon of Cunaxa for a father. Sionell was ashamed of herself, even while wondering once more if she was supposed to feel that way.

"Of course, my dear." She patted Meiglan's hand and rose. "Go to sleep."

Rialt was in the antechamber, explaining to the maid that Meiglan had been upset by a dream. Sionell waited until he pronounced the wine suitable in taste and temperature for soothing a frightened lady to sleep, then took him firmly by the arm and led him out of the room.

Before she could speak, he did. "My lady—the description she gave—"

"Yes," she said evenly.

"Down to the detail of the rings."

It was exactly what she had been thinking, but to hear it aloud from someone else brought a paradoxical denial to her lips. "I think you're placing rather too much significance on—"

"Of course." His face wore no expression at all. "Good night, Rialt. Thank you for your help."

"Good night, my lady."

There were candles lit in her bedchamber, and Tallain was missing. Sionell crawled back into bed and stared across the room at the tapestry that had been Pol's wedding gift. A flight of bright dragons soared through deep blue skies above Tiglath, every detail stitched with exquisite accuracy—down to the section of wall demolished by the Merida in the year of Pol's birth. Tallain's father had decreed that the rubble be left symbolically unrepaired. "The walls Rohan will build for us will be stronger than any stone."

Tonight Sionell saw other symbolism in that battered wall. She had seen to her own defenses for two years now, building them of marriage and motherhood and the demands of ruling over her adopted holding. She loved her husband deeply and honestly, and adored her daughter; she was challenged and satisfied by her life as Lady of Tiglath. There was only that one small place where the grown woman had been unable to build an adult defense against a girlhood dream.

Had Meiglan truly dreamed tonight? Or had she merely *said* that she dreamed?

Whichever, Sionell now understood why the girl was here. It was so ludicrously obvious that she kicked herself for not realizing it before.

She is everything he has never seen before in a woman.

Pol had been surrounded by strong, capable, confident women all his life. None of them could even remotely be described as delicate and shy. Despite her looks, Tobin was about as frail as a plow-elk; Sioned possessed the power and fierceness of a she-dragon; Audrite's gentle manners covered a tough, brilliant mind; Hollis, the quietest of them, had all the meekness of a sandstorm.

Miyon's scornful treatment of this fragile child was enough to rouse anyone's protective instincts. But no one had ever in their lives insulted Sioned, Tobin, Feylin, or any of the other women Pol knew by thinking or suggesting they required protecting. Their husbands would have laughed themselves into apoplexies at the very notion.

But Meiglan. . . .

And she was so damned beautiful.

Her differences alone would attract him. Her father's ill-usage would help. And her beauty would do the rest.

Pol wasn't that big a fool. He'd see through this. He had to. The thought of his falling into Miyon's trap was ridiculous.

The thought of him married to Meiglan was insupportable.

When Tallain's interest had been brought to Sionell's attention after the last *Rialla*, she had fought an interior battle which was more than just a war between head and heart. Strongly attracted by both the person and the position of the Lord of Tiglath, still her emotions and mind also drew her to Pol. Hers had been the choice of which portion of each to heed. Now she struggled with the same confusion of feeling and intellect.

She was genuinely fond of Meiglan—or at least felt genuinely sorry for her. Practicality forced her to admit that dowering the girl might bring extremely important concessions from Miyon—whom Tiglath must deal with much more immediately than Dragon's Rest ever would. But she was also jealous, an emotion bolstered by the certainty that no Choice would be politically or personally worse for Pol than Meiglan. Miyon would use the girl against him any way he could. Pol would be twenty times a fool if he married her.

Still—he wasn't *that* blind. And if he didn't see it, Rohan or Sioned would.

And if *they* didn't, Sionell would waste no time in pointing it out to them.

Tallain came back and collapsed into bed with a martyred sigh. "One story, two glasses of water, and three lullabies," he reported before she could ask. "Sionell, I will adore any children you give me. But *please* do me the favor of having them one at a time! Twins would be the death of me!"

"Once Antalya is their age, you'll think she *is* twins."

"I was afraid of that. What was all the fuss?"

"Meiglan had a dream."

"Oh. Good thing we put her father in the other wing—Goddess knows how long it would've taken to calm her if he'd been there jeering at the poor child."

She hollowed out a comfortable position in his arms and smiled. She had never regretted marrying Tallain, never mourned for an instant that he wasn't Pol. "Good night, love," she whispered in the darkness. "Gentle dreams."

"Mmm," he responded. "I'm holding the best one . . . not the *sweetest*, perhaps—not with your temper—but definitely the best."

"Oh, keep talking," Sionell purred. "I *love* it."

"And me."

"And you."

"I know," he said smugly.

"Conceited swine."

Chapter Fourteen

Stronghold: 26 Spring

Fifteen years in the rich coastal lands of Goddess Keep had not blunted Andry's Desert-bred reaction to spring. He still watched the fields respond to the lengthening days with wide-eyed wonderment, and knew his Sunrunners often grinned behind their hands when he expressed his amazement at the yearly renewal. But as he rode with Oclel and Nialdan down from Feruche that spring, his companions laughed openly at the stunned silence with which he greeted the Desert's incredible blooming.

"You'd think he'd never seen a flower before," Nialdan teased.

Andry finally found his voice. "You don't understand. All you're seeing is what you've seen all your life. What I'm seeing is a miracle."

One that Sorin would never witness.

Andry had spent two days at Feruche, the first time he had ever been to his brother's castle. It had been nearly as painful as that abrupt, searing moment when he'd known Sorin was dead. Feruche was permeated with his twin's energy, thoughtfulness, and disciplined taste in design and decoration. Every stone, every timber, every tapestry had been selected and set with care and purpose; the castle was a marvel of beauty and strength, neither dominant, each existing within and complementing the other. Andry walked hallways Sorin had planned, slept in rooms Sorin had embellished, ran his fingers over wood carved to Sorin's specifications, stood in the great hall where Sorin had sat to administer justice. Anguish, deadened somewhat by the long, exhausting ride from Goddess Keep, had returned full force. He had spent the night before last in Sorin's private chambers, looking out

at the moon-drenched sand. And at last he had given way
to tears, as he had not done even when the first brutal
impact of death had slammed into his senses.

Riding the last measures to Stronghold after spending
the previous night in the open—there being no reason to
stop at Skybowl with Riyan at Tiglath—sorrow had at
first been eased by the stupendous bounty all around
him. But Sorin would never see it. And from grief it was
but a short pace to anger.

He blamed Pol. But he blamed himself even more for
not seeking out every *diarmadhi* in all the princedoms.
The one foolish action in all Lady Merisel's long life had
been allowing her enemies to flee just punishment. The
histories were silent on why she had not pursued and
eradicated them as they deserved. It could not have been
because they were unidentifiable.

Sunrunners, violently ill when they crossed water,
couldn't swim a stroke. There were tales of *faradh'im*
who drowned in shallow, placid water where even a child
could have floated safely. But sorcerers had no such
difficulties. This would make a useful trap when Andry
chose to spring it. Sorin's death had convinced him that
he should make that choice soon, before anyone else
could die at *diarmadhi* hands.

Why had Merisel not destroyed those who had cost
Lord Rosseyn his life? In all his study of the scrolls,
Andry had come to know almost everything about her
but that one puzzling thing. He had reviewed her actions
and through them had deduced her reasons for taking
them, reasons that revealed her as a strong, shrewd,
brilliant woman. In truth, at his initial reading of the
histories she had dictated in her old age, he had fallen a
little in love with her. But where at first he had imagined
her as a combination of his fiercely proud mother, his
fiery Aunt Sioned, and his formidable great-aunt Andrade,
for the last nine years the face Merisel wore in his thoughts
was very much like Alasen's.

Only Sorin had ever really understood Andry's despair
at losing Alasen. Now that solace was lost to him as
surely as Alasen herself. Three children she had given
Ostvel now: two daughters, Camigwen and Milar, and
the son born two summers ago. Sorin, at Castle Crag on
business for Pol when Dannar was born, had reported

that the red hair that seemed to have vanished from the
Kierstian line with Sioned had made an emphatic reap-
pearance in Alasen's son. Sorin had understood that Andry
craved word of her, any scrap of information that would
prove her decision the right one. He was not a selfish
man, nor a vindictive one; he cared for her still and
wanted her to be happy. Yet it was like worrying a sore
tooth: exquisitely painful, impossible to resist.

His fury against life for making him the one man
Alasen loved and feared in equal measure had faded. He
had even sent small gifts to celebrate her children's births.
Odds were that at least one and possibly all three would
be *faradhi*-gifted—and he intended her children to become what Alasen would never be. Practically speaking,
the Sunrunners could not afford to lose the strength of
the Kierstian heritage that had produced Sioned and Pol.
More personally, Andry wanted the link these children
would provide to their mother. He would supervise their
learning and come to know them as people, the daughters and son who might have been his.

He had even stopped thinking *should* have been his.
Sorin had helped him to see that the truest expression of
love for her was to let her go. He might still believe that
her greatest happiness and fulfillment would have come
at his side, with earned rings of Sunrunner rank glittering
from her slender fingers. But the choice had been hers to
make. He had learned to live with it. The years had at
least distanced him from the pain.

By way of Donato, Castle Crag's Sunrunner, she and
Ostvel had sent word of their grief at Sorin's death.
Alasen had grown up with him in her father's castle of
New Raetia, where he had been Prince Volog's squire.
She grieved as if she too had lost a brother. But if Andry
had hoped for a more personal message, he had not
admitted it to himself. What would be the use?

"Is that it? Are we nearly there?"

Oclel's voice roused him and he glanced to the craggy
hilltop indicated by a pointing finger. "That's the Flametower," he said shortly, and the change in his voice from
the excited awe of his last words made his companions
stiffen.

The fire burning within the Flametower was invisible
during daylight, but at night became a beacon across the

Desert. It had blazed for the nearly thirty years since his grandfather Zehava had died after being gored by a dragon. When Rohan died, his fire would be extinguished as Zehava's had been. The huge circular chamber would then be scrubbed clean—by Sioned if she survived him—and Pol would light new flames, his own, from the Fire called by Sunrunners to burn Rohan's corpse. Pol would then hold both Princemarch and the Desert as High Prince. It should have given Andry great satisfaction that the man who would become the most powerful prince on the continent was a Sunrunner and his close kinsman. It did not. He hoped Rohan's fire burned for another thirty years.

Andry had never approached Stronghold from this direction before. Nialdan and Oclel had never been in the Desert at all. Riding north from Radzyn, the great keep was visible for forty measures. But coming down from Skybowl and Feruche, all that showed was the Flametower, the bulk of the castle hidden by an outcropping of rock like a finger half-crooked into the dunes. As the three *faradh'im* rode around it, Stronghold abruptly appeared in all its blunt, massive power.

Nialdan whistled; Oclel gave a soft exclamation. Even Andry, who had been here countless times, was impressed by the sudden view of thick walls, huge towers, and pennants flying from the gatehouse. Princemarch's violet flag rose there, too, on a staff just as high as the Desert blue with its golden dragon; Radzyn's red and white, Skybowl's blue and brown, the blue and white of Remagev, and the red and orange of Whitecliff all flew below those of the two princes in residence. The colors proclaimed pride and power and prestige; Andry was irked with himself for not remembering to bring along his own plain white banner which by tradition would have flown at equal height with those of princes. It was a small point, but neglect of any of Goddess Keep's perquisites was undesirable. People, especially *these* people, needed to remember exactly who he was.

The approach led up a narrow defile and through a tunnel carved from solid rock, under the guards' quarters and the main gates to the outer courtyard. Another gate would lead them through to the central court, where

Andry was betting that only his parents would come to greet him.

The trio had been spotted. Andry reined in and held up both hands to identify himself with rings and bracelets that jealousy hoarded the sunlight. As the dragon horn sounded and gates were opened to him, he imagined what would be happening within the castle. His mother's insistence that she be the one to handle him would be obeyed by everyone except his father. Maarken might attempt to join them, but a glance from Chay would send him back to his seat. They would wait for him on the main steps, expecting anger, hurt, sullen resentment.

Andry decided to confound them.

***

Dinner that evening in the Great Hall left Nialdan and Oclel speechless. In honor of the Lord of Goddess Keep, Rohan had ordered his cooks to heights of artistry and his chamberlain to extremes of elegance normally reserved only for the New Year Holiday or visiting princes. Dragon's Rest had been built in part for the kind of show a High Prince was supposed to lavish on his guests; Stronghold was all the more impressive in its finery for being designed as a defensive fortress from cellars to towers. The beauty of Dragon's Rest hid its carefully planned military strength, but for sheer magnificence nothing could compare with Stronghold bedecked for a formal occasion. Massive stones garlanded with flowers and greenery presented the aspect of a brawny warrior in ceremonial armor: muscle covered by polished silver and softest silk, but ready for battle just the same.

This was not lost on Andry, though he was used to it. His whole family was like that: steel wrapped in velvet. Nialdan and Oclel were as awestruck as Rohan obviously intended them to be. It vaguely irritated Andry. Still, he had the family pride in the family seat, and his sense of humor allowed a private salute to Rohan's instincts. Anyone would think more than twice about opposing the High Prince in anything after seeing Stronghold at its most impressive.

And, too, he knew that the display was not merely for his two Sunrunners. It was practice for Miyon of Cunaxa's expected arrival.

Sioned told him as much flat out. "Tallain isn't having

much luck with him at Tiglath. So I suppose Miyon will be here fairly soon." She made a face. "And as a good, dutiful princess, I'll have to dance with the snake."

They were more or less isolated at the high table. After the meal Rohan had left his wife's side to confer with Feylin about, inevitably, dragons; Maarken and Pol were trying to master the art of juggling greased sticks as demonstrated by a pair of traveling entertainers who had shown off their skills between courses. Tobin and Hollis were laughing at their frustrations. Of the others, Walvis endeavored to convince Chay regarding some finer point of estate management, with pretty Ruala of Elktrap listening avidly. Morwenna, displaced from the usual Sunrunner's seat by the presence of *faradh'im* more high-ranking than she, watched the whole with a gaze that for all its dark Fironese tilt reminded Andry forcibly of Andrade's shrewd blue eyes. He could sense her even when he was not looking at her, watching and judging, ignoring Nialdan's and Oclel's attempts at conversation.

"What do you think he wants?" Andry asked in response to Sioned's last remark.

"You're Desert-bred, you know exactly what he wants."

"Preferably Radzyn Port," Andry acknowledged with a little smile. "Will he settle for anything less while he lives?"

"He'll have to. But you're right, of course. It's damned irksome to have him always sneaking around up north."

"At least he'll be here for a while where you can watch him."

"Mmm. Sometimes I think his merchants are even worse than he is."

"They're only trying to survive, Sioned."

"I have no objection to that. Where I begin to get irritated is when they equate their survival with our destruction." She gave a comical grimace. "Not an entirely new experience."

Andry sipped his wine, then said, "I've been wondering when you'd get around to mentioning the dragon-killer."

"I've been wondering if I dared." She met his gaze forthrightly. "I admire your self-command."

It was recognition of his unexpectedly placid manner thus far, and suspicion of it. His easy manner and his quiet entrance into Stronghold had not gone unnoticed—he hadn't thought it would. He nodded noncommittally.

"You were always honest with me as a little boy," she murmured.

"You may have noticed that I've grown up."

"Don't spar with me, Andry."

"Why not? Do you fear you'd lose?"

Looking for a frown, he received a smile—and remembered that Sioned had had far more years of training under Andrade than he. "You speak as if there were some matter of contention between us, nephew."

"Isn't there?"

"Are you determined to make it so?"

He desperately wanted to abandon his pose and was within a breath of doing so when she spoke again.

"Have you ever counted up the times I've lost?"

Though his body remained motionless, his spine went rigid.

"Come, Andry. We're on the same side, you know," she told him in quiet tones.

Her green eyes captured his in a trick Andrade had taught all her senior Sunrunners. Andry had learned it on his own—and how to escape it. He did not look away, but instead concentrated everything he was in his eyes. All his knowledge, all his gifts, all his will bored into her. In the space of a few heartbeats she ought to have wavered. But her gaze stayed level and calm.

"You have indeed grown up," she said at last.

He was the one who broke contact then, understanding at least a part of her strength. This fiercely passionate woman had learned in the course of her life that passion unleashed was passion that destroyed its user. The things that drove her might be much the same as those driving him—but she knew patience, and careful power. There was in her a centered place where passion and restless intellect alike were stilled and calm. It was the same quality often sensed in Rohan, and he wondered suddenly who had taught it to whom.

And just as quickly it occurred to him that Pol did not possess this quiet center. He had not yet been tested as his parents had been. He had not yet been hurt.

Relenting a little, he said with a slight smile, "It always

takes a long time for one's family to stop seeing one as a little boy playing at dragons."

"So your father said with much bewilderment this afternoon. I think you startled him, Andry. He also made a very disgruntled remark about getting old."

"Him? Never."

Her expression softened again. "That's the first honest reaction I've had from you all night. My dear, I confess that sometimes I haven't dared feel things for fear they would overcome me. But we're your family. Sorin's family. We grieve for him just as you do." Sensitive fingers rested on his arm. "We need your comfort and you need ours."

Tempting. But betraying in the end. If he gave in to what he felt it would overcome him, as she had said. If he rendered himself vulnerable in one area, he would be defenseless in others. It should not have been such a shock to realize he didn't trust his own family not to take advantage of any weakness. After all, they didn't trust him, either.

In her eyes was so accurate an analysis of his private thoughts that he cursed silently; he was not as unreadable as he'd thought himself schooled to be by now. Sorrow flickered in her expression. She removed her hand from his arm and gestured a squire over.

"Arlis, more wine for Lord Andry."

"At once, your grace."

More than anything else, the titles underscored a moment lost, perhaps forever. They were not family anymore, but Lord of Goddess Keep and High Princess. Andry took refuge in asking the young man if he would be knighted at the *Rialla* this summer, and a brief conversation about Arlis' grandfathers Saumer and Volog ensued. But he could not shake the feeling of desolation, of being isolated within the home of his ancestors.

***

"So you see we have to do something to increase the number of available caves, and this year if possible," Feylin concluded, and sat back in her chair. "Otherwise. . . ."

"I understand." Rohan gave an irritated hiss of a sigh. "I haven't time for all this," he muttered.

"Sunrunners, sorcerers, and dragons," she summed

up. "Plus that Merida-loving bastard of Cunaxa. Almost makes you wish somebody else wore that circlet, doesn't it?"

He rubbed automatically at the silver crossing his forehead and she smiled wry sympathy. "Better me than you, is that it?" he suggested.

"Infinitely better. I only worry about dragons. And Remagev. And my son and daughter and grandchild—" She grinned at him. "But I'm curious. Which problem are you going to address first, and what are you going to do about it?"

"Andry. I'm going to invite him for a private chat."

Gray eyes narrowed as she glanced to the center of the high table. "Sioned already tried that. It doesn't look as if she got anywhere."

"I didn't really expect her to," he admitted. "Have you any suggestions?"

Feylin only shrugged.

"Out with it," he ordered with a half-smile.

"I was just remembering the siege of Tiglath."

"Yes?" Feylin was the type who would eventually speak her mind without prompting. She just enjoyed being prompted.

"The Merida surrounded us, you'll recall. And then my solid gold fool of a husband led the charge that annihilated them."

"After they'd breached Tiglath's walls, wasn't it?"

"Exactly." She nodded her satisfaction.

"Feylin, would you care to expl—" He stopped. "Oh. I see."

"Nobody ever accused you of being stupid." She lifted her wine cup to him approvingly.

He slanted a thoughtful glance at Andry. It made sense. He could use the rest of the family to surround Andry from all sides, then allow him to think there was a weakness in Rohan's own position—and thereby trap him. Using military metaphors to describe an under-handed action against his own blood-kin left a very sour taste in his mouth.

But no one had ever accused Feylin of being stupid, either.

Tobin and Chay had unwittingly begun the maneuver this morning. They had met their son alone, but the only thing they had shared was a formal expression of grief over Sorin's death. Andry's coolness had puzzled and hurt them—an emotional strain on him, surely. He loved his parents deeply. Sioned had come at him from another direction. Rohan would have to wait for a detailed report of their conversation, but that Andry was looking uncomfortable was a good sign. Maarken could be next; Andry adored him and Maarken was now the only brother he had left. If he still held out, Pol could—no, Pol must be perceived as Rohan's weakness that would lure Andry in.

And what in the name of the Goddess and all her works was he *thinking?*

Disgusted and feeling unclean, he got to his feet. Feylin's hand on his arm stopped him.

"He's no longer a child, Rohan," she murmured. "He rules Goddess Keep and does it very, very well."

Rohan stared down at her. "I can't lay a trap for my own kin."

"You're an honorable man. Will he behave the same?"

"If he doesn't, he's not Chay's son. Or my sister's."

Her eyes turned the pale gray of new steel. "Because he *is* their son, he will believe as powerfully and completely in his own truths as you do in yours. Belief is much more dangerous than deception." Then her gaze softened and she gave his arm a gentle squeeze. "I know you, Rohan. You only lie to people who deserve nothing better. Walvis was already cast in your mold when he came to you as a squire, but you had the final forming and polishing. Gold I called him, and so he is. So are you. But lying to people who matter tarnishes you both. And no, I wouldn't have either of you any other way." She gave a rueful shake of her head. "But it would be so much easier if you were."

Rohan smiled down at her. "And you'd love to be ruthless, wouldn't you?"

"It'd be a help."

"Don't try. It doesn't suit you. I can be ruthless enough for all of us."

"But not with Andry?"

He pulled in a deep breath. "No. You're right—I *would* feel tarnished. And, Goddess knows, I've enough muck sticking to me after thirty years of rule."

"None where it shows." Feylin slid her hand into his and pressed it.

He remembered her words later on when, according to his original plan, he invited Andry upstairs. Perhaps the dirt wouldn't show if no one but he and his nephew witnessed it.

Sioned, obedient to Rohan's glance but not liking the exclusion, left them alone in the outer chamber, saying she was too sleepy to sit up late over wine. Arlis served them, then bowed his way out to wait in the hall if Rohan should require him.

"He'll make an excellent prince," Andry said to begin the conversation.

"I hope his grandfather agrees with you. Volog's been helping rule Isel since Saumer's death two winters ago, complaining constantly that he's too old for so much work." He paused to take a sip of wine. "But you know, I think he was devastated when Saumer died—though he'd never admit it. Sometimes losing a lifelong enemy is worse than losing a lifelong friend."

"They worked together fairly well those last years."

"Yes. But Volog will be as glad to hand over Isel to Arlis as I was when Pol was ready to take on Princemarch by himself."

"Latham can't rule Isel in his son's place?"

"As regent, he's fine. But the Iseli think of Arlis as the heir, not his father."

"Also reminiscent of the way you handled Princemarch."

Rohan shrugged. "It was the only wise solution."

"Wisdom seems to be in short supply in Gilad these days."

"You always did have an interesting way of putting things." Rohan smiled.

A bit unwillingly, Andry's mouth lifted at the corners. But few people were able to resist the High Prince's smile, no matter their grievances against him. Rohan hated having to use it on Andry.

"Let's be wise and state things plainly, shall we?" he went on. "This Sunrunner of yours has put us all in an awkward position."

"I wanted to thank you for getting Gevlia out of the dark. That was an incredibly cruel thing to do to her, and for that alone I'm going to fight Cabar on this."

"I can't side with you and I can't side with him,"
Rohan warned. "I can't stay neutral, either. It'll come
down to my deciding the disposition of the case and we
all know it."

"Surely you understand my position," Andry said
smoothly. "Gevlia is *faradhi*. No one has the right to
judge her but me."

"Cabar insists she was not acting as a Sunrunner, but
as a physician."

"Nonetheless, she *is* a Sunrunner."

"Andry—"

The young man made an impatient gesture. "What do
you think Aunt Andrade would have said?"

"Exactly what you're saying now. And my reply would
have been the same." He shook his head. "So many
times I've listened to myself throwing words at a problem—
endless words, as if the sheer numbers of them would
crush the difficulty into the dust. Words are the weapons
of the civilized man, I tell myself. There's nothing that
can't be solved if people only talk to each other instead
of reaching for their swords."

"If Cabar reaches for his, he'll be in for a shock."

Rohan's eyes narrowed. "So. It's true, then." He saw
the shift of candlelight on Andry's shirt as shoulder muscles tensed.

"Is what true?"

"Don't play games with me, Andry. I know about
your—what are you calling them? Ah, yes. *Devr'im*."

"You've been a ruling prince the length of my life and
have ten times my experience at these little skirmishes."
Andry shrugged. "Especially with rulers of Goddess Keep.
But though I may not be Andrade, I have my own—"

"Games and secrets? Do you suppose such things make
you her worthy successor?" Rohan knew he should not
grow angry, or at least should not give in to it. But he
was tired of this and sick with the knowledge that Feylin
had been right. He was used to this kind of conversation
with other princes who tried to outwit him. But to encounter it within his own family—irritation got the better
of him and he snapped, "Do you think it a secret from
me that during one of your little practice 'wars,' the
mother of your son *died*?"

Andry turned white to the lips. But his voice was low

and controlled as he said, "Othanel believed in what I'm doing."

"Can't you see the danger?"

"More danger than you know." The bleak reply startled Rohan. Andry got to his feet and put down his untasted wine. "You're still trying to talk your way to a solution. Do you seriously think these sorcerers will sit still long enough to listen? Have a care, High Prince. You're going to need me and my *devr'im,* perhaps sooner than you know."

Rohan waited until he was at the door, fingers on the crystal knob. "The Sunrunner will not be handed over to you on your order."

Andry froze. "I *will* be the one to judge her. Not Cabar, and not you. It is my right."

"By whose reckoning?"

"The same that put you where you are. Power itself. Would you give up any of yours? Of course not. Don't expect me to."

Rohan shook his head sadly. "You hang on hardest to the very thing you least understand. Have you considered what your brother would have said to all this?"

Andry's whole body stiffened as if a sword had gone into his heart. "Sorin is dead, his soul scattered to the Desert winds."

And then Rohan understood the mistake he had made tonight. "Andry—you're not alone. We're here, your family, those who know you and love you best. Don't turn away from us."

The young man whirled around furiously. "You did that to me long ago!"

"The choice to become a Sunrunner was yours."

"There was none other I could make! Why should I have stayed here to run some insignificant little holding when I could be what I am now? Ambition runs in the family—why do you condemn mine? Andrade wanted me to rule Goddess Keep and all *faradh'im.* If the power that gives me doesn't suit you, then too damned bad! And while we're on the subject of ambition, look to your son!"

Rohan spoke quietly. "It would be futile to point out that, like you, Pol is in exactly the position Andrade intended. But I will tell you one thing. You turned your face from everyone but Sorin. Now that he's gone, there's nothing to hold you to us but our love for you. I see now that you have none left for us."

Blue eyes went wide with sudden unexpected pain. Rohan stood, speaking gently.

"Andry, you haven't lost us. But we're afraid of losing you."

"Afraid of losing me, or afraid *of* me?" came the bitter reply. And in the next instant he was gone.

Arlis, pushed summarily aside in the hall, hovered in the doorway for a moment. He was still young enough to be offended by Andry's brusque treatment but old enough—and prince enough—to show it only with a brow arched at Rohan.

"I don't think he even saw you," Rohan said tiredly. "Never mind. Go to bed now, Arlis. I'll do for myself, thank you."

"As you wish, my lord."

The weariness was profound as he went through to the bedchamber. His wife sat at her dressing table, brushing her hair.

"Sioned, I am a fool."

"Granted," she replied serenely. "What have you done this time?"

"I said all the wrong things it was possible to say." He flung himself into a chair. "I questioned his judgment, threatened his power, insulted him, hurt him, and came damned close to taking him over my knee."

"That about covers the mistakes you could have made with him," she agreed.

"Am I getting old and stupid? I'm supposed to be clever. I'm supposed to know how to handle people."

She faced him, compassion soft in her eyes. "People, my love. Not family. The problem is that you care too much about him."

Rohan nodded. "Feylin said much the same thing this evening."

"What are we going to do now?"

"I haven't the slightest notion."

"I think you do," she murmured.

He shifted uncomfortably, then admitted, "Pol asked me why it is that I never act until I'm forced to. It seems I'm forced to now. Who was that cousin of Cabar's who approached Pol? Barig? He should still be at Swalekeep. I want him summoned here. Do it yourself, Sioned, as a direct order from the High Prince."

"Every bed at Stronghold will be full, then. I just spoke with Riyan on moonlight and gave Tallain permission to bring Miyon here."

"Damn!" But after a moment's thought he added, "No, that will be all right. I'd rather have him watch my little demonstration of power with his own eyes."

"Which will properly warn him—and impress on him that the laws of the High Prince are superior to those of any other princedom and even of Goddess Keep."

Rohan gaped at her. "How can you know what I'm going to do when I've barely started to work it out myself?"

She smiled. "I know you, *azhrei*. Now come to bed."

Chapter Fifteen

Swalekeep: 26 Spring

Princess Chiana dismissed her maids with a gesture, barely waiting for the doors to click shut behind them before plunging into the depths of her huge standing wardrobe. A few moments later she emerged gleefully with garments clutched in her hands. Shucking out of her bedrobe and nightdress, she made quick work of buttons and laces and stood before three angled mirrors to judge the effect.

Chiana smiled. She had kept her figure after her pregnancies and at almost thirty had a waist like a young girl's, shown off to excellent advantage by a snug tunic and tight belt. Her hips curved sleekly in leather breeches that clung like a second skin. The clothes were basically for riding, but there was a marked difference: the light green tunic was cut like a soldier's and across the breast leaped the black deer of Meadowlord, antlers lifted like swords.

At the bottom of a clothespress in the corner was the final piece of the ensemble. Chiana struggled into it, acting as her own squire as she fastened silver buckles. At last the stiffened leather was secure. She struck a martial pose and grinned at her reflection. With boots rising to mid-thigh and carnelian-studded body armor covering her chest and spine, she was the perfect picture of the warrior-princess.

Thought of her rank sent her to another wardrobe, where she removed a locked coffer. The helm inside was also of stiffened leather braced with gold. Around the brow circled a wide band of gold, which above the nose-piece swirled up into another running stag, its eyes and antlers set with more carnelians. It was difficult to get all her heavy auburn hair hidden beneath the helm, but she managed. When she strutted before the three mirrors again, she laughed out loud.

All she needed was to mount the Kadari mare purchased at the last *Rialla*, a magnificent horse black from nose to tail with white feathering at hooves and ears, and her presentation would be complete. But it was to be no idle masquerade for amusement. Tomorrow she would ride out wearing her warrior's armor in earnest, and by the end of spring Castle Crag and all of Princemarch would be hers.

Troops waited in secret for her arrival. Strategically scattered along the border, they had been assembling slowly, stealthily, since the New Year Holiday. They waited for her to lead them up to Rezeld Manor, where Lord Morlen had also assembled all those who owed him service. He had been a real find—the work of the red-haired steward Mirris, who was in Cunaxa arranging another army. Morlen and his family had succeeded for years in pretending poverty to hide their considerable resources. But he had been unable to fool High Prince Rohan, who had claimed his share of Rezeld's bounty, mainly in stone used to build Dragon's Rest. Morlen had conceived a loathing for his princes that made him easy to convince when Mirris had put forth certain proposals. And now the man waited with more than three hundred soldiers at Rezeld for Chiana to lead them against Prince Pol's gorgeous new palace.

The number of troops Morlen was able to assemble had been a shock to him as well as to Chiana, until Mirris had explained that there were many in the Veresch who wished a prince of Roelstra's blood back at Castle Crag. Chiana laughed again as she remembered Mirris' explanation.

"Their loyalty is to those who ruled them for five generations. Of course they will flock to your grace's banner—the noblest of the late High Prince's daughters. And I wouldn't be at all surprised if along the way from Dragon's Rest to Castle Crag, hundreds more joined your grace's armies."

The notion was intoxicating. Mirris himself had been a find of no small importance. Chiana turned a straight chair around before her favorite mirror, straddling the chair as if it was her black horse. Sunlight glinted off the gold and carnelians scattered around her armor and helm. As she nodded graciously to her imagined armies, the stag at her brow seemed eager to vault mountains.

"Mama! Mama!"

Furious, she jumped out of the chair as the chamber door swung open. Who had given Rinhoel permission to come in here? But when had he ever waited for permission to do anything? Her anger evaporated and she reveled in the child's beauty. Not even Ianthe's sons could have been so like their grandsire. Rinhoel was tall for being not quite seven winters old, lanky but strong. His hair was night-black, his eyes pure green without a hint of hazel; his kinship to Roelstra was as obvious in his looks as it was every time he opened his mouth. She caught him in her arms and he reached for the stag on her helm.

"No, greedy one, don't ruin Mama's armor!" She set him down hastily and went to kick the door shut. "Have you escaped your squires and tutors again?"

"They wanted me to read boring things," he informed her. "I don't need to read at all, Mama. I hate it and I'm a prince and people will read to me when I order them!"

"True," she admitted, taking off the helm to let her hair cascade down her back. "But often there are messages you won't want anyone to know about. That's why you must learn to read well and quickly, my own. You wouldn't want to depend on someone else to read to you what must be kept secret." She had a sudden idea, and, being a mother intensely concerned with her son's education, she acted on it at once. Turning the straight chair around again, she said, "Rinhoel, shall I tell you a secret?"

"Yes! Tell me now!"

He claimed the hand she held out to him and suffered himself to be lifted onto her lap. She watched their reflections in the mirror. "Mama is going away tomorrow for a little while."

"Where?" he demanded. "To battle? Is that why you're dressed like a soldier? I want to come!"

"Not yet, darling. But very soon. While I'm gone, I'll send you letters every day and tell you everything that's happening. You wouldn't want anyone else to read them, would you?"

"They'll be secret?"

"Of course. From everyone but us. Between a princess and her princely son there are no secrets." It was amazing how much pleasure the titles still brought her.

"But you weren't going to tell me you were going."

"I would have this evening if you hadn't burst in on me all unmannerly." She squeezed him. "Look in the mirror, Rinhoel. Can you see yourself wearing this same kind of armor, riding a beautiful big horse into Castle Crag?"

"I don't want Castle Crag, I want Dragon's Rest."

Chiana told herself that naturally a little boy would desire a place he had seen rather than one he had not. Her official excuse for bringing him with her to the last *Rialla* had been that she could not bear to be parted from him. True enough. But it was another secret between them, solemnly sworn even though he had been only four years old, that she had shown him the palace halls and gardens whispering of the day Dragon's Rest would be his along with the rest of Princemarch.

"You will certainly own it soon. But remember that Castle Crag belonged to our ancestors for many generations, and we'll rule from there—the way your grandsire did and his grandsire before him."

"I'm not supposed to tell Father about this, am I?" he asked shrewdly.

"It'll be our secret, Rinhoel. Think how much fun it will be to receive my letters and know things that no one else does! So you must practice your reading all the time, my darling. Do you understand?"

"I'm not a baby."

"No, you're not. You're my prince, aren't you? And together we'll ride into Castle Crag—after we take Dragon's Rest, of course."

Rinhoel considered, then nodded acquiescence. He hopped off her lap and recovered the discarded helm. Chiana watched in delight as he put it on and marched back to her, wielding an imaginary sword.

"And *that* to Prince Pol and all Sunrunners!" he cried, thrusting toward her heart.

She applauded and together they laughed.

***

Swalekeep—like every other princely seat, all the major and a good many of the minor holdings—had a resident *faradhi*. But unlike most court Sunrunners, Vamanis usually had very little to do. There were other places where his kind were tolerated, and some where they were openly suspected. But no Sunrunner was so thoroughly ignored as Vamanis. He saw their graces of Meadowlord only when a message had come in from elsewhere, for tradition dictated that the Sunrunner speak directly to those he served. Prince Halian and Princess Chiana never used him for communication with other princes or with their own *athr'im*—which to Vamanis' way of thinking was surpassingly stupid. Why send couriers when one had a Sunrunner at hand? But they obviously did not trust him. Part of *faradhi* ethic was to respect the privacy of such communication no matter what it might be—although he had to admit that under young Lord Andry, that tradition was becoming as flexible as many others. There were things Vamanis swore Lord Andry could have known only because a court Sunrunner had broken the oath of secrecy. Vamanis' own training had been under Lady Andrade, and she had been a stickler for tradition. But convincing those at Swalekeep of his honor had proved impossible. Especially forbidden him was the usual Sunrunner duty of helping instruct the children of the house. So he rarely had anything to do.

Fortunately, he had other interests and resources. His mother had been a silversmith, his father a cook in their home city of Einar, and Vamanis exercised both talents when he wasn't exploring the countryside, idly courting several pretty women, reading, or conversing on sunlight with friends who lived anywhere from Snowcoves to Dorval. It was a pleasant life all in all, devoted to private pursuits. But after three years it was beginning to bore him. He had just completed his twenty-eighth winter, and his rings made him one of the elite of his world. There were many other things he could do with his life and he often felt as if his gifts were starting to rust. This summer he intended to petition Lord Andry for another posting, and let someone else enjoy this cushiony existence for a few years.

Vamanis was in the kitchens conferring with the pastry cook about a delicacy for that evening's meal when an abrupt message on the sunlight streaming through an open window caught his mind. In her characteristically brief, dignified, but friendly fashion, the High Princess requested that he inform Lord Barig of Gilad that the High Prince earnestly desired his presence at Stronghold. Vamanis paused an instant to savor the elegant pattern of Sioned's colors; he had seldom been touched by them, and her mastery and her glow were a rare treat. After promising to convey the request, he tendered his respects and sighed faintly with the loss of her. Now, there was a woman and then some, he told himself as he went to find Lord Barig.

Duty required that he inform Princess Chiana first. Thus he went upstairs and asked to be admitted to her private chambers. One of her squires arrogantly demanded to know his purpose. Vamanis was tempted to read the boy a lecture on the respect due Sunrunners, but then decided this was too minor a matter to stand on ceremony he hadn't much use for anyway. So he merely smiled and waited patiently while the squire took the request to his mistress.

Chiana saw him alone. She wore one of her plainer gowns and only a few of the diamonds she so adored and that her husband lavished on her. Vamanis noted that she had on a bracelet of twisting silver wires he had fashioned for her during his first year at Swalekeep, when he had still entertained hopes of being a real court Sunrunner instead of an ignored lackey.

"Your grace honors me," he said with a bow.

She saw the direction of his gaze. "Oh—you mean the bracelet," she replied, and he was reminded that she could be a surpassingly beautiful woman when she chose to smile. "Actually, I was about to send for you, Vamanis. But first tell me your news."

He did so, watched her slight frown, and then asked, "How may I be of service to your grace?"

"Service? Oh. I would have asked one of the resident crafters, but I was going through my jewels and was reminded how clever and delicate your work is. The frame of my mirror is ready to break. Can you fix it for me?"

If he had hoped for some *faradhi* task, he did not show his disappointment. He advanced to the mirror, admiring the workmanship. Somehow a piece of silver had been bent near to breaking, a section of vine that twisted down the left-hand side.

"Not too serious, your grace," he reported. "I'll have to remove this bit here to reshape it, then reattach the vine."

"But it can be repaired?"

"Of course." At least it would give him something to do. "I'll need my tools. With your grace's permission, I'll go fetch them and—"

Suddenly he could not speak, not even to cry out. It was as if something had trapped him inside his own skull and deprived him of all will and volition. He could see the princess in the mirror, her diamonds striking light like glass shards into his eyes. He could not even blink.

A word left his mouth, resonant and complex, a sound he could not have remembered or duplicated. Chiana froze instantly. And Vamanis suddenly knew what was being done to him. With him.

"Is everything prepared?" he heard his own voice ask.

"Everything," the princess answered.

"Everything in secrecy?"

"Everything," she repeated.

"Excellent. You have done well, Chiana, and soon you will have your heart's desire." Vamanis stared at the princess in the mirror.

"Soon," she said, eyes alight with eagerness.

"Remember none of this, as you remember nothing of our conversations. But you *will* remember to take the mirror with you."

"I will remember about the mirror."

A spasm took hold of his throat like a strangling fist. His eyes were abruptly blind, his senses opaque. Part of his mind screamed for help.

And a voice answered.

Heard of this technique, have you, Sunrunner? Using another's eyes and ears to observe is a faradhi *trick not taught to many. But I have actually used your voice. Impressive, don't you think?*

Oh, Goddess—the mirror—

Of course. A fortuitous little piece of damage to the frame, wasn't it? The voice, rich and gloating, laughed inside his mind. *You Sunrunners know certain things but by no means all. I see your face as clearly as you do, for I am indeed using your eyes. But you're looking flushed, Sunrunner. Feeling feverish and ill, aren't you? I think you are becoming very sick, and will remain so. And in your sickness you will not remember this as anything other than a fever dream.*

Monster! he screamed.

I? You faradh'im *are the monsters, perverting ancient knowledge, turning it soft and bloodless! Although I'll admit that this Lord Andry you don't entirely approve of has some interesting notions about power. You may rest easy, Sunrunner. He won't live long enough to carry them through. Return to your chamber now—you're feeling very, very ill, aren't you? You need to be alone and in the dark. The light hurts your eyes. You must stay out of the sunlight.*

Vamanis staggered against the mirror, toppling it and most of the princess' brushes and jars of makeup and scent. Heat raged through his whole body, a fever that set his very bones ablaze. Chiana's angry cry split his head open and he collapsed onto the fallen mirror.

"Get up! What's wrong with you?" The princess kicked him to one side and he groaned. "Clumsy idiot! You could have broken my mirror!"

He wasn't sure why, but he knew that the mirror could not remain whole. He reached for it, light reflecting off his rings like knives into his eyes as he fisted his hand.

Chiana's foot descended on his wrist. His eyes teared with frustration and failure, his fingers uncurling helplessly as the fever drowned him in darkness.

***

Chiana paced impatiently as her squire righted the mirror and assessed the damage. Only that one silver vine had needed mending before—she couldn't quite recall how it had been bent, but that hardly mattered; now the complex knotwork at the top had come loose. That lout of a Sunrunner would have much to answer for when he recovered from his sudden and mysterious illness. She had had him removed to his own chamber.

"Well?" she snapped.

"Intact, your grace, but for this bit here. I think it can be repaired by tomorrow evening, your grace."

"I won't be deprived of my favorite mirror for even

half that long. Fix it tonight. I don't care who you have to wake up to get the work done!"

"Yes, your grace. At once." The squire departed, the mirror borne carefully in his arms.

Chiana paced some more, fretting. She wanted that mirror with her when she left tomorrow morning. No need to live like a complete barbarian in the field—and when she occupied Dragon's Rest, it would be satisfying to put something of her own in Prince Pol's private suite.

"Chiana? What's the trouble here?"

She spun around as her husband entered the chamber. "A slight accident. Nothing to be alarmed about. But Vamanis damaged my beautiful mirror!"

"I'm sure it can be mended." Halian gestured and the squire bowed himself out. "The master of horse tells me you've ordered that Kadari mare saddled early tomorrow. Would you like some company?"

"How sweet of you, darling," she purred. "But you know how fond I've grown of a solitary ride now and then. It clears my head of all the wretched politics."

Duties he had no talent for, and that would have been utterly neglected if not for her. After years of wishing his aged father dead and burned, Halian had played at being prince for a little while and then gladly shoved the burdens onto her. That she had been more than willing to shoulder them did not counter her disgust at his laziness. There was much to be said for a prince's early death; it allowed a son to rule while still young and vigorous, before he had grown too accustomed to constant leisure and lack of power.

During his years of waiting for Clutha to die, Halian had become fond of horses, drink, his illegitimate daughters by a long-dead mistress, and some discreet wenching now and then. Had it been anything other than discreet, Chiana would have dealt with the women as her mother Lady Palila had done with her father's other mistresses. It was his total indifference to the wonderful son she had given him that really rankled, but she had learned to shrug it off. Though his dedication to his pleasures left her free to rule as she pleased, any respect she had ever had for him was gone. She had craved power all her life; Halian had lost the desire many years ago. Power was too much work.

"As you like, my love." He gave her an idle caress. "What was Vamanis doing in here?"

She had almost forgotten the Sunrunner's news. "The High Prince wants Barig at Stronghold. One can guess why." Even Halian would be able to figure that one out. "Lord Andry will have gone there after his stay at Feruche. Do you think they'll decide about this stupid Sunrunner there, or put it off until the *Rialla*?"

"Whichever, it really doesn't concern us."

She had not quite given up exasperation at his obtuseness. Would he never understand that everything that occurred in all the princedoms concerned them? But she had something else on her mind now, a possibility that had not previously occurred to her. Barig's cousin Prince Cabar disliked and distrusted the Desert and the Sunrunners; if Barig could be brought to support her in exchange for her support against Andry, then he might very well threaten Rohan with the Giladan armies in support of her claim to Princemarch. And with Gilad would come Grib. Cunaxa was already assured.

Could she convince Barig to her cause in a single evening?

Perhaps. Perhaps. At least she could hint at remarkable doings and suggest that he be ready to advise his prince in her favor. He was not a stupid man; he would comprehend that she intended to move.

She gave Halian a bright smile. "Of course it has nothing to do with us, dearest. Nothing at all."

Chapter Sixteen

Stronghold: 35 Spring

Feylin, Lady of Remagev and counter of dragons, loathed crowds. The entire population of Stronghold stood waiting in the hot sun, for Rohan had ordered up princely honors for Miyon's arrival from Tiglath. Not because the Cunaxan expected it, though he would—or deserved it, for he didn't—but because such display would be an unmistakable reminder to a man lacking in subtlety. Only a moron would fail to be impressed by the sight of the castle guard, wearing battle blue and harness, lining a pathway all the way through the tunnel into the main courtyard. Rohan's family and vassals, arranged in strict order of precedence on the main steps, were impressive in and of themselves.

The Lord and Lady of Remagev were of minor importance in terms of prestige, though few were closer personally to the High Prince. Walvis had been Rohan's squire and had, in fact, know him longer than Sioned had. But Remagev, once a holding in possession of Rohan's cousin who had died without heirs, was technically lower in rank than Tuath Castle or Faolain Lowland or Whitecliff, and certainly far below the crown jewel that was Radzyn. But though Walvis and Feylin had as little use for the protocol of position as their prince, standing on the fringes of the highborn assembly afforded a much better view. They could watch everything without being noticed, unlike Chay and Maarken and their wives, who were front and center and themselves the objects of many sharp eyes.

Feylin shifted her shoulder beneath the deep blue silk of her formal tunic. It was hot and she regretted the layers of clothing necessary for this absurd welcome as much as she begrudged the time it took away from her studies. When the dragon horn sounded, she was mentally reviewing statistics that had come in through Sunrunner means only that morning. The count of dragons this year was seventeen sires, eighty-five females, and sixty-three immature dragons not yet old enough for mating. Those numbers had held more or less steady for three cycles, reassuring her that the population had stabilized. But it was still dangerously low. And disaster had happened at Feruche two years ago, when five caves had collapsed. A total of only thirty-six caverns were now available there and near Skybowl—which meant that forty-nine of the females would die.

Feylin had worried at the problem until her wits ached, but there was only one solution: persuade the dragons back to Rivenrock with its one hundred seven lovely, spacious, *perfect* caves, unused since the Plague. Dragons had died by the hundreds then at Rivenrock and had shunned the place ever since. But if they did not return there or find other caves, their numbers would not increase to a level Feylin considered safe.

If they would only use Rivenrock, all eighty-five females would produce at least two and, with very good luck, four hatchlings each to fly from the caves. Call it three apiece, which would make it—

"Stop that," her husband whispered in her ear, startling her.

"Stop what? I wasn't doing anything."

"You're counting dragons on your fingers again." He tugged playfully at the dark red braid trailing down her back. "I'm willing to put up with your maps and anatomy diagrams at meals and even your muttered calculations while we're in bed—"

"I never!" Feylin exclaimed.

"You do so. As your sweet-natured, long-suffering, adoring husband, I'll endure your dragons most of the time, but the least you can do is pay attention to the arrival of your own children." He grinned down at her.

Feylin glanced around. The chamberlain was calling out Miyon's titles and all eyes were fixed on the gates, so she felt safe enough in giving Walvis her sweetest smile—and an elbow to the ribs. "*That* for your sweet nature!"

He grunted with the impact, a sound lost in the shouts

and cries that greeted Miyon's entrance. Feylin forgot dragons in the satisfaction of knowing that the people of Stronghold gave not a damn about the Cunaxan prince; they were welcoming Tallain, Riyan, Maarken's two children, and her own Sionell and Jahnavi.

She evaluated the familiar faces quickly. Tallain was wary beneath the bland facade which he did even better than Rohan, from whom he had learned it. Sionell was serene, but there was a strained look around her eyes. Riyan's tension showed only in his tight grip on the reins. Jahnavi was poised, alert, but innocent of the undercurrents disturbing the others. Grace notes were provided by Chayla and Rohannon—riding without lead reins, Feylin noted approvingly—who bounced excitedly on their ponies at being part of this grown-up spectacle. She saw Hollis direct a quelling look at the children and smiled when Chayla straightened up and kicked her brother into proper decorum that lasted all of two paces.

Miyon's expression was not as easy to read. He nodded amiably enough to the crowd, but his smile was a mere stretching of his lips and his eyes were black frost. Yet there was a sleek, smug look about him that puzzled Feylin. Rohan and Sioned wore their most charming aspects—a dead giveaway to anyone who knew them well. Fortunately, Miyon did not, and accepted their welcoming smiles as if he were returning in triumph to his own keep.

Feylin whispered as much to Walvis, who nodded. "He'd certainly *like* Stronghold for his own. I remember the first time he was here, years ago, he inspected things as if making mental notes on what he'd change when he took possession. Feylin, my love, did you have to poke me so hard?"

She reached an inconspicuous hand to rub his side. "Sorry. But you *will* be provoking. Jahnavi's grown—as usual! And Sionell looks lovely, doesn't she?"

"Worried," he said, blue eyes narrowing.

"Probably about Talya," Feylin responded, not believing it. "I wish she wasn't too young to make the journey from Tiglath."

"We'll go inflict ourselves on them for the summer. But I'm surprised Ell didn't stay behind with her."

"She must have had an excellent reason for coming along."

"And you'll have it out of her before dusk," Walvis murmured. "Tallain's a smart boy—you notice there's a soldier of his for every one of Miyon's? He's taking no chance that there's a Merida in the group."

The very mention of the Desert's enemies sent sparks into Feylin's eyes. Walvis saw it and tickled her nape with the end of her braid.

"Settle down and smile," he advised. "They'll be up here in a moment, and Jahnavi will think you're angry with him for not writing more often."

"Well, I am." But she smoothed her expression just the same.

Rohan and Sioned descended exactly one step to show respect for a fellow prince, spoke formal words of welcome, and gave the traditional wine cup which Feylin wished could have been laced with poison. Pol was duly greeted, then Andry. Protocol did not permit the introduction of vassals, not even the powerful Lord of Radzyn Keep, but Feylin almost succeeded in hiding a grin as Miyon recognized her husband. At barely nineteen, Walvis had commanded the Desert forces that had defeated the Merida in 704, and his prowess as a warrior was well known. Twenty-four years had put a little gray into his hair and beard, but had also added mature muscle and not a coinweight of excess flesh. There was a very simple reason for this: Remagev, aside from its fine goats and glass ingots, also produced soldiers trained personally and superbly by Walvis. And Miyon knew it.

Tallain had mounted the steps behind the Cunaxan prince, Riyan at his side. Sionell and Jahnavi were next, Chayla and Rohannon firmly in hand. But before Feylin and Walvis could greet their own offspring, the twins had broken free and were clambering all over Maarken and Hollis. The strict formality of the occasion was thus happily broken, and even Miyon chuckled.

It was then that Feylin saw the girl. Wearied by the long ride, looking as fragile as a windblown flower, still she was exquisite. Beneath a soft cap that protected her from the hot spring sun tumbled masses of pale golden hair, each strand a separate curl like spun sunlight. A delicate profile was turned away from the warm and easy welcomes exchanged between friends and family; the girl bit her lip as she was utterly ignored.

Sionell drew back from her father's embrace and turned, beckoning the girl up the steps. "This is Lady Meiglan of Gracine Manor. Meiglan, come meet my parents, Lord Walvis and Lady Feylin."

"I—I'm honored to meet you, my lord, my lady," the girl whispered.

"Welcome to Stronghold, my dear," Walvis said kindly.

Feylin pressed the girl's trembling, gloved hand. Her own Sionell looked as if she could ride another four days without feeling it, but this frail child ought to be tucked up in bed until tomorrow morning. "It's a long journey through the Desert from Tiglath—you must be exhausted."

"I am, a little," she admitted.

"You can go upstairs as soon as you've met their graces," Sionell said.

The girl shrank back, eyes lifting at last. They were velvety brown; with her golden coloring and dark eyes she resembled nothing so much as a terrified fawn. "Oh, no, please—not now, my lady!"

"Oh, come," Sionell encouraged with a bracing smile, "whatever you've heard about the High Prince's passion for dragons, he hasn't yet turned into one!"

"And neither," said Pol from behind Meiglan's shoulder, "have I."

The girl turned. Feylin could not see her face, but suddenly she saw Pol as a stranger must: a creature fashioned of sunlight. It glowed on his fair head, lit the planes and angles of his face, glinted off the tiny silver wreaths of Princemarch embroidered around the throat of his violet tunic, was outshone by his quick smile.

"Here you are at last," he said to Sionell. "But I'm disappointed. You didn't bring Talya with you."

"I see she managed to enchant you when you met her at Feruche," Sionell said with a smile. "But she's much too little for such a long trip, Pol."

"You look none the worse for it. Marriage and motherhood suit you perfectly, Ell. You've never been prettier."

Crumbs from the loaf, Feylin thought, exchanging a glance with Walvis, and was grateful that their daughter had never deluded herself into believing she could make a meal of them.

Sionell thanked him and gracefully introduced Meiglan. The girl said nothing as Pol bent over her wrist and welcomed her; Feylin kept one eye on him and the other on Sionell, and saw the same absolute self-possession in each. But there was something wrong here. She could sense it in every nerve.

Pol held Meiglan's hand between his, leaning over her solicitously. "Allow me to escort you out of this heat."

She nodded wordlessly and they went into the cool dimness of the foyer. An instant later Chayla and Rohannon clambered up Pol's legs, nearly toppling him. Having greeted and been made much of by everyone else, they now claimed their fair share of Pol's attention. He knelt to hug them, demanding to know what kind of trouble they had caused at Tiglath. Chayla gave an indignant squeal and Rohannon applied to Meiglan for witness that they had behaved perfectly.

At last the girl smiled. She bent slightly and murmured something Feylin didn't quite hear. Rohannon told Pol, "See? Lady Meiglan says so. We went to bed on time and we were very good and didn't bother anybody. Talya was the one who kept waking everybody up—and Lady Meiglan, that night she had her dream."

The girl's cheeks turned scarlet and her whole body stiffened. A frown quirked Sionell's brows. And the sudden crack of Prince Miyon's voice through the foyer shocked everyone so much that after his first word, all was silence.

"Meiglan! Why are you still here? You're filthy. Go upstairs at once!"

She cringed back, as white-faced now as she had been crimson a moment before. Chayla and Rohannon actually jumped. Pol stood, a flash of irritation swiftly banished from his eyes with obvious effort. Before he could say anything, Sionell stepped smoothly into the breach.

"It's my fault for lingering, your grace. After that long ride the thought of all those stairs is a little daunting." She distributed smiles all around, then took Meiglan's arm and drew her toward Rohan and Sioned. The girl stumbled slightly, frozen with terror that made her look even more like a frightened fawn. "May I present Lady Meiglan of Gracine Manor to your graces? And I must apologize again, Prince Miyon, for not allowing you the introduction of your daughter."

Rohan and Sioned were too experienced to show any

startlement, and calmly made the girl welcome. Pol was younger. For an instant he simply appeared stunned.

Usually Feylin found people about half as interesting as dragons. But she could add up words and looks as well as statistics, and the sum made little Lady Meiglan very interesting indeed. She saw the girl upstairs and into her chamber with her maid in attendance, then firmly claimed her daughter's arm and walked her down the long hallway toward her own rooms.

"Your explanation," Feylin said. "Now."

"You're not going to like it," Sionell murmured.

"I already don't like it."

Sionell shrugged and went to a little alcove overlooking the bustle of the courtyard. The third-floor corridor was deserted but for the guard near the stairs; all the servants were busy fetching and carrying down below. Seating herself on a low wooden bench carved with dragons, she looked up at her mother. "As nearly as I can tell, Miyon has a very interesting plot going."

"And that child has something to do with it?"

Sionell gave a quiet sigh. "She has everything to do with it."

When her explanation was over, Feylin gave a low whistle between her teeth. "My, my," she said. "How did I ever come to have such a clever daughter?"

***

Sionell went down early to the Great Hall. The servants, still setting the tables, gave her a few curious glances, and she busied herself with the flowers as an excuse for being there.

Early evening light shone through the window wall onto silver from Fessenden, crystal from Firon, and delicate ceramic plates from Kierst. All very impressive, Sionell thought sourly. Rohan hadn't missed a trick.

Neither had Miyon. Pol already felt sorry for Meiglan—who, when Sionell had visited her briefly a little while ago, was still in partial shock at seeing the man from her dream made real. But Miyon had not reckoned on Sionell, who was determined that Meiglan would *not* present Pol with a lonely little figure trembling in a corner.

"I can't make her clever," she had explained to her mother, "and I can't turn her into a sparkling wit. But nobody could look pathetic partnered at dinner or in dancing by Tallain or Maarken or Riyan."

She consulted the servants about the seating plan at the high table and was appalled to discover that no order had been given to put Meiglan there.

"Set another place at once," she said.

"But, my lady, I've had no word from her grace—"

"With all that her grace has to do, it's not surprising that it slipped her mind, is it? Please see to the extra place immediately."

When the squires arrived—Arlis, Edrel, and her own brother Jahnavi would be serving the high table tonight—she gave specific instructions about who was to be seated where. They blinked a little at her rearrangements, but only Jahnavi drew her aside and leveled their father's piercing blue eyes on her.

"I know you, Ell," he said flatly. "You're up to something."

"Don't be silly. Nobody thought to seat Meiglan at the high table."

He made a face. "Somebody's heard what a charming dinner partner she is."

"And don't be nasty, either. Or a snob. She can't help it if she's shy."

"There's shy—and then there's boring. All right, all right," he said hastily as her brows rushed together in a frown. "But I still say it's a dirty trick to foist her off on Riyan and your own poor husband for the evening."

"She knows them well enough to talk to them. And with her father halfway down the table, she might even relax and enjoy herself."

"Don't make any bets. It took her all that time at Tiglath to say six words at meals. And this is Stronghold. I mean, look at the place."

Sionell was familiar with its elegance and splendor, but to Meiglan this castle would seem stupendous. Sionell fussed with the flowers, telling herself that at least the girl would not be cowering all alone at one of the lower tables. And with distance between her and her father, at a table populated by people she already knew, Miyon could not possibly humiliate her.

Sionell had reckoned without Miyon's grasp of strategy. He totally ignored his daughter all during the meal.

It was as if she did not exist, sitting between Tallain and Riyan in her soft pink gown with its high lace collar. Sionell wore a vibrant shade of green that not even Sioned could wear; the bold coloring and dark red hair bequeathed by Feylin allowed her more vivid hues than Sioned's fire-gold looks could support. But she knew the instant she saw Meiglan that the green gown had been a mistake. More delicate and fawnlike than ever, she made Sionell feel like a plow-elk.

But if Miyon had decided that his daughter did not exist, Pol was fully aware of the fact; frequent glances down to her end of the table proved it. He had to lean over his plate to catch sight of her. Sionell began to wonder if it had been adequately impressed on him exactly who the girl was.

"He must know she's impossible," Feylin had said that afternoon.

"He's not stupid, Mother. But no one must *tell* him she's impossible, or he'll think up a dozen reasons why she isn't. I can think of one right now—that an alliance would end the disharmony between the Desert and Cunaxa. Miyon could scarcely continue to support the Merida if his daughter is Pol's wife."

Pol's wife. The words echoed in her mind as she intercepted yet another glance from those blue-green eyes. She smiled and fingered the sapphires around her neck—present at Antalya's birth—as if thanking him once more for them. But he barely noticed.

Tallain, however, did. "You're wasting your time, my love," he whispered.

"What are you talking about?"

"It's impossible to distract a man from the source of his distraction." Tallain shook his head. "He's being painfully obvious about it, isn't he?"

"Disgustingly so." She signaled Jahnavi to serve her another pastry.

"Don't worry. She's lovely, of course, but Pol isn't a fool."

"Most men are fools when it comes to such things." She gave him a sidelong smile. "You certainly were."

"I still am. And you know it. Shall we be foolish together and shatter precedent by dancing only with each other instead of everybody else?"

"Oh, you'll have to lead poor Meiglan out once or twice to start her off. If Chay or even Maarken is the first to ask her, she'll faint with the shock."

"I suppose so. Ell, are you by any chance concealing something from me?"

She froze with her laden fork halfway to her mouth and stared at him. "I beg your pardon?"

He gestured to the pastry. "We stopped for something to eat on the road today, so you can't be starving to death. And the *last* time you devoured everything in sight. . . ." He trailed off, one brow arching.

"When was—oh!" She blushed. "No, I'm not." Then, rallying from her momentary shock, she laughed and added, "Though it's not from lack of trying!"

Tallain gave a modest shrug. "I'm compelled to admit it, in consciousness of duty done—"

"Idiot," she accused fondly.

"Well, I try." He grinned. "But in the meantime, if you're not eating for two, then stop eating!"

She made a face and finished off the pastry. But when Jahnavi came to pour taze, she shook her head to the sweets that accompanied it. Regretfully; nowhere but at Dragon's Rest and Castle Crag did one taste such marvels as spice seeds wrapped in candied fruit and covered in caramelized sugar.

Between courses various musicians had appeared singly, but now the whole household orchestra assembled. As servants moved the lower tables out of the way, many of Stronghold's retainers took up instruments. Rohan's mother had pleaded for years with his father to hire a suite of musicians, but Zehava's reply had always been that he did not intend to support twenty or thirty parasites. Rohan was of the same mind. So music at Stronghold was provided not by professionals but by the castlefolk themselves. The quality of the entertainment had never suffered for it. As a lively tune began to set feet tapping, Sionell gave her husband a pointed look.

He grinned again, but obeyed her overt hint and asked Meiglan to dance. The girl blanched, stammered, and was not permitted to refuse. Riyan, without prompting, claimed a dance for himself after Tallain. Seeing her thus securely launched, Sionell leaned back and sipped her taze, satisfied.

The Cunaxan prince might ignore his daughter, but nobody else would.

Rohan partnered Lady Ruala while Sioned did her duty by Miyon. Andry led his sister-by-marriage into the set. Sionell found herself claimed by Maarken, who, having eyes, had noticed Pol's preoccupation.

"Your little friend is quite a success," he told her when the figure allowed him close enough to whisper in her ear. "Watch—Pol will be next."

Pol was indeed casting impatient looks at Meiglan while he exchanged the bows and gestures of the dance with Tobin. Sionell glanced around at the other highborn women in the Great Hall—beautiful, vibrant, confident women, sure of themselves and their worth. Despite the damage done by Miyon's deliberate cruelties, Meiglan could not help but learn from their example. And, indeed, she made a pretty picture, guided gracefully through the steps by Tallain, her pink gown swirling.

But Pol did not vie with Riyan for the second dance. He surrendered his aunt to her younger son and made directly for Sionell.

It was a slow tune requiring a half-embrace that, with a partner one desired, could become more than mildly flirtatious. Sionell put her fingertips on Pol's shoulders and looked him straight in the eye. Part of her would always respond to him. But she was no longer a lovestruck child.

His first words to her as they glided across the blue and green tiles shattered her notions of his good sense.

"Tell me about Lady Meiglan."

Subtle as ever, she thought. "What did you want to know?"

"Everything."

"She's very young, very beautiful, and very innocent. But you can see that with your own eyes."

"Do you like her?"

"Yes."

"Do you trust her?"

"As far as anyone Desert-born and Desert-bred trusts any Cunaxan."

Pol frowned.

The dance called for a flirtatious "escape"; Sionell's hands slid down Pol's arms until she was poised lightly at his fingertips, connected to him only by that tentative touch.

"Miyon will use anyone and anything to get what he wants." She made the required crossover step to her left; Pol countered, blocking her. As the movement was repeated to the right, she added, "What he wanted this spring was to come to Stronghold."

"And here he is," Pol said.

Her wrists were grasped and she was drawn in close once more. "Yes. Here he is."

"And Meiglan with him. How do you think he'd react if I showed interest in her?"

"I think he's counting on it," she said bluntly.

"So do I." He spun her around twice so that her green gown flared, then stood behind her with his hands on her waist again. "But I don't think he's counting on *her* reaction to *me*."

Sionell gave him a startled glance over her shoulder. "Why, you vain, self-centered, conceited—"

Pol only laughed. "Don't be redundant, Ell!"

For an instant as the dance ended he pulled her back against him. Then he surrendered her to his father before sauntering over to claim Meiglan right out from under Chay's nose.

"He's making a complete fool of himself," Rohan muttered as a country dance began. "After Tilal and Kostas fought over Gemma, he told me to kick him if he displayed the same imbecility. I have the feeling my boot will connect with his backside rather soon."

Sionell picked up her skirts to execute quick, complicated steps, then placed her hands once more in his. "He knows she's unsuitable and that Miyon brought her here on purpose."

"Did he tell you as much?" When she nodded, he smiled. "You made very sure he realized it, didn't you? Good girl. Still . . . I wonder."

The ladies again separated from their partners for individual footwork. This was Sionell's favorite dance and she was very good at it. But as she whirled around she caught sight of Meiglan, frozen in place and mortified by her lack of knowledge. Pol wore his most charming smile as he demonstrated the steps. The girl hardly dared breathe.

Sionell was a little late in clasping Rohan's fingers again. He was adroit in covering the mistake and, mercifully, said nothing.

Miyon beckoned several of his servants to him as the dance ended. A gesture had them clearing a space at the end of the Great Hall, only ten or so paces from the huge doors. Tables were pushed against the side walls, chairs were stacked atop them, and into the area thus provided was brought an immense stringed instrument.

"Knowing Prince Pol's fondness for music," he said with a silken smile, "I thought he might enjoy listening to our Cunaxan *fenath*." Then, imperiously, "Meiglan!"

Sionell's fists clenched on the folds of her gown as the girl turned white. Exhausted by the long ride, stunned at recognizing Pol as the man in her dream, edgy with the strain of a formal dinner in the Great Hall of Stronghold, and humiliated by her ignorance of dancing, the last thing the girl needed was a command to perform on this huge and aptly named "string wall." Sionell was furious with herself for underestimating Prince Miyon.

Meiglan moved woodenly toward the instrument, walking the entire length of the chamber from the high table where everyone had resumed their chairs, the eyes of a hundred and more servants and retainers on her from where they stood along the walls. She approached the harp, hesitating, then circled around it so she faced the high table.

The instrument was obviously an expensive one; Sionell could see that even though she knew next to nothing about music. The frame was made of polished Cunaxan pine inlaid with gold and enamelwork, the tuning pegs decorated with pearlshell. Higher at one end than the height of a very tall man and narrowing to barely an arm's length, it rested on a cushioned stand that elevated the shorter end and kept its strings in reach. But it was still wider than anyone's outstretched arms and looked impossible to play.

Meiglan checked the tuning, nodded to herself, and drew six slim little hammers from a velvet pouch hung at the tallest end of the harp. Arranging them between her fingers, three to each hand, she cast an anxious glance toward the high table and bit her lip.

Miyon let the silence drag out, then said, "In times past, the *fenath* would be tuned to a single chording and set outside for the wind to play. Most people now use the lowest strings for one chord, the middle for another, and the high for yet a third."

Andry nodded. "It was also used before a battle."

Raised brows greeted this piece of information. "You know about the *fenath*, my lord?"

Andry gave a half-smile. "It was left at the top of a windy hill and tuned to a terrible assonance that scraped enemy nerves raw. I'm confident that the Lady Meiglan will show us its gentler music."

"Certainly. There is no battle being waged here." Miyon showed his teeth. Then he snapped his fingers at his daughter. "Begin!"

A few notes ventured timidly into the silent Hall, trembling with the tremor of Meiglan's hands. Another chord, struck wrong—then suddenly there was a ripple of music, sweet and clear as new rain down a green hillside creek. The tune danced around and beneath and through an undercurrent of delicate chords. Meiglan began to sway gently back and forth as the notes flowed from strings low and high, skirts swinging in time to her music.

A breathless enchantment equal to a Sunrunner's power darted through the evening air. Beyond the strings and the swift, graceful hands Meiglan's face was glowing, soft, fully alive. Some women might save a face such as this for a lover, for a coveted jewel, for a dream fulfilled, for a life's passion. Thus did Sioned's eyes shine when they rested on her husband, or when she wove sunlight for the sheer joy of the flight. *Faradh'im* knew what spells they cast and the effects of their art. This girl had no consciousness of anyone but herself. A small aloneness was Meiglan, an isolated island of solitary magic.

A slow movement tugged Sionell's gaze around. Pol had risen to his feet, hands braced on the table, body canted slightly forward. His lips were parted and his eyes were fixed on the slender, swaying form that brought forth such music, such incredible music.

The strings sang one last graceful chord, ending with a single high, pure note.

"My precious treasure," Miyon said, smiling.

Chapter Seventeen

Castle Crag: 30 Spring

Late for an appointment with her steward, Alasen hurried down the hall from the nursery. Dannar was teething, and reacted to the usual salves with roars of outrage that turned his comical little face redder than his hair. The only sure way of settling him down was a song from his father, but Ostvel had already been up half the night with the child so the rest of the castle could get some sleep. Their youngest possessed a truly remarkable set of lungs and wasn't shy about using them.

"I'm getting too old for this," Ostvel had sighed when he finally came to bed at dawn. "At least the girls waited until they could walk before they started running the keep. It can't just be that he's male—Riyan never screeched like that."

Alasen's talk with the steward was directly related to the screeching; there had to be *someone* else at Castle Crag who could sing Dannar to sleep. She rounded a corner and started for the stairway, then broke into a run as she heard her daughters' voices in excellent imitation of their little brother.

The shrieks that echoed to the rafters did not unduly alarm her, for giggles soon followed. But she knew her girls and was positive that disaster was imminent for some part of the keep. Camigwen and Milar were themselves indestructible, as last winter's exploit involving a chandelier and a ladder had proved.

Now, instead of two small figures swinging merrily from a ceiling fixture, Alasen was presented with an impromptu sledding party on the stairs. A gigantic silver bowl meant to hold an entire night's portion of soup had been pressed into service. The handles were gripped in

Jeni's determined fists as she shot head first toward the landing at breakneck speed, Milar clinging to her back like a leech. Alasen was relieved to see they had piled dozens of pillows against the wall to cushion the impact, which was still considerable enough to knock the breath out of them. Pillow seams split and feathers flew like snowflakes.

"Again!" Milar cried from the middle of the blizzard.

"Once more here, then we'll try the circle stairs." Jeni sorted out arms and legs, brushed herself off, and hefted the bowl. As she turned to make the climb again, she saw her mother.

Alasen was trying very hard not to laugh. Guilty faces decorated in feathers, they were adorable. Besides, the wild ride had looked like terrific fun.

"The circle stairs, hmm?" she asked.

"We didn't hurt anything, Mama," Jeni hastened to explain. "That's why the pillows. And we didn't even dent the bowl. See?" She hefted it up for inspection.

Milar chimed in with, "You said be 'specially quiet today so Papa can sleep after being up all night with Dannar, so we picked stairs where he wouldn't hear us."

Alasen bit her lip. The incident this winter had been explained with the excuse that, having been told not to disturb their papa's peace, they had chosen to climb a chandelier in a chamber on the other side of the castle from his library.

Jeni added, "This was just a test, really. We could go much faster on the circle stairs."

"I daresay you could." Alasen bit her lip, then glanced around. No one had appeared in response to their gleeful shrieks, but that wasn't surprising. Previous escapades had seen half a dozen servants successfully bribed beforehand. She wondered briefly what Milar, the more conniving of the pair, had thought up this time, then gave in and grinned down at her daughters. "Shall we go try it out?"

If Donato was shocked to encounter a Princess of Kierst and her daughters hurtling down a staircase in a serving bowl, he gave no sign. When they tumbled to a laughing halt two paces from him—with predictably disastrous consequences to the pillows piled there—he helped them up and brushed them off with perfect aplomb.

"Do you want to try?" Milar offered. "It's almost as good as the snow this winter."

"Perhaps another time, my lady," Donato replied courteously, plucking feathers from her pale brown hair.

Alasen recognized a certain look in the *faradhi*'s eyes and all the fun went out of the morning. "I think you'd better take this back now," she told Jeni. "Your lessons are *supposed* to begin immediately after breakfast."

"Mama!" both girls wailed.

"Do I have to call someone to escort you? Go on. Oh—and on your way find Iavol and tell him I'll see him before noon. Hurry, now!"

They left dejectedly, the bowl dragged along between them. Donato watched them go, a fond smile on his face.

"Goddess help the men who try to tame them," he murmured.

"Ostvel says we'll have to find each a nice, calm, tolerant husband with an excellent sense of humor. But that's many years ahead of us, and you didn't come looking for me to discuss Jeni and Milar. What's wrong?"

Donato touched her elbow. "In private, my lady."

Really worried now by his request for privacy—for through the years Pandsala's servants had been replaced by trusted people loyal only to Ostvel and Alasen—she stayed silent until they had climbed back up the circular stairs to the oratory. Thick, heavy fog formed another wall a finger's breadth beyond the glass, blocking the view of the Faolain gorge below. Alasen seated herself on one of the chairs, folded her hands, and waited for Donato to speak.

"This fog came up quickly, didn't it?" he said. "It was clear last night."

"And what did you see on moonlight that you've been thinking about ever since?"

"My lady, I've been trying to puzzle something out all night. I waited to consult you, hoping the fog would lift and I could get a clearer look by sunlight, but—" He shrugged. "You know that I keep regular watch on all Princemarch's holdings and take a look at the borders every so often as well."

She nodded. Donato's observations were occasionally very useful—for instance, when he caught Geir of Waes in a little smuggling off the coastline three years ago.

Ostvel was bothered by what he thought of as spying, but Alasen quashed his doubts with the simple logic that people who had nothing to hide would never even know they had been seen.

"It may be nothing." Donato shrugged uneasily and sat down across the aisle from her. "But—has Ostvel or his grace authorized any military exercises around Rezeld?"

"Ostvel has not," she replied with total confidence. "I doubt if Prince Pol has, either. How many troops and horses are we discussing here?"

"The manor can stable twenty horses and could conceivably pack about a hundred extra people into the hall for sleeping." He hesitated. "Alasen, camped in the fields nearby were at least three hundred, possibly more. I can't think where they'd be keeping the horses—in the woods, perhaps. And if they've bows and spears, they're as hidden as the horses. I won't be sure until I can get a better look."

"What about banners, colors of any kind?"

"None. I'm not familiar with how one prepares for war. We'll have to ask Ostvel what else I should look for when I go back."

Alasen frowned. "Who could Morlen be thinking of warring *against*? Surely not us. Castle Crag is impenetrable. And not Dragon's Rest, either. That would be ludicrous. It would take twice three hundred soldiers and then some even to make the attempt. If there were brigands to be chased out of the mountains again, he'd apply to us for help while Pol's at Stronghold—and to you as a Sunrunner, to let him know where they're hiding."

"It makes very little sense, my lady—unless Morlen has the assurance of more troops from someone."

Alasen rose. "I'm going to talk to Ostvel about this. Donato, keep alert for any break in the fog. If it doesn't clear by noon, then we'll have to send you out in search of some usable sunlight."

He contemplated the swirling gray outside the oratory wall. "I hope this really is fog up from the river and not a cloud hugging the ground. Otherwise I'd have to ride all the way to the top of Whitespur."

Ostvel was fast asleep, snoring gently. Alasen paused a moment, urgent worry fading a little as the familiar tenderness crept through her. His dark hair was going gray and the lines carved on his face by twenty years in the Desert were deeper, but in slumber he looked nearly her own age. His sensitive mouth curved softly, its almost vulnerable lines belied by the strong bones of brow and nose and cheek bequeathed to their son. Not a beautiful face as masculine beauty was usually reckoned, but a face she had grown to love very much.

"Ostvel," she whispered, brushing the hair from his forehead. "Dearest, I'm sorry to wake you, but we must talk."

He grunted and rolled away from her touch. She shook his shoulder.

"Ostvel!"

"Go 'way," he muttered, hunching into the quilts.

"What a welcome for your loving wife," she chided. Climbing onto the bed, she knelt at his back and tickled his nape with one finger. "Come on, I know you're awake."

"If you were a loving wife, you'd let me sleep." He flopped onto his back and glared up at her. "Better still, you'd teach our pest of a son some manners, so I could sleep nights like the honest, hardworking *athri* I am. Very well, I'm awake. What is it?"

She told him.

"Damn." He flung back the quilt and strode to the dressing room. Alasen followed, demanding to know what he thought he was doing.

"We can't wait for the fog to lift," he explained as he pulled his warmest clothes from the closets. "Donato and I will have to ride up Whitespur now, as soon as possible."

"But why? I know the activity at Rezeld is suspicious, but— "

"It fits in with a few other puzzling things I've noticed this last year." His head disappeared for a moment beneath a thick knitted-wool shirt. "Why, for instance, Morlen has asked Pol to secure him a quantity of iron at the *Rialla* bargaining this year. He says he wants to reinforce Rezeld using the new techniques devised at Feruche and perfected at Dragon's Rest—but how could he do that without tearing down his whole keep? My guess is that he's going to need replacement iron for things he's melted down to make spears and arrowtips for this little comedy."

"Ostvel!"

"Hand me those other leggings, will you, my love? Moths have been at these. There's something else. Chadric wrote of a curious circumstance in a letter recently. Someone contracted for a great deal of silk. It was a huge order and he filled it, of course, at a tidy profit. But once it reached Radzyn, it vanished before the shipping duties were paid."

"Lord Chaynal never mentioned—"

"It would have shown up on the account books only at next New Year. I doubt he's had the time or inclination to do his bookkeeping recently." Ostvel stamped his feet into his riding boots and reached for a heavy tunic. "Chadric thought the colors involved might interest me."

Alasen frowned. "Not Rezeld's colors."

"Indeed not. Cunaxan orange. And Merida brown and yellow."

She stared at him. He gave her a tight smile and bent to kiss her.

"Why would one need so vast a quantity of silk? Summer tunics, of course. For an army. Moreover, an army heading for the lower Desert. Cunaxan wool would kill them quicker than Desert swords."

Alasen found her voice again. "Why didn't you *tell* me this?"

"Because none of it fit before now." He hesitated as he pulled on his gloves. "Even after nine years with you, I suppose I'm still in the habit of fretting on my own. Forgive me."

She nodded, and that was the end of the issue. "Go have the horses saddled. I'll find Donato and while he's getting dressed I'll have the kitchens put together a meal."

Ostvel took her waist in his hands. "Have I told you recently—"

"That I'm wonderful?" She smiled. "Just bring yourself back in one piece, my lord, or I'll have your teeth for tunic buttons."

***

Ostvel had spent his early youth at Goddess Keep and his first wife had been *faradhi*, so he was as intimately familiar with the process of weaving sunlight as anyone not gifted could be. He knew what kind of light was needed, and how much, and for how long. So when

Donato would have stopped halfway up Whitespur to risk a Sunrunning, Ostvel forbade it.

"That cloud over there would trap you before you'd gone past Castle Crag. Don't be an idiot."

"The more I think about all this, the more I want to hurry and the more nervous I get."

"Which is precisely why you need a nice, strong fall of sunlight."

Donato squinted at the snowfield ahead. "You're going to make me ride through that muck, aren't you?" He sighed and stroked the neck of the sturdy little mountain pony beneath him. "At least we're not on those great fire-eaters Lord Chaynal gave you."

The uncertain gray light muted the brilliance of the snowy peak rising up before him. What had been torrential winter rains in the lowlands had covered the Veresch in the heaviest snow within living memory. Castle Crag had become a glistening fantasy in ice, silent until the children had discovered that this strange frozen stuff they usually saw only on mountaintops was tremendous if chilly fun. But all was eerily quiet now, except for the crunch of broad hooves on snow and soft exhalations that sent clouds into the frosty air.

It was noon and they were nearly at the top of Whitespur before both Ostvel and Donato were satisfied with the sunshine. They refreshed themselves with a bite to eat and some wine, huddling beside their ponies for warmth. Then Donato faced east, toward Rezeld Manor.

Ostvel saw his eyes go blank, unfocused. How many hundreds of times had he watched a Sunrunner at work? Chances were that he himself possessed a glimmer of the gift; his elder son was a *faradhi* trained and skilled, and whereas eight years old was young to show the signs, last summer Jeni had flatly refused to join a sailing party on the Faolain. Ostvel was pleased that at least two of his children were gifted. He had always wondered what it might be like to weave light, to fly without dragon wings, to revel in the flush of power through body and heart and mind. But he had also seen what possession of the gift had done to Alasen, the pain and terror that had taken years to fade. And he had also seen Sionell's anguish that her lack had rendered her an unsuitable match for Pol, even if he had ever noticed her as a woman. Ostvel had always honored and valued *faradhi* powers in his youth; ambivalence about them had crept slowly into his mind, beginning the night Sioned had almost killed Ianthe using those powers.

Donato stumbled suddenly against the pony's shoulder. Ostvel steadied him, knowing better than to distract him with questions before he had fully returned. In a moment the Sunrunner had caught his breath. He chafed his gloved fingers, looking stunned.

"They're all gone! It's like nothing was ever there!"

"You mean they've marched."

"I mean there's no sign of the encampment I saw last night! No scars of cookfires on the ground, no hoofprints, no evidence." He shook his head. "Ostvel, I saw what I saw last night."

"Look again," was the grim reply.

It took a few moments. Meeting Ostvel's gaze again, he kneaded his laced fingers together to warm them. His voice was expressionless as he said, "Lord Morlen's lady is in the courtyard with her daughter. They're standing in front of a mirror combing their hair dry. The servant holding the mirror steady is Fironese. The little boy holding the hair ornaments is trying not to drop them—it's all bloody *nothing!*" he spat. "What I saw last night is gone!"

Ostvel paced a few stiff steps away in the snow. All at once he looked back over his shoulder. "Why are you rubbing your hands?"

"It's cold."

"Not that cold. What's wrong with your hands, Donato?"

The Sunrunner pulled off one glove with his teeth. His fingers were shaking. "Sweet Goddess," he whispered. "They feel burned."

"Sorcery." The word hissed in the white quiet of the mountainside. "You slammed right into it. *Faradh'im* work with sunlight by day—no need for this by night, not with all the clouds and the moons rising so short a time." He kicked one booted foot into the snow. "But there's sun over Rezeld today."

"It's impossible. They couldn't hide a whole army—"

"Then perhaps you were only dreaming last night," Ostvel growled, knowing very well Donato had not. "How do we know what they can and can't do? Andry himself admits that Lady Merisel didn't tell everything she knew in the scrolls. The point is, we've got to get word to Rohan. From Rezeld to Dragon's Rest—"

Donato interrupted. "Pol is his own Sunrunner. He's at Stronghold. There's nobody at Dragon's Rest to warn."

"They'll have to send a messenger through the mountains, then. And a small troop with him to see that the news gets there. Contact Sioned at once."

While Donato obeyed, Ostvel paced. He could not imagine life without *faradh'im,* but in the end they were useless against those who understood their limitations.

Donato was pale and drawn by the time he returned from Stronghold. But he was also angry. "I couldn't find her. Andry was the one who answered. He said she's otherwise occupied. But I told him everything." His lips twisted. "He assured me he'll inform Sioned—but I know he didn't believe a word."

Ostvel nodded slowly. "Somehow that doesn't surprise me." Donato was one of the old guard, like Morwenna, who had chosen service elsewhere rather than continue residence at Goddess Keep and watch *faradhi* traditions shatter. It was no secret that Andry wanted his own representatives at all courts. Several years ago he'd sent a young woman to be Donato's second; though pleasant in her person and quite skilled, she was so obviously loyal to Andry that Ostvel had wasted no time in packing her back to Goddess Keep with a polite but firm refusal of the offer. The episode had insulted Donato, irritated Ostvel, mortified the rejected Sunrunner, and infuriated Andry.

"I saw what I saw," Donato repeated stubbornly.

"Perhaps he *did* believe you, and chose not to indicate it," Ostvel mused.

Donato's jaw dropped slightly. "Wherever else his ambitions might lead him, he could hardly want the destruction of Dragon's Rest!"

Ostvel only grunted.

The Sunrunner thumbed one of his rings nervously. "Are you going to tell me about these? Why they hurt?"

"Not now. But thank the Goddess for it, my old friend," he said more gently, trying to ease Donato's eventual shock when he learned he, too, had *diarmadhi* blood.

After helping Donato onto his pony, he mounted and

they rode down the mountain, back into the fog that still blanketed Castle Crag. He saw the *faradhi* to his chambers for a well-earned rest, then climbed up to the oratory and stared out at the gray mist. Eventually he almost smiled. Sorcery might have disguised whatever was happening or had happened at Rezeld, but Ostvel would need no magic to hide what he was about to do.

Only a short while later he stood beside Dannar's cradle, watching the boy sleep. He stroked one finger lightly over bright red hair, remembering when Riyan had been this small, this defenseless. His paternal reverie was broken by a smile as Dannar's sleeping face screwed up in a terrible grimace.

"Ah, now, none of that, my lad," he whispered. "You must be very good while I'm gone, and let people sleep nights."

The mere sound of his voice settled the child, and a great yawn was followed by a drowsy mumble. Ostvel tugged unnecessarily at the blanket—a gift from Rohan and Sioned, woven in Desert blue and Princemarch's violet to signify his relationship to both, with a touch of Kierstian scarlet around the edges to honor Alasen. So much royal heritage wrapped around so small a child. . . . He smiled again. Camigwen had always accused him of being a perfect shatter-shell around babies.

A soft voice behind him made him turn. "Everything's ready."

"Thank you." He did not need to ask if Alasen had accomplished it all in secret. "If anyone asks—"

"Donato is indisposed and you're out checking the herds again after the winter rains," she finished for him.

They left the nursery and went to their own rooms. Donato and two male guards waited there, dressed warmly and carrying small satchels. Ostvel accepted his own pack from Alasen, then turned to his escort.

"I trust you or you wouldn't be here," he said simply. The guards gave him brief, proud nods. He led them through the anteroom to the bedchamber. "My lady?" he asked. "Will you do the honors?"

Alasen walked unerringly to the fireplace, touched a carving in the form of a star, and stepped aside as a narrow section of stone slid soundlessly back, revealing a dark passageway. "This leads to Prince Pol's rooms," she informed the dumbstruck guards. "And thence down about a million stairs to the river. I hope you're in good shape," she added wryly. "Remember to douse the candles before you emerge from the passage, and don't use any light in the boat. And—" She faltered slightly. "And take good care of my lord."

"With our lives, my lady," one of them said, and followed Donato through the opening, each carrying a lighted candle. The second man hung back, tactfully studying a tapestry as Alasen turned to Ostvel.

"I'd come with you, but you know how I feel about crossing water," she told him.

He framed her face in his hands. "I wish you'd reconsider about having Sioned or Riyan contact you with news Donato will send them."

She shook her head. "They'll have enough to worry about without adding me to the list. I'll be fine."

He didn't press the point. Leaning down to brush his lips against hers, he was startled when she flung her arms around his neck and clung to him.

"Be careful." Then she let him go as abruptly as she had embraced him. "Hurry."

A few moments later, holding a candle high as he negotiated the narrow passage, he heard the whisper of stone sliding shut behind him. He was gambling that four men could get to Dragon's Rest in the same time an army could march there from Rezeld. The swift-flowing Faolain would take them to a landing where they would commandeer horses. At his age he was not looking forward to a forced ride, but with a little luck they'd make it in time.

As for the reason he was doing this crazy thing—he pushed hard on the star carved into the wood paneling of Pol's bedchamber and led the way through the opening. He supposed it was the habit of half a lifetime to look after his princes' interests. There was no one at Dragon's Rest of sufficient authority to counter Lord Morlen, so it was his duty as regent in Pol's absence to forbid this unlawful undertaking. *Flimsy*, he thought; *nicely attentive to Rohan's law, but no man who raises an army against his prince is going to be bothered by a little thing like legality. Besides, you've never commanded a defensive action in your life, unless you count Stronghold in 704*

*when the Merida attacked, and even then it was Maeta and
Myrdal who ran things.*

He called a stop halfway down the interminable stairs
so the four of them could rest their legs before knees
turned to mush. During the brief respite, he continued
examining his motives. There was no Sunrunner at Dragon's Rest to receive Pol's orders at a distance. It was
essential that Donato be there. But this excuse held up
only little better than the other. If Andry was prompt
about relaying Donato's message, even if he didn't believe it, then someone would arrive at the palace about
the same time as Ostvel.

If Andry told Rohan and Sioned. Not *when*.

His real reason was that of the few people he trusted
absolutely, Andry was not among them. Rationally, he
knew there could be no motive for Andry to conceal
what was going on, but trust was not a thing rationally
arrived at. Ostvel wanted to *be* at Dragon's Rest, to
warn, to lead if necessary, to defend his princes as he had
done for nearly thirty years.

Chapter Eighteen

Stronghold: 32 Spring

Stifling a yawn, Rohan slid his arms into the shirt his squire held out for him. Sioned was seated at her dressing table mirror, sunlight bathing her in gold as she braided her hair. A morning like any other, except for her silence. He nodded permission for Arlis to retire, guessing that his wife desired privacy. He was right; she waited only until the door closed before speaking.

"I suppose that girl is going along."

"I suppose so."

Last night Pol had proposed an expedition to Rivenrock Canyon to view the dragon caves. Rialt had gone ahead early with a dozen servants and the open-sided pavilion where the party would be served a simple meal before a leisurely ride back in time for dinner. The ride was a pleasant day's diversion and, considering the discussions awaiting him, Rohan almost wished he had been asked to be diverted.

"It'd be nice to go with them," he went on. "But we do pretty much as we please the rest of the time, and pay for it on days like this."

"Who's first today, Miyon or Lord Barig?"

"Which one would you prefer to avoid?"

"Have I a choice?" She gave him a sour smile.

"Both breathlessly await our summons." He fastened the cuffs of his shirt and bent over to peer at his hair in her mirror. "You know, I never see the gray except when Pol's here."

"Speaking of whom. . . ." She gave him frown for frown in the mirror. "You've been putting me off for four days and—"

"Sioned, I can't fix my mind either on Miyon's schemes

256

or Barig's arguments if I'm distracted by what's going on with Pol."

"You wouldn't have sent Arlis out if you weren't ready to discuss it. And discuss it we will." She spun around on the cushioned stool. "Miyon's never been able to best us any other way, so now he's resorted to low cunning. Dangling this girl in front of Pol—"

"Don't you think Pol knows that? I *told* you, Sionell made it clear to me that he's perfectly aware of why Meiglan is here."

"Then why is he falling headlong into the trap? And in case you hadn't noticed, he's not a boy. He's a man. You'd better hope he thinks with what's between his ears instead of what's between his legs!"

Rohan told himself to be patient. "So why don't you talk to him about it?"

"I did," she replied shortly and turned to the mirror again, picking through a jewel case with quick, angry fingers. "Yesterday."

"What did he say?"

Her voice dripped sarcasm. "That it's only good manners to be polite to someone so obviously shy and unused to company. That he wants to learn more about her music. That he admires her looks. That I can't seriously be suggesting, Mother, that he should snub her because of who her father is." Sioned snapped the case shut. "That I ought to mind *my* business, not his!"

"Pol never said that."

"He implied it!"

Rohan put his hands on her shoulders, rubbing the tense muscles. "My love, you've been jumpy ever since we learned who this Ruval really is. I think you're being a little too sensitive."

"Don't patronize me," she warned. "Ruval is something else you won't talk to me about, and don't think I don't know why." She glared at him in the mirror. "Jumpy, am I? Sensitive? Pol's behaving as if he's about to Choose an enemy's bastard daughter, Ianthe's sons have suddenly appeared out of nowhere to challenge his right to Princemarch—with sorcery involved—and I can't even express what I feel in decent privacy to my own husband?"

"Sioned!" He had rarely seen her so upset. "There are

threats here, I'll admit, but Pol's not a child. And he's not fool enough to take Meiglan as his wife!"

"Do you believe that?" she demanded. "Do you? If you answer yes, you're a liar."

"You and I made a promise to tell each other the truth. Or at least never to lie, which doesn't quite amount to the same thing, as you've demonstrated on several occasions. So—yes, the prospect of a Cunaxan as the mother of my grandchildren revolts me. But until Ruval comes out from whatever rock he's hiding under and Pol comes to his own conclusions about Meiglan, there's not a hell of a lot I can do, is there?"

Sioned relented. Placing her hands on his where they rested on her shoulders, she said, "I've been frightened before, Goddess knows. Pol's been in danger before, his rights in doubt. But—"

"But you and I were always acting on his behalf. Protecting him, making the decisions for him. This time he's on his own. We have to trust him, Sioned—and trust in the training we gave him."

"Yes," she replied slowly. "He's not a child. But there's an innocence about him, Rohan. I can't quite explain it. A quality of being . . . untouched somehow, even though he's a grown man and a ruling prince—and no stranger to women."

"Unlike his extremely backward father," Rohan murmured, smiling a little.

"Oh? I heard about when you were eighteen and had been in your first battle and were quite full of yourself."

"Myrdal told on me, I suppose. Did she also mention I was so full of victory wine that I remember almost nothing of that whole night?"

"Almost?" She arched a brow.

"Well. . . . Enough to know what I wanted when I finally met you."

"Exactly. And Pol knows enough to know what *he* wants from this girl."

"She has a name, you know."

"Don't divert me from the issue," Sioned told him severely.

"Very well." He pulled a chair into the sun and sat down; since they were obviously in for a long discussion, he decided he might as well be comfortable. "Let's talk about trusting Pol's wits and judgment. Do you or don't you?"

"In everything else, yes! He's proved himself as a prince and as a man—"

"Has he? I wonder."

"And what is *that* supposed to mean?"

Rohan propped his elbows on the arms of the chair, lacing his fingers together. The great Desert topaz surrounded by emeralds shone on his hand. "I worried sometimes that my son would come to resent me the way I resented my own father. Oh, I loved Zehava and admired him deeply, for all that we were nothing alike. But by the time I was twenty or so I was frantic to rule a princedom I thought I understood better than he did." He smiled wryly. "A fine piece of adolescent conceit, you'll agree."

"Pol doesn't feel that way at all, Rohan."

"No. We're lucky that way. He has his own princedom to govern, so he doesn't have to covet mine in order to prove his talents. He's not even sure he *wants* to be High Prince—he's perfectly willing to let me wrestle with that for the next fifty years or so. So there's no jealousy or rivalry between us."

"Of course not. But I don't understand—"

"Let me finish. When I put Princemarch in his name instead of mine it wasn't only because he has blood-right to it, while my claim was only spoils of war. I wanted him to grow up thinking of Princemarch as *his*, to know that he would rule it long before he gets the Desert as well. By now he has every confidence in himself as a prince and a man.

"But, you see, he never really had to *work* for it. He's never been given things outright—he had to earn his way from squire to knighthood, and, Goddess know, Urival and Morwenna were strict enough with *faradhi* training. You and Ostvel and I put him through an equally tough school when it came to governing. But he's never fought for and won anything, either. The way I had to fight Roelstra that summer to win my own respect as a prince—and to win you."

Sioned tapped her nails on the dressing table. "And Pol hasn't done that yet. Rohan—do you think he needs to?"

"I think everyone needs to take the risk in some form or another. How else to discover one's possibilities?"

She was silent for a time, mulling over his words. More than anything else about her, he loved this: that she listened to him with all her gifts. She never meekly agreed with him simply because he was her husband and the High Prince. If she thought he was wrong she said so; if she accepted his reasoning she explained why, almost always confirming his own thoughts with things he hadn't considered. Precious as she was to him as his wife, she was essential as his princess.

At last she spoke. "It's natural for the young to be impatient to test themselves. To take the risk, as you said."

"They have to announce their arrival as adults," he said, smiling.

"Yes, but that's not what I meant. They can afford to risk everything because they don't really know what life is about. They don't know that the things worth daring all for aren't grand or glorious, really." She tucked one bare foot beneath her, frowning slightly. "You played Roelstra for a fool because you loved the game—and only afterward found out why you'd played it."

"For the right to wake up in my own bed each morning with you at my side. The right to live in peace, without my sword constantly to hand." And to teach his son—not the formal things, not law or history or rule, but mending a bridle, or how to whistle. Not great issues, but the little everyday things no one thought anything about until circumstances destroyed them. "The risks we take make us appreciate a peaceful life *without* risks. Pol doesn't understand that yet. He hasn't tested himself. What he'll face soon is the risk of everything—but he doesn't even know what 'everything' is."

"And we can't do it for him this time. Rohan, do people go on taking risks if they don't win what they set out to win—or prove themselves to their own satisfaction?"

"Perhaps the risk must be great enough to teach us our limits as well as our possibilities." And perhaps, he thought, one had to know war—of whatever kind—before one could embrace the slow and patient sameness of days that make up peace.

"Do you know what really frightens me?" Sioned asked abruptly. "What if what you *do* win isn't enough?"

"That's something Pol has to decide."

Haunted green eyes met his. "Rohan—"

"His decision, Sioned. His risk. Not ours."

Rebellion flickered, was extinguished with a weary acceptance he had never seen in her before. "You're wiser than I, my love," she murmured. "But then, you have less to lose. You won't give these sorcerers their real identities, so I will. They're not just Ianthe's sons. They're Pol's half-brothers. I've dreaded this since the night I took him from Feruche. It's time, Rohan, I can feel it. I risked my life and Tobin's and Ostvel's to claim him— and I'm about to risk losing him because of what I did."

"Sioned, I've said this time and again and you never seem to hear it. Ianthe had the bearing of him, but he's your son, not hers."

She said nothing, merely stared down at her hands.

"If you didn't believe that, you never would have taken him from Feruche that night."

"Of course *I* believe it!" she cried. "But will *he*? That's another decision he'll have to make—which of us was his true mother!"

"If you doubt what choice he'd make, you don't know him."

"Don't talk as if we won't ever have to tell him the truth! When he finds out I've lied to him his whole life—"

"You weren't the one who begot him of rape. If we're portioning out guilt, mine is the dragon's share."

"But I was the one who created the lie. Rohan . . . I could stand it if he rejected me. I think I could, anyway. But it would kill me if he rejected himself. His life is based on two facts: he is a prince and a Sunrunner. How will he feel when he finds out that what he thinks are Sunrunner gifts are really signs of sorcerer's blood?"

Rohan leaned forward and grasped her unwilling hands in his own. "*Listen* to me. You have to trust him, Sioned. He'll be angry and hurt at first. He won't understand. But we're his parents. He loves us."

She gave him a cynical little smile. "We've already judged ourselves, Rohan, and been found guilty. We'd better hope Pol decides differently, and is more forgiving."

***

At that moment Pol was deciding nothing more weighty than whether or not to take the stretch of dunes before him at a gallop. Though his stallion, Pashoc, had better manners than to test the bit, there was an impatient dance to his steps that could only be expected of a son of Rohan's old war-horse. He wanted a run, and he wanted it *now*.

Pol was tempted. He glanced back over his shoulder at the others—Maarken, Hollis, and their children were grouped with Andry and Nialdan; Feylin and Sionell rode with Riyan, Ruala, and Meiglan. Guard duty was shared among six of Miyon's men and six of Stronghold's, riding at a discreet distance though the Cunaxans looked as if they wanted to be closer. But no one rode ahead of Pol, and he could let Pashoc have his head at any time. *That* would shake them all up a bit, he thought with a hidden grin. His own people were nervous enough about this little expedition today without his bolting off into the distance unescorted.

Still . . . he shared the horse's impatience, mixed in with a dose of recklessness and a perverse desire to startle. Pashoc sensed his choice in the fractional shift of weight in the saddle and hands on the reins, and the instant Pol touched his heels to sleek flanks, the stallion was off like an arrow.

"Pol!" yelled Maarken, the shout fading as wind rushed through his hair and hooves pounded on packed sand. The Desert blurred to pale golden light around him, edged by fierce blue sky. Pashoc reached for more distance with every stride, slowing only a little going up each dune, gaining speed on the descents. Pol laughed and imagined himself with dragon wings, skimming over the bright world far below.

At last he signaled a slower pace. As the stallion pulled back from full gallop to canter to a walk that expressed his impatience for yet more speed, Pol surveyed the landscape, breathless not from the ride but from amazement.

The Desert, usually golden-white accented by dusty green scrub along the Vere Hills, was alive with color. A fabric of flowers spread across the dunes like silk draped over the sweet curves of a woman's body. The patchwork of brilliant orange and vivid scarlet and deepest turquoise changed to bronze and dark crimson and violet in the hollows, accented by traceries of water-rich green, all of it stitched to a background of white-gold sand. Around Stronghold the Desert had bloomed this spring, but here water and long-dormant seeds had burst into wealth worthy of Meadowlord or Syr.

Pol nearly leaped off his horse to plunge his hands into that incredible treasure of color. But the sand-muted thud of hooves behind him recalled him to princely dignity just in time. He turned in the saddle, unsurprised to find it was Maarken and Andry who had caught up to him first. The horses they rode were Radzyn breed, as long-legged and swift as Pashoc.

"Can you *believe* this?" he called out, gesturing to the hills. "It's as if the Desert itself has a pattern everyone can see, not just a Sunrunner."

The brothers reined in nearby. Andry shook the hair from his eyes and gave Pol a wide smile. "Nialdan and Oclel teased me for being so stunned by the colors," he confided. "Nobody not Desert-born can understand our reactions to this. And being *faradhi* makes us all the more sensitive to it."

Maarken nodded. "You should have seen the twins at New Year, when the south began to bloom. They came back from a ride covered in flower-dust and reeking of perfume—the little monsters actually *rolled* in a field of rock-roses!"

"Stark naked," Pol guessed, and his cousin laughed. "Sounds wonderful, but I think we'd shock the ladies if we tried it."

"Are you joking? Hollis and Sionell would join us!" Andry grinned. "Nialdan's the one who'd have a fit—he has such exalted ideas of highborn behavior."

Maarken's brows lifted. "Then you've never told him about the time we—"

"I have a position to uphold," Andry informed him haughtily, but his eyes were dancing the lie to his tone. "Anyway, he'd never believe I was ever a little boy who followed my criminally inclined eldest brother into mischief."

"Criminally inclined?" Maarken took a playful swing at his shoulder. "And what d'you mean, followed me?

You were the one who thought up the exploding goat bladder filled with pepper."

"Inspired," Pol contributed. "I tried it at Graypearl once, but a fish bladder didn't produce the same effect. Besides, I couldn't wash the smell off my hands and got caught."

"We had the same problem," Andry reminisced. "And tried to solve it with half a jar of Mother's hand cream."

"Which gave us away as surely as goat-stink would have," Maarken added. "We three little wretches smelled suspiciously sweet, and our fingers were so slippery that none of us could hold a spoon that night at dinner!"

They shared more memories of childhood escapades while waiting for the others to catch up. Pol was almost sorry when they did. His relationship with Maarken had always been comfortable and affectionate, but it was a very long time since he'd shared such easy humor and companionship with Andry.

He wondered how much effort the Lord of Goddess Keep had to put into pretending to like the Ruler of Princemarch—as much as the Ruler of Princemarch was giving to pretending he liked the Lord of Goddess Keep?

Pol was a little ashamed of himself. They didn't have to be their titles *all* the time. They were members of the same family, with the same blood and the same heritage and the same love of this Desert that belonged to them all.

When the others approached, Maarken fixed a stern gaze on the younger men. "If either of you tell Chayla or Rohannon any of this—"

"Us?" Andry sent an innocent glance toward Pol, who grinned.

"Let 'em think up their own trouble to get into. From what I hear, they're already quite creative."

"And will only get worse." Maarken sighed. "They're own parents' revenge, you know—grandchildren. I wouldn't be surprised if Father put them up to the unstitched pillows trick last winter. Every time anybody sat down. . . ." He grimaced.

"I never tried that one," Andry said thoughtfully.

"I'll have my brats teach yours someday," Maarken offered generously.

"*Too* kind!"

"What's a brother for?"

Pol laughed and reined Pashoc around to greet the late arrivals. As he had expected, Meiglan was last, riding the most placid mare in the Stronghold stables. Sionell and Feylin had stayed with her, and one of Miyon's guards, for it was obvious that she was far from being an expert horsewoman. He smiled encouragement at her and when the party was fully assembled once again, led the way along the trail to Rivenrock.

Feylin cantered up to ride beside him. "I trust you're through practicing for the races," she said.

"How did you know I was going to ride this year?"

She looked startled. "Are you really?"

"Of course." He smiled. "It's something of a tradition in the family, after all, to win our Chosen lady's wedding jewels in a race."

He admired her self-control. A momentary tensing of her shoulders and a flicker of a frown were the only indications of her reaction.

"It's about time you did something about that," she replied easily. "Am I to assume you have someone in mind?" She didn't wait for an answer, as if she had no desire to hear one. "I've always thought the *Rialla* an absurd way to find a spouse. All those young people thrown together in an artificial situation, expected to discover each other's characters and make an intelligent Choice based on eight or ten days' acquaintance."

"The alternative is a grand tour of the princedoms, in equally artificial visits that put even more pressure on the people involved. At least at the *Rialla* there's comfort in knowing there's a score of you all in the same fix."

"Mmm. Still, it's a terrible risk to take with one's future."

"We can't all be as lucky as you and Walvis, to find each other during a war—as honest a situation as one could encounter, don't you think?"

"Now that you mention it, yes," she replied forthrightly. "You see what a person really is. The circumstances aren't any more normal than that cattle show at the *Rialla*, but the people are a lot more honest."

"Perhaps I ought to start a war. Just a *little* one, to improve my chances of finding a suitable wife."

She regarded him sourly. "I pity the girls who succumb to that handsome face and silken tongue of yours."

Pol laughed. "I can't claim credit for either—I get them from my father."

"He never saw fit to use them the way you do. How many dozens is it now?"

He bowed in his saddle. "I'll send you a list so you can express your sympathies to them."

Feylin gave up and laughed. "You're a mannerless, arrogant, impudent pest!"

"So I've been told." Pol winked at her. "But let's talk about something more interesting—like dragons. We'll make a cave count today, I suppose?"

"For all the good it will do." She shook her head. "They'll never return here, Pol. Sioned tried to get it across to her little dragon that it's safe, but the creature didn't seem to understand."

"Mother told me Elisel howled even at a mental picture of Rivenrock."

"Yet she was convinced to share Dragon's Rest. It frustrates Sioned that she can't make it clear that the caves are safe to use again."

"I don't understand that," he said. "Elisel wasn't even hatched when the Plague struck. How could she know?"

"How can we understand how their thoughts work? I've held a dragon's brain in my two hands, and aside from the obvious similarities in shape and differences in size, I didn't learn a damned thing. You and Sioned have communicated with them—but I've also seen Chay and Maarken hold long conversations with their horses that I could swear the beasts understand."

His brows arched. "Touching dragon colors is slightly more sophisticated a process than having a chat with a horse!"

"Yet we comprehend both animals to about the same degree."

Pol ruminated for a time, staring at the trail from between his horse's ears. "Ostvel thinks the old legend about Castle Crag being carved out by dragons is true. Other caverns in the Faolain gorge there are perfect. But no dragons have ever used them. Why did they abandon *those* caves?"

"Summer isn't warm enough there to bake the eggs properly."

"But it must have been once. The evidence argues for it—and for a change in climate. When the dragons found their eggs didn't hatch, they adapted to the change." He gestured to the land around them. "Like the insects feasting off the flowers, and the birds feasting off the insects. They found a banquet in the Desert that hasn't been seen in a hundred years. Dragons are smarter than insects or birds, and in a lot more need."

"It's an interesting theory," Feylin granted, "except for one thing. When dragons presumably hatched in the caves around Castle Crag, they numbered in the thousands. How many caves are there above the Faolain? A hundred? The dragons wouldn't have noticed the loss of a hundred females' hatchlings. I'm sorry, Pol, but they simply abandoned Castle Crag the same way they did Rivenrock, for equally good reasons to the dragon mind."

"And you're the one who's always saying dragons are smarter than anybody gives them credit for!"

"They are. But they're not people. Sioned persuaded them to share the valley at Dragon's Rest. All that means is they're smart enough to comprehend an offer of free food—not a very exalted concept, you'll admit."

Pol scowled at her. "But the dragon I touched understood that I wouldn't hurt her, that I'd take her vengeance on those who killed her. And she told me quite plainly that any attempt to heal her shattered wing was doomed to failure. The concepts of help, revenge, and healing are fairly advanced."

"Did she really communicate those things, Pol? Or was it your own mind and emotions projecting human thought and feeling into the dragon?" She paused and ran her fingers back through her hair. "In any case, your argument about Castle Crag won't work. Dragons have used the same caves for hundreds and hundreds of years. No stories, rumors, or even legends describe them looking for new ones. So we can't count on a perceived need motivating them to return to Rivenrock."

"They range out to find food," he challenged. "When the Plague decimated herds in the Catha Hills, they expanded their territory into Syr and Gilad."

"And they readily accepted the offer of sheep raised

just for them at Dragon's Rest, where they were accustomed only to stop for a drink," she agreed. "But I give your own analogy back to you: the insects and the birds. It doesn't take much mind power to find and take advantage of a food supply."

"Oh, all right," he said with a sigh. "I'll concede. But I still say that dragon knew exactly what I was talking about and was a lot smarter than you'll admit."

"You were the one who touched her colors. Only you can say what you perceived."

"Gracious of you to say it," he grumbled. "Even if you're obviously unconvinced."

She laughed. "Give me facts, my prince! Good, solid statistics—"

"Or a dragon corpse you can take apart to figure out how he works!" Pol grinned back at her. "Come to think of it, it's highly appropriate that you met your husband during a war—you're a bloodthirsty woman, my lady!"

Riyan rode up then, saying, "Apologies, my prince. I don't mean to interrupt, but—"

"But you have something to talk over in private," Feylin supplied, smiling. She swung her mare neatly around and trotted away.

"What is it, Riyan?" Pol asked.

"I don't think anyone ought to go mucking about in any of the caves, do you?" It was said in casual tones, but with one brow arched significantly.

"Ah!" Pol said. "Naturally not. It might be dangerous."

"No one knows if the walls or ceilings might collapse."

"Or what sort of animal might have established a den."

Their gazes met in perfect understanding; none of these eminently sensible reasons had anything to do with why people must not explore the caves where shells shone with gold.

Pol said, "I was hoping for a chance to talk with you. I've been considering what's to be done about Feruche."

Riyan gave a soft sigh. "I can't imagine anyone but Sorin as its *athri*, but I suppose someone has to run the place. Do you have anybody in mind?"

"Who else would I give it to, Riyan?" Pol smiled.

"Me?" The young Lord of Skybowl gaped at him. "Why?"

"Because it's with in easy distance of Skybowl, you're

demonstrably capable of it, and I don't want anyone else to have it."

"But it should be saved for one of your family! Maarken's bound to have other children—"

Pol shook his head. "No. And don't let on that I told you. Hollis found out at the Mother Tree that Chayla and Rohannon are all the children she'll ever have."

"But—your own younger sons, or your daughters—"

"What's the matter? Don't you want Feruche?"

Riyan bit his lip. "Alasen and I had this conversation years ago. She thought that as my father's eldest son, I ought to have Castle Crag after him. But I'm Desert-born, Pol—and I don't want to live anywhere else."

"Feruche is only a day and a half from Skybowl, and nobody's asking you to give up your primary holding. And it's not as if being the vassal of two princes is going to be a conflict, when the two are father and son! What's the real reason? I know very well you're not afraid of the work."

"It's—what I already said," Riyan replied softly. "I can't imagine anyone but Sorin there."

"And I can't imagine anyone he'd want to have it more than you. Or anyone who'd make of it what he intended it to be. If you won't accept it for yourself or for me, then accept it for him."

Riyan hesitated. "May I have time to think it over, my prince?"

"Take as long as you like—as long as your answer is yes. With the new trade agreements we're sure to reach with Prince Miyon, I need somebody there I can trust to carry out a few plans."

The older man laughed. "Goddess! You're Rohan's son to your fingertips, aren't you? He makes plans stretching years ahead before he's even told the people those plans include! My father says that Rohan's the only man he ever knew who reminisces about the future! Very well, I'll hold Feruche for you—but with the understanding that if you need it at any time for a second son or a daughter's dowry, it will revert to Princemarch."

"And *you're* the only man I know who'd take a magnificent keep with one hand and give it back with the other!" Pol shook his head in comical amazement. "I'll accept your conditions for now. But I have a suspicion that sooner or later you'll have sons and daughters of your own to dower, my friend."

"The sooner the better, according to my father. The 'What, not married *yet*?' looks come fast and thick at your age, but wait till you get to be mine!"

"Oh, I don't intend to wait that long," Pol said.

Sudden raucous yells heralded the beginning of a surprise ambush. Chayla and Rohannon rode up at speed to besiege Pol and pelt him with blossoms. He cowered in his saddle and shouted for help, which brought the Stronghold guard thundering up in earnest. The adults heroically hid grins as the disgruntled soldiers solemnly accepted the children's apologies. Then Andry created a gentle whirlwind that sent the flowers spinning around the delighted twins.

"What's the good of knowing how if you can't do it for fun sometimes?" he countered when Maarken said something about wasting his energies to entertain a couple of monsters.

"I see now why one has to be at least fourteen to begin training," Hollis laughed. "Can you imagine the chaos otherwise?"

By the time they reached the gold silk pavilion Rialt had brought earlier, everyone was starving. The canopy was set up just below the spire that stood sentinel over the entrance to Rivenrock. It was here that Pol's grandfather, Prince Zehava, had taken mortal wounds battling a dragon; Rohan had killed the same dragon somewhere in the canyon. Here, too, the Hatching Hunts had been held before Rohan outlawed the triennial butchery. Pol could not conceive of doing any injury at all to a dragon, let alone going out to fight one as proof of prowess. And the thought of ambushing the hatchlings as they emerged into the sun, wings still damp and eyes dazzled, sickened him.

But he understood why Rohan had killed the dragon that had killed Zehava—the last one slain until the three that Princess Ianthe's son had slaughtered. Rohan had promised Zehava that dragon's death, but it also announced his own strength. Pol thanked the Goddess that circumstances made it unnecessary for him to provide a similar demonstration of his abilities with a sword. Indeed, his father's whole life had been dedicated to making sure Pol did not have to live by the sword at all.

He lazed back on the thick carpet spread under the pavilion, full plate and wine cup in easy reach. Outings like this with just his family were much less formal—bread, fruit, and cheese to make a meal on while seated in the shade of a dune or a rock outcropping. But he had acquired a taste for elegant frivolity at Dragon's Rest, where guests expected more than a loaf, a water skin, and the hard ground. Besides, his present companion deserved elegance.

Lady Meiglan sat on a cushion to his right, slim and dainty in a riding outfit of creamy beige accented with orange embroidery. She had gained enough confidence around him—and away from her father—to answer harmless questions. But he had still not decided if her shyness was genuine or deliberate.

Pol had always known that Miyon's trade treaties were secondary to some other plan; that he was supposed to think Meiglan *was* that other plan had occurred to him rather more slowly than was comfortable for his conceit. He gave the Cunaxan prince full marks for choosing his diversion well. Pol's wits had not worked with the usual speed because she was indeed enchantingly lovely.

So he had decided to become enchanted.

His amusement at this conscious resolve tugged the corners of his mouth up. This game would be almost as good as one played thirty years ago: the only point in which his father could top him was the number of females he'd played off against each other.

Rialt and Edrel had been scandalized by Pol's opening gambit two mornings ago as they'd helped him dress for the day. Critical attention paid to clothes, from a man who usually put on whatever was given him without knowing or caring what it was, had astonished them almost as much as his words.

"Did you notice her eyes? Like a pool kept secret in the forest, in autumn when leaves drift down to darken the water. But when she smiles, the sun shines. What do you think, Edrel—the agate, for seduction?" He'd held up a plump stone set in a silver earring.

Rialt's scowl had answered for the pair. "Amber would

be more appropriate—for protection against danger! My prince, please recall who this girl is!"

Pol only laughed. "Definitely the agate."

Rialt gestured Edrel from the room. "You can't seriously be—"

"—attracted to a pretty girl? Come now, Rialt. You know me better than that." He sprawled in a chair and grinned. "I'm only attracted to the really *beautiful* ones."

"If you desire her, fine. Goddess knows, she's lovely. But you don't have to make such a show of it! And you certainly don't have to treat her to a display of the family charm!"

"Why not? She's a princess—of a somewhat irregular sort, true. But one doesn't go about seducing even bastard princesses, Rialt. I'm ashamed of you for even suggesting it."

"But there are a hundred reasons why you shouldn't notice her at all, let alone make much of her! First, she *is* illegitimate. Second, she's too young. Third, she's Cunaxan. Fourth—"

"I beg you, *don't* give me the entire list! Besides, I could think think up a reason in favor for every one you think up against." The expression of shock on his chamberlain's face was delightful; Pol wondered why his father had never told him this could be so much fun. "First, bastardy doesn't really matter much. Second, she can't be much younger than Sionell was when she married Tallain. Third, what better way to make peace than to make love? And fourth—she has but a single fault."

Rialt's fiery blue eyes widened still more. Pol laughed. "Don't you want to know what it is?"

"I can't wait," he spat.

"It's only a little one," he said, playing it out to the end. "Rather easily remedied." He paused. "Her fault is that she's not my wife. Yet."

"Pol!"

At last he took pity on his friend. "I really have you fooled, don't I?"

Rialt sank bonelessly into a chair.

"A moment to treasure!" Pol allowed himself to gloat a moment, then sobered. "No one must know about this, not even my parents. Just you and I, or it won't work. I've a pretty good idea of what Miyon is up to with this

girl. And I'll need your help, the way my father needed
Walvis thirty years ago. Have you heard that story?"

It took a couple of tries before Rialt could form coherent words. In the end, he said only one. "Roelstra?"

"Exactly. Miyon's not overly burdened with wits, but
he's capable of copying someone else's plan. One of
Roelstra's innumerable daughters was supposed to marry
Father, give him a son or two, and then become his
grieving widow—and regent while the little vipers grew.
It was a clever idea and might even have worked if
Father really had been the fool he pretended to be for
Roelstra's benefit."

"And if not for your mother. But—Lady Meiglan can't
possibly be a party to this!"

Pol shrugged. "She looks as innocent as a new morning, but who can say? I don't want to hurt her unnecessarily if she really doesn't know anything about her father's
plot. Still, I have to play along—only the game is going
to be mine, not his grace of Cunaxa's. That's why you
have to help me. Make sure people know how worried
you are about my interest in her. I'll have enough trouble
being obvious without being *too* obvious—it wouldn't do
for anyone who knows me well to guess what I'm up to."
He grimaced. "I warn you, I'll start sounding and behaving like a madman."

"Why change your style now?" Rialt laughed. "Just
make sure you don't get overwhelmed by your own game.
And if the girl really is the innocent she appears, this
isn't fair to her."

That was the only problem, Pol reflected as he watched
Meiglan smile at some remark of Ruala's. Now, *there* was
a fascinating young woman, he acknowledged, and it was
obvious that Riyan thought so, too. But there was something about Meiglan that did attract him, and he was
powerless to analyze exactly what it was. Certainly she
was beautiful, and in a way vastly different from other
women he knew. But though Pol was deeply sensitive to
beauty of any kind, from the glory of the Veresch in
springtime to the delicate grace of Fironese crystal, he
had never been a slave to his senses. Her music be-
witched him, but music always had. He decided that what
intrigued him was the uncertainty. Was she truly as she
seemed, or did her vulnerability mask a ruthless mind?

He would find out eventually. But for the present he was sure of two things. First, she represented danger—either through total knowledge of the way he read Miyon's plan for marriage and death, or in total innocence that really might enchant him. Second, until he discovered which it was, he must conduct most of his act out of her sight and hearing. If she was conversant with Miyon's aims, it would not do for her to think she was succeeding; if she was not, he had no wish to cause her pain. His conversations with Feylin and Riyan that day would be duly reported to his parents; just sitting beside her would work as well as if he openly flirted with her. Come to think of it, he mused, she probably didn't know *how* to flirt.

It worried him a little that he was deliberately fooling those who loved him. But he had little choice. And his father had done the same thing, after all. Still, even though he had taken a page from Rohan's book, he was very different from his father. Rohan had learned how to wait—indeed, preferred to wait while things developed on their own. Usually it worked for him; sometimes it did not. But Pol was not made that way. He had to *do* something, could not merely allow things to happen to himself or others. He had to influence events, turn them in directions he wanted them to go. He supposed in time he would discover the kind of patience his father had. But for now. . . .

After the meal some of the group mounted up once more to ride into Rivenrock Canyon. Pol chuckled under his breath as he saw Riyan's attempts to gain Ruala's sole companionship foiled by the twins. They had taken a liking to her and insisted she ride with them—graciously allowing Riyan to join them. Maarken and Hollis chose to linger in the pavilion for a comfortable chat with Andry and Sionell. Meiglan, however, came along. Whether she wanted to or had been told to was open to speculation.

Feylin played tour guide as they rode into the canyon. Nialdan, Andry's other *faradhi* companion, listened in abject wonder as Feylin described the cycle of dragon mating: first the devouring of bittersweet plants, then the cliff-dance and the sand-dance during which the females selected their mates.

"Afterward, the she-dragon walls up her eggs to bake through the summer. When the little beasts hatch, they gobble their weaker siblings to give them the strength to break down the walls. They breathe fire to dry and toughen their wings—and to roast their first meal."

Nialdan gulped. "I see," he said shakily.

Feylin had a grin and went on remorselessly, "Yes, back when the dragons were using these caves, it was said that when the walls finally came down you could smell broiled dragon meat all the way to Radzyn. Ask Lord Andry sometime. He'll tell you."

The big Sunrunner gave a faint nod, eyes wide.

"Of course, that's nothing to the mating stink. The sires give off the most appalling stench. You may be wondering how I know so much," she added blithely. "Some years ago I had the great good fortune to carve up a dead dragon. Remarkable creatures. Incredible structure to the wings, of course, but the stomach and brain were nearly as interesting, once I'd washed all the blood off."

"Indeed, my lady," Nialdan managed, looking rather pale.

Pol glanced around and was relieved to find Meiglan out of earshot, riding between Chayla and one of the Cunaxan guards. He turned his horse in their direction and was amused to see the man bow and ride off; none of Miyon's people got very near him, and had probably been given orders that whenever he approached Meiglan, they were to back away.

"What do you think of the canyon, my lady?"

"I—I can imagine the dragons here, my lord, even though I've never seen one."

"Never?" Chayla exclaimed. "Oh, but you have to! They're beautiful!"

"If his grace my father allows it, then perhaps we'll stay long enough to see them."

"Only another few days," Pol supplied. "They'll fill the skies with their wings and their challenges to each other. It's not to be missed."

"Can we go look in the caves?" Chayla asked. "Please?"

"Not today, sweetheart. Didn't your papa ever tell you what happened to him and his brother when they tried it once? A baby dragon popped out and nearly scared them to death!"

"And *your* papa and Sioned scared the dragon away," she finished. "But there aren't any dragons here now."

"No." He squinted up at the canyon walls. Darkness gaped here and there, natural caves carved even larger by dragons. They must return here or they would never reproduce in the numbers that would ensure their survival.

"I wish they'd come back," Chayla sighed.

Meiglan regarded her curiously. "Do you remember them so clearly, then? You couldn't have been very old during the last mating."

"Dragons fly over the Desert every year. Oh, you have to stay to see them, Lady Meggie! Pol, tell her she has to stay."

He smiled at them. "I'll do everything in my power to assure it."

Rohannon trotted up and challenged his sister to a race—supervised by Riyan and Ruala, so Pol allowed it. When he and Meiglan were alone, he turned to her once more.

"Chayla called you 'Meggie' instead of Meiglan."

The girl flushed. "It's—a nickname, my lord, given by my nurse. Chayla happened on it by accident, I think."

"The old word for honey-pine is 'megna,' isn't it?"

She nodded. "Nobody's called me that in many years, my lord."

"Does your nurse think you're too old for nicknames now?"

"She died when I was about Chayla's age."

"And you loved her very much."

"Yes," she said unwillingly, as if admitting to emotion was dangerous.

Pol was ashamed, but an apology was impossible. He knew without being told that the only love in her short life had been connected to that nurse; Goddess knew, she received none from her father. The fact that she had not mentioned her mother in connection with the tender nickname hinted at no affection from that source, either. Pol realized again how lucky he was in parents as in all else.

"Shall—shall we join the others, my lord?" Meiglan asked warily.

The somber expression brought by his thoughts had alarmed her; she looked as if afraid she had said something wrong. But there was nothing he could do to apologize or make amends except give her a reassuring smile.

He left her in Nialdan's care and rode with Feylin down the canyon, talking dragons and trying to imagine what it had been like when they used Rivenrock. But there was no *feel* of dragons here as there was at other cavern complexes.

The sounds of hoofbeats and laughter rang off the stone as the children raced their ponies. Pol noted that Riyan had finally managed to separate Ruala from the others, and grinned to himself; the sooner the better, indeed. Elktrap was a formidable dowry. Ostvel would be pleased. But Riyan might get a little ragged around the edges, supervising Skybowl, Elktrap, and Feruche—

Suddenly someone screamed, and Feylin lurched forward in her saddle as another horse's shoulder plowed into her own mount's hindquarters. Feylin's mare kicked back instinctively, but the second horse was already galloping back down the canyon. Pol's heart stopped for an instant as he saw that the rider wore cream and orange, and thick golden curls whipped back from her face.

He swore and dug his heels into Pashoc's sides. Though Meiglan's mare was no match for the stallion, she was Radzyn-bred for strength. Panic gave her wings. As the distance between them narrowed too slowly, Pol wondered what could have spooked the usually placid animal to bolt. The reins had escaped the girl's hands entirely and she had both arms flung around the horse's neck. If the mare stumbled on the reins and fell—

He rejected the image of her slight body pitching over the mare's head to shatter on stony ground. Riding low over Pashoc's neck, he urged the horse to greater speed. They were out of Rivenrock now, thundering past the gold pavilion out on the dunes. The mare began to tire. At last Pol was able to lean from his saddle and grab one of the dangling reins. Another few moments, and the mare had slowed to a shuddering, exhausted walk.

Meiglan still had a death grip on the horse. Pol spoke her name several times without response; she clung trembling to the mare's neck. He stopped both horses, leaped down, and bodily pried Meiglan from her saddle.

It seemed she didn't much care what she hung on to, as long as there was something to hold. His ribs nearly cracked with the terrified strength of her arms. He stroked her disordered hair, murmuring wordlessly to soothe her. At length she gave a long, quivering sigh and her muscles relaxed enough so he could breathe freely again.

"There now," he said softly. "You're safe, Meggie. All over now."

All at once her head jerked back and two huge brown eyes stared up at him in horror. "You—!" she gasped.

"Yes, just me. Nothing bruised or broken? You're quite all right?"

She stumbled back from him, hands at her mouth, those great eyes even darker in contrast to the golden curls tangled around her face.

"It was very brave of you not to scream and frighten the mare even more," he went on, wishing she wouldn't look at him as if he had grown two heads and a dragon's tail. "And you're stronger than you look, to have hung on and not fallen off." His ribs could attest to that.

Her hands twisted together and she shivered again.

"You're not hurt, are you?" he asked, fairly sure that she was only shaken.

"I'm sorry!" she blurted out. "I'm sorry! Please believe me, my lord!"

Pol realized that her slightest transgression, whether her fault or not, was probably punished by her father as if she had purposely planned it to irritate him. And she expected the same harsh words from him.

So he said nothing at all. Instead he surrounded her gently with his arms. Anger warred with aching tenderness for this frail, frightened girl—and with growing knowledge that this was exactly what he was supposed to feel. The mare's headlong panic was no accident. But had Meiglan planned it, or her father?

Eventually she stopped shaking and stepped back. She would not look at him as she whispered, "Please forgive me, my lord."

"Don't be silly," he said, and cursed himself for the quick answer when she flinched. "I only meant it wasn't your fault the mare bolted. You have nothing to be sorry for."

She met his gaze again. "You won't—you won't tell my father?"

He looked down into the big brown eyes, trying to decide if their anguished entreaty was honesty or artifice. And suddenly he was ashamed that he had ever suspected her at all. Meiglan was innocent. She must be. However it had been done, her life had been at stake in this little plot. Would it have pleased Miyon, Pol thought furiously, if the girl had died in pursuit of him?

"I won't tell your father anything except that you were very brave."

"Oh, thank you, my lord," she breathed, the passionate gratitude in her eyes confirming her innocence. Not even the surety that this fierce instinct to protect had been planned for him could keep him from feeling it. He told himself he would feel the same toward anyone so utterly without defenses.

Chapter Nineteen

Stronghold: 33 Spring

Rohan was irked by Andry's absence from the audience granted Lord Barig and the two Giladan lawyers, but he was compelled to admire his nephew's tactics. By riding off to Rivenrock today he showed his contempt for Prince Cabar's claim to jurisdiction over the Sunrunner—while making sure he would know exactly what was said by deputizing Oclel to sit in. The presence of a mere *faradhi* instead of the Lord of Goddess Keep was an insult that Barig noted with a glower to which Oclel responded with a bland stare. Rohan hid his own annoyance and endured the first portion of the audience with admirable patience, all the while wishing he could be out riding in the fresh air. They sat in the Summer Room, named by Sionell years ago for tapestries depicting the Desert in that season; the hangings were a constant reminder of beauty Rohan would much rather have enjoyed in person rather than stitched in bright wool.

Oclel played his part to perfection. He listened to Barig's case and the lawyers' amplifications, pleasant face below a shock of fair hair revealing nothing. Rohan's speculative gaze returned to him many times as he wondered what Andry had instructed him to say and when he was supposed to say it. At last the lawyers finished presentations of precedent nicely calculated to appeal to Rohan's sense of tradition, and Barig summed up.

"It is therefore our position, your grace, that this person Gevlia, originally from Isel, by acting as a physician rather than as a Sunrunner, is punishable by the laws of Gilad. These have been formulated through hundreds of years by a score of noble princes and most recently by his grace my cousin Prince Cabar, and we of Gilad bless his wise rule over us and trust that it will continue for many long years to come."

Rohan drew breath to thank Barig for his words, but Oclel beat him to it.

"My lord," he said to Barig, "as the wisdom and the years granted to his grace of Gilad are Goddess-given, your gratitude might be more properly expressed to her."

Mildly said, severely meant. Rohan saw Sioned regard Oclel with renewed interest. The lawyers puffed up indignantly, but Barig was surprisingly undisturbed.

"I have noted," he said thoughtfully, "that the name and graces of the Goddess are emphasized more and more often these days."

"Appropriately so, my lord," Oclel replied.

"Ostentatiously so," Barig riposted. "Last night in the Great Hall, for example. I do not know how things are done at Goddess Keep, where no doubt the Goddess spends more time than she does at other places. But at his grace's palace of Medawari we do not make a ritual of gratitude for food and drink we and not she worked to produce."

Sioned interposed, "I'm sure that proper thanks are given to the Goddess for the richness of Gilad, just as is done here in the Desert—where this year we have been especially blessed."

"Agriculturally speaking, your grace," Barig observed smoothly, "the rain produced the flowers. If anyone ought to be thanked, surely it is the Father of Storms—who also drowned and thereby ruined a goodly portion of everyone's fields and herds last winter. Tell me," he added, turning to Oclel, "did he and the Goddess have a lover's quarrel, do you think?"

Oclel's brows arched. "We can scarcely comprehend their natures, my lord. They certainly should not be mocked!"

"I'm sure he did not mean to do so." Sioned spoke with steel beneath the silk of her voice. "I think Lord Barig is simply unaccustomed to the thanksgiving used at Goddess Keep, where naturally things are more formal than elsewhere. I found Lord Andry's words quite lovely."

"As did we all," Barig said hastily, hearing the warning in her tone.

Oclel's response was honeyed. "Then your lordship can be relied on to institute similar thanksgiving at

Medawari in future. It would certainly find favor with the Goddess."

Not to mention with Andry, Rohan thought. "I'm sure Lord Barig will discuss it with his grace of Gilad," he said aloud. "Interesting as this is, I suggest that we return to the matter at hand." His tone indicated that they had better, or else. Both men nodded and Rohan continued, "I'm most interested by your lordship's analysis of Prince Cabar's position. I'm confident that as Lord Andry's representative, Oclel would be equally eloquent." Thus he neatly deprived the Sunrunner of any chance for further speechifying—and brought a wisp of a grin to Barig's face. Rohan didn't even have to glance at Sioned for her to start weaving with the threads he'd given her.

"The way I understand things," she said, "not the guilt but the trial and punishment of this unfortunate woman is in dispute. Andry believes it his right as Lord of Goddess Keep and Cabar believes it his right as ruler of Gilad. But has anyone considered the rights of this Sunrunner?"

They stared at her. Rohan leaned back in his chair and let his lids droop slightly as he listened and watched. How he loved the patterns of her mind. . . .

"Has anybody even talked to her? Found out what her side of this is?"

"She has been questioned, your grace," Barig began.

"Questioned? Do you mean 'interrogated,' my lord? Did anyone ever ask her why she agreed to treat Master Thacri in the first place? Surely she is horrified that she made a mistake."

"If you'll forgive me, your grace," Barig said stiffly, " 'sorry' will not feed Master Thacri's wife and children."

Oclel said, "No one ever claimed that it would, my lord. It seems to me that the question is not whether she was negligent in causing this man's death, but whether he would have died anyway. She was the only physician available. She attempted to heal him, as was her duty as a Sunrunner sworn to give help when and where needed."

"The attempt failed," Barig said in a flat voice.

Sioned looked momentarily irritated by this interruption of her argument. "Her youth and inexperience must be taken into consideration. She is only—what, twenty-three? Twenty-four?"

One of the lawyers had the temerity to speak to the High Princess. "That makes no difference, your grace. The man is dead, and through the woman's fault. The law is quite specific that restitution must be paid."

"And what about justice?" Sioned exclaimed. "If the law is to have any meaning, then *right* must be done. Barbarians know only one definition of a crime and only one punishment for it. Should the man who steals a loaf of bread to feed his starving family be given punishment equal to the man who steals just to prove he can? Civilization's privilege and duty is to think, reason, and be merciful. But to seek compassionate justice is also civilization's curse. After all—simple, barbaric restitution is so much easier."

Rohan nearly stood up and applauded. It was now his turn to speak, according to their prior agreement. But he had not expected so much passion from Sioned, so much heartfelt belief. Thirty years ago he had felt utterly alone in his commitment to the rule of law rather than that of the sword. But then she had appeared, first in Andrade's fiery conjuring and then windblown and weary in the Desert near Rivenrock. He had never been alone since, not in heart or mind or spirit. He spent a moment in wordless gratitude for the gift of his wife, then spoke.

"Her grace has made an excellent point. This Sunrunner does have rights, just as anyone does from the Sunrise Water to Kierst-Isel—peasant, prince, and Sunrunner alike. I have no wish to intrude upon Lord Andry's right to discipline his *faradh'im*. Nor do I desire to usurp the right of Prince Cabar to punish wrongdoers within his princedom as the laws of Gilad give him the power to do."

Oclel, Barig, and the lawyers all looked puzzled by this speech. Only Sioned knew exactly where he was going with this; a tiny smile played around her eyes as he stitched the final design.

Rohan paused, then said, "Neither do I mean to deprive this Sunrunner of *her* right."

"*What* right?" Barig was betrayed by astonishment into the exclamation.

"To be judged by Lord Andry," Oclel said with a silken smile that left his face with Rohan's next words.

"To be judged by *me*."

Sioned waited just the right amount of time for this to

sink in, then said, "The thing that rankled Lady Andrade most in her years of rule at Goddess Keep was the long-standing tradition that Sunrunners are citizens of all princedoms, their only true overlord being the High Prince. Of course, the reason she objected to this was because the High Prince was Roelstra. When my lord husband was acclaimed, she willingly confirmed his rights in this matter." She smiled. "Lord Andry naturally reaffirmed them."

Rohan said pleasantly, "All persons swear loyalty to someone. The common folk to their *athr'im*, they to their princes, the princes to me. Goddess Keep is held not from the Prince of Ossetia, but from the High Prince. Therefore, just as when people marry out of their own lands, when Sunrunners go to Goddess Keep they come under the rule of that place.

"Because Gevlia is a Sunrunner, Lord Andry does indeed have the right to decide her punishment. Because the offense occurred in Gilad, Prince Cabar also has the right to judge her." He leaned forward slightly and lapsed into a stern royal plural. "It is our opinion that each made a serious mistake in claiming jurisdiction to the exclusion of the other, forcing us to decide between two equal claims. And we tell you now that neither will be the one to decide this matter. *We* will. We are High Prince. Gevlia's right under very old laws is to be judged by *us*."

Barig sprang to his feet. "Outrageous!"

"No. Justice. Her grace the High Princess wisely pointed out that it is a difficult thing, being civilized. Both Lord Andry and Prince Cabar seem rather more interested in the degree of restitution rather than in justice. We promise you that *we* shall seek the latter."

It was a terrible insult that neither could reply to when spoken by the High Prince—and which would be duly reported to Cabar and Andry for suitable reply on a level approaching Rohan's. But they had forced him into this locked room. It was their own fault that they had underestimated him and, rather than use either of the doors they had so smugly provided, he had chosen to climb out an unsuspected window instead.

But he was furious that he had been put in this position to begin with. He knew his decision would be perceived as an arbitrary action of the autocrat he wasn't. Neither Cabar nor Andry would be satisfied, the other princes would feel threatened, and the whole mess already left a bad taste in his own mouth. And then there was that poor young woman. She was not an abstraction of an issue. She was a person caught in wretched circumstances.

He eyed Barig, Oclel, and the lawyers for a moment, then said brusquely, "Thank you for your attendance upon us. You have our permission to withdraw."

All four left with frowns. Rohan did not much care. He sprawled back in his chair and blew out a long sigh. Sioned poured wine and handed him a cup.

"What will her punishment be?"

"Damned if I know," he admitted. "Barig's right, the man's family must be compensated—monetarily, at least. Andry will have to disgorge a bit, which won't make him happy at all." He grimaced at the understatement. "But I think Gevlia will have to perform some service as well. I just can't decide what."

"This will follow her for the rest of her life."

"I know. What's worse, she undoubtedly knows it. What future for a Sunrunner found guilty of murder by accident and incompetence? You *faradh'im* are so much more visible than the common people, after all."

"She did the best she could."

"But failed. Somehow I'll have to find a way of having her publicly pay her debt while restoring her confidence in herself. But you know, out of this may come something I've spent years trying to find a good excuse for doing."

Her brows arched. "And now I'm supposed to guess what."

He grinned at her. "Mm-hmm."

She rose to pace slowly back and forth before the gigantic tapestry of the Desert in spring—but not a spring like this one. No artist could have guessed at this year's glory of flowers. Rohan indulged himself in appreciation of beauty just as glorious as far as he was concerned: his wife's. His gaze followed the graceful swirl of rustling silk skirts, the supple lines of shoulder and arm, waist and hip. But her frown and her occasional mutterings ruined the picture of regal perfection. He would not have had it otherwise; what use had he for a lovely lackwit?

At last she spun on one heel to face him. "You're going to do something about training physicians, aren't you?" she accused.

Rohan nodded. "I'm surprised it took you this long to think of it. I gave you enough clues," he teased.

Sioned ignored this remark. "A school, I take it. Like the scriptorium on Kierst-Isel."

"More or less. The only available training in medical arts is at Goddess Keep or as apprentice to a working physician—not all of whom are of equal skill. A school would allow standardized techniques, shared knowledge, and improved treatments—or so one hopes. What do you think?"

"I think you're a devious son of a—dragon. Is there anything you can't turn to an advantage of one sort or another?"

"Haven't run into one yet," he replied immodestly. "Andry won't like *this* much, either. He'll see it as a threat."

Sioned blinked in surprise. "But Sunrunners will continue to be trained—"

"Of course! Aside from their importance in communications, having someone with at least a basic knowledge of medicine at all holdings is essential. But if they wish to be certified, practicing physicians. . . ."

"They'll need credentials from your school. Where will it be?" She grinned suddenly. "How about Gilad?"

"You can be rather devious, yourself."

"It might mollify Cabar a little. But what are we going to do about Andry?"

Rohan shrugged. "He'll get used to it."

"I doubt it. Rohan, we must tread carefully with him," she warned.

"On the contrary, my love. It is Andry who must learn to walk a little more softly around *me*. Those scrolls Urival and Morwenna brought with them weren't read only by you and Pol. In them I discovered my right to decide certain Sunrunner questions."

"But there are limits."

"And wise ones. I confess to sharing Andry's admiration for this Lady Merisel. She seems to have been a remarkably crafty woman." He laughed. "I have a taste for the type. I'd even bet she was a redhead."

***

Sioned was in the Great Hall, staring in wonder at the flowers Rialt had brought back to decorate the dinner tables when Andry stormed through the open doors. She watched him stride up the center aisle and engaged herself in a private debate. Then, deciding that his anger did not merit a gawking audience, she gestured to the servants. They abandoned the dozens of vases and beat a hasty retreat, closing the double doors behind them.

"Is it true?" Andry demanded.

Sioned met his blazing blue eyes for a moment, then picked up a small, sharp knife and began trimming stems. "Yes."

"He has no right. None! It's given to *me* to judge a Sunrunner!"

"I presume Oclel told you Rohan's reasoning. It's all perfectly legal."

"That doesn't make it right!"

She poured water into a vase and selected flowers for it. "Then petition for a change in the law. For now, it stands."

Andry pulled in a long breath obviously meant to steady himself. "Sioned, you're a Sunrunner. Even though you don't wear the rings, even though you've been High Princess for so long—surely there's some loyalty left in you for the traditions of Goddess Keep. Would you see those rights and privileges smashed for the sake of your own power? That's not worthy of you."

Sioned refused to be baited. "Neither is it worthy of you to imply that I would place power above what is right and just. I forgive you for it because I know you're angry. But if you'll think about this, you'll understand that it was the only thing Rohan could do."

"What he *should* have done was force Cabar to hand Gevlia over to me! I wouldn't have found her innocent—is that what you were all afraid of? I don't dispute that she's guilty of causing Master Thacri's death. But Sunrunners are disciplined by the Lord of Goddess Keep. Not the High Prince!"

One vase filled, she started cutting flowers to fit a shorter one. "I don't think you entirely appreciate the position you and Cabar placed him in."

"Oh, come now, Sioned. Surely you're not complaining that you've had yet another chance to demonstrate how powerful you and Rohan are!"

She slammed the knife on the table so hard the empty vases rattled. "Lord of Goddess Keep you may be, but it hasn't taught you much about what power really is!"

"Lord of Goddess Keep chosen by Lady Andrade—who taught all of us about power!" he snapped.

Sioned forced calm into her voice, reminding herself that this was a proud and potentially dangerous man. And still so young—only twenty-nine. "Andry, I was a Sunrunner long before I was a princess. Do you forget that I pleaded with your parents to allow your training as a squire to end so your chosen life as a Sunrunner could begin?"

"And have you come to regret it?" he asked bitterly.

"Don't be a fool. I don't always agree with you. I didn't always agree with Andrade. We all have our own functions, duties, responsibilities—"

"And Rohan has usurped mine!"

"You gave him no choice! Can't you see that? There can't be one code for Sunrunners and another for everyone else! The woman's negligence brought about a man's death. You yourself admit her guilt. You and Cabar both came to Rohan, agreed to abide by his decision—"

"And he made the wrong one!"

Sioned gritted her teeth in exasperation. "What do you think Cabar would do if Rohan gave her over to you? What would *you* do if Cabar was allowed to decide her punishment? Use your brains, Andry! Rohan's laws provide the only sure justice. That's his duty as High Prince."

Andry met her gaze coldly. "His duty. His laws. His power. Just exactly the way he likes it."

"You don't understand him at all, do you?"

"I understand him perfectly. I've watched him lead the other princes around by the nose every chance he gets. He loves to exercise his power as High Prince and there's no use pretending he doesn't. And he's as jealous of those powers as—"

"When has Rohan ever acted arbitrarily? When has he ever done anything simply because he felt like it? You've watched him at work for two *Riall'im* since Andrade died. You're right, he uses every trick he has to bring the princes to agreement. But have you ever considered why?"

He shrugged. "It amuses him, I suppose. Very well, Sioned, read me the lecture. I'm a little old for the schoolroom, but we won't quibble about it."

She controlled her temper with an effort. "Punishment for crimes—even the definitions of crimes—used to make no sense at all. There were two dozen laws about horse theft and Goddess alone knew how many penalties, depending on whose horse was stolen and what it was worth and how long it was in the thief's possession—Rohan studied law all his life, and *he* couldn't follow all the ins and outs of such chaos. His work has been to organize all the confusion. Every *Rialla* he hacks away at it a little more, persuading the other princes to agree to *one* law and *just* punishment. Law is now associated with him. As High Prince it's his responsibility to arbitrate—"

"And why shouldn't the laws have his name on them? It's only the reality. *His* laws, Sioned—*his* power."

"The duties of the High Prince haven't changed. Rohan hasn't done anything Roelstra couldn't have done if he'd been so inclined. But because Rohan does so much through the law that affects people's everyday lives, it's perceived that his power is the greater."

"It *is* greater. He uses it."

"That's exactly what he *doesn't* do."

"Then let him prove it. Let him *not* use this so-called right he has over Sunrunners, and give judgment to me, where it belongs."

Her patience snapped. "Where you'd like *all* power to belong, isn't that so, Andry? How dare you prate about traditions when you've tossed them aside without a thought! How dare you accuse Rohan of grasping for power when it's *you* who reaches out both hands! Lord of Goddess Keep will never be enough for you, will it? Don't think I don't know precisely what you're up to with your emphasis on the powers of the Goddess and your change in *faradhi* traditions! You're the one who's jealous of power, Andry—especially of what will come to Pol when he's High Prince!"

He turned white, and went as still as stone, not even breathing. Then he sent the vases crashing to the tiled floor with a violent sweep of one hand.

She heard the furious snap of his bootheels as he strode from the Great Hall, but could not watch him go.

Servants came in—silent, hesitant—to clean up shards of glass and pottery. Sioned stared down at her hands. Of all the rings she was entitled to wear, only her husband's emerald gleamed there.

"Well, beloved," she whispered, "I made a fine job of that, didn't I?"

She wiped her hands on a towel and decided she'd better go upstairs and warn Rohan that because of her, Andry was one step away from becoming their open enemy.

***

Rohan and Pol were also discussing the ramifications of power—or, rather, Rohan was talking and Pol was listening. The events at Rivenrock and the outcome of the morning audience having been briefly recounted, they sat alone in the Summer Room.

"Nobody's going to be made happy by this," Rohan sighed. "It's what usually happens when I use my authority as High Prince."

"But there wasn't anything else you could have done."

"No. But that's not how it's going to be perceived. And perception is all, you know," he added ruefully. "The scriptorium at New Raetia is a good example. I contracted with several princes for the physical makings—hide for parchment and bindings, ink, and so on—but I *ordered* each prince to provide copyists. It was the only way to reproduce the volumes at speed. I used Desert wealth to buy the materials, but I couldn't buy the people. So I made it an order of the High Prince. And nobody approved, even though the future advantages ought to have been obvious."

Pol said, "But by now everyone's cooperating for the good they get from the library. The same thing will happen with the school for physicians."

"One hopes so. Still, it's *my* decision, you see. *My* use of power. *My* name that gets associated with it all."

"It may take everyone a while to understand, but—"

"Oh, it always takes more than a while. I never deluded myself I could accomplish it all in my lifetime. Laws, in particular. How do you correct such a mess in thirty years? I could've decreed things and made the princes bow down to my authority. But I don't think I would have lasted long if I'd tried. Not even Roelstra attempted to rule all the princedoms by decree.

"Almost everything I've done has been through the *Rialla*, slowly enough so no one gets too nervous. I let them thrash out an issue among themselves and mostly they end up agreeing with me. When they don't, there's usually something wrong with my reasoning and I have to rethink my position. As often as possible I've let them believe the whole thing is *their* idea. But I'm still High Prince. I'm the one whose name goes at the top of the parchment."

"You're proud of it, Father, don't try to fool me," Pol said with a smile.

"Of course! But that doesn't change the fact that however much benefit comes from the laws I initiate, however careful I am to bring the other princes into the process, some still think I just wave my hand and say, 'This shall be done because We order it so!'" Rohan laughed shortly. "Goddess, if it were only that easy!"

"You're more tender of their feelings than they are of yours. And it's not fair. You're right almost all the time."

"Ah, so you're experienced enough to see that I've made mistakes—and impudent enough to throw them in my face!" He laughed more easily this time.

"Oh, there haven't been that many," Pol reassured him, grinning. "But it's a little daunting, you know. And another reason I wouldn't mind at all if you lived forever. You're going to be difficult to follow."

"Did I ever tell you I felt the same about my own father?"

"But you two were so different from each other. You always knew you couldn't be the kind of prince he was, so you never tried to live up to what he was. *I've* always known that to be like you is the best ambition I could have."

Rohan was absurdly flattered. "Just don't ever start believing that you're always right, Pol. I haven't been—as you so ungraciously pointed out! And you won't be, either. Listen to the other princes. Know what their prejudices are, where their self-interest lies. Don't rule them—guide them. If you can't present an issue in ways that satisfy them, then you're probably acting in your own favor. And they'll scent it as quickly as a hungry dragon does fresh game."

He shifted in his chair and frowned. "Along the way something happened that I never intended. Roelstra projected power through his personality and the art of the well-timed whim—and the equally well-timed art of causing fights that only the High Prince could settle. He didn't care much about the thoughts of ordinary folk. But what I've done touches people's lives. And now they look to me to effect changes—with my name on them. So it seems I have more power and use it more often than is true."

"As long as the work gets done, what does that matter?"

"It matters a great deal. A jealous prince—Cabar is a prime example—is a dangerous one. He can make trouble. I took the decision about this Sunrunner out of his hands. He'll see that as a threat to his power. Wouldn't you?"

"If I was the suspicious type, certainly." Pol paused for a moment. "The new school will make it easier for Cabar to swallow."

"But not for the others. At the *Rialla* this summer I intend to order each prince to contribute at least two physicians for the teaching staff. The benefits won't become clear for some time, just as with the scriptorium. But this time I intend to have someone else's name associated with it—yours, if you're not careful!"

"Mother's!" Pol laughed. "She was the one who thought of putting it in Gilad to soothe Cabar."

"Not a bad idea, but she'd never agree. Besides, it wouldn't do us much good. Everybody knows at least half of my best ideas were hers to begin with. And that when I use 'we,' I mean the two of us." Rohan hoped Pol would consider the advantages of having a wife who shared his work as well as his bed. From what Rohan had seen of Meiglan, she was hardly the type. Yet it suddenly occurred to him that perhaps Pol didn't want or need that kind of woman.

When Pol spoke, it was of filial and not marital relationships. "When I was little I used to get into all sorts of trouble just to get you and Mother away from your work—"

"You think I need reminding?" Rohan chuckled. "After you left for Graypearl we'd get a whole season's work done in a single day—and then sit staring at each other, cursing the quiet."

Pol smiled. "I guess I did demand a lot of attention. And you always gave it to me. But when you and Mother disappeared into your study, I wanted to be there, too.

Have you talk to me the way you talked to each other, about important things. Oh, I was far too young to understand any of it, but—do you know what I mean?"

"My father kept me wrapped in silk until I was eighteen years old. I do understand, Pol. When you grow up around powerful people, it's only natural to want to be in on it. It's not until you're older that you realize the responsibilities."

"Andry would say it's the gift of the Goddess. He seems to find that justification enough for all the changes he's made."

Rohan shrugged. "I don't presume to know the Goddess' mind on this."

"Ask Andry. He seems to have her ear these days."

"Belief is becoming less personal and more public, isn't it? Ostentatious, as Barig said this morning. If Andry has his way, the gentle and very comfortable relationship we have with the Lady is going to change. I find that sad, Pol."

"These long speeches of Andry's worry me. It's as if he's emphasizing his own importance by emphasizing the name of the Goddess. Connecting himself to her."

"Giving a perception of greater power than he in fact possesses?" Rohan shrugged. "Perhaps strength is justification enough for use of power. After all, if you've got it, why not use it?" He was pleased to see Pol grimace.

"If that's so, may the Goddess have mercy on us all."

"I agree." Rohan stretched the tension from his shoulders and sighed. "By now power is expected of me. I don't think I'll be disappointing anyone this time. Not even you," he added.

Pol cleared his throat. "I know I've said some harsh things in the past. I understand why you wait, Father, I just haven't learned your patience yet."

"Mine was a hard school. Your mother and I have tried to make yours a little easier without sacrificing the most important lessons. And this is one. Few people really understand the limits I impose on myself."

"My own limits are what I'm trying to define," Pol said seriously. "I wanted to talk about—well, I don't think you're going to approve, but—"

He broke off as they heard Arlis' adamant voice from

the other side of the door. "I'm sorry, my lord, but it's impossible. His grace is—"

"I don't give a damn if he's making love to his wife!" Barig roared. The door was flung open. Arlis tried to block the furious Giladan, saying, "Forgive me, your graces, but—"

"Do you know what's happened?" Barig waved a parchment from which a ribbon and a broken seal hung. "Do you?"

"Not until you enlighten us, my lord," Rohan replied. "Please calm yourself and tell us what news Prince Cabar has sent." The pink ribbon was Gilad's, and the characteristic grayish tinge to the parchment.

"She's dead! The miserable woman is dead!"

Pol caught his breath. "The Sunrunner?"

"Who else?" Barig rattled the parchment at him. "Because of you, she was allowed the sunlight, a daily walk at noon, and for all I know used her arts to contact other Sunrunners. Then she pretended to be ill one noonday, delayed her walk until later—and when she went out at dusk, she—"

"Oh, Goddess, no," Rohan whispered. "Shadow-lost. Deliberately."

"Yes, deliberately! It took her two days to die. His grace's Sunrunner tried to keep her alive, but it was hopeless. And I know who's to blame! He'll never admit he ordered her to do it, but he's as guilty of murder as she was!"

"Lord Barig!" Rohan made his voice a whiplash under which stronger men than this had flinched. "We have no desire to hear unsubstantiated accusations." He rose and held out his hand for the letter. Barig surrendered it with poor grace. Scanning it quickly, Rohan felt the muscles of his neck and shoulders twist with repressed fury. "We share Prince Cabar's shock. But we are disgusted by his suspicions. You may so inform him when you reply to this." He let the parchment drop to the carpet as if it was too foul to touch. "Arlis, be so good as to find Lord Andry and bring him to us."

"At once, your grace." After a warning glare at the Giladan, the squire bowed himself out.

Barig had recovered some of his aplomb and his words were tinged with as much sarcasm as he dared use to the

High Prince. "This changes nothing. The guilt is still there, and the right of Master Thacri's family to restitution."

"Don't you understand what this woman did to herself?" Pol exclaimed. "That she used the very craft that *was* her life to *end* her life?"

"An unfortunate end, your grace. But self-chosen."

"Yet you just accused someone of ordering her to it," Pol snapped. "Make up your mind, Barig. Give your supposed culprit a name, if you dare!"

"I am not required by his grace my cousin to be insulted by—"

"By the next High Prince," Rohan pointed out. "We suggest you choose your words and your attitude most carefully, my lord. It would be unfortunate if Prince Cabar were held responsible for them."

Barig knew when he was outmanned. He made a jerky bow in Pol's direction, a lower one in Rohan's. "Your grace's permission to withdraw?"

"Granted." Rohan waited just long enough for the door to close, then sank numbly into his chair.

Pol picked up the letter. "Andry's going to spit fire." After a moment's pause, he added without looking at Rohan, "You don't think there's anything in Barig's accusation, do you?"

"Of course not." He shook his head. "Pol—I saw a Sunrunner die that way once. His name was Kessel. Merciful Goddess, to die that way, shadow-lost, mindless —ah, why couldn't she have been patient just a little longer?"

"Perhaps she thought she was doing the right thing. Perhaps she only wanted to escape. Whichever, Barig had a point. It doesn't really change anything."

"No." He paused. "It might be better if I told Andry myself."

"I'll stay, if you don't mind. Father, what's to be done if Cabar makes a public accusation?"

"He won't." Rohan straightened his shoulders. "His grace of Gilad has certain . . . vulnerabilities . . . known to me." He gave Pol a tired, bitter smile. "Knowledge of secrets is also power, my son."

Chapter Twenty

Stronghold: 33 Spring

Marron stood guard duty in the Great Hall during dinner, a tall staff hung with Miyon's heavy orange banner wearing a groove in his shoulder. The evening had begun with another of Andry's invocations to the Goddess. He had quite an audience; even the most humble castlefolk were permitted to dine in the presence of the High Prince, except for those actually serving the meal, on duty at the gates, or at posts of honor inside. It disgusted him that Rohan chose to break bread with the commonality instead of banishing them to the stables and kitchens where they belonged. He saw nothing of the easy sense of community among the people here, nothing of their affection for their princes that came from associating with them in every aspect of their lives.

When the meal was over, Marron would partake of the same excellent food, seated with the other servants at reset lower tables. But with his ancestry and his powers, by rights he should be sitting at the high table—now, this moment, eating off fine Kierstian plate and drinking from delicate Fironese crystal. That he would soon be able to do as he pleased at Stronghold was small comfort. He had had enough of playing lowly servant.

The strain of this charade was wearing on his nerves. Constant vigilance to make sure the face presented was not his own was bad enough. It was exacerbated by the equally nerve-wracking alertness required to stay out of range of those Sunrunners whose *diarmadhi* blood made them sensitive to the spell he had spun around himself. And on a more personal level, he was damned sick and tired of following orders and being a good boy.

He had taken this duty night after night so that Mireva

and Ruval could have time to make further plans and still know what went on at meals. He had volunteered to sleep in the stables, ostensibly to guard Miyon's precious horses, in reality to make sure no one came upon him when he slept and resumed his true shape. He had followed orders to escort Meiglan on today's ride, though it had been chancy keeping out of Riyan's way. He had frightened Meiglan's horse with a brief but vivid conjure, giving Ruval time to sneak up to one of the caves for who knew what purpose. He had succeeded in every task given him—other people's tasks that gained other people's ends. He had endured years of bowing to that bitch Chiana, and after this spring of consorting with lowborn guardsmen he'd had enough. The disguises would be over with sooner than Mireva or Ruval thought.

He absorbed the details of the Great Hall with a discerning eye. Intimately familiar with Swalekeep's ancient elegance made a bit garish by Chiana's taste, he found Stronghold a marvel of classic beauty and strength. Only the best for High Prince Rohan, he told himself sourly. Exquisite dinner service, magnificent tapestries, furniture carved of the finest Syrene woods, candles from Grib giving soft white light instead of oily, smoking torches—though this was a warrior's castle, always battle-ready, it was also that of a prince.

Marron was a prince. And before he was done, he would be High Prince in his grandfather's place, with the castles of two lands to choose among for his residence. He shifted the banner from the bruise on his shoulder and, after a moment's consideration, decided to spend spring at Dragon's Rest, summer at Castle Crag, autumn at Feruche, and winter here at Stronghold. There would be pleasure trips to Radzyn and other places as he desired, and Elktrap would make a fine hunting lodge. . . . He grinned to himself. If Mireva and Ruval thought he would meekly accept Feruche as his only payment for all he had endured, they would have to think again.

His stomach growled a demand for dinner, and the Tiglathi guard standing nearby with his lord's banner glanced over with a sympathetic smile. Marron gave a little shrug in reply. Tonight's gathering was not the grand banquet ordered up for Miyon's arrival, and so music and dancing would not follow into the night. But the highborns were taking a long time over their taze. With the rumors of the Sunrunner's death in Gilad, it was amazing that a formal meal was taking place at all. He would have thought they'd all eat in their rooms.

The food here was spectacular, even that served to the common folk. The flesh Marron had lost at Tiglath from unaccustomed physical labor was returning to his belly. He wondered enviously how these Desert people kept their figures; Rohan had the waistline of a man half his age, and the High Princess showed off a lissome shape tonight in a simple blue dress that slid along her like water.

Marron changed his stance again in irritation as the squires went around with still more pitchers. Then he squinted up to the high table and frowned. It was not taze that was being poured but wine, and into tiny crystal glasses like the ones Chiana used for sweet fruit cordials. A toast, then. Marron grimaced. That fool Miyon had probably signed some agreement or other—not that any of it meant anything. Neither Rohan nor Pol would be around long enough to fulfill any bargains.

He caged his impatience as best he could, knowing that his own plan as well as Mireva's required him to wait just a little longer. She wanted him to assist in Ruval's challenge to Pol, but Ruval was not going to have the chance. Marron would be the one to claim that right. He would couch it in a demand for Feruche, but with Pol's defeat not just that castle but all of Princemarch would be forfeit. And his dear brother could try as he might to dislodge him. Marron had what Ruval did not: Chiana's trust and, through that, her army.

The noisy chatter in the Great Hall fell to whispers as Pol got to his feet and raised his glass. The crystal glowed dark sapphire blue in candlelight blazing from wall sconces and tables. Only the best here, Marron thought again— the Gribains demanded outrageous sums for their candles and these were the finest, burning clear and bright amid huge vases of flowers. Not that any candle would dare gutter in the presence of the High Prince, he added spitefully.

Pol waited for silence. Marron doubted he would make any remark about the dead Sunrunner. No one had confirmed the rumors, and the Giladan courier had known nothing useful when Ruval had casually questioned him a short while ago. Lord Andry was looking tight-jawed, Marron noted with a tiny smile. Sunrunner deaths were a thing he'd have to get used to.

Pol began to speak in a crisp, admirably carrying voice. Even at the far end of the huge hall, Marron heard every word.

"The death of my beloved kinsman, Lord Sorin of Feruche, has left a void in all our hearts. He was everything that a man should be, and more. He loved the Desert and its people."

Marron smiled to himself. *Rest assured I will cherish your princedom, too, Starborn, once it is mine.*

"But most especially Sorin loved the wondrous castle he created. Feruche is his from its foundation to its topmost spires. Every stone was planned and placed by him. Sorin's it is, and always will be."

Mine it will be, and all else with it!

"His loss is a grievous one—to his family, his friends, to all of us. It is a sorrow to me to have the giving of Feruche. I had hoped Sorin would give it to his eldest son. But I think he would wish to see his beautiful castle ruled by a man who was close to him in friendship, who will make of Feruche what Sorin would have made of it himself. It is with confidence that I give it now to Lord Riyan of Skybowl."

The blood roared in Marron's ears and he shook with rage. It was *Pol* he must challenge for possession of Feruche, not some lowborn Sunrunner without a drop of prince's blood in his veins, *Pol* who must own Feruche now that Sorin was dead. How dared he do this? He simply could not give it away, could not ruin Marron's chance to thwart Ruval and gain everything for himself.

"No!"

His shout was drowned by cries of Riyan's name as everyone lifted their glasses. But a moment later a woman shrieked in stark terror. Marron's fury had overcome his sorcery. As he strode up to the high table, his second face and form shimmered away.

***

The scream at the end of the Great Hall found hysterical echo at the high table. Meiglan's face was a horrified mask, her eyes gone black and her skin dead white.

Nearly lost in her piercing cry was the shatter of crystal and the soft groan Riyan gave as he dropped his glass and clutched his trembling fists to his chest.

An old woman ran to Meiglan and hauled her bodily from the room. Rohan saw this from the corner of his eye, grateful that someone had had the sense to remove the girl before her screams infected the whole room. He forced himself to stand straight and still, even though the fragments of Sunrunner heritage in him flinched in response to Riyan's pain, just as Sioned was quivering at his side. He was High Prince; he could show no reaction and especially no weakness.

And no foolishness, as Andry was still young enough to do. He shouted an order for his *faradh'im* to seize the man whose lineaments were shifting, changing, hovering between one face and another in obvious struggle to resume his false shape. Nialdan and Oclel ran down the center aisle and got within arm's reach of the man before a circle of cold white fire sprang up in defense.

Rohan could have told Andry it wouldn't work. He kept silent as the Sunrunners fell back. The enemy had strength; Rohan had been expecting a manifestation of it for many days now, and thus was not as shocked as he might have been. Still—none of them had ever heard of this aspect of *diarmadhi* power, the ability to alter one's face and form. None of them knew how to deal with it. Now, of all times, patience was needed. Strength had been shown; Rohan hoped that waiting would expose weakness. There was noting else he could do.

At his shoulder, Pol whispered, "It's Ianthe's younger son. I recognize the red hair. And where one is, the other must be as well."

Rohan nodded. "He must be among Miyon's suite. The search must be conducted by Riyan. Have him take Morwenna with him. They're the only ones who can sense sorcery through their rings."

Pol blinked as his old teacher was identified as part-*diarmadhi*, but recovered quickly. "I'll have all the Cunaxans rounded up at once."

Sioned murmured, "Get Rialt to do it. I have the feeling you're to be a featured performer in this little play."

Miyon had recovered from his stupefaction by this

time, and gestured for the red-haired man to be brought forward—as foolish an order as Andry's had been. Behind the wall of icy flames as tall as his head, the man had begun to laugh. When he walked the rest of the long aisle, Nialdan and Oclel warily trailing him, it was because he chose to do so. The fire formed a cloak around him.

Miyon braced his fists on the table before him. "I am horrified!" he exclaimed. "A sorcerer posing as one of my own guard!"

Rohan slanted a look at him. The shock had been genuine, but not the protestation. Just as he'd expected. "We understand," he said, knowing Miyon would not hear the irony.

"Do you, my lord? To discover one of that foul race has been in charge of my safety for Goddess knows how long?" Miyon gave an artistic shudder.

"You have our sympathies," Sioned told him. "Perhaps you would care to withdraw, my lord. Your nerves must be quite shattered."

Miyon gaped for an instant before recovering his dignity. A flight of dragons couldn't tear him away from this spectacle.

"No?" Sioned went on. "Very well, then. You must have a great interest in this, after all."

"Self-interest," Tobin supplied ingenuously from nearby. What she really meant and what Miyon had to pretend she meant were entirely different things.

"Naturally I wish to know how this came to pass, my lady," he said to Tobin, who nodded as if she believed him.

Andry spoke up impatiently, outrage blazing in his eyes. "Confine this man at once! There must be some way to—"

"And what would you suggest?" Sioned asked. He had no answer and no chance to think of one, for the man had reached the area before the high table.

He made a sweeping movement with one arm and the fire vanished. In a ringing voice he called out, "I am Marron, grandson of High Prince Roelstra and rightful Lord of Feruche, where I was born of the Princess Ianthe! I am willing to prove my claim against the usurper Pol at a time and place of his choosing!"

If he had expected pandemonium, he was doomed to disappointment. Absolute silence greeted his announcement. Rohan merely lifted a brow.

Pol said, "If I was disposed to entertain this absurd claim, which I am not, I would point out that Feruche belonged to Lord Riyan the moment I placed its ring on his finger."

"It is *you* I challenge, not him!"

Andry had gasped on hearing the name, and now said in a tone of deadly quiet, "This man murdered my brother."

"I am a prince. My person is inviolate unless formal charges are brought against me—and even then I cannot be forcibly detained." Marron smirked. "Read your own law, High Prince."

"It's one we haven't gotten around to changing," Rohan admitted with mild regret. "As for formal charges—the murder of Lord Sorin is primary among them."

"I killed him in self-defense," Marron shrugged. "He attacked me. If every man who slew an enemy in battle was tried for murder, half the high table here would be long gone. And in any case, no one but a gathering of princes can judge me. I am sworn to no one, I am no man's vassal. I am a prince."

"That's open to debate," Pol snapped. "I myself saw you helping to kill a dragon. And *that* law applies to everyone, no matter what station!"

" 'Helping'?" Marron grinned at him. "That's a matter of interpretation. There is no means by which you may arrest or detain me. And you still haven't answered my challenge."

Riyan stepped around the high table, still pallid, still rubbing at his fingers. "I accept for Prince Pol. Goddess forbid that he should dirty his hands on you."

"I do not accept! I challenge Pol, not you!"

"And I say Feruche is mine, and it is me you will fight!" Riyan shouted. "Will it be swords, you bastard excuse for a prince, or sorcerer's tricks?"

"Neither," Andry said. "This man has admitted to murdering my brother. His death is mine."

Marron swung to face him, suddenly wary. In the next instant Riyan groaned and doubled over, his hands twisting into claws as Marron's sorcery lashed out. Before anyone could draw another breath, Fire engulfed Marron's body, gold and crimson and so intense that Nialdan and Oclel cried out and shielded their faces. But defense came too late. Andry spread his arms wide, calling down yet more Fire. And when it subsided, there was only the stench of charred flesh and a pathetic scattering of blackened bones on the tiles.

***

"He knew somehow about the rings, what they signified," Riyan said.

Ruala nodded. "Even in the brief time since I met him, I've learned that it doesn't do to underestimate Lord Andry."

They walked together through the back gardens, where Princess Milar's fountain blossomed taller and stronger than ever in this spring of abundant water. The little stream that meandered through the lush green grass and flowers had overflowed all winter, and even now was barely contained by its banks. Firepots glowed along the pathways and glittered from the little bridge arching over the stream. The stars were bright enough tonight to illumine all but the grotto, and it was to this place that Riyan guided their steps.

She had been the one to come to him. After Rohan, looking sick and stunned, had ordered everyone out of the Great Hall, Riyan had sought the coolness of the fountain. It was only memory that burned around his fingers, but memory was enough to make him plunge his damnably shaking hands in the water. Ruala had found him there.

She paused at the apex of the little bridge and looked up at the stars. "It was a brave thing you did, accepting challenge on Marron's terms of sorcery."

Riyan shrugged. "I was so furious I didn't really know what I was saying."

Ruala smiled at him. "Yes you did. I've come to know you, too, in the short time since we met at Elktrap."

"And do I worry you as much Andry does?" he asked, inviting her to flirt with him.

She was in no mood for it; her look turned serious and she said, "He's changing everything. All the traditions of Goddess Keep. I don't know why anyone was surprised when he killed Marron using his gifts. I expected it."

"I should have, too, I suppose. But Sunrunner training is so strong—it's not something any of us can even consider, even if we're threatened. And I really *wasn't* thinking straight, you know. My rings had turned to fire. I keep wondering why that happens."

Ruala hesitated. "If you promise not to interrupt, I can explain."

He watched her face for a long moment, the dark green eyes shadowed to black, the strong lines of nose and cheek and jaw softened by starlight. Taking her arm, he walked with her down the pathway again in silence.

"My family is very old and has lived very isolated," she began. "In the Veresch, memories are long. The mountain folk still prefer their dialect of the old tongue. I speak it myself a little—one has to, in order to deal with them. And sometimes they treat the old ways as if the new did not exist. Things you Sunrunners are only now rediscovering through the scrolls, some people in the Veresch have always known."

"What do you know about the scrolls?" he demanded.

She gave him a slight smile. "You weren't to interrupt. But no matter. My grandfather despaired of my ever believing any of the family stories. But this spring has taught me how true they are. How else could Andry have defeated a *diarmadhi* if he hadn't learned it from the scrolls? Oh, it's not stated openly. You have to be as devious as Lady Merisel herself to discover the method."

Riyan stared at her. "How do you know all this?"

"I might not have credited my grandfather's tales, but I listened to them."

"Lord Garic," he said suddenly. "The same name as Lady Merisel's husband."

"It's a rather common name in the Veresch," she said easily. "Something else he told me was that the ceremony of giving the rings is a simple one, but potent. The very gold you *faradh'im* use is charged with power. Some say Lady Merisel cleaned out an entire mine on Kierst and had the gold brought to her at Goddess Keep to be imbued with power. Lord Gerik and Lord Rosseyn helped her as long as they could, but not even they had the strength to endure five days of it. She was more powerful than any of us can imagine. Rings made from this special gold are given to a Sunrunner rather casually—although

I'm told Lord Andry makes it more of a ceremony these days. But it doesn't matter. The spell is already in the gold. That's Lady Merisel's gift to Sunrunners. The warning when sorcery is nearby—*if* they possess sorcerer's blood themselves."

"I don't understand. Why would she do that, if she spent her life working against *diarmadh'im*? Logically, the power in the rings would be a trap for those trying to pass themselves off as Sunrunners."

"Tell me, my lord, does the fact that you have *diarmadhi* blood inevitably make you evil?"

"There are a lot of people who are going to be asking themselves exactly that," he replied bitterly.

"The only answer that counts is yours." She stopped walking and looked up into his eyes, her own strangely intense.

"My answer is 'no.' Of course it doesn't. And I see your point, my lady—character determines how power will be used, not the source of that power."

"Ah." She sighed softly and continued on toward the grotto.

"You don't agree?" he asked, confused.

"Certainly I agree. But how much easier it would be if one could say, 'Here is a *faradhi*, who always does the good and right thing, and there is a *diarmadhi*, who cannot.' People would prefer it so."

"Andry would," he mused. "He doesn't dare touch *me*, but I've always felt that anyone else would be wise to hide it from him." Ruala nodded sadly. Riyan pulled a branch of Sioned's willow out of her way and said, "So the reaction was set into the gold rings as a warning. Wait a moment—the silver ones burn, too."

"But not as much. Originally *all* Sunrunner rings were gold. Perhaps they changed some to silver when the supply began to dwindle, and mixed some of the spelled gold into the making. That would be sensible, but I don't really know." She glanced up. "Why do you think the rings of a Lord or Lady of Goddess Keep are always taken at death and melted down to make the successor's rings?"

"You know a great deal for having lived—isolated," he commented warily.

She ignored his rather obvious hint. "Not that it signifies with Lord Andry, that he had new rings made. The gold and silver are the same. And he has no Old Blood. But once the special gold runs out. . . ."

Riyan saw that he would have to be blunt. "Why didn't your grandfather say something, tell someone?"

"The sorcerers haven't threatened in generations. But they've come into the open again, and Lady Merisel's wisdom is serving you very well. They can't work their spells around Sunrunners such as you without giving themselves away—and without their spells, they are relatively harmless."

They came to the waterfall that tumbled down mossy rocks from the hidden spring and stood quietly for a time, listening to the night. Its sounds were very different at Skybowl: water surged gently there, did not dance and chatter like this. The stars reflected off slow ripples across the lake, did not dart and tease the eye with glinting swiftness off the spraying drops. At Feruche, Riyan thought suddenly, there was no open water at all. Strange that he'd been so unwilling to accept it from Pol this afternoon, and yet by evening was ready to risk his life to keep it.

"You know a lot about the *diarmadh'im*," he said at last. "And about the Sunrunners. I'd like to hear Lord Garic's stories sometime."

"You're welcome at Elktrap whenever you like, my lord. It would please my grandfather very much to see you again."

Riyan looked down at her. He would risk it; somehow he had to risk it. "And would it please you? Would *you* welcome me, Ruala?"

She met his gaze steadily, and it seemed all the stars concentrated their brilliant light in her eyes.

When a playful night breeze tossed water at them like handfuls of diamonds, they were much too busy kissing each other to notice.

***

Pol dismissed Edrel as soon as he entered his own chambers and let his clothes fall where they would, careful only of the gold belt buckle given at his knighting. Restless, sickened by the night's events, he paced a carpet made of thin, nubby Fessenden wool and tried to find some center of calm within himself.

He hadn't felt equal to staying with his family as they heard Andry out. He knew how the conversation would go—Andry would say again what he had said when the Fire had died and Marron with it: "He killed Sorin. He deserved to die." No Sunrunner ethic, no consideration of orderly process of law, no argument in the world would ever convince Andry that he had done something terribly wrong. And beneath the angry frustration he knew the others shared, Pol was afraid.

He could not have endured being near his cousin another instant. So he had left with Rialt on the pretext of finding and confining the rest of Miyon's suite so Riyan and Morwenna could test for the presence of sorcery. But Riyan had disappeared. Considering the jittery state of Pol's own nerves after this night's business, he didn't have the heart to track him down.

He doubted anything else would occur before tomorrow, anyway. Long ruminations about the brothers and what Ruval said the day Sorin died had convinced Pol that Marron's action was unexpected, not part of the master plot. Ruval was the elder, and his would be the serious challenge. Pol had been waiting for it. Tomorrow, next day, the day after—it would come soon enough. But not tonight.

A breeze had come up with the rising moons, and Pol stood at the windows to feel its coolness. The Desert smelled different this year, rich with water and flowers, unlike the usual clean aridity, almost the fragrances of Dragon's Rest. His grandmother Milar's fountain rose nearly twice its normal height with increased flow from the hidden spring. As Pol looked down on it, he considered a long walk in the gardens to clear his head. He saw a man and woman strolling idly from the direction of the grotto, holding hands. The pleasure of recognizing Riyan and Ruala as they stopped for a kiss was welcome distraction from the uncomfortable jumble of his feelings.

But not distraction enough. Turning from the windows, he walked the length of his bedchamber again, soft carpet and then chill stone beneath his bare feet as he made the circuit over and over. His thoughts circled, too: Andry, Marron, Ruval, the dead Sunrunner in Gilad, Miyon, dragons, Meiglan—especially Meiglan.

She was providing exactly the distraction her father

had intended. Pol muttered a lurid curse, but whether it was directed at Miyon or himself, he wasn't sure. He'd thought to trap everyone else into thinking him in love with the girl. But by now he was beginning to think it was himself he had trapped.

She'd be gone soon, temptation with her, and at the *Rialla* this summer he'd find a woman more to his taste. Older, more self-assured, capable of being High Princess. Beautiful, of course, but smart and clever as well. Someone like Sionell had turned out to be.

And yet. . . . He could not imagine beauty more compelling than Meiglan's when she stood before her *fenath*, swaying gracefully back and forth as she plucked magic from the strings.

Just as her father had intended.

Pol stripped off his trousers and underwear and flung himself across the bed. *Clever prince*, he accused in disgust. He ought to be thinking about the challenge to his power that Ruval would surely make in the next day or two. Instead he was conforming to plan by fretting over Meggie. There, he had even given her the tender nickname. He doused the candles with a thought and determinedly shut his eyes. He'd be no good to himself or anyone else if he didn't get some sleep. He needed a clear head tomorrow.

There was a whisper of lace and silk in the darkness, barely audible above the splash of the fountain below, and a faint fragrance he recognized at once. He sat straight up in bed, quickly hauling the sheet around his naked body, and heard her catch her breath.

"No—please, my lord—no light!"

"Meiglan? What are you doing here?"

"I—I made them let me in," she breathed, gliding closer to the bed, a slender drifting shadow hinted at by moonlight.

"They told me you were sleeping. Surely you ought to—" He could hardly believe her women would allow her out of her bedchamber, let alone into his.

"I had to see you! I had to be near you—I'm so frightened, my lord, it's all been so terrible, this whole day—"

"It's all right now, Meiglan. Nothing to be afraid of."

"Not here," she said softly. "I feel safe with you."

Pol drew in a shaky breath. Knowing he should not, that more definite sight of her would be dangerous, he gestured the bedside candle into being. Her whole body flinched and he automatically reached for her hand. It was small and chill in his palm. And he'd been right; the candle was a mistake. She wore a nightdress with a pale silk bedrobe over it and dark lace over her hair. She shifted her head and the veil slid to the floor. Her golden curls seemed to have a luminescence all their own, and their perfume was intoxicating. She took a step closer and he began to feel dizzy.

"You came to me at Tiglath," she breathed, trembling. "Sent by the Goddess in a dream. I didn't know until I came here—but it was you, even to your rings." She gestured to the moonstone that had been Lady Andrade's, the amethyst of Princemarch. "You're *faradhi*, my lord. Tell me what my dream meant. Please."

"I—I don't know." He cleared his throat and let go of her hand. *She* must be the dream. This wasn't possible. He felt strange, light-headed, his whole body tingling but not in the usual manner of desire. "Meiglan—"

"Let me stay a while," she begged. "Just until I'm not so frightened."

He nodded, and she sat at the foot of the bed—out of reach, for which he was grateful. Goddess, she was magic itself by candlelight, all gold hair and dark eyes and cloud-pale skin. She must know that. Why else would she be here? He felt betrayed by his own perceptions, furious that he had been so utterly wrong about her. Her father had planned this, too, and Meiglan was about as innocent as a harborside whore.

One way to be sure.

He got hold of her hand again and eased toward her across the bed. Memories of other seductions tumbled through him—there had not been as many women as Rialt teased him about, but there had been enough. And there had been Morwenna. Dear, lusty, laughing, wry Morwenna, who had come to him in the guise of the Goddess that hadn't fooled him for an instant, informing him that she had taken it upon herself to correct any bad habits he might have learned.

"Don't be so clumsy! And remember there are paths and paths of pleasure. Oh, come now, Pol—subtlety! If

you haven't learned any better than that, it's a good thing I'm here to teach you!"

Teach him she had. He stroked the back of Meiglan's palm, turned it over to place a kiss in its hollow. With his other hand he untied the loose knot of her nightdress and before long had it off her shoulders. She was quivering, eyes closed, head tilting slightly back to expose the delicate line of her throat. An open invitation for his lips, he noted with a tight smile. She was no more a virgin than Morwenna, and he would prove it to himself and be rid of the aching tenderness caused by her supposed vulnerability.

But he was finding it difficult to breathe. The closer he got to her, the more his head spun. She lay back across the bed, her fingers locked with his, the golden cloud of her hair spread over white silk sheets. Her body was curving and slender and the only difference in color between her skin and the silk she lay upon was the faintest glow of rose, teasing at his *faradhi* senses.

Pol lowered himself half-across her, looked down into her face that seemed hazy in the soft fog of her incredible hair. He buried his lips in the curve of her shoulder. She gave a soft cry that was his name as his knee parted her thighs. Head reeling, he took her mouth, not caring anymore that he was supposed to be doing this, that she had come here with this in mind. He was drunk with her face and form and scent, his senses all awry, as if he'd plunged into some boiling lake whose water seeped into his blood through his skin, depths where there was no air to breathe and he would drown—and not give a damn about the death.

Neither his tastes nor his vices included raping little girls. But this was no child-woman whose body arched against his, no virgin whose nails dug into his back and buttocks, no inexperienced innocent whose kisses matched his in passion.

"Find out what a woman wants," Morwenna had instructed. *"How she likes to be touched. Where your touch will do the most good! Be responsive to her mood— sometimes, just as will be true of you, she won't be certain which path she'll want to take. This is especially so if she's not experienced. But finding out can be very pleasurable!"*

Meiglan knew exactly what she wanted and how she wanted it. Pol gave it to her—quickly, fiercely, without caution or finesse or caring about anything other than his lust.

When he was done, he lay on his back and stared up at the bed curtains. Bitterness like Sunrunner's Fire seared his pride. Himself so clever, he mocked, and she so innocent. He had discovered the truth of her, and the disappointment and shame burned his heart to ashes.

"Now . . . now I am yours," she whispered beside him.

He turned his head and saw the sweet joy illuminating her face. The dizziness increased. False, all of her false, some part of him repeated, and now that he was not touching her he could hear that voice again. He rose and went to the windows. The night air froze the sweat on his naked skin.

"My lord?" Her voice was soft, hesitant, half-fearful again. "Have I displeased you?"

Pol clenched his fists. Moonlight and the cool breeze washed him in pale silver, and he shivered. "Why would you think that?"

"I–I know nothing of the ways of a man after—after. . . ."

He spun around. "Liar!" he hissed. "Who are you really? Not that timid frightened child you've been at such pains to show me! Who are you?"

"My lord—why are you angry?" She sat up, her hair tumbling around her, clutching the sheet to her breasts. One hand stretched out, pleading with him. Her eyes were like two black hollows in her face, filled with night.

"What's the plan now?" he demanded in a fury of betrayal and wounded pride. "Claim that I raped you, so your father can invoke the law? *You* were the one who came to *me*, my lady! Who'd listen to a rape charge from a woman who slinks into a man's bedroom dressed like a hired whore?"

She gasped and cringed back. "Why are you being so cruel?" she breathed. "I thought you w–wanted me—"

"I want you to get out. Now." He stayed where he was in the clean moonlight, knowing that if he approached her he would probably strike her. Besides, there was a better repayment. In silken tones he said, "I doubt your father will be happy with your failure."

"Oh, no! Please don't tell my father about this! He'd kill me!"

Pol nodded. "Yes, I think he might."

"My lord—oh, Pol, please, you must protect me from him—"

He laughed aloud. "You can't be serious! Looking to me for protection? Is there no limit to you?"

She gave a terrified sob. He turned his back and stared sightlessly down at the fountain.

At length she stopped crying, and he heard the rustle of her discarded nightdress. "My lord?" she asked in a small voice. "Will you at least help me return to my chambers without—without anyone seeing me? I could not bear the shame."

"A little late for that, isn't it?" he snapped. But a lack of witnesses was to his advantage, as well. In fact, he had been wondering why no one had burst in on them yet. Perhaps Miyon had counted on his being so besotted that one taste of Meiglan's sweet white flesh would bring a formal Choice, in which case witnesses to a "rape" would be unnecessary.

He said, "Very well. I'll make sure—"

He forgot what he'd been about to say as a wave of nausea swept over him. He staggered back against the window frame, barely hearing Meiglan's cry of his name. Colors whirled all around him, catching him up in their brilliant power, drawing him helplessly along thick ropes of woven light far from Stronghold.

Chapter Twenty-one

Dragon's Rest: 33 Spring

Ostvel was beyond exhaustion. This morning he had awakened from a brief rest—more like a dead faint—to find abused muscles stiff, his very bones bruised. The damp spring night had put an ache into every joint in his body, but the pain was so familiar by now that it was as if he had never felt anything else. Oddly enough, his head no longer swam with the thick confusion of weariness. Everything had become clear as Fironese crystal. All considerations of trusting or not trusting Andry, all political permutations of an army's march on the palace, all intricate webs of motive and reason and responsibility had resolved into a very simple thing. It was so obvious, really. He must ride to Dragon's Rest. He supposed he was lucky he still had some idea why.

The two guards, Chandar and Jofra, were doing better than he. But then, they were younger. Donato had looked awful during the whole journey—which might have been three days or three years by now, for all Ostvel knew. The Sunrunner had struggled bravely but uselessly against his reaction to crossing water. Ostvel had a vague memory of holding his friend's head over the side of the boat as Donato vomited and then collapsed in groaning misery. The Faolain's swift current had taken them downstream faster than Ostvel had calculated, and they had almost missed the landing. Still, any time gained had been offset by the difficulties of getting Donato fit to sit a horse. They had ended by having him ride pillion until noon, which had slowed them down even more. But then he had declared himself equal to holding the reins instead of merely getting a mindless grip on Jofra's belt. And they had been riding ever since, with stops only for a little food, a few moments' rest, and fresh horses.

These were more difficult to find than Ostvel had thought. Though as lord of Castle Crag and former Regent of Princemarch he could commandeer any horse he chose, he knew animals of better quality would be forthcoming if money were offered as well. He'd been in luck with the first change, for the minor *athri* whose possessions included the landing had an eye for good horseflesh. But inspection of another holding's stables the next day had produced nothing worth riding, let alone risking a princedom on.

He had been lucky again this afternoon, finding four sturdy mountain ponies perfect for the approach to Dragon's Rest he had in mind. It had taken the greater part of his purse to secure them, their owner being naturally suspicious of a man he'd never even heard of, but Ostvel had not allowed Jofra to convince the man with his sword. Especially not after the news that a great many horses and soldiers had been seen passing that way only the previous night.

"We're not too far behind them, then," Ostvel had sighed as they rode off. "They should get there by dark. And so will we."

They could not enter the valley the usual way. They must go up over the hills and approach from the western flank. And now, at midnight, when Ostvel was barely conscious and sodden with weariness, he reined in very suddenly at the sight of the palace down below him.

"All serene," Jofra muttered. "Shall we ride down and warn them, my lord?"

Ostvel rubbed his throbbing temples and upended his water skin over his head to wake himself up. The shock of cold water made him shiver. But it did not entirely clear his head. Now that his simple goal had been reached, his mind infuriatingly muddled again. The hillside wood was protection from a chill breeze, but the darkness felt thick and menacing.

"Too serene," Chandar said, frowning.

"Donato? Donato!"

The Sunrunner jerked upright in his saddle and mumbled something. He looked worse than Ostvel felt.

"Wake up, man. Tell us what you see down there and at the valley entrance."

"What? Oh—yes." He swung off his pony and groaned

softly as a joint cracked. "Goddess in glory! Sitting this brute is like being in a sailboat during a storm."

"How would you know, Sunrunner?" Ostvel smiled faintly. "Tell me what's going on down there or I'll take you back to Castle Crag the way we left it."

Donato gave him a black look. "If so, I'll make damned sure to throw up all over *you*." He walked gingerly toward the moonlight at the edge of the trees.

"My lord?" Chandar asked. "Has anyone ever even thought about defending Dragon's Rest?"

Ostvel had helped plan the palace. Familiar thoughts came easily enough to reassure him about the state of his wits, and he consciously polished them on well-known ideas. "Its situation is its best defense. The valley narrows to the south, the only approach for an army. You can ride four horses abreast, but that's it. The area is regularly patrolled, even at night. The two towers are placed to defend against frontal assault, which is the only kind that can be made here. There's a guardhouse halfway down the valley on the eastern slope. Invaders could make things difficult, but they can't possibly take the place."

Chandar looked thoughtful. "I don't mean to argue, my lord, but it seems to me that this isn't a regular kind of army."

"How so?"

"I've been considering it. Where would Lord Morlen get so many people? From the Veresch. And they don't think like soldiers trained elsewhere. Some of our own guards at Castle Crag are mountain folk, and they tell me there's almost no place they couldn't take if they set their minds to it. And I don't believe it's boasting, either, my lord. I think they'll attack the expected way, up through the valley. But I also think they'll come down out of the hills—*un*-expectedly."

Jofra spoke up. "I'll go take a look if you like, my lord. Over on that ridge would be a good place to muster."

"Do that. But be careful and be silent about it. If Chandar's right, they may be waiting for you."

The guard dismounted and vanished into the trees. Donato came back then, shaking his head. "Nothing unusual at the palace—unless you count a couple of servants dallying in the rose garden by moonlight. And nothing at all down the valley."

"How far did you look?"

"To the narrows."

Ostvel rubbed his forehead. "I don't like this. Where are they? The man we bought the ponies from said he'd seen them last night. If they've melted into nothingness, then perhaps you're right about their plan of attack, Chandar."

"I'll go look again, out beyond the valley," Donato offered, and returned to the moonlight.

"And then there's the sorcery," Ostvel muttered to himself.

"My lord?"

"Nothing." He dismounted, caught himself against the saddle as his knees buckled, and bent to rub his aching thighs. "I'm too old for this sort of thing. Does it seem to you as if the palace has been warned?"

Chandar shook his head. "Not at all. You see the horses down the valley, my lord? They ought to be in the stables, ready to be saddled in a hurry. Yet there they are in the paddocks as if this were any other spring night."

"The guards commander could be trying to present as normal a face as possible, to lull the invaders into feeling secure."

"Not with horses out of quick reach."

"Damn." So he'd been right about Andry. But why would Andry want Dragon's Rest besieged?

Donato was fairly staggering back to them. Chandar jumped down from his saddle and caught the Sunrunner before he could fall.

"Ostvel—you were right, they're out there! Hundreds and hundreds of them! Even more than I saw at Rezeld! And the banners are raised now in their camp." He gulped in air. "Meadowlord's black deer!"

"Meadowlord? What in the name of the Goddess does Halian think he's doing?" Ostvel felt his brain whirl again, but with shock that chased all the exhaustion away. An idea occurred to him. "Donato—your rings. No burning?"

"None."

Then their sorcerers were not at work tonight—obviously, or Donato would have seen peaceful, empty space instead of encampment and banners. Ostvel paced away from the two men, thinking quickly. Dragon's Rest did not know the danger it faced. Halian's forces did not know someone was aware of their presence. There might be a hope.

He spun around. "Chandar, what are the chances of organizing a raid? Tonight, now, as soon as we can get down to the palace."

"If it's done in total silence, my lord, and if Prince Halian's army is caught unawares—but the narrowness of the valley entrance works against defenders as well as against invaders. Four horses abreast is no way to run a surprise attack."

"Donato! What kind of horses did you see?"

The Sunrunner frowned. "A pretty wide mix. Mostly those feather-hoofed Kadar horses, but a good selection of Radzyn breed and a lot of mountain ponies. Why?"

"I was hoping you'd say just that. If the ponies are still tethered down below, then their owners won't be up on the heights getting ready for their own surprise attack. When Jofra comes back, I think he'll confirm. Donato, find Pol at Stronghold. Sioned will do. But *not* Andry. Avoid him at all costs. Say what's happened and what we propose to do about it."

"At once, my lord."

Once more he walked out into the moonlight. While he was working, Jofra returned with exactly the news Ostvel had hoped for: signs of reconnoitering, but no troops waiting in the hills.

Donato took a long time about it, but finally joined them again. "I found Riyan out in the gardens with some untrained girl who was trying to hide her colors from me. He's going to inform Rohan, Sioned, and Pol. But he says to start on his authority anyway while we're awaiting formal word."

"Excellent." They remounted and rode slowly down the steep slope, not wishing to provoke general alarm. A pair of guards galloped up from their regular patrol and, recognizing Ostvel, heard him out. But by the time he had explained everything to the commander and the stabled horses were being readied as quickly and silently as possible, the moons were on a swift descent. Donato remained outside to receive Sioned's message. When preparations were well underway, Ostvel joined his anxious wait.

"Tell me about the rings," Donato said suddenly.

"I'm surprised you haven't asked before now."

"You had other things on your mind. Tell me, Ostvel."

"It happens to Riyan as well. When sorcery is being done, usually nearby."

Donato gave him a sharp look. "To Riyan—not to Sioned or other Sunrunners?"

"Only to those with *diarmadhi* blood as well as Sunrunner gifts," Ostvel said levelly. "Lord Urival was one."

A short silence. "Sweet Mother of All—you're telling me I'm—"

"You have the heritage. So does my son, through his mother. You knew Camigwen. Was she a sorcerer? Was Urival? Is Riyan?"

"Am I?" Donato asked bitterly. Then he stiffened and his eyes lost focus. Ostvel was long familiar with the sight of a Sunrunner at work. He held his breath while moonlight seemed to glow brighter around Donato's weary face. When it was over, the man stumbled against Ostvel.

"It—it was Sioned—but Andry more than she—Goddess, you've no idea his power—"

"Donato!" Ostvel shook him.

"He just—he wove himself through the light, treated her as if she was a single thread in a huge tapestry that was only him—"

"Damn him!" Ostvel snapped. "Tell me what was said!"

Donato straightened a little, breathing heavily. "Sorry— they turned me inside out." He raked the hair back from his face and went on more calmly, "Before he entered the weaving, Sioned told me about the Sunrunner in Gilad. She's dead, Ostvel—purposely shadow-lost."

"Oh, no," he breathed.

"Rohan took the decision about her away from both Andry and Cabar. Andry's furious, of course. And then he was there, like a blanket smothering us both. He knows everything. I got the feeling he'd been waiting for this. Before I was flung out of the weave—and I'd love to know how he did it—he said something about taking care of it himself. Sioned seemed . . . trapped somehow. Almost helpless." His bewildered eyes met Ostvel's. "I've known Sioned since she was at Goddess Keep. I know how strong she is. Andry was late into the weaving, but he took it over as if we were both first-ring novices. He took us completely by surprise."

"And he says he'll handle things? How can he, from Stronghold?"

"I don't know. But he seemed absolutely confident of it."

"I can't trust him," Ostvel muttered. "I can't believe he can work at such long range."

"Sioned did, years ago."

"I know. I watched her do it. But I can't believe Andry would risk what she did. Look at the moons. They'll be down in only a little while. What light can be used then? Donato, I don't *trust* him!"

"Then let's get busy with our own work."

"You're too exhausted to stand, let alone ride."

"After that nightmare of a journey here from Castle Crag, don't you tell me what I can or can't do. Come on."

Mounted troops rode out of the stables in groups of three and four, harness muffled by rags. Archers slipped silently down the valley in slightly larger groups and disappeared up the vine-planted slopes into the woods. Ostvel, a black Radzyn stallion under him and a stiff drink inside him, cantered out of the stables last along with Donato and Jofra. Chandar had gone on ahead with Laroshin, the guards commander, to organize things.

Will it work? Ostvel kept asking himself. He couldn't trust Andry to defend Dragon's Rest—didn't think he *could*. He had witnessed Sioned's weaving that had protected Rohan from treachery years ago, during the battle with Roelstra. With her at Skybowl, he had watched as Tobin and even the newborn Pol, barely Named that very night, were helplessly caught in Sioned's working. At the field of battle, Andrade and Urival and Pandsala had been used, too, as Sioned grasped at all the power she could reach. But hers had been an act of desperation, an instinctive creation of starlight to raise a dome around the combatants.

Andry had no such stake in protecting Dragon's Rest. A defeat for Pol would be a vast satisfaction to him, especially after his humiliation over the right to judge the Sunrunner in Gilad. What motive could he possibly have for keeping this great symbol of Pol's power and prestige safe?

By the time the riders had assembled at the hillside guardhouse, word came that the archers were well on their way to their assigned posts. As Donato dismounted, the last moonlight transfixed him.

Eighty men and women watched wide-eyed as the Sunrunner was caught in a powerful weaving. Ostvel feared it might be Andry again, but when Donato returned to them, he was smiling.

"The High Princess relays word from the High Prince. He approves our plan, but has a refinement of his own to add if we think it wise."

"Anything," Laroshin grunted. "In fact, I wish he was here!"

"So does he, to hear her grace tell it. But we have his orders, if not his sword."

Rohan's suggestion was that the archers attack from the rear, driving the invaders up through the narrows in as much confusion as they could cause. As they burst into the valley, they could be pounced on from either side and slaughtered, with no retreat possible.

The commander chewed his mustache and nodded. "His grace knows tactics."

"He's had experience in war that he never wanted," Ostvel said.

"But here's the best part," Donato went on. "Not just arrows but Fire will chase them forward. *Sunrunner's* Fire."

Ostvel looked at him worriedly. "Are you up to it? It's been a hellish trip and you've been using yourself up tonight at speed."

"Are you saying I can't manage to place a bit of Fire where it'll do the most good? I'm not old and feeble yet!"

"Sorry." Ostvel grinned suddenly. "Jofra, escort our lord Sunrunner here to a suitable spot for Fire-raising."

When they were gone, Laroshin surveyed his troops. "It'll take a while. Well after moonset, I'd say. Let's divide up now and make ready for the flood. But if Prince Halian's nails are so much as scuffed, I'll have the culprit strung up by the short hairs. His grace has quite a few things to answer for and I want him in shape to do so." He glanced at Ostvel. "Agreed, my lord?"

"Agreed." Ostvel glanced around as a squire came up and offered him a sword. He shook his head. "I'll stay to the rear, if you don't mind. I was never much good with a sword."

"That's not what I hear," the commander said. "All of us know about the battle for Stronghold."

"That was many years ago."

Laroshin grinned at him. "How old is your younger son? Not quite two?"

Ostvel couldn't help laughing. "Success with *that* sword has nothing to do with this kind!"

"It's my experience that a man who wields the one with excellent results isn't too old to use the other."

"Well, if you put it *that* way. . . ." He accepted the fine blade, tested its weight and balance, and nodded his satisfaction. The exchange was a useful antidote to nerves among the soldiers; Ostvel had played along for just that reason. It was suicidal, really, pitting eighty mounted troops, the same number of archers, and Sunrunner's Fire against an army of many hundreds. But surprise was a useful weapon, too. He hoped the Goddess would be interested enough, amused enough, or impressed enough by this crazy undertaking to lend her considerable support.

When the moons vanished over the hills, everything was in readiness. Ostvel looked up at the stars, remembering once again the night after Pol's birth. Kneeling on the lip of Skybowl's crater on a night of no moons, listening to Sioned Name the child after the stars themselves. Watching the infant's face as she wove his raw strength into the starlight and flung it hundreds of measures away to where Rohan battled Roelstra. Holding the terrified baby in his arms after the work was done. Realizing only then what he and she and Tobin had done by taking this child of Rohan's body and Ianthe's—and trying not to think about the moment when he'd plunged his sword into Ianthe's breast.

Someday Pol would find out. Ostvel had argued for revealing the truth while he was still young enough to be flexible, to understand in a child's terms: *"We wanted you and loved you too much to let her keep you from us."* But it was too late for the simple love that would have eased a little boy's understanding and acceptance. Pol was a grown man now. The reassurance of being loved and wanted more by Rohan and Sioned than by Ianthe would not be enough. He would see politics and power, be shocked by the years of deceit, feel betrayed unto his soul.

He should have been told long ago. But somehow Ostvel could not help wishing that his own part would never be discovered. Pol would eventually forgive his parents and Tobin. Ostvel doubted he would forgive his mother's executioner.

A murmuring among the waiting troops took him gratefully from his thoughts. He looked toward the narrows and concentrated. There—a faint yellowish glow, the distinctive pale gold of Sunrunner's Fire.

"Ha! There it is! Too early and the wrong direction for sunup," Laroshin whispered smugly.

Ostvel nodded, watching in fascination as the radiance slowly intensified. And there were sounds now, shouts barely heard on the night breeze, distant hoofbeats. He shifted his grip on the sword and told himself that young son or no young son, his thrust with this kind of blade wasn't what it had been. He would be fifty-five this summer, not twenty. He'd keep well to the rear of the battle, knowing that Alasen would skin him alive if he came home with so much as a scratch. He didn't want to think about what would happen if he didn't come home at all.

Stampeding horses and mountain ponies had entered the narrows; the thunder of their passing echoed off the rock walls. Ostvel jumped as the swiftest burst into the valley and his Radzyn stallion snorted at this invasion of his home turf. Laroshin signaled his soldiers to hold. They'd wait until the army itself came running through, chased by Fire and arrows. But it was a long, tense wait and Ostvel felt the muscles knotting in his shoulders.

The runaway horses galloped past. They probably wouldn't stop until they reached the lake at the top of the valley. As their hoofbeats pounded into the distance, there was a period of almost-quiet, punctuated by the cries of arrow-shot men and women. From the echo, they, too, had reached the narrows.

"Hold, hold," Laroshin breathed. "Wait till they're in position."

The first enemy troops staggered into the valley, followed by scores of others as arrows and Fire pushed them into the trap.

"Hold," came the low-voiced order. "Not long now. Look at that, we can herd them like stray lambs!"

"I never saw a lamb that brought its own sword along to the slaughter," Chandar muttered.

Many of the fleeing soldiers indeed carried weapons. That they had snatched up swords even in their panic spoke well for their training. Ancient years though he had claimed for himself earlier, Ostvel's blood heated at the prospect of a fight. Bred to war, the horse beneath him stirred and quivered, eagerly catching his excitement.

No longer harried by arrows, a knot of invaders paused to regroup. One of them shouted for the rest to gather around her. About a hundred scattered troops assumed formation and started warily forward.

"Damn," Laroshin growled. "If she inspires them to disciplined battle, the rest will join as they arrive." He lifted one arm to signal imminent attack.

But the Meadowlord soldiers abruptly stopped cold. They broke ranks and fled shrieking to collide headlong with the main army now pouring from the narrows. The defenders watched in stark amazement as waves of people pushed forward by arrows and Fire and panic struck some invisible barrier and fell back screaming in horror.

"What in all Hells—?" Ostvel forgot his self-imposed strictures about staying to the rear and urged his horse down the slope. Chandar swore and followed, and then Laroshin and the rest of the troops. But it was not a charge into battle Ostvel led. There would be no blood shed tonight.

He rode closer and closer, gaping at the spectacle. He ignored Chandar's plea to ride back to safety. He was as safe here as in his own bed at Castle Crag. The rush forward and terrified ebb backward fascinated him. It was as if men and women were being flung against a great glass wall that nothing could break through.

Trapped between the assault behind and the eerie barrier ahead, the army of Meadowlord collapsed in on itself like a castle with its support beams torn out. The defenders of Dragon's Rest had nothing to do but watch.

"The High Princess' work?" Laroshin asked.

"I don't know. Perhaps." He glanced upward. No moons; only stars to work with. Stars that were a *diarmadhi*'s source of power and light.

Chapter Twenty-two

Stronghold: 34 Spring

Sunrise heralded a new spring day, warm and glowing and perfect. Andry was exhausted by the night's work, but was damned if he'd show it, especially not to those gathered in the Summer Room. None of them had slept; all of them looked grim.

"You let it happen!" Pol was saying furiously. "You *knew* Dragon's Rest would be attacked, and you let it happen!"

Andry shrugged. "And what could you have done from here? Pol, we've been over this at least ten times."

Oclel, seated at his side and silent until now, said, "My Lord is correct, your grace. There was no time to send troops from Stronghold. The only hope of discouraging the attack was through *devri* means."

Sioned, opposite Andry with Chay and Tobin flanking her, lifted her gaze from contemplation of her hands. "Let us talk about your means," she suggested quietly.

"You saw. You were part of it—though I didn't mean for you to be caught up in the weaving. Nor you, Pol."

The young man stood beside his father's chair, glowering. "I'd like to hear your explanation. You learned this from the scrolls, of course."

"Of course. It's a subtle variation on certain Sunrunner techniques."

"Subtle?" Pol burst out. "You grabbed onto every *faradhi* mind in range and forced us to participate in Goddess knows what? That's your notion of subtlety? A thing so powerful that it turned scores of people into babbling half-wits?"

"A consequence of strength on the weak-minded. I don't understand why you're arguing the methods, Pol.

They contacted the barrier and what they saw there has temporarily—"

"It had damned well better be temporary," Pol snapped.

"And what about your soldiers' arrows and swords? How temporary is death? My way, they're alive and will probably recover."

"Probably." Sioned let the word fall into a heavy silence.

Andry shrugged again, annoyed. He'd saved Dragon's Rest, and now they were quarreling over the outcome. But what else should he have expected? he asked himself sourly. "Normal ways of defense wouldn't have worked. My way was the only way. Fewer died, the invaders were so frightened that no one will ever approach Dragon's Rest again, and they were all very neatly trapped. I understand Ostvel will be conducting interrogations today. I'll be very interested in how Chiana explains herself—not to mention Geir of Waes. Oh, and your own vassal, Lord Morlen, who caused the army to be assembled within Princemarch itself."

Pol stiffened at the veiled insult, but his voice was silken as he replied, "I'm more interested in why so many plots and so much sorcery went undetected, even though regular observations are conducted from Goddess Keep."

Andry narrowed his gaze, hating Pol just as much as Pol hated him. "You seem to be calling me a spy—and an incompetent one at that. It also sounds as if you'd prefer to see your palace gutted rather than accept help from a Sunrunner."

Chay intervened before they could start shouting at each other. "I think we all simply want to know what was done and why, Andry."

"I told you, Father. It's an old technique used by Lady Merisel in battle against the *diarmadh'im* long ago. It worked for her—and it's worked for me, Goddess be thanked."

"The idea, my lord," Nialdan said in respectful tones, "is that—"

"I want to hear it from my son." The quicksilver gaze never left Andry's.

He'd thought the time long past when his sire could make him feel twelve winters old again. He kept resentment from his voice as he answered, "There are fears in everyone. This particular weaving is constructed to provide a mirror. It's not unlike what I did to Marron. Only that reflected his own spell back at him. With the technique I used last night, visions of fear, no matter how deeply hidden in the mind, are reflected at the one who encounters the barrier. The formal name for it is *ros'sálath*, the warrior's wall of dreams."

"Nightmares," Pol corrected sharply.

"Andry. . . ." Tobin's eyes looked tortured. "I saw what happened. You and Nialdan and Oclel caught me up in it, too. But I don't understand why you could do this thing so readily."

"I'm sure you knew about it before now, Mother. Even if Maarken and Hollis said nothing, Pol has his spies, too."

Pol forced himself to stand immobile. He ached to smash that sarcastic half-smile off Andry's face, but willed his body to absolute stillness. There would be other, more satisfying, ways of revenge. He told himself to be patient.

Rohan had been silent this whole time. Now he got to his feet, and Pol watched with his usual awe—and a little envy—as his father effortlessly commanded all eyes. *How does he do that?* Pol marveled. Analyzing the sheer force of his father's presence, Pol realized it came mostly from the way he held himself—straight, proud without arrogance —and from his eyes: clear, watchful without wariness, giving away nothing. This was a man one could not impress with wealth or power or blandishments, only with qualities of mind and character. At times like this his power was an almost visible thing. Whether one was his enemy or his ally, this man's respect was a thing to be coveted.

Pol could hear power, too, in the quiet authority of Rohan's voice as he said, "We all knew. What we don't know is why. You learned well from Andrade. She would no more have explained herself than you intend to do right now. But consider this, Andry. What you do as a Sunrunner and what I do as High Prince are interconnected things. What each of us does reflects back at the other—much like your nightmare weaving. Your murder of Marron last night—"

"It was justice," Andry said coldly.

"It was murder. It made a mockery of justice. Worse, it broke the vow you made never to kill using your gift."

Andry's eyes widened and he gave a startled laugh. "You can't possibly think you're going to punish me for it!"

"Murder does not go unpunished in this princedom. Use of power does not go unnoticed. We choose now to use our own."

The royal plural stunned Andry. "He killed Sorin! He deserved to die! Who had a better right to do it than—"

Rohan paid no heed to the outburst and continued implacably, "We do not harbor murderers in our princedom. You have three days to remove yourself from our lands. Set foot here again on pain of arrest and trial for murder."

Andry's face went death pale. But there was more.

"Further, whatever princedom we see fit to inhabit for whatever amount of time, we forbid you to be present in that princedom. We lift this restriction for the *Rialla* every three years, and for two days preceding and following."

"You have no right—"

Rohan's temper flared at last. "We have every right! Be grateful we don't order you confined to Goddess Keep!"

Surging to his feet, Andry challenged, "And how would you go about it?"

"This *ros'salath* of yours might prevent us from entering—but we could also prevent you from leaving. Further—"

"How dare you?" he cried. "I refuse to be sentenced for a crime that was no crime, by someone who has no authority—"

"Further," Rohan repeated, "any use of the thing you term *ros'salath* for other than direct defense of Goddess Keep is forbidden for as long as we are High Prince. You deemed it necessary to learn, necessary to teach, and now necessary to use. Whatever the reason, consider your motives carefully. Rest assured that we will do the same." He stared Andry down. "Your grandfather said once that the promises of a prince die with him. When Pol rules here, he may decide as he pleases about these things. But while we live, Lord Andry—"

"You have no right!"

"We have every right," Rohan said again. "Or had you forgotten that tradition states and ancient scrolls confirm that *faradh'im* hold Goddess Keep of the High Prince? How long, do you think, would it take for us to make good a revocation of that gift?"

Andry gasped.

"You've not inspired trust among the princes," Rohan observed coldly. "Or even your own senior Sunrunners."

The struggle for control made a battlefield of Andry's features. He mastered himself and turned to Pol. "You think yourself well-educated in the scroll Urival stole for you, don't you? You think you can defend yourself from what will come when—when the princes have had enough of a Sunrunner High Prince. Think again, cousin!"

Pol didn't much care what Andry thought or believed; he was railing against the consequences of his father's lack of action. Why hadn't something been done before now? he cried inwardly. Why did it have to come to this?

Rohan spoke again. "We strongly suggest you accept your punishment, my Lord. It is mild indeed, compared to that which we might have chosen."

Andry appealed to his parents. "You can't let this happen!"

"*You* let it happen," Chay told him gravely, his face twisted by grief.

"Mother!"

Tears ran down Tobin's cheeks. "Andry—don't you see? You left no other choice."

He turned to Maarken, beloved eldest brother, only brother now. There was no succor there either, and equal grief. Andry's expression hardened as he turned to Rohan again.

"I understand, High Prince. You see me as a threat. You're afraid that my power is greater than Pol's, so you want to make me as impotent as you've made your other enemies. I am no enemy of yours, High Prince—nor even of your son. You understand nothing about me or my intentions. I saved your precious palace for you, and this is how you repay me. Oh, I accept the punishment. By law I can do nothing else—you made your precedent yesterday, when you took judgment of a Sunrunner from me. How clever of you," he snarled, "how expert in the use of your power. As High Prince you have jurisdiction over us all."

"We are pleased you understand that," Rohan said.

"Make sure you understand *this*, High Prince. I will leave the Desert and never return. I will even abide by your restrictions on my movements. But I will do as I like at Goddess Keep. Someday you and yours will call out for *devr'im* to protect you. Be warned by the Lord of Goddess Keep—you *will* need us."

He raked the group with one last icy glance, then strode from the room with his Sunrunners behind him.

Rohan went to his sister. "Tobin . . . I'm sorry."

She gazed up at him, her black eyes liquid with anguish. "I lost one son this spring," she whispered. "Now I've lost another."

***

Pol stood irresolutely in the antechamber of his suite, unwilling to enter the bedchamber where the smell of Meiglan and what they had done last night surely lingered. When Edrel appeared from the inner door, carrying an armful of bedclothes, Pol turned away to hide his flinch. He'd been right; the sheets carried her perfume and the scent of sex.

The boy deposited his silken burden in a large hamper, then approached Pol. Wordlessly he held out a delicate veil of taze-brown lace. Pol accepted it helplessly. His earlier shame was nothing compared to this.

"Edrel," he began.

"I've put fresh sheets on the bed, my lord. Your lady mother relayed an order for you to rest."

"I couldn't. Not after—" Neither could he meet the squire's gaze. Thirteen innocent winters old; he couldn't remember what it had been like to be that age, and untouched. "Edrel," he said again, but did not go on. He had no right to upset the squire with talk of what had happened, especially not to ease his own mind. If he felt soiled, it was his own fault.

"You really ought to try to rest, my lord," Edrel said.

"If you wish." He started for the bedchamber door.

"My lord?"

He forced himself to turn and face the boy. But in those guileless black eyes there was the same trusting admiration as always. "Yes? What is it?"

"I'll come back in a little while with some food."

Pol nodded and fled into the next room. The bed was pristine. He sprawled in a deep chair by the windows and stared at the view of cliffs and sky, trying not to think of anything.

His brain did not cooperate. Meiglan was part of it, but mostly it was Andry and the punishment Rohan had decreed. Not that Pol disapproved; it was only what his cousin deserved. The law was the law, no matter what. But something in him argued that if only his father had *done* something before this, no punishment would have been necessary and Andry would not now be an open enemy.

And what of his threat—promise, really—that sooner or later they would call on him in their need? Was it only to frighten, or had he truly seen into the future? Pol knew his mother had done so several times. He wished he'd inherited the gift from her. Since he hadn't, he must rely on his instincts and his other gifts. And they demanded that he act.

Marron was dead, but his brother was here somewhere at Stronghold. Pol could sense it all along his nerves. The waiting was intolerable. Today, tonight, tomorrow—when? A challenge would come and he would have to face it—*re*act instead of *act*. He was not made the way his father was, he could not be that patient.

Yet what could he do? The curse of using power wisely was to keep from using it until absolutely necessary. He had been taught that all his life through lesson and observation, and had believed it. But not this time. He must do something. He must control events, make them happen, instead of waiting for them to force him into a corner. He was prince and Sunrunner with power to act as he chose. What good was power if one didn't use it?

Pol pushed himself out of the chair and left his suite. At the very least he could find out whether Riyan or Morwenna had discovered other sorcerers in their midst.

He met the new Lord of Feruche on the main stairs, accompanied by Rialt. Ruala was with them. Even the seriousness of the day could not dim the joy she and Riyan had found in each other.

"No luck," Riyan said. "But Ruala says there's one guard missing."

"If they can change their forms, my lord," she said to Pol, "then he could be anyone, anywhere."

"I took the liberty of ordering the gates shut so no one can leave without written permission from your father or mother." Riyan shrugged. "It'd be nearly impossible to duplicate their seals, but. . . ."

"Who knows what these people are capable of?" Rialt finished.

"Actually, Ruala has a pretty good idea," Riyan said. "It seems we ought to listen more closely to the legends of the Veresch. She never quite believed before, but she's been witnessing the truth of them all spring."

Pol gestured up the stairs. "I need all the information I can get, my lady—legend, rumor, and especially fact. If you're not too tired, perhaps you can educate me."

"I'm not tired, my lord."

Rialt was frowning as he regarded Pol. "But *you* are."

"I can't afford to be."

They climbed the stairs and went down the hall toward the library that had been schoolroom to generations of princes, Pol included. As they passed a junction of corridors, Ruala suddenly gasped.

"What is it?" Pol caught her arm. "What's wrong?"

"Can't you feel it?" She was trembling and clutched at his shoulder for support, her gaze seeking Riyan. "Can't you sense it through your rings?"

He lifted his hands, staring white-faced. "Sweet Goddess —it's faint, but it's there. Ruala, where's it coming from?"

She took a few steps forward. Rialt helped her; Riyan was beginning to shake with increasing pain. Then Pol felt it, too, a jarring dislocation of his thoughts and senses, a dizziness, a dry ache in his head of colors and sounds and textures that weren't really there. It felt oddly familiar, but he couldn't think clearly enough to identify it. Ruala lifted her face to him, shock superimposed on shock as he caught his breath.

"You, too?" she whispered.

Rialt stared from one to the other of them, mystified. "What is this? And whatever it is, where's it coming from?"

Ruala squinted down the hall that glowed with morning sun, hurting Pol's eyes. "There," she said, pointing. "There—"

***

Mireva met Ruval in the stables. He drew her quickly and silently into the small tack room where he usually slept and shut the door. She sank wearily onto a bench, rubbing her face with her hands.

"What in all Hells do we do now?" he rasped. "Chiana and her so-called army are lost to us! That fool Marron ruined everything—"

"Be silent! Let me think!" She had been doing little else during the long night and morning.

But a strong dose of *dranath* had restored her somewhat, though her weariness was still profound. Panic had a way of draining the spirit as well as the body. She forced herself to rally and speared Ruval with her gaze.

"Riyan will test all Miyon's suite for signs of sorcery," she said, taking worst things first. "You'll have to relinquish that form and use another."

"Don't I know it! I stole some other clothes." He gestured to a bundle on the floor. "You'll have to help me work the change. Damn it, Mireva—"

"Settle down. We can overcome Marron's stupidity, but not if you persist in acting like a witless fool instead of a prince."

"Just give me another face for a day or so, and I'll show you a prince," he retorted.

A few moments later it was done. Ruval's dark hair was now gray-streaked, his blue eyes brown, his smooth chin showed a deep cleft. Mireva worked a few lines into his face to support the impression of a man twice his true age, then leaned back against the wall and sighed tiredly. "There. Commit this to memory. And for fear of the Nameless One, don't get it confused with the other!"

Ruval stripped off his shirt. The tunic of service to Cunaxa had been burned that morning. "How did your little tryst with Pol go last night?"

"Total success, but for the shock of its conclusion. Andry caught him in a weaving," she said. "I thought Pol would embrace 'Meiglan' with vows of love, which would have been useful. But his attitude was quite unexpected." She grinned suddenly. "He believes her to be a lying, cheating little whore. And that's even better, because now he doesn't trust his own judgment and perceptions. The blow to his pride in his cleverness was a devastating one."

"Naturally 'Meiglan' wept and pleaded."

"Naturally. I really did have a wonderful time—until Andry interrupted."

"Well, we won't have to worry much about him." Ruval finished dressing in the plain shirt and vest worn by most servants at Stronghold.

"What have you heard?"

"You mean I know something you don't?" He laughed again. "It seems he's been banished for all time to Goddess Keep. At least, that's the rumor. I doubt even Rohan would attempt to cage him there physically, but the effect will be the same. One of Miyon's people saw him tear out of the Summer Room in a rage guaranteed to freeze the balls of anyone who saw him. And the rumors have been flying ever since."

"Ah!" She rocked back and forth, chuckling. "Delicious!"

"Some say he's got until tonight to clear out, some that he's been given five or six days."

"It doesn't matter. He'll never help Pol defend against your challenge now. Perhaps this business with Chiana wasn't such a disaster after all."

Ruval chortled. "Oh, it's not because of what he did with the *ros'salath*."

"Then why—?"

"You won't believe it! Rohan's punishing him for the murder! Have you ever heard anything more insane? I overheard one of the stewards say with the most pompous pride that his grace obeys the law, no matter what. Even though Marron was a threat and a murderer himself, Rohan's laws must be followed and Andry must be punished!"

Mireva choked on laughter. "A truly honorable idiot—let's hope his son is the same!"

"Pol will be that much easier to defeat." Ruval grinned down at her. "For, as we both know, I have no honor at all." He paused, his fingers cupping her chin. "So you had a wonderful night with him, did you?"

"Very," she purred.

"I've never seen you wearing Meiglan's face. It might be interesting."

"When you hold Princemarch, I'll wear whatever face most pleases you."

"When I hold Princemarch, I'll have Meiglan herself or any other woman who pleases me."

She jerked her head away. "Do you think you won't need me anymore once you're at Castle Crag?" she snapped. "I made you and I can destroy you."

"But you won't." He gave a harsh laugh. "I'm the only one you have left, Mireva. I'm your only hope now that both my brothers are gone. And that, my lady, is the power *I* possess over you. I suggest you remember it and behave accordingly."

He left her seething with impotent rage. Mireva calmed herself with an effort. After a time she returned to the keep, where she mounted the steps to Meiglan's chambers and locked herself in with the still unconscious girl. She spared a vicious glance for the youthful golden beauty so helpless in the bed, then rummaged in a coffer for a certain bracelet. Marron had stolen it and its mate from Chiana's colossal collection before he'd quit Swalekeep.

She fetched a shallow basin of water and lowered herself onto the Cunaxan carpet. The bracelet tinkled down into the water and she cradled the bowl in her lap, fingers spread. There was enough *dranath* in her still to facilitate the spell. Her pride was soothed by the swift sureness of her gifts.

Chiana was pacing before a banner of pale Meadowlord green. The mirror was set nearby in obedience to strong compulsion. It reflected the princess and Morlen of Rezeld. Both were frightened. Mireva could imagine their conversation, necessarily low-voiced with so many guards nearby wearing Princemarch's violet. Ostvel would arrive soon, Mireva was sure, to begin asking questions that, thank the Nameless One, none of them could answer in ways damaging to Mireva. But there was a risk that the Sunrunner with *diarmadhi* blood would be there as well. She had encountered him several days ago while shielding the army with the mirror; the touch had been unmistakable. The mirror must be destroyed before he could comprehend its uses.

She gathered herself and clamped down on Chiana's readied mind. It was simplicity itself to turn her, fix her gaze on the mirror, draw her toward it. Mireva's peripheral vision showed her Morlen's slack-jawed stare of surprise, affording her momentary amusement. Chiana moved like a sleepwalking child.

Mireva concentrated, suddenly furious as her contact with Chiana increased and she saw that Marron had played on Chiana's ambitions for her son. After all the effort it had taken to persuade the princess that Rinhoel's claim was hopeless, Marron had insidiously undone her work, knowing Chiana's lust would be the greater in her son's cause alone. Doubtless he would have killed Rinhoel once Princemarch was safely in his hands. A clever plan— for which Chiana would be the one to pay.

The princess stood sightlessly before the mirror, her pale, soft, beringed hands lifted in tense fists. An instant later the mirror lay in blood-covered shards on the ground. Chiana's mouth stretched in an unheard scream of pain and she fell to her knees amid the shattered glass, her fingers slashed to ribbons and dripping crimson.

Mireva watched a few moments longer from a narrow splinter of mirror, then withdrew. "Thus ever for those who disobey," she murmured.

And the door of Meiglan's bedchamber crashed open, the lock forced and the wood splintered, and three pairs of *diarmadhi* eyes transfixed her.

Chapter Twenty-three

Stronghold: 34 Spring

The old woman acted with stunning speed. The effect of her sudden blaze of sorcerer's power on their senses was devastating. Pol, Riyan, and Rialt were strong, athletic young men—but she ensnared them with her strange gray-green eyes and they had no more chance against her than newborn infants.

Rays of sunlight became swords of golden crystal plunging into their eyes. The very air turned to tiny needles tipped with acid stabbing their skin. Their own cries were transformed into black knives sinking into their skulls. And with these knives came unconsciousness—but not surcease from pain.

By the time sense returned to Pol's lacerated mind, the old woman was gone and Ruala with her.

He gathered his legs under him, but his knees didn't seem to be working right. Riyan was similarly sprawled nearby. Rialt, lacking the gifts that had made the attack much worse on the other two, was already on his feet. He gave Pol a hand up and steadied him when he tottered.

"Gentle Goddess," Pol breathed when he was sure his voice would hold steady. "What in all Hells *was* that?"

"Sorcery enough for her to escape with Lady Ruala," Rialt said bitterly. "Are you all right, my lord?"

"I will be." He helped Riyan to his feet.

Rialt had started for the door. "We have to find them, though Goddess knows how much time they've had to disappear in."

"Where do you suggest we look?" Riyan asked in bleak tones. "It's hopeless, Pol. You and I both know from playing here as children that there are scores of places to hide in Stronghold."

"Just follow the trail of felled servants and guards," Rialt suggested.

Pol shook his head. "Once they're out of here, the only person she'll have to control is Ruala, to keep her quiet. Who'd look twice at a servant helping a lady to a place where she could rest?"

"Well, they can't get out of the castle," Rialt maintained. "Riyan's order to the guardhouse—"

"She got past the three of us. What difficulty would a few guards pose? We could turn Stronghold inside out and not find them unless we were very, very lucky. You said yourself we have no way of knowing how much of a lead they've got."

Rialt nodded unhappily. He went to a bedside table and poured wine from the pitcher there. Pol glanced around, suddenly realizing whose chamber they were in. Meiglan lay in a froth of white silk and lace, looking as innocent as he had only yesterday believed her to be. He absently accepted a wine cup from Rialt and was just about to drink when Riyan dashed the goblet from his hand.

"Smell it," he said, holding out his own cup. "I didn't show much talent in medicine at Goddess Keep, but I learned how to recognize certain odors. One sip of that and you'd be laid out on the floor until noon."

Not having inherited his mother's nose for wine, Pol could detect nothing out of the ordinary. But he was more concerned with why the wine was drugged—and who it was meant for. He stared at Meiglan. She was barely breathing.

"She's been drugged," he said slowly. "But why?"

"Silence?" Rialt guessed. "She was removed from the Great Hall last night in hysterics. She might know something."

"I don't give a damn what she knows or doesn't know!" Riyan's patience had snapped. "Not when that *diarmadhi* witch has Ruala—"

"Hostages aren't harmed until demands go unmet," Pol said grimly.

"There's another interesting thought," Rialt added. "Why Lady Ruala? Why not you, my lord? You're more valuable to a sorcerer undoubtedly in harness with

Roelstra's grandson. They could kill you outright and claim Princemarch."

Pol was still gazing at Meiglan. "It has to be done publicly. I have to acknowledge Ruval's right to challenge, then accept it prince to prince."

"And by taking Ruala," Riyan said with anguish thick in his voice, "he's ensured your acceptance."

"She'll be safe enough until then." Pol approached the bed. "Silence," he said, echoing Rialt's earlier suggestion.

The chamberlain nodded. "The old woman was one of her servants, brought from Cunaxa to Tiglath and now here. What is it Lady Meiglan can't tell us as long as she's drugged into a stupor?"

"And how long has she been so?" Pol lifted the girl's wrist, felt the pulse flutter weakly like a tiny bird trapped within the delicate cage of bones. "Rialt, find one of my mother's maids and have her keep watch in here. And post guards outside the door. No one is to enter this room, not even her own father. I don't think there'll be any more trouble from sorcery here, but when she wakes I don't want anybody but one of us hearing what she has to say."

"Not even her other serving woman?" Rialt asked.

"No." He set down her hand and rose. "We'll stay here until you return."

"Very good, my lord."

With Rialt gone, Pol turned to Riyan. "How did Ruala sense it, even before your rings began to burn?" he asked quietly.

"You know as well as I. And we both know something else, too." Riyan held his gaze steadily.

Pol replied unwillingly, "We three felt it out in the hallway. Rialt did not—and I know very well he hasn't a drop of Sunrunner blood. Either Ruala is one of us, a Sunrunner, or she and I are the same as you. *Diarmadh'im.*"

"The rings would argue for the latter." Riyan spoke without emotion.

"Doesn't it bother you that—"

"That she may be what I am? My mother was of the Old Blood. So was Urival. It's not one of my prejudices," he replied with a shrug.

"She must know what she is. Why hasn't she said anything?"

"Wouldn't you keep it secret?" Riyan would not look at him.

"Secrets are exactly what I'm concerned with. If this is true, and I really am—" He tried to keep his voice level.

"It can't come from your mother, Pol. She's full-blooded *faradhi*. Her rings don't burn in the presence of sorcery."

"She hasn't worn any Sunrunner's rings for as long as I've been alive. It might come from my father. And if it does, our whole family—" He pulled in a deep breath. "If they don't know, how can I tell them? And if they do know, they've been lying to me my whole life. Keeping it secret. Secrets give *power*," he quoted bitterly.

"Andry can't learn this one," Riyan warned.

"Damn Andry! He can take his *devr'im* and his Sunrunner rings and—"

"Rings—that's the reason, Pol, it's not that you're *diarmadhi* at all!" Riyan snatched up Pol's right hand. "This is Andrade's ring, isn't it?"

"What does that have to do with—"

"It didn't burn the way mine did. No burning, no sorcerer's blood. The gold is special—a ceremony, something Lady Merisel did to it, Ruala says. This would still have the power within it."

Pol hesitated, then said, "No. It's not the original. It didn't fit me. We took the moonstone out and used dragon gold to make a new setting."

Riyan gripped Pol's hand for a moment, let it go. "That doesn't prove or disprove anything."

Making an effort, ashamed of his reaction to the prospect of sorcerer's blood, Pol said, "I am or I'm not. It's not important right now. Ruala is."

"If they hurt her, I'll kill them with my bare hands."

"She'll be safe, Riyan. They need her to keep me cooperative. And it won't be long now. The challenge is sure to come within the next day or so. They can't hide forever. And even if they got out the gates—the Desert's not a place to spend more than a single night, even in spring."

Riyan nodded, but his rings glinted as fists clenched and unclenched in impotent fury.

Rialt came back with two guards and a maid who wore the emerald-green badge of personal service to the High

Princess. Pol gave his instructions tersely, then said to Riyan, "Come on. It's time my father knew of this."

Yet he could not help one last look at Meiglan. She could have taken the drug last night to prohibit any questioning after—after. He wanted to believe she had, was desperately afraid she had not. For if sorcerers could shape-change, the woman he had been with last night might not have been Meiglan at all.

***

Chay and Andry stood on ramparts that overlooked the Desert beyond the cliffs sheltering Stronghold, father and son struggling one last time to understand each other. The one, a powerful *athri* and renowned warrior who had seen sixty winters, had never been comfortable with *faradhi* abilities despite being surrounded with Sunrunners. The other, half his father's age and Lord of Goddess Keep from his twentieth year, had instigated changes in Sunrunner practices that had culminated last night in something the ungifted would never comprehend. Each knew the other's doubts and prejudices as men; but they were father and son. They had to try.

"Listen to the word you just used," Chay said. "*Magic*. It's something I heard maybe a dozen times in my youth."

"It's a convenient term—"

"For something everyone used to take for granted as simply a part of life. What Sunrunners did was just what they did, not magic." He braced his hands on the stone wall and squinted into the sunlight. "We used to say 'arts' or 'skills' when we spoke of Sunrunners. Now we're beginning to say *magic*. Andry, don't you hear the difference?"

"If people choose to call it so. . . ." He shrugged. "What we do isn't ordinary."

"It's damned inexplicable to somebody like me. People fear what they don't understand."

"Father!" Andry began to laugh. "You've never been afraid of anything in your life, much less your own wife and sons!"

"It isn't me I'm talking about. A Sunrunner at work is an odd sight, but it's not threatening if you think of it as a skill like—like skills in war. Magic is something else entirely."

"You and I are different kinds of warrior, that's all. Besides, what you've seen is respect, not fear."

"Is it?"

"Exactly the same respect that you receive when you carry your sword at your side," Andry said firmly.

"Ah, but any other man with a sword can meet me on equal terms." Chay began picking at the mortar between stones. "Swords are useless against what you did last night at Dragon's Rest."

"I'm not interested in Dragon's Rest right now. What concerns me more is that you seem to be blaming me for something. I'd like to know what it is."

Chay was silent for a moment, then turned and folded his arms across his chest. "Not blame. It's a responsibility you and Andrade share. She began it by marrying her sister to Zehava and then Sioned to Rohan. She pushed Sunrunners into the lives and bloodlines of princes. That made you more visible."

"And what of it? We're meant to serve—and not just princes."

"But don't you see that you're being woven into the everyday fabric of life? You've put *faradh'im* in all princely courts and every major holding. You're working on the minor ones. When Sunrunners were remote beings, nobody had to think much about you. But now people must deal with you more directly."

"And isn't Rohan's name attached to all the new laws that have found their way into people's everyday lives? He's the most visible High Prince in a hundred years. People are dealing with *him* a lot more directly, too. I don't see the difference. Besides, it's not my fault if people choose to believe we're some mysterious—"

"What happens when news of your *devr'im* spreads, as you know it will? Use of Sunrunners as—as weapons of combat—Andry, it's so complete a departure from what you've always been that only a fool wouldn't be afraid of it!"

Andry hesitated. Then, because this was certainly the last time he would ever stand here with his father looking out at the land of their birth, he said, "You don't know what I've seen."

"Seen?" The furrows deepened on Chay's wide brow. "Explain yourself."

Andry bit his lip. "Forgive me, but I must have your word not to repeat any of this."

Chay stiffened. "My *word*?"

"I'm sorry. Believe me, I wouldn't ask if it wasn't so important. Please."

A reluctant nod. Andry sighed his relief. The knowledge was suddenly too much for him to live with alone; this was the one man in the world he could share it with.

"Father, the day I became Lord of Goddess Keep, there was a . . . a vision." He conjured it in memory and as he forced himself to relive the horror he heard its shadow in his voice. "Hundreds of dead. Castles lying in ruins—terrible destruction. Unimaginable battles in a war we're destined to lose if something isn't done. Yes, the *devr'im* are a departure from tradition. Didn't Andrade shatter precedent by marrying Sioned, a fully trained Sunrunner, to a prince? For all I know, this war will come about because Pol is who he is, Sunrunner and prince both. I don't know. I can't be sure. But I've seen the agony, Father. I'm doing all I can to defend against it. Do you think I'd stand meekly by? Would I be your son if I did?"

The gray eyes searched his. "You saw all this?"

"I've seen Graypearl gutted," he murmured. "Medawari in Gilad, Faolain Riverport—even Stronghold, even Radzyn." Chay gave an involuntary flinch. "All in ruins," Andry insisted. "As dead as Feruche before Sorin rebuilt it." He choked at mention of his twin.

"I don't *dis*believe you," Chay said slowly. "But . . . could you be doing things that will bring your—vision— into being that much faster?"

"You've never had much use for *faradhi*, have you? It doesn't matter, I suppose. I believe in what I was shown. And I also believe I've been given the means to defend against it. What other use for the Star Scroll? And if a growing fear of Sunrunners saves thousands, is the price too high?"

"If fear is the price, count the cost to yourself, my son."

"How can I make you see?" he cried. "I'm not seeking power for its own sake or to set myself up as Pol's rival. Whatever I do, it's not greed or ambition that drives me. I'm terrified of what the future looks like."

"Be careful what you sacrifice to that future," Chay warned.

"I would sacrifice my own life if it would stop what I know is to come."

For the first time his father looked truly shaken. "Andry—you're right, I don't understand Sunrunners. I ought to. I've lived with your mother for—Goddess, thirty-eight winters now!—I've two *faradhi* sons, and it looks as if my grandchildren will be Sunrunners as well. The destruction you tell me is coming—"

Andry stiffened. "You don't believe in it."

"*You* do," Chay said softly. "So I must."

He had never felt so proud or so humble in his life. He put one hand on his father's arm, unable to speak. But the moment of warm communion dissolved with Chay's next words.

"I said before that people fear what they can't understand. It's also true that they can't be afraid of something they *do* understand. You're turning Sunrunner arts and skills into magic. It's not merely that you can do things the rest of us can't. You're rubbing our noses in it. These invocations to the Goddess, all the words taken from the old language that no one understands, elaborate rituals within your own community—"

"Who's been watching?" he demanded. "Pol? Sioned?"

The gray eyes held his in a level stare. "Your brother. And he doesn't much like what he's seen."

"Maarken?" The betrayal crippled his breathing for a moment. Alone—he was alone in this. Forbidden his home, undefended by his own parents, suspected by his family—and now this. Maarken, spying on him.

Chay's voice was heavy with weariness. "Andry, is it truly respect you're after? Wouldn't it be better to strive for trust? To work in the open so all can see and understand?"

"You *do* fear me," he whispered. "All of you do."

"You're my son," Chay rasped. "I want to trust you, but you're making it almost impossible. Why didn't you come to us when you first heard about the army marching on Dragon's Rest?"

"Why are you objecting to the use of Sunrunner power against Desert enemies? Isn't that what Andrade wanted?"

"She wanted a line of princes who were also Sunrunners.

Not Sunrunners behaving as if they had all the rights and privileges of princes."

"Oh, I understand now," he said, bitterly angry and hurt. "All of you were amazed that I'd lift a finger to defend Dragon's Rest! You thought I'd watch laughing while it was destroyed!"

"Andry!"

"It's true, though, isn't it?" he raged. "Well, Ruval *can* destroy Pol for all I care! Neither of them matters. Compared to the horror that's been in my mind for nine years now, no one else matters at all!"

"Except you?" Chay asked harshly.

Andry froze for an instant, then turned on his heel and strode off.

***

Rohan listened to Pol and Riyan without question or comment. When they had finished he said only, "Come with me." He led them to the library and office he shared with his wife and locked the door. This coupled with his silence made the young men fidget slightly. But their eyes popped half out of their skulls when he opened the secret place where the translated Star Scroll was kept.

"This is a copy of what Meath found on Dorval years ago. The original and another translation are at Goddess Keep. You know about the Star Scroll, Pol, even though you've never seen it. Urival and Morwenna taught you some of what's in here. But only your mother and I knew where it was hidden. When I put it back, I'll show you how the compartment works. One day you may have to get at this in a hurry."

Pol came forward as he set the case on the double desk. But Riyan held back. Rohan glanced over at him.

"What's wrong?" he asked, knowing full well what troubled him.

"This is . . . a lot to trust me with," Riyan said uneasily.

Rohan smiled slightly as he unrolled the parchment. He'd guessed right—not too difficult. The son was much like the father, and he'd known Ostvel for half his life. "I trust you with the secret of dragon gold," he pointed out.

"But—*this*—" Riyan faltered.

"You're as curious as I am," Pol said impatiently. "Stop equivocating and get over here."

Brows arching at his son's vehemence, Rohan held the

scroll open at its first page. "Urival insisted on reproducing this section exactly as it appears in the real thing. Two words and a border of stars."

" 'On Sorcery,' " Riyan whispered, standing at Pol's shoulder.

"Yes." He wound the scroll down to its opening sections. "The cunning part about the original is the interior code. It seems Lady Merisel was scholar enough to want this knowledge preserved. But she was also wise enough to hide what it contains from casual perusal. This is a decoded version. Everything in it is accurate. Which is why it's kept hidden."

"How much of this has Mother tried out?" Pol asked.

"Not much. She, too, is wise." He sat and began searching for the sections he wanted.

"Is there anything about shape-changing in here?"

"Nothing."

"Pity. It might have been useful."

"And dangerous," Riyan murmured.

Rohan chose to ignore the byplay. "Pol, you've remarked before that I wait for events to develop, that I don't act until I must. I have my reasons—even though I know you don't always agree with them." The Star Scroll spread out page by page, telling of power he could never possess—and didn't want to. "Nine years ago I let the pretender Masul live long enough to challenge your claim because rumor can become more real sometimes than truth. He had to be heard and defeated publicly or your right would always have been in doubt. What I didn't count on was sorcery. And Maarken nearly died because of my mistake."

"But that wasn't your fault—"

"I'm High Prince. That made it my fault—and my responsibility to kill him before he could kill Maarken. My mistake, my fault, my responsibility. That's what being High Prince is." He gestured for Riyan to hold the top of the scroll while he secured the bottom. "I determined then not to repeat the error. When Urival brought this to Stronghold, Sioned wasn't the only one who studied it. I know this scroll backwards, and the histories Meath found with it. They enabled me to invoke my rights in the matter of the Sunrunner in Gilad."

"You knew all along," Riyan said admiringly. "The words were there for you to use, and you did."

Rohan leaned back in his chair and blew out a long sigh. "Words," he repeated. "I told Andry the other day that all my life I've thrown words at problems. They're the weapons of a civilized man, or so I keep telling myself. But we're not civilized, none of us. We always have our knives within reach." He ran his fingertips over the parchment. "What are these words but a different kind of knife?"

"Power," Pol said flatly. "More effective than any knife."

Rohan heard him with sadness. The innocence Sioned had spoken of, the quality of being untouched, was gone from Pol's eyes and voice. He had not been sheltered in the ways Rohan had been, but it was clear he could no longer be protected.

"I knew all along that neither Andry nor Cabar would give up a whit of their privileges. But I had to wait until they petitioned me for a decision. I was hoping they'd work it out between themselves and spare my having to use the power given me by the scrolls. But each of you has power—the hidden knife, if you will—that's out of my reach. In this, I'm blind. But you're a Sunrunner, Pol. Riyan, you're gifted in both ways. Sorcery is without doubt the means Ruval will choose. So I give you this knife."

All the bright gold and bronze glints had left Riyan's dark eyes. "I still say that's a lot to trust us with."

To burden you with, he thought, hiding his melancholy behind a calm answer. "I wouldn't give it if I didn't trust you."

Pol bent over the scroll and read aloud, leaning one elbow on the desk. " 'The *rabikor* is bound only by rules agreed to before battle. Learn the traditions well, therefore, lest your opponent catch you in your ignorance and legally cast aside all honor, to your defeat.' " He glanced at Rohan. "*Rabikor*—that's 'crystal battle' in the old language."

"A descriptive and accurate name. Rather too beautiful though, for a fight to the death."

"Just a moment," Riyan protested. "Does that mean if

the other man knows the rules but you don't, he doesn't have to adhere to them?"

"Exactly. He's bound only by what's agreed to. Any unstipulated tactic is fair. I suggest you learn this section word for word," he added with deceptive mildness. "Anyone who breaks the stated rules, even if he wins, forfeits all rights and claims to whatever he challenged for. Read on."

Pol continued, " 'The first of the rules is this: that battle shall be between two persons only. Interference by another person is forbidden. Second, all Elements may be called upon as skill and power allow. Third, the Unreal may be used at any time.' " He frowned. "A reference to conjuring up horrors, the way Andry did."

"The part about all Elements worries me," Riyan confessed. "We can call Fire, of course, and Air—but spinning Water and Earth into it isn't something we ordinarily do."

"Learn," Rohan said succinctly, and Pol grimaced.

"Fourth, *perath* shall be constructed by three persons for each combatant. Within this dome of interwoven light the *rabikor* is fought. If any of the six die during the battle, they shall not be replaced.' " He looked up again. "*Perath*? 'Needle wall'? No—'talon'!"

"A tribute to dragons, one supposes. It keeps anyone from getting in—or out. The victor destroys the *perath* at battle's end."

Riyan hesitated. "Is it that dangerous, that its makers can die of it?"

"Evidently."

Pol continued, " 'Fifth, physical touch and weapons of iron, bronze, gold, silver, or glass are forbidden.' Damn. I can't take care of Ruval cleanly, it seems. I have to beat him through sorcery."

"Only if you agree to that condition," Riyan reminded him. "If it doesn't come up, you can do as you like."

"Hmm." Pol considered, looking troubled. "What's to keep us honest in this, Father? Not the witnesses. None has the power to enforce a forfeit if the rules are broken. Besides, Miyon's against us, Barig's representing a prince who's furious with us, and as for Andry—" He stopped and grimaced again. "He's not fool enough to want a sorcerer in my place, no matter how much he hates me."

Rohan nodded. "I trust you appreciate the irony. You're perceived as a Sunrunner even though you weren't trained at Goddess Keep. Your defeat would shake confidence in all *faradh'im*—not a desirable outcome as far as Andry is concerned. Oh, yes, he'll support you. He can't do otherwise."

"I don't know," Pol said, openly doubtful. "He was angry enough to make a lot of threats. But I still don't understand why either of us should keep to the rules."

Rohan shrugged. "Honor, on your part. The ancient ways on his, or so one hopes. Perhaps he's confident that you don't *know* the rules."

"Pol . . . take a look at the sixth one," Riyan murmured.

He read it to himself, then blanched and read aloud. " 'Sixth, the use of *dranath* is imperative. It shall be taken publicly in equal amounts by each combatant.' Father—*dranath* addicts, doesn't it?"

"Yes. It won't make for a pleasant time as it fades. But neither will one dose chain you." He deliberately forgot Sioned's experiences with the drug, Hollis' terrible climb out of addiction.

"We have some available?" He shrugged irritably. "Stupid question."

"Forgivable," Rohan answered. "It's not every day one has to plan a battle against a sorcerer." He rose. "I'll leave you two with the scroll now. Read it through from here to the end. It'll tell you how to function with *dranath* in your blood, and some specifics that may help you defeat Ruval."

Sioned was waiting in the hall and silently took his arm as they walked to their suite. When they were alone in the bedchamber, she flung her arms around him and shook.

"Hush," he whispered. "Sioned, sweet love—it'll be all right, I swear it."

Her voice was muffled against his shoulder as she said, "Rialt told me. Rohan, it's worse than we ever suspected."

He held her away from him, frowning. "What is it? What's frightened you?"

"Ruala was the perfect choice as hostage. She's *diarmadhi*."

"What?" Rohan's head spun. "Are you sure?"

"She sensed the sorcery before Riyan did with his rings."

"So he and Pol told me. But that doesn't mean—"

"Doesn't it? They'll call for the *perath*. They need three against three *faradh'im*. Marron was to be part of it, I'm sure of it. This woman Mireva is the second. And I know who they had in mind for their third."

He felt his fingers clench on her shoulders. "Riyan," he whispered.

She nodded. "With Marron dead, they were crippled. But they have Ruala, and she's of the Old Blood. She can be drugged into it—all that's really needed is her power, not her conscious cooperation."

"And Riyan won't let her go through it alone. We've both seen the looks they give each other. What they demand of him, he'll do."

"He'll have no choice."

Rohan paced away form her, thinking furiously. "He's in with Pol reading the Star Scroll now. That should help him."

"The *perath* can kill."

"So can I," he said.

"Rohan—no! It's gone too far for that! And how would you do it? You saw Andry destroy Marron—what you didn't sense was the effort it cost him, even though he knew more or less what to do!"

"Sioned, I can't let Riyan and Ruala fight that battle for me. I delayed too long in killing Masul nine years ago. I won't let—"

"There's more," she interrupted. "And worse."

He laughed harshly. "Of course there is. There *always* is."

Sioned hesitated, not looking at him. "I went in to see Meiglan. Edrel met me outside her rooms and asked if she was all right after last night. I thought he meant when Marron's false shape vanished." She wrapped her arms around herself, trembling. "I told him it seemed she'd been helped to sleep shortly after it happened and had been sleeping ever since. And he—he said that wasn't possible because he found a lace veil belonging to her in Pol's room this morning. But she *couldn't* have been the one who left it there."

Rohan's throat closed as if a fist gripped it.

"Can you possibly imagine that pitiful child sneaking into a man's chamber, even on direct threat from her father? Besides, she was taken away in hysterics last night and I can't see her making a quick recovery."

"You . . . have evidence," he managed around the terrible constriction of fear.

She nodded. "I know some medicine. Tobin knows more, and Feylin more than both of us combined. Her mother was a physician. I had them confirm what I suspected. The amount of drug in Meiglan's wine produces identifiable levels of unconsciousness as it works. When I left her, she was in the last stages. The drug *must* have been given only a little while after her so-called maidservant got her out of the Great Hall. Pol didn't leave us until much later than that."

"It won't work, Sioned." He heard the desperation in his voice and tried to control it. "You can't be sure whether or not the amount of drug was changed, added to since—"

"Both Tobin and Feylin confirmed it!"

"All three of you could be wrong!"

"But you know we're not." She wilted into a chair. "You know it as well as I do, Rohan."

"Gentle Goddess," he whispered with no voice at all.

"Ianthe couldn't change her shape, so she changed your perceptions with *dranath*," Sioned told him in lifeless tones. "This woman Mireva—what she must have done—would Pol have sensed sorcery? Even if he didn't, once he finds out about Meiglan, he'll put it together. I don't know what to do. I don't know how to protect him."

"We can't. Not anymore." He knew it now for certain, and there was a strange relief in the knowing. "He must be told who he is."

She sprang to her feet, terrified. "No! Please, Rohan—please!"

"It's time. It must be tonight."

"No!"

"Would you see him die because he can't use power he doesn't know he has?" he lashed out.

Green eyes blazed in a face the color of chalk. "We could tell him he gets the *diarmadhi* blood from one of us, we could—"

"Lie to him? Again? When do the lies stop, Sioned? Who are you protecting now—Pol or yourself?"

"And what happens when he finds out the man who wants his death is his own brother?"

"He'll just have to accept that, won't he!" Rohan turned for the door, but her next words stopped him in mid-stride.

"The way you accepted him when you returned to Stronghold that winter? You could barely look at either of us! I'd brought you a son you didn't want, and Pol was living reminder that you weren't perfect! Shall we tell him that, too?"

He heard his voice become the chill, brittle one he used when forced to address someone he loathed. "He will be told who is he tonight. You may attend or not, as you choose. But he *will* be told."

Chapter Twenty-four

Stronghold: 34 Spring

By sunset Stronghold had been turned inside out. The guards and Sunrunners scoured the area around the keep while light lasted, reporting nothing out of the ordinary. Rohan expected as much. Ruval and Mireva would assume there'd be a search of this kind, so he had to provide it. He hoped the show would satisfy them so that his next gambit would come unanticipated.

But before he began it, there was Pol.

They met in the library again at Rohan's request. Pol had just arrived when Sioned entered and sat down on her side of the double desk. Rohan would have bet half his princedom that she wouldn't come, especially after their clash today—that she would flee this thing she had dreaded for so long. But she met his eyes squarely, unflinching.

Pol had pulled up a chair near Sioned's desk, curious at his parents' tense silence. "What is it you wanted to talk about?"

Rohan locked the door and leaned back against it. He had struggled with the words a thousand times, trying to imagine this moment, to find the right way to say it that would spare Pol and Sioned any pain. But the words escaped him, and there must be pain.

Sioned folded her hands atop her desk, her shining head bent, the graceful lines of her throat and shoulders highlighted by candleglow. Rohan had lit the candlebranch earlier, knowing that if she had done it by Sunrunner means, the flames would leap and flare with her emotions. Refracted light from the emerald ring on her left hand trembled slightly, the only sign of her terror.

Aware that he was delaying the inevitable, he glanced

around the room. Tapestry map, books, parchments piled on the desks, boxes containing the seals of their princedom —perhaps he should have chosen another place. This was, after all, a political room. But it was too late to move to a private chamber, one in which they could be people and not princes.

Drawing in a deep breath, he began. "Pol . . . you are everything we ever wanted in a son." The young man's head tilted to one side in a gesture of puzzlement. "You know your own strengths. You've explored your abilities as a prince and learned how to use your *faradhi* gifts with confidence and wisdom. You *are* a Sunrunner."

"That's made painfully obvious every time I cross water," Pol said, smiling a little. "What are you trying to say, Father? That my Sunrunner skills can defeat Ruval's sorceries? If so, keep talking—because I'm dreading it, even knowing what's in the Star Scroll."

Sioned murmured, "You have no cause to fear, Pol. You *are* everything we ever dreamed you would become." She hesitated, glancing once more at Rohan. "And you are everything you always were, no matter what you might hear about—about who you are."

Blue-green eyes widened. "Mother! Don't tell me you're worried about that old rumor?"

"What rumor?" Rohan asked, sharp-voiced.

"I heard it first while I was at Graypearl. The gist of it is that I'm not really your son—that Mother couldn't have a child with you. Some say my real father is someone here at Stronghold, and others say a Sunrunner was brought here in secret. It was merely insulting until they got to the part about Mother only marrying you because Lady Andrade told her to, and that she never loved you at all. *That* made it ludicrous! I always laughed it off— and so should you," he added with gentle chiding to Sioned.

"I never heard that one," Rohan mused.

"There are others. All of them just as ridiculous. Mother, don't concern yourself with—"

"Pol, please!" She shied to her feet like a nervous cat and paced to the other side of the desk. "Just listen. Don't make this any harder."

Obviously bewildered now, Pol looked to his father for an explanation. Rohan said softly, "There's no easy way to tell it. Pol, do you believe that possession of *diarmadhi* power is inherently evil?"

"I've already been through this with Riyan. If I ever did believe that, which I don't, he's ample evidence otherwise." He shifted impatiently, flinging a look at Sioned. "Will you please just tell me whatever it is you feel you have to tell me?"

Her shoulders straightened as though she was bracing herself. She stood behind Rohan's desk chair, gripping its carved wooden back. She drew a slow breath—but Rohan spoke first.

"You are a Sunrunner, Pol," he said. "But you are also *diarmadhi*. You are my son, but not hers. Your mother was Princess Ianthe, youngest daughter of High Prince Roelstra and his only wife, Lallante."

Shock froze the young face. His eyes went blank, his skin colorless. Rohan watched confusion, denial, suspicion, a hundred emotions play across his son's features. At last Pol's lips moved in a deathly whisper. "Why would you tell me such a lie?"

Rohan could hardly breathe. Sioned clung to the chair so hard her hands were bloodless.

"How?" Pol's voice was harsh, hollow.

Sioned answered. "I lost every child I ever carried. All failings of a princess are forgivable but one: failure to bear a son. But I—I saw myself in a vision of Fire and Water. I was holding a newborn. You. So much your father's son that there could be no doubt you were his. Yet I knew I would never conceive again." She stood very still, staring down at her hands. "You know that Ianthe held your father captive at Feruche. I was there, too. When she was certain she was pregnant, she let us go."

"I do not excuse myself, Pol," Rohan said quietly. "I—"

"The first time," Sioned went on as if he had not spoken, "she went to him while he was drugged with *dranath* and fevered from a wound. She . . . pretended to be me. She wished an heir to Princemarch and the Desert both, her vengeance on him for Choosing me instead of her."

"The second time, I raped her." Rohan heard the revulsion he'd sworn he would never reveal, and cursed himself. "I prefer to believe you were the result of that first—" He stopped, swallowed hard. "When—afterward—I joined our armies already in the field. Sioned stayed at

Stronghold and emptied it of all but a few servants. Tobin and Ostvel were here as well."

Pol flinched. "Then . . . they've always known. Who else?"

"Chay. Myrdal. Maeta." She pronounced the names slowly, reluctantly.

"And the servants?"

"All dead now, but for Tibalia." Her eyes, liquid with anguish, beseeched him. "People who love you, Pol. Who—"

"—don't hold it against me?" For the first time there was an edge to his voice, a strange spark in his blue-green eyes.

Rohan said softly, "She kept watch. She waited just as if she was the one carrying you in her body. You were *hers*, Pol. Do you understand? She'd seen you in her arms. *Our* child."

"I watched Ianthe grow big with the son she had stolen from me. From him. Her time came early. Ostvel and Tobin and I rode to Feruche." She looked up then, memory swirling in her darkened eyes. "I took you from her in secret, reclaimed what was mine. I brought Feruche down around itself with Fire. Everyone thought that the child she bore died with her. But he did not. *You* are that child, Pol. We went to Skybowl. Few saw us there—the workers had all become warriors in defense of the Desert. Skybowl was nearly as empty as Stronghold. For those who did see, there was . . . an explanation."

"A lie," Pol said in a toneless voice.

"Yes," she agreed steadily. "That I had expected the birth of my own son to occur in midwinter. That I had started for Skybowl on whim, Tobin and Ostvel in attendance. I . . . was not myself that summer and autumn. I don't remember much about that time—not from the night Ianthe took me, put me into a cell without light . . . I think perhaps I went a little mad." Her hands twisted around themselves. "My actions were understood to be part of this. It was plausible. Women with child have strange fancies sometimes." A deep breath to calm herself, and she went on, "We told them at Skybowl that you were born along the way. That night I Named you with Ostvel and Tobin witnessing. And also that night—"

"I killed Roelstra," Rohan said curtly. "You've heard how it happened. A dome of starfire constructed all the way from Skybowl, catching into it every *faradhi*-gifted mind there and at the battleground—including you. Roelstra knew you had been born. He didn't know his daughter was dead."

"Wh–who killed her?"

Rohan met Sioned's haunted eyes.

"Oh, Goddess," Pol breathed. "*Mother*—"

"No!" Rohan exclaimed.

"I didn't kill her." Sioned looked at Pol and her eyes were hard. "But I wanted nothing more in the world. She imprisoned us, tortured your father, shut me away from the sunlight—and she would have raised you to be as foul as she was. I couldn't let that happen, Pol. She had the bearing of you, but you were never her son." Her voice held a note of pleading now. But Rohan recognized that even in her anguish she had managed to avoid revealing another truth: that Ostvel was the one who had killed Ianthe. They could never tell Pol that.

"Then . . . then Ruval is my half-brother," Pol said slowly, as if awakening from a long sleep to find that even words were strangers. "And my life is a lie."

"Pol!" Rohan went to him, grasped his shoulders. "You are no different now than you were before you knew! What's changed? You were born of princes, you are *faradhi*, and you are my son. And Sioned's." He stared into his son's face, willing Pol to say words that would free Sioned of her terror.

"No different?" the young man asked incredulously. "Knowing I'm *diarmadhi*, that I'm the child of rape, that my father killed my grandfather, that my mother—" He gave a small, choking laugh. "*Which* mother?"

"Pol—"

"No *different*?"

"Are you anything less than you were before you knew?" Rohan snapped.

"I'm *more*," he replied in soft, deadly tones.

Rohan stood away from him. "This can only change you if you let it. Ianthe may have birthed you, but you were never her son. *Never*. Do you feel any kinship to Ruval? Any pull of brotherhood? Who was it who nursed you, raised you, loved you, taught you—"

Sioned moaned low in her throat. Rohan turned to

her, stricken by the look in her eyes. What she had always feared had come to pass. Pol was blaming her, rejecting her—for something Rohan had done.

He faced his son once more. "This is no easier for us than it is for you. If we'd had a choice—"

"You never would have told me. That's obvious. You would have gone on letting me believe a lie!" He surged to his feet.

"That you're Sioned's son? Is that truly a lie? Pol, look into yourself. Are you Ianthe's?"

"Why didn't you tell me?" Pol cried. "Why did you keep it secret?"

"If you need to blame someone, blame me," Rohan said.

"Do you know what they planned for him, Pol?" Sioned spoke with deliberate harshness. "Do you know what they would have done, your birth-mother and her sire? He and Ianthe were to marry. Once an heir was born, Rohan would have been killed. The Desert would become part of Princemarch. Ianthe's son would rule both as High Prince once Roelstra was dead. Do you want to claim such people for your own? They had nothing to do with your life!"

"Except that they gave it to me! And things haven't worked out too differently, have they? I've got Princemarch, and eventually I'll have the Desert and be High Prince— Goddess, it's all happened as if my—my *grandfather* was still alive!"

"Stop it!" Rohan commanded. "I killed Roelstra because he needed killing, not because I wanted his power for either of us. If you believe otherwise after so many years, you're a fool! All this was my doing, Pol. All of it. It's my fault that they plotted against me, my fault that your mother was captured and shut away in the dark and—"

Sioned made a small, animal sound, her hands lifting as if to ward off the memory of rape, darkness in her eyes that would devour her if the words were spoken. He bit his lips closed and dug his fingers into his palms, speaking again only when he could do so with relative calm.

"I raped Ianthe and I killed Roelstra and I allowed you to think you're what everyone believes you are. All these things you may blame me for. But Tobin knows the truth of your birth, and Chay, and Myrdal, and Ostvel—and so did Maeta. Would she have given her life for you if she believed you to be truly Ianthe's son? Do any of the others watch for signs of Roelstra in you? Your real mother is here before you, not in the ashes beneath Feruche!"

At last Pol looked at Sioned. She had wrapped her arms around herself, shivering, eyes huge with pain and pleading. He stared at her a long, silent time, without accusation or understanding. Then he turned and left the room.

**

He didn't know he was running until there was nowhere else to go.

The door to the uppermost chamber of the Flametower stopped him. He stared at the carved wood without comprehension for some moments, then slammed it open with one shoulder, colliding instantly with a blast of searing heat from the constant fire. The door reeled on one hinge; he shoved it closed, leaned back, tried to catch his breath. Intense firelight stung his eyes and all the colors he had ever seen or dreamed whirled in the center of the windowed room, reaching out as in *faradhi* vision to assault his senses.

Air rasped into his lungs. He staggered to a window, unable to breathe around the ache in his chest. Lied to, betrayed, deceived—and by the two people he loved and trusted and honored more than anyone in the world. He cried out a wordless, mindless protest. This could not be happening to him. It wasn't right, it wasn't fair—how could they have lied to him? They were supposed to love him, to want the best for him. And yet they had done this thing to him.

The cool scented darkness of the Desert spread beyond Stronghold. Above, the night sky was drenched with stars. He clenched his fingers on the stones as if he could tear them asunder, push them into the placid garden of roses and water below, then take flight like a dragon into the sky.

That was what had brought him up here. The need to escape, to find freedom, solitary and wild, to flex the muscles of his wings and fly. He stared down at his useless hands and a low groan of rage broke from his throat.

Fire blazing behind him soaked him in heat and sweat, and he knew that if he turned he could conjure visions in that Fire. He could bring into being scenes of the past.

The Star Scroll had taught him that today. A rape, a stolen child, a castle gutted by Sunrunner's Fire. Scenes to bear silent witness to the lie that was his life.

Or he could urge the flames higher, hotter, and in them be consumed.

"Pol?"

He swung around, livid with fury that someone had dared intrude. "Get out!" he snarled before he even recognized the young woman who stood beside the drunkenly tilting door. Her dark red hair was already thick with sweat that sheened her skin. "Leave me alone!"

Sionell hesitated, then moved inside and managed to wrench the door shut behind her. She leaned back against it as he had done, her voice almost casual as she said, "You're lucky I'm the only one still about at this hour to see you tear through the hallways like an avenging dragon."

Small solace that no one had witnessed his flight. Sionell had. And he would never forgive her for it. "I don't have to answer to anyone—least of all you!"

"Now, that sounds just like the arrogant little boy I used to know. The one who found me such a nuisance. You still do, I take it."

"Don't make me order you out of here, Sionell. Just go!"

Her brows arched. "Once when I was about eleven winters old, your mother interrupted one of our constant arguments. She told you that a prince who has to remind others of his rank isn't much of a prince."

His whole body stiffened at mention of his mother. Not his mother. His mother was Princess Ianthe, dead the night of his birth.

"What is it, Pol?" Sionell asked, more softly now. She raked damp hair from her face, blue eyes shadowed by a concerned frown, and took a step toward him. "We've known each other a long time. You can talk to me, you know."

"Really?" he asked in cutting tones. "I can talk to you, tell you anything, no matter what, and you'll love me just the same?" Some vicious part of him wanted to hurt someone else as deeply as he'd been hurt. It was Sionell's misfortune that she happened to be handy. "Do you think I haven't known all these years?"

That struck home. All the natural color drained from

her face, leaving ugly red patches on cheeks and fore-head where the fire's heat blazed against white skin.

"Go back to the husband you Chose because you couldn't have me," he taunted. "Go back to him and leave me alone."

"You bastard," she breathed.

Laughter scraped his throat raw. "Truer than you know, my lady! My father the prince and my mother the princess—only not the one everyone thinks!"

Stark bewilderment replaced mortal hurt in her eyes.

"Ianthe!" he shouted. "My real mother was Princess Ianthe!"

"No—that's not possible—"

Her shock confirmed his worst fears. He would see it in everyone from now on, everyone. They would know whose son he was, and whose grandson.

"It's true. They told me tonight—finally told me the truth of who I am!"

Sionell rallied with infuriating swiftness. "What of it? What about your own truths? Are you defined by a woman dead for—"

"For the length of my life, less one day! Now you know—so get out!"

"No," she said quietly, and stepped closer to the fire.

"Don't you understand? You're supposed to be *clever*, aren't you? I'm Roelstra's grandson, just like the man I'm supposed to kill! He's my *brother!*"

"And what of it?" she repeated.

"You haven't heard the best part yet! Can you guess, Sionell?" he jeered. "Does your cleverness extend to it? Have you figured out that I'm sorcerer's blood, just like my brother?"

"So is Riyan. So was Lord Urival. *What of it?*" she cried for a third time. "Does this makes any difference in what you choose to be?" Long fingers again pushed sweat-soaked hair from blazing blue eyes. "Will you choose your own life or trap yourself into what you think your ancestry makes you?"

"Leave me alone!" he shouted. "You can't possibly understand!"

"I understand you perfectly," she replied with a serenity that enraged him. "I always have. I just never knew it until I stopped loving you and started seeing you for what you are."

Stopped loving him? There was a sudden hollowness inside him that he never would have believed possible.

"You're arrogant and insufferable and self-centered," she continued icily. "The natural result of too much pride in too many gifts. And too damned smart for your own good."

"Thank you for that comforting list of my virtues," he snapped.

"Incomplete," she shot back. "But that's not important right now. What matters is that you're also strong enough to live as your intelligence and your heart say you must. Not as you think two dead people wanted."

"My whole life is a lie, Sionell! I'm not *me*, I'm—"

Her temper suddenly ignited. "You're a fool! Maybe you're right. Maybe being Roelstra's grandson *is* enough to overcome all you are, all you've been taught, all the love and guidance lavished on you from the day you were born! Maybe you'll forsake all that when you face Ruval, turn into some vicious—Goddess knows I've seen cruelty enough in you tonight! You didn't spare me much." She paused, sudden suspicion tightening her features. "And you didn't spare your mother either, did you? Pol, how *could* you?"

"She's not my mother!"

Sionell crossed the distance between them and struck him across the face. "Damn you," she hissed, breathing hard. "Cruelty and disloyalty make a fine start! You're right, Pol, you're just like your grandsire! Why don't you let Ruval kill you? That way you won't have to spend your life proving to everyone else what a monster you really are—the way you proved it to me tonight!"

She wrenched open the door and the gush of air snagged at the flames. The next instant she was gone.

***

Rohan stood alone, unnoticed and unremarked in an alcove near the main stairs. He wasn't exactly hiding, but he did want to observe without being assaulted with endless questions while at his order every room in the keep was emptied.

It was considerably past midnight. The general tone of conversation was therefore querulous if not downright irritable as servants, squires, guards, and highborns alike descended the stairs. Muttering and complaining, they crowded into the foyer, which was dimly lit by four tall standing branches of candles. To pass the time while he waited for the castle to clear, Rohan wagered with himself that he could guess what they'd say. Most of it was fairly predictable.

"What's going on?"

"How do I know?"

"We already searched from Flametower to the cellars—"

"It's the High Prince's order. Just do it!" This from an underchamberlain to a group of drowsy-eyed maids he was herding downstairs.

"But why order everyone out?"

Rialt, taking the last steps two at a time, said, "Whatever the reason, look lively. It's bad practice to keep a prince waiting."

Hollis and Maarken, carrying their sleepy children, said nothing. Morwenna came downstairs with bedrobe askew, grumbling under her breath about an honest day's work deserving an honest night's slumber. The duty guards were polite but firm as they ushered castlefolk and Miyon's servants out to the courtyard.

"This is an outrage!" announced Lord Barig. His Giladan lawyers agreed with him. Rohan mouthed the next, inevitable words along with his lordship: "I demand to know the meaning of this!"

Nodding to himself, Rohan saw Barig waylay Arlis, who stood in the foyer encouraging people to assemble swiftly in the courtyard. The young man listened with grave politeness, shrugged an apology, and gestured to the doors.

Andry was predictably silent, but Nialdan rumbled, "It's the middle of the night! Why are we being rousted out of bed?" To which Andry replied softly, "Doubtless to witness something both entertaining and instructive. Aren't you glad we were given three days to leave?"

Sionell came down the stairs wrapped in a thick robe, her hair dripping. Rohan's brows shot up; it was a little late at night for a bath. Tallain was waiting for her in the foyer. Rohan could not hear the words they exchanged, but as she huddled into the curve of his arm his protective tenderness was eloquent. Rohan tried to puzzle it out as noisy squires and young servants trooped past. Something had hurt Sionell. More than that, he realized, something had made her feel unclean. He had felt the same impulse himself at times, a need for cool cleansing water. But the cause of her distress was a mystery. Pol's infatuation with Meiglan, perhaps? No, Ell was too sensible for that. Come to think of it, where was Meiglan?

Chay went by with Jahnavi, complimenting the boy on his instinctive grab for his sword—a true warrior's reaction on so abrupt a wakening. "By the Goddess' grace, I hope you won't need it," he added.

Miyon was next. Rohan bet himself that the Cunaxan prince would echo Barig's words, maybe with a "How dare he?" thrown in. But Miyon surprised him. He descended the steps unruffled and unconcerned, a much more telling reaction than if he had stormed into the foyer with loud complaints. Rohan shook his head. The man was too confident, and too arrogant to hide it.

It took Walvis and Feylin both to support Meiglan down the stairs. From his post in the alcove Rohan heard Feylin's gentle encouragements before he actually caught sight of the girl. Her appearance shocked him. She could barely walk. Her bright curls looked crushed, her dark eyes dull and only awake enough to be frightened. She clung to Feylin as Walvis steadied her with an arm around her waist. After the last step she paused, swaying, eyelids fluttering as if she was about to faint.

"Meiglan!"

Her father's roar straightened her body like a whip across her back. Walvis looked murderous; Feylin, disgusted. Rohan was about to step forward and deflect Miyon's wrath when Pol appeared out of nowhere and strode to the girl's side. Deftly he took charge of her from Walvis. But she was too terrified to notice the identity of the man whose strong arm now supported her.

Miyon had stopped halfway to her, his upraised hand falling to his side. But he did with words what he did not dare do physically, not with Pol there. "How dare you trouble the Lord and Lady of Remagev with your worthless person!"

Meiglan clutched at Pol's shirt. "Father—I'm sorry—what have I done?"

"Goddess, what stupidity! Did you think this assembly was called for you?"

It was obvious that she did, that she believed a public humiliation in front of the whole castle would be his ultimate cruelty. The confusion in her drug-hazed eyes slowly gave way to pathetic relief and she sagged against Pol.

He directed a single, quelling look at Miyon, then said, "I'm pleased to see you up and about, my lady."

Rohan expected her to collapse when she recognized Pol. Instead, though she turned even paler if that were possible, she managed to straighten up and compose herself a little. She trusted him. Rohan found that very interesting. And he decided that Miyon and his *diarmadhi* allies would pay not only for their crimes but for using this innocent child.

As the foyer cleared, he leaned against the wall, hands deep in his pockets, reviewing his next actions one last time. Much depended on his knowledge of the people involved—but he had picked up a taste for gambling from his wife. A tart mental reminder that Sioned never bet except on a sure thing only brought a wry smile to his lips. He couldn't afford to be that cautious. Not now.

Arlis, who had known where he was all along, approached the alcove. "It took a bit longer than I had hoped, but Stronghold is emptied, my lord."

"Good. I hope Barig didn't insult you too much."

Arlis grinned. "I confess he goaded me into a display of bad taste—I had to remind him I'm a prince of Kierst and Isel."

"I excuse you—and I tremble for your dealings with Cabar once you're ruling your island. Instruct five pairs of guards to go through all the rooms a last time. They're to stay together, mind. Oh—and have Myrdal sent to me."

"At once, my lord. I'll make it fast. They're getting restless outside."

"Dear me. And it's such a lovely night," he mused, shaking his head.

Arlis gave a snort. "Six years with you have taught me that tone of voice means you're up to absolutely no good."

"I'll have to remember that if we ever find ourselves on opposite sides of an issue at a *Rialla*. I should've realized it was a bad idea to foster a future ruling prince in my household."

"I wouldn't have missed it for anything. I just wish I knew what you were up to this time." The squire left through the main doors to command the search.

Rohan sat on the alcove bench, content still to wait—

and to let the others grow as restless as they liked. Pol wanted him to act. Well, it had never been said of him that once he decided a thing, he hesitated in carrying it out. He hoped that one day Pol would understand that a High Prince acted only when he must—and then ruthlessly.

The ten guards came and went through the foyer without noticing him. Myrdal hobbled in a little while after, white hair flowing down her back, dragon-head cane tapping impatiently on the stones.

"Well?" she snapped. "Where are you, boy?"

Rohan emerged from the shadows. "Here. I apologize for disturbing your rest."

The old woman eyed him shrewdly, missing nothing of his black clothes enlivened by touches of Desert blue and gold embroidery. "Dressed as High Prince, I see, while the rest of us are in bedgowns. Not very subtle, Rohan."

"I'm not dealing with subtle people, Myrdal."

"Granted. Well, then, what do you want of me?"

"Your knowledge. You know places within Stronghold where nobody else believes there could *be* places."

"And you think the sorcerers are hiding in one of them? Hmm. You may be right. This is a very old castle."

"You know it better than I do—and I'm the one who owns it."

"I suppose it's time I told you," she admitted. "Your great-grandsire Prince Zagroy knew all the secrets, but he was a possessive sort and didn't quite trust his son. So he entrusted the knowledge to my mother."

"His illegitimate daughter," Rohan said.

Myrdal grinned at him. "Possibly, possibly. In any case, my mother shared it with me, and I told most of it to Maeta. I thought she'd have a daughter or son of her own to pass the knowledge to. But it seems I'm the last." She lowered her ancient bones gingerly onto the third step, sighing. "Some of the secrets you know. Can you tell me what they have in common?"

"They operate by hidden catches, they're all built into stone and none into wood, and—" He stopped, staring down at her with his mouth open.

Myrdal nodded. "Never had to think much about it before, have you? The trigger is always marked with a star or a sunburst."

"You've shown me five—no, six. Two with a star, four with a sunburst. For Sorcerers and Sunrunners?"

"Think of how many times this keep has changed hands," she suggested.

"Damn it, I don't have time for guessing games!"

"Impatience was always a failing of yours," she chided. "You've controlled it remarkably well recently; now isn't the moment to give in. To answer your question, yes, it has to do with who put the secret into the castle. Some are fatal. There's one in the Flametower that lands one rather precipitously in the cellars."

"That's a structural impossibility," he stated.

She only laughed.

"Oh, all right," he said grudgingly. "Were the Sunrunners as lethally inclined?"

"In general, no. My mother had their only death trap walled up and its symbol effaced from the stones. Something to do with a knife-lined floor."

He stared in spite of himself. "Here? In Stronghold?"

She shrugged. "You've kept the peace as High Prince. Times weren't always so easy. When the *diarmadh'im* were here, they sought and learned the *faradhi* tricks—a favor the Sunrunners returned when they retook the castle. They went on like that for about thirty years, merrily setting traps for each other."

"The histories make no mention of it," he challenged.

"Would you write down all your secrets? I gather you're interested in places that could hold a few people in reasonable comfort."

"I need to find them quickly, Myrdal," he said.

"The sorcerers and their Merida assassins specialized in quick escape routes—like the one at the grotto. But hiding holes were put into Stronghold by *faradh'im*."

Rohan caught his breath. "And they'd need sunlight more than anything else!" He thought rapidly. "An outer wall, then—and southern exposure to get the most light."

"Very good. Help me up, boy."

He did so as the guards returned. Arlis came to him with negative reports. "Not even a stray bedbug, my lord."

"I should think not!" Myrdal sniffed. "Princess Milar spent the first year of her marriage having them all hunted down. Why, I remember—"

Rohan interposed gently, "Arlis, bring my wife and

son here, please. I need Lord Chaynal, Lord Maarken, and Lord Riyan as well."

"Yes, my lord."

Myrdal squinted up at him in the gloom. "Have you thought what you'll do when you find your sorcerer?"

He put his hands back into his trouser pockets. "I have an idea or two."

"She'll throw everything she's got at you," the old woman warned.

"I know. But she doesn't know what I intend to do to *her*."

"I doubt you'll be able to kill her."

"So do I."

Myrdal thumped her cane on the step. "Don't play coy with me!"

Making innocent eyes at her, he replied, "I wouldn't presume."

"Oh, as you like, then," she muttered. "You haven't changed since the day you were born."

"But I have, you know," he said seriously. "I've learned how to be afraid."

***

Pol helped Meiglan into the torchlit courtyard, pleased that she seemed to be growing stronger with each step. A tinge of color had returned to her lips and cheeks, she breathed more easily, and her eyes were brighter, more lucid.

There were hundreds of people currently in residence at Stronghold. Every last one of them—save a telltale few Pol looked for and did not find—jostled for space in the courtyard. Confusion there was; guards posted at strategic spots made sure there would be no chaos. Pol heard snatches of conversation as he and Meiglan descended the outer steps, and it intrigued him that while junior servants and the strangers from Cunaxa and Gilad and Tiglath all speculated on what the High Prince had in mind, those who knew his father simply waited in silence. Their long service here had bred a trust he had never thought about before. But it was not blind faith; it was the certainty of experience that whatever the difficulty, Rohan would solve it the cleanest and quickest way possible.

Pol escorted Meiglan to a place beside Walvis and Feylin. She murmured words of thanks to the couple for their assistance.

"Not at all," Feylin replied briskly. "Actually, I'm astonished you were able to stand up, let alone walk. That sleeping potion was one of the strongest I've ever encountered."

"Are you feeling better now, my dear?" Walvis asked.

"Yes, my lord." She cast a brief glance at her father, who was out of earshot. "I–I need to explain what happened, your grace," she said to Pol.

"I wish you would," Feylin told her with frank curiosity.

A deeper color mounted her cheeks, and she again looked toward Miyon.

"It will be between us," Pol reassured her.

Meiglan gave him a strangely dignified nod. "Thank you, your grace. But I d-don't have anything more to fear."

He stared down at her, taken aback. "Not here, of course," he said, groping for words. "You're quite safe, my lady."

"Perfectly," Walvis agreed. "I can understand that watching that man's face changing into something else altogether was startling—I admit I had to pick up my jaw with both hands."

"It's what I saw when the change was complete, my lord. I *recognized* him."

"As what?" Pol asked, unable to keep suspicion from shading his voice.

"Before we left Castle Pine, I came upon my father talking with a man while another approached. He was very displeased and s–sent me away." The catch in her voice at remembered ill-usage tore at Pol's heart. "That man was one of them. I–I recognized his red hair."

"So when you saw his real form. . . ." Feylin encouraged.

Meiglan shivered. "I'm sorry for my behavior. But I—when I knew who he was, and Mireva came to take me out of the Great Hall—"

"She drugged you to the eyebrows to keep you quiet," Feylin said.

"It's my fault," Meiglan said miserably. "I was the excuse and the opportunity to bring sorcerers within this keep."

Walvis took her hand. "Nonsense. Nobody could possibly blame you."

Pol watched the huge dark eyes fill with tears of gratitude. But she did not weep. He tried to be logical, tried to examine her story rationally. If all was as she had said, then she could not have been in his bedchamber last night.

Meiglan's form, but not Meiglan. Mireva.

The twist of physical sickness in his guts told him he had best not dwell too long on that idea. Meiglan was what mattered now. Did he believe her? Suspect her? Trust her?

What had she to lose at this point? Everyone now knew who the *diarmadh'im* were. There was no danger to them in telling her tale. He saw her dry her tears with her sleeve, a childlike gesture that brought a renewed ache to his chest. Did he dare believe? What if it really had been her last night, not Mireva? What if this was just one more lie designed by sorcery and her father?

But she had just handed him her father on a golden plate. Miyon had been seen with Marron and Ruval, Miyon had taken them into his service. Pol had been sure of Miyon's complicity before, but now he had proof.

Of a sort, anyway. If he could believe her.

She looked up at him, beseeching his forgiveness and understanding. He opened his mouth to speak, not knowing if he would accuse her or accept her.

"Your pardon, your grace, but the High Prince commands your grace to attend him within the keep."

He swung around, startled by Arlis' voice and formal phrasing. "What? Why?"

"The High Prince did not share his reasons with me, your grace. But he was most insistent that your grace obey him immediately."

Pol looked down into Meiglan's dark eyes, tortured. *Decide—one way or the other!* He saw his fingers caress the lingering drops from her cheek. Her lips parted in fearful wonder at his touch. Unable to bear even this tenuous contact with her, he turned and followed Arlis up the steps.

Chapter Twenty-five

Stronghold: 34 Spring

Sioned felt wrapped in darkness, shut away from the sun as she had been in Ianthe's dungeon, touched with the madness of that long-ago time. Weeping had cleansed neither her eyes nor her heart; she felt sick, her eyes throbbed, her whole body ached. She wanted to crawl to her bedchamber and huddle in that darkness like a wounded animal.

She stood silently by the closed doors of the Great Hall. When Pol came into the foyer, her control wavered for a moment. Candles revealed shadows around eyes already bruised with strain. There was darkness about him now, where before there had always been only light.

He saw her and glanced quickly away. Sioned fixed her gaze on the emerald resting heavily on her hand, remembering how she'd wrested it from Ianthe's finger. Claimed back everything that was hers. How young she had been then, only a few years older than Pol was now, how certain of herself and her vision. But what was a wound on her shoulder seen in Fire and Water was a scar on her cheek in reality. Andrade had told her long ago that conjured visions came to pass if one worked to make them happen. The difference between what she had seen and what had occurred, symbolized by that crescent-shaped scar on her face, had never troubled her before tonight. Now it frightened her. Perhaps it meant she had been wrong to take Pol, wrong to destroy Feruche.

Yet as she risked looking at him, doubt drained away. Even if he never forgave her, even if he wasn't her son, he was Rohan's. All his gifts of strength and pride, intelligence and power, would have been twisted had Ianthe had the raising as well as the bearing of him. What

Sioned had done, the way she had done it, had not been wrong.

"Father?" Pol was saying. "What's the trouble?"

"Wait until the others arrive. I only want to explain his once."

"What others?"

"Until you have something useful to say, be silent!" Rohan snapped.

Pol stiffened, answering coldly, "As you wish, your grace."

Myrdal snorted. "Well, well. Prickly as *pemida* cactus tonight, aren't we?"

The situation was saved by the entrance of Maarken and Riyan. Rohan had insisted that Arlis make the summonses formal; the two young men took the hint and made their bows to the High Prince, not speaking until spoken to. Rohan acknowledged them with a nod and the words, "I trust your various talents are in working order even in the middle of the night."

"Our gifts are at your grace's command," Maarken affirmed.

Chay entered, Andry beside him, in time to hear Maarken's words. Andry's lips thinned as his brother offered up Sunrunner abilities to a prince's use. He approached Rohan boldly enough, saying, "I'm pent up here like everyone else, even though we both want me gone—you may not wish *my* presence, but you may require the Lord of Goddess Keep."

"We welcome your presence, my Lord," Rohan answered quietly.

Mollified but wary, Andry nodded.

Sioned did not join them. She waited in the shadowed doorway, watching Pol's face.

"We have ordered Stronghold emptied of all its obvious inhabitants," Rohan said. "Now it's time to take care of the unobvious ones." Without further explanation he took Myrdal's arm and helped her up the stairs.

The others followed, expressions reflecting various degrees of confusion, curiosity, and concern. Still Sioned held back. And what she both wished for and feared came to pass. Pol mounted only two steps before he paused, turned, and came to where she stood.

Sioned held her breath. She forced herself to look into

his eyes as he halted before her, his eyes that were
bitterly ashamed.

"I . . . I'm sorry. I never doubted that you love me."
He touched the scar on her cheek. "I just—I never
expected this kind of proof. That you'd risk so much for
me."

Sioned framed his face hesitantly, afraid he would pull
away. He did not. Her eyes stung with tears.

"I loved you before you were even born," she murmured. "I saw you and you were mine. I Named you,
taught you, gave you everything that had meaning for
me. But you're not mine anymore, Pol." His eyes widened in protest and she shook her head. "Let me finish.
You belong to no one but yourself. That's what it means
to leave childhood behind. No one can possess anything
of your heart unless you choose it so. Whatever you feel
for me—"

"I love you," he said. "Please don't cry, Mama."

Tears rolled down her cheeks. "Oh, damn—I swore I
wasn't going to—"

"Shh. I *love* you." Pol gave her a quick, hard hug.
Then, stepping back, he held out one hand. "We'll have
to hurry or we'll miss it."

She swept tears from her face. "Yes." Managing a
smile, she added, "Your father does so hate to be deprived of an audience when he's being clever."

***

It had taken no special cleverness to figure out that
those he sought were almost certainly hiding somewhere
within Stronghold.

Rohan reasoned this way. It was unlikely, considering
Riyan's quick order to the gatehouse, that they had managed to escape the castle. If they had, sorcery would
probably be necessary to conceal their movements. Sioned,
Maarken, and Morwenna, all of whom knew the surrounding hills and dunes intimately, had searched by
Sunrunner methods and found no trace. Riyan, with both
diarmadhi blood and *faradhi* rings, had sensed nothing
on his own forays. Soldiers both mounted and on foot
had undertaken a more conventional exploration with the
same negative results. The chances of successfully hiding
from so many were remote. Mireva, Ruval, and Ruala
were not outside Stronghold.

If they were not without, they must be within. But Riyan's tours of the keep from cellars to battlements had revealed no hint of sorcery either. Physical search by servants and guards had proved equally fruitless.

Every indication affirmed that the three were neither inside the castle nor outside it. But not even a sorcerer could vanish into thin air. Still, there were places in Stronghold that could create that impression.

Rohan knew they must be laughing, safely concealed in his very castle while he made a fool of himself trying to find them. What profit in leaving? How much more formidable they would see, after all, if the challenge came from within Stronghold itself, as if they already had command and possession of the keep. It was what he would have done. They must be waiting here for a ripe moment to reveal themselves.

Rohan had had enough of waiting.

Given the clues by Myrdal—stubborn old she-dragon, he told himself with an inner smile both fond and exasperated—he led his little group to the southern side of the fourth floor. On the way upstairs Myrdal whispered instructions about which rooms contained secrets. Though she rejoiced in teasing him without mercy, she did so only in private; the privileges of a High Prince did not include being made a fool of in public. So he entered the maidservants' quarters with perfect confidence, blessing her tender regard for his image.

Riyan gestured candles alight without being asked. By their glow the room's features were revealed: a row of beds along one wall, covers tumbled; a carved screen around the private space for Tibalia, the benevolent despot in charge; standing wardrobes that sectioned off the sleeping area from chairs and tables scattered casually before the windows. It was to this wall that Rohan went.

Chay said, "I hate to ask, but would somebody please tell me what we're supposed to be doing?"

Maarken answered him. "Finding a couple of unwanted guests. Andry, Riyan, we'll have to be ready for just about anything."

Rohan felt carefully along the junction of walls. "I regret I've never heard of a way to prepare for countering an attack by sorcery. I'm relying on your instincts."

"What do *yours* say, Rohan?" Chay asked.

"That this is the logical place. Mireva would have been in here several times during her stay. Our tyrannical Tibalia is as strict with guesting servants as she is with our own maids, so Lady Meiglan's pair would have found themselves spending evenings here instead of roaming the castle."

"Which gave the witch ample opportunity to find what we're looking for now," Myrdal finished approvingly. "Very good indeed, my prince."

"Why waste time on places she didn't go? It isn't as if she was free to explore. And I can't convince myself that all the secrets of Stronghold are known by every *diarmadh'im* in the—aha!"

The sunburst pattern was half-hidden in a decorative carving of flowers. Gesturing the others closer, he held his breath and pressed down.

Nothing happened.

He felt the stones all around the sunburst, trying to discern in which direction the wall would give. "Damn it all, where is it? There's got to be a catch here someplace. Myrdal, help me with this."

"I only know about the fool thing, I've never actually worked it before," she grumbled, but obeyed.

"Riyan," Pol said, and his presence startled Rohan, "you remember the defense we read about today. We'll weave it now, just in case."

Rohan glanced over his shoulder, saw his son standing protectively in front of Sioned. Her face was tense, but the terrible hurt had left her eyes.

"The Star Scroll?" This from Andry, in sharp tones.

"You've used it," Pol said aggressively. "Why shouldn't we?"

Rohan's fingers probed and pushed, twisted, tugged, and tested. Swearing under his breath, he drew back slightly. "Look here, you can see where it fits into the wall. There's a little seam in the stone. But it won't work!"

"Maybe they fouled it somehow," Chay suggested. Then, with an odd look at Myrdal, "How many of these little secrets *are* there around here?"

"A lot more than in Radzyn," she replied smugly. "I think this one's hopeless. I've opened plenty of others and they all work perfectly. Chaynal's right, it was broken somehow."

"Deliberately?" Sioned asked.

Rohan sighed. "It doesn't much matter. So much for my first brilliant idea. We'll have to try another—" He broke off and stared at the stone carvings.

"Father? What is it?"

He ignored his son, addressing Myrdal instead. "You said they traded control of Stronghold back and forth, finding out each other's secrets, putting new ones in."

"Yes, but—"

He ran his fingers over the stone, inspecting each shadow. "By logic, this is the room. All the others would be difficult to explore without getting caught. She wouldn't want to draw attention to herself. This has to be it."

Sioned reluctantly pointed out, "But the sorcery, Rohan. We can't know what she's able to do. Nothing ever prepared us for shape-changing. There could be any number of other things—"

"But only one star carved into this wall!" he interrupted triumphantly.

"By the Goddess' works and marvels," Myrdal breathed.

"Careful," Chay warned. "They might be expecting us."

Rohan was counting on it. He looked again at the Sunrunners. "Ready yourselves. We're not likely to be welcomed with open arms."

There was an exit to his own bedchamber marked with a star, something Myrdal had shown Sioned years ago. One pressed gently on the carving until it gave, then turned it to the left. He held his breath again as he manipulated the star symbol, hoping it worked the same way.

It moved. The seam parted—slowly at first, then faster. A gap opened from head-height to floor, grew wider as a section of stone slid back. Something rustled within, a heavy sound that set his heart beating rapidly with excitement and apprehension. He stood his ground.

From the blackness leaped a hatchling dragon colored the slick red of fresh blood. Its head reared back on a furious shriek, wings spread wide, gleaming claws ripping at the air. It doubled in size as it surged into the room, roaring a challenge. The creature was every nightmare of *dragon* that ever was, down to the flames that spewed toward the ceiling beams from jaws powerful enough to snap a man in two. The throat pulsed as another gout of fire hissed forth. Another hideous roar, a flexing of the massive muscles in the wings—and blazing ruby eyes fixed on Rohan.

He had looked into dragon eyes before. None had been like this. Will drained from him like water into sand. He was nothing. The flames would burn him to nothing, crisp his flesh and bones to ash on the blackened stones. . . .

"Rohan!"

The word barely made sense to him. His name? Yes. Sioned's voice. Sioned—

She screamed his name again and this time he responded, terrified not for himself but for her. He tore his gaze from the dragon's compelling ruby eyes and realized with vague astonishment that he had toppled to the floor. The dragon loomed over him; he could see its wing lifting to block out the ceiling like a blood-red cloud across a white sky.

But it should have been black. The fire should have scorched whitewashed rafters and stone. *Unreal.* He scrabbled for purchase, and had barely regained his feet when the dragon lashed out with blade-sharp talons. They passed right through him and left him whole.

He laughed up into the hot, glowing eyes, dizzy with relief. The dragon was not a shape assumed by Mireva herself, but a conjuring, harmless as morning mist. Into the gaping darkness of the hiding hole he shouted, "If this is the best you can do, try again!"

The dragon vanished. In its place stood a young man with dark hair and Ianthe's eyes, a death's grin on his handsome face. "Better, High Prince?"

Rohan crossed the distance separating them, confident that this was illusion, too. But the taunting laughter was real. The knife that plunged into his shoulder was real. The pain was real.

"No!" Riyan staggered forward, hands contorted in familiar agony. He slammed into Ruval, knocking him down. The blood-stained knife clattered to the stones. Chay's boot descended on the blade as Ruval's fingers groped for it.

Riyan's abrupt sundering of the defensive weave left Pol momentarily blind. From behind its protection he had seen the conjured dragon, a terrifying sight but one he knew could not harm his father. It had no substance. His senses—Sunrunner? Sorcerer?—told him without his conscious awareness.

But the knife was real. As he sensed its solid steel panic flooded his whole body, shattering the weave as surely as Riyan's sudden departure from it. But Ruval moved too fast. Pol's vision cleared and he surged forward, ready to kill. Before he could get there, Riyan had twisted around to clasp the shaking form tight in his arms. They rolled against the wall beside the gaping blackness, Ruval protected by Riyan's body. Chay, not as vulnerable to the lash of sorcery against his consciousness, rushed forward with a knife.

"No!" Riyan cried again. "It's not him! My rings are burning the flesh from my fingers—it's not Ruval! It's Ruala!"

Pol stared down in shock as the tall, muscular shape shifted to a slighter one with slender curves and tangled black hair. Trousers and shirt and tunic were all that remained of the illusion of Ruval.

Rohan recovered first. He pulled Riyan and the dazed, half-conscious young woman to their feet. Then he winced and leaned against the wall, clutching his arm. Sioned pried his fingers away from the wound. Her scowl worried Pol, but her words dispelled his fear. "As if you didn't have enough scars, you great fool!" She ripped the sleeve off and tied it around his arm to stop the bleeding.

Rohan made a face at her rough handling that, even more than her scolding, indicated the wound was not serious. Turning to Pol, he said grimly, "She's still in there. Unless there's an escape built into that hole."

Maarken pushed by his father, who was helping Riyan and Ruala to nearby chairs.

"Maarken—no!" Pol exclaimed, but his cousin was already ducking past into the darkness. There was a blaze of light, a startled cry of pain, and Maarken stumbled back against Pol.

"Merciful Goddess," he breathed. Then, rallying, he said, "Well, at least we know where she is."

Andry came to his brother's side. "You idiot—she might have killed you. Are you all right?"

Maarken nodded. "Shaken a little. There's quite a bit

to this sorcery," he said with deceptive mildness. "We can't go in, that's obvious. But if she could have escaped, I think she would have done it by now."

"I don't know about the rest of you, but I have no taste for waiting her out." Andry turned. "Sioned, can you weave some sort of protection for yourself and the others?"

"Yes, I think so, but—"

"Please do so." He met Pol's gaze in sardonic challenge. "Well? Shall we see which of us she most wants dead?"

"Interesting decision for her," he replied. "Ready?"

Andry nodded. He murmured something under his breath then called, "Did you hear me, creature? Your choice! The Lord of Goddess Keep or the next High Prince! Which of us would be easiest for you?"

"Whichever of us you destroy, the other will come in after you!" Pol shouted.

Laughter floated from the darkness. "Which of you has the courage to come to me for your death?"

"No!" Rohan hissed behind them. "Don't go in! Bring her out!"

"Can you face me?" Mireva taunted.

"Can you face us both?" Pol jeered.

"The two of *you,* working as one?" She laughed uproariously. "You'll combine forces when dragons fly the seas instead of the sky!"

Pol met and held Andry's gaze. His cousin whispered words in the old language that for a moment confused Pol. *Fire dream?* Andry gestured impatiently and suddenly Pol understood. Nodding, he readied himself.

Two forms coalesced from Sunrunner's Fire. One of them became Pol; the other, Andry. The conjurings drifted into the blackness. By their light Pol saw the shape of the room, the woman standing within—alone and still laughing. His fury at being cheated of Ruval showed in a flare of his conjuring. The next instant he cried out and lost control completely as Mireva assaulted his Fire with her own. It was white and cold and it seared every nerve in his body.

"Try again, princeling!"

"Shall I show you how it's done?" Andry said, voice acid with contempt for them both. Pol's jangled senses

reeled as power flowed smooth and strong from Andry.
It was an almost casual display; no effort showed on his
face or in his eyes. But Mireva fell back, and the white
fire guttered out.

"Pol! Grab her—she's lost the spell, she's vulnerable!"
Andry cried.

His head was a mass of needles and the orders he gave his
limbs were so garbled that he moved like a badly jointed
puppet. But he flung himself forward, crashing into Mireva.
The Fireglow vanished as they sprawled onto the hard stones.

Pol went for her throat. The loose and wrinkled skin of
age suddenly firmed to youthful suppleness and the face
above his throttling hands was the exquisite face of Meiglan,
framed in the light of her golden hair. His grip faltered.
Even though he knew it was illusion, he faltered.

His mind was a storm. Like lightning branches across
the Desert sky, firebolts ripped through his brain. He
fled them. But Meiglan's face with Mireva's gray-green
eyes laughed from every corner of thought. Spasms leaped
through his muscles as in his mind he ran screaming. But
there was no escape.

It was Mireva's face again, a ruby glow of triumph
deep in the eyes. But only for an instant. Horror sliced
through him and another burst of lightning as the face
changed again, dissolving into formlessness, reshaping as
a nightmare. The neck he clutched grew leathery, the
face above it became a leering, hideous mass of blotched
sores and shedding scales. Horns tipped with blood
sprouted from the forehead; curving fangs and a forked
tongue protruded from slimy lips. The thick body writhed
beneath him; more hands than were possible touched his
body in obscene caresses. A shriek echoed endlessly in
his skull, a howl half laughter and half feral hunting call.

But the gray-green eyes with their crimson light were
still Mireva's.

Her mistake saved his sanity. He was within an instant
of abandoning the struggle in stark terror when some
lingering portion of reason screamed that it was illusion:
no matter how horrible, only illusion. Fear brought a sob
to his throat, but he dug his thumbs as hard as he could
into the neck, seeking to crush bones. He concentrated
on the sight of his own hands, the moonstone ring, the
amethyst of Princemarch, the whitened knuckles, the

infuriating weakness that made his fingers jerk and quiver so he could not get a death grip.

Hands very like his own reached down. He tried not to look at them, fearing they were another conjuring. But one finger wore a topaz circled by emeralds. The hands worked quickly near the angle of the massive jaw. And the monster roared in agony.

"Hurts, doesn't it?" said Rohan.

Mireva writhed on the floor as if from a mortal wound. Pol drew back, stunned by the thing's sudden disappearance. Rohan pushed him aside and deftly tied the woman's wrists together with a length of thin wire. Then he grasped Pol's shoulders.

"Are you all right?" Pol nodded mutely and Rohan sighed with relief. Rocking back on his heels, he wiped sweat from his face and asked more softly, "Well? Does my version of taking action meet with your approval?"

Pol flushed crimson and looked away. Candlelight spilled from the outer room across Mireva's upper body. She lay quiet now, her head lolling to one side. And then Pol saw it—a thin gleam of silver twisted through her earlobe. No, not silver: steel. He stared at his father with equal parts astonishment and admiration. Rohan smiled tightly.

"It won't kill her. They're not as vulnerable to iron as Sunrunners are. But if she makes the slightest attempt at sorcery, her new earring will cause her the agony of all Hells." He shrugged. "Inelegant, but effective."

Pol made it to his feet on the second try, with his father's help. "Why didn't you just kill her?"

"Because there are still others like her. And our possession of her might be of some worth against Ruval. Besides, I have something else in mind for her. Something infinitely more fitting."

Pol had never before seen another person's death in his father's eyes. He wondered suddenly if this look had been given Ianthe. His mother.

Rohan rubbed absently at his wounded shoulder. "I believe there are suitable accommodations in the cellar—holdovers from our barbarian past," he added ironically. "If you and Maarken would be so good as to escort her there when she comes around—but I see she's recovering already."

"Rohan? Are you going to stay in there all night?"

Chay's exasperated voice heralded his shadow in the doorway. "What's going on?"

"Patience," came the reply. "Go outside and tell everyone they can return to their beds, please. We're almost through here."

"What about Ruval?" This from Sioned. "He's still here somewhere."

"Is he?" Rohan mused. "I wonder."

Prodding Mireva's ribs with his toe, Pol asked, "Well? Where is Ianthe's eldest spawn?"

Mireva glared at them. "Hidden where you'll never find him, in the walls of this very castle!"

Rohan smiled. "Thank you. You just informed me that he's *not* here. If he were, you would have bragged of his escape to entertain yourself with watching me search the castle for the rest of the night. Let's see, how would he have gotten out of Stronghold? Ah, of course. The guards I sent out looking for you today in the hills. I thought that might be a mistake, but—never mind."

She spat feebly at him, the truth of his deduction in her eyes. Pol was beyond mere amazement now. He could only stare and wait for his father's next unsuspected gambit. But if he had been expecting something spectacular, he received only a tired smile.

"I think it's time we all got some rest," Rohan said. "Tomorrow may be rather busy."

They hauled Mireva out. Andry approached her with the curiosity of a scholar looking upon some new and unsavory discovery.

"So," he said. "This is a sorcerer's face."

She lurched to her feet, wrists already raw where she had struggled against the wire binding her. "So," she sneered, "this is a weakling Sunrunner's face."

His brows shot up. "*You* are the one imprisoned here, not I."

"Not for long." She flung her head back defiantly, the steel wire shining from her earlobe.

"Spare us your threats," Riyan snapped. He stood nearby, Ruala within his embrace. "There'll be no protection for Ruval now. He'll have to fight Pol fairly."

"Ah," Sioned murmured, casting a surprised look at Rohan.

Pol had only just realized it, too. By depriving Mireva

of sorcery, the starfire dome of the *rabikor* could not be fashioned. Riyan and Ruala were safe.

"You think you've won, High Prince," Mireva taunted. "Think carefully. You don't know where he is, what he's doing, what he knows and how he will use it." She turned her laughing gaze on Pol. "How much good will your Sunrunner tricks do you against the full power of a *diarmadhi*?"

Andry answered her. "They seem to have worked rather nicely against you."

"Not for long," she repeated.

Mydral thumped her cane on the stone. "I've had enough of this piece of filth," she announced. "Get her out of my sight."

Pol and Maarken started for Mireva, Andry a step behind them.

"Three strong young men to guard one poor, helpless old woman?" she mocked. "You must fear me even more than I thought."

"Don't flatter yourself," Pol told her. "They're coming along to make sure I don't kill you on the spot."

"Do you think you could?"

He smiled with fatal sweetness. "I know it. But I wouldn't want to deprive you of the sight of Ruval's death."

They took her belowstairs. There were people in the hallways now, returning to their interrupted sleep at Chay's order, eyes popping with curiosity. Not only did this ordinary-looking old woman merit an extraordinary escort, but three small fingerflames of Sunrunner's Fire lit their way down the stairs. Pol knew that before anyone's head rested on a pillow again, word would spread throughout the castle. Everyone would believe that the threat was gone, whatever it had been, and they were safe. His father had that effect on people.

As he descended the cellar stairs behind Mireva, he realized that his own apprehensions had eased. Goddess, how cunning Rohan was. First he had shown Pol the Star Scroll with its spells to work with and its traditions of the *rabikor*. Then had come the revelation about Ianthe to let him know that he was Ruval's equal in power if not in formal training. Now Mireva was rendered helpless, and by an innocuous piece of steel wire that would interfere with any attempt to use sorcery; there would be no powers but his own and Ruval's when the challenge came. Tension still coiled in his belly, but Pol knew he would face the man unafraid. His father had given him that.

And his mother. Sionell was right. It must have cost Sioned her soul to tell him. And he had repaid her with cruelty. He would make it up to her with more than the brief words he'd been able to manage earlier. To Princess Ianthe he might owe his existence, but to his mother he owed his life.

And to Sionell, the humblest of apologies.

"Here," Maarken said, breaking into Pol's thoughts. "Grandfather Zehava showed me this when I was little. It's where he kept those rare idiots who offended him twice." He gestured Mireva into the tiny room with a sarcastic flourish. "Before he personally escorted them out to the Long Sand and left them there."

"Why not do the same for me?" she asked.

"You heard his grace," Maarken reminded her. "He wishes you to watch your last hope die."

She smiled. "If he does, which is by no means certain, it won't be until he's settled the debt of Segev's death with your murdering bitch of a wife."

Pol saw Maarken turn white in the sudden reactive blaze of conjured Fire. Then Mireva was pinned to the back wall by her throat.

"If you even so much as *think* harm against my wife or my children, I'll kill you myself," Maarken hissed, shoving her higher up the stone. "And I warn you, I am neither as powerful nor as civilized as my brother or my cousin. It would take me a very long time, and I would make sure every instant was exquisite agony. So guard even your thoughts, witch. Someone will be listening."

Pol *had* seen death in Maarken's eyes before, but not like this. Even Mireva was taken aback. Maarken let her drop to the stone floor, dazed, and spun on his heels. He left it to Andry and Pol to secure the door.

Pol made a swift visual inspection of the cell. It was absolutely bare, without so much as a blanket to lie upon or a piece of straw to set afire for light. There were no windows. The heavy iron door did not even have a slot for passing in food and drink. Evidently his grandfather had meted out a ruthless justice; once it closed, that door would open only to remove the prisoner for transport to a quick death in the trackless wastes of the Long Sand.

It occurred to him that probably in just such a room, Ianthe had imprisoned Sioned.

"There's nothing here she can use, even if she could get her hands free," Andry observed. "The way Rohan tied the wires, she'd slice her hands off at the wrist before she could get loose." Andry regarded her for a long moment, then slammed the door shut with a clang. "So now we wait."

Pol secured the lock. "It won't take long."

"Are you prepared for it? For what he'll try to do to you?"

He thought his tiny fingerflame closer so he could see Andry's face. "Don't tell me you're concerned."

His cousin shrugged. "Better you as High Prince than Roelstra's grandson."

Pol kept reaction from his face. "I thought you'd see it that way." Then he sighed. "I'm sorry. I didn't mean to say that. I wanted to thank you for your help tonight. You didn't have to, but you did."

"That's right," Andry said, nodding, and they started up the steps.

Pol's next words came at even greater price, but he said them. "We worked well together. I think that shows we could continue to do so."

Andry gave him a quizzical look. "What was it she said? 'When dragons fly the seas instead of the sky'?"

"Why do you have to make things so difficult?"

"I have my duties and responsibilities. You have yours. If they clash—well, at least we won't be accused of conspiring together toward complete tyranny. Isn't that a desirable outcome? Won't it be reassuring to the other princes?"

Pol stopped him with a grasp on his arm. "Stop this, damn it! Andrade and Roelstra were checks on each other's power—and lifelong enemies. We don't have to emulate them."

"You're a dreamer, cousin. You think of what *could* be. I must think in terms of that I know is to come."

Pol kept hold of his temper with difficulty. "You keep mentioning this mysterious future. What exactly are you afraid of?"

For a moment he thought Andry might tell him. Then his cousin shrugged. "If you live long enough, maybe you'll find out."

His grip tightened. "You don't think I'll defeat Ruval?"

"On the contrary. I think you will. But you have other enemies. Stray *diarmadh'im* looking for revenge for killing their leader and their prince. Stray Merida—there are always stray Merida. Chiana cannot be discounted. Nor Miyon." Andry paused. Then, with mock solicitude: "Tell me, if you end up marrying the girl, do you think the knife in your back will have his handprint on it—or hers?"

Pol let him go as if the contact burned him. "It's a damned good thing you've been forbidden this princedom."

"Remember that when the future I've seen comes to pass."

They glared at each other by the angry flicker of two small flames. After a few moments Andry shrugged once again and continued up the stairs. Pol waited until he had regained control of himself, until the cellar door had opened and closed again behind his cousin.

"The last word—this time," he vowed. "Never again."

Fortunately, he had calmed enough to listen to what he said—and grimace. So much for what he thought he'd learned tonight. He had acted swiftly and decisively with Mireva, and he had hung on long enough for his father to carry out his plan. And that was the difference between them: Rohan had known exactly what he was doing and Pol had not. Pol had acted on instinct and emotion. His father worked from sure knowledge and patient reasoning, those things that were Rohan's greatest strength.

Maarken might indulge in quick fury, but Pol must not. Particularly not regarding Andry, who seemed to have mastered the art of angering him. Nor, he realized suddenly, regarding this mysterious future threat. While he felt no duty toward Goddess Keep and none of the awed deference most people, especially Sunrunners, accorded its Lord or Lady, he could not but respect Andry's certainty that this threat would appear. Pol was living testimony to the power of *faradhi* visions.

Patience. The ability to wait, to think things through, to act only when one understood. To use power and strength where they did the most good. To be certain of when, how, where, and why one acted. To be cautious always—and ruthless when necessary. To know exactly what to do. Rohan and Sioned had built peace on those qualities. He suddenly despaired of ever matching their wisdom.

Had either of his parents been aware of the towering virtues Pol ascribed to them, they would have gaped with astonishment and then roared with laughter. Their catalog of mistakes, miscalculations, and misapprehensions was no less than anyone else's—and they would have been the first to admit how often they had acted on blind instinct without any patience whatsoever.

Yet as he climbed the last flight of stairs, Pol's reprimands to himself taught him much more than if his perceptions had been more accurate. Some other time he would examine history and conclude that perfection was not among his parents' attributes. But for now, exhortations to patience, caution, and knowledge were of much more use to him.

They allowed him to listen with a quiet mind and a calm spirit as Ruval's challenge echoed on the last starlight just before dawn. Pol heard the arrogance and the anger, the insults and the impudence, and knew they covered fear. He stood in a windowed hallway, in a pool of bright white light, smiling. And made no reply. His answer would come tomorrow when noon sun baked Rivenrock Canyon.

Chapter Twenty-Six

Stronghold: 35 Spring

Tobin stormed into her brother's chambers a little after dawn, her rage reminding him forcibly of their parents. The flash fire temper was Milar's; the blazing black eyes, Zehava's. As he heard her out, he wondered idly what they would have thought about this present pass. Not to mention a few other things he had done in his life. . . .

"—as clearly as if the bastard was standing next to me!" Tobin was fuming, pacing up and down before the bed where he lay propped on soft pillows.

"What took you so long to get here?" he interrupted.

"I was with Hollis and Maarken, trying to keep the babies from having hysterics!" she shouted. "First you roust everyone out of bed in the middle of the night, and then Ianthe's bastard scares the children half to death!"

"Are they all right?" He was half out of bed, ready to go to Chayla and Rohannon even though there was nothing he could do.

"Once they wake up from the sleeping draught we had to give them!" Tobin glared at him.

Rohan settled again with a long sigh. "Listen, do me a favor. Don't tell Pol. He'd be furious, and that wouldn't help him at all."

"Furious? I'll show you furious! I'll geld that impudent whelp, shrieking his challenge to every Sunrunner in the keep! I—"

"And to every Sunrunner in reach of starlight," Rohan interrupted.

That stopped her in her tracks. "What?"

"Sioned confirmed this morning at sunrise. Or, rather, she received messages from Donato at Dragon's Rest and Meath at Graypearl. Currently she's contacting several

387

other friends. I suspect the sky will be as busy today as it was last night."

Tobin sat at the foot of the bed. "And what are you going to do about it?"

"It's Pol's fight now, not mine. I've done all I can."

"All you can?" she echoed incredulously. "You could find Ruval the way you found Mireva and—"

"The time for killing Ianthe's sons in secret was years ago, before anyone knew they existed. Hollis got one of them, Andry the second. The third belongs to Pol."

"And what if he loses?"

"He won't."

"You're very sure of yourself!"

"No, I'm sure of *him*." He raked both hands back through his hair. "I have to be. I was right about where Mireva was hiding, and I was right about Ruval's means of escape. His horse trotted in just before dawn, wearing Stronghold saddle and harness, and one of our guards was found trussed up in a tack room in the stables. I've been right about almost everything, and I'm right about Pol, too. I have to be," he repeated.

"No one's ever doubted that you're clever," she snapped. "And I have no doubts about Pol, either. But Ruval is an entirely different threat than the pretender was nine years ago."

"I disagree. The threat isn't just to Princemarch. Masul tried that, thinking that all he need do was appear at the *Rialla* to be acclaimed as Roelstra's true heir. I see now that Alasen was right, and this was the *diarmadh'im's* first move back to power. Masul never knew. If he'd won, Ruval would eventually have killed him and taken Princemarch after being revealed as Ianthe's son. But we can't think just in terms of land and castles. Look at the way Ruval's done it, Tobin. How many Sunrunners heard the challenge last night and his claim to Princemarch? One hundred? Two? All of them, touched by starlight, sleeping or waking? Pol's the next High Prince, but he's also a Sunrunner. Kill him, gain his lands and his position, and the *diarmadh'im* have a power base to work against Andry and all other Sunrunners."

She scowled at him. "And my honorable fool of a brother feels he must meet this challenge head on instead of killing the whoreson outright as he should."

"If I'd found him last night, perhaps I would have

killed him—or let Pol do it. Though I think Andry would have given him a fight for the privilege. But I can't do that now. Too many people know."

"And what does *Pol* know?"

"Everything."

She caught her breath and all the fire went out of her. "Oh, Rohan," she whispered.

He looked down at his hands. "It was the hardest thing I've ever done. And Sioned—but he understands. He may even forgive us, in time. He had to know, Tobin. He needs the advantage that knowledge of his other power can give him."

"Against his own half-brother."

He nodded. Kicking back the covers, he rose and shrugged into a thin, pale silk bedrobe. "Arlis is taking a long time about breakfast."

"Don't change the subject." She stopped again, scowling. "Wait—you said that two of Ianthe's sons are dead. *Hollis* killed one?"

"Nine years ago. Segev. Sent by Mireva to infiltrate Goddess Keep, probably to steal the scrolls Meath found that year. That's just a guess, based on the fact that he worked with Andry and Hollis on them. But Urival recognized him and told Pol about it before he died. Pol told us last night, after the challenge. Mireva made a threat about Hollis, that she'd pay for the murder—"

"In Maarken's hearing?" A fleeting glint appeared in her black eyes.

"Yes. I'm surprised she survived it, myself. In the tack room where the guard was found, there were also several things belonging to Hollis. And one of Chayla's little shirts and a pair of Rohannon's shoes as well. I don't like to imagine what they planned to do with them."

Tobin sucked in a breath, her eyes kindling again. "I'll kill that witch myself!"

"I think you'll approve of my method of execution," he responded grimly.

She nodded, satisfied. "So Pol knows all of it now." Her gaze sharpened. "Even my part, and Ostvel's?"

"Not that he killed Ianthe."

"Don't ever tell him."

"As far as he's concerned, she died in the Fire." He paced to the windows, bracing his fists on the ledge.

"You know, Tobin, if Masul had won Princemarch, I would have had to go to war—and with enemies I hadn't yet guessed at. I owe Maarken and Hollis more than they'd ever acknowledge. Without them, there would have been terrible battles and thousands would have died. Instead. . . ." He shrugged again. "We have an intimate little war. Only one of them will emerge from it alive. They're on equal footing now, Tobin. Both young, strong, and powerful, with exactly the same blood-claim through their mother. . . ."

"If it came to war, our people would fight. They'd insist on fighting for you and Pol."

"Why should thousands suffer for the sake of a few? When I vowed never to raise my sword again in battle, nobody heard that I vowed the same thing for my people." He turned to her. "To defend them from attack, yes. But if we *are* ever attacked, my incompetence will have caused it. I'd have no right to ask them to go to war for a fool.

"I won't ask it now, either. Because I *was* a fool years ago. Somehow, in spite of my stupidity, I gained a son who's my pride and my hope. What I did at Feruche is my responsibility. It shames me that Pol is suffering for what I did. But, cold as it may sound, better him than the men and women who're sworn to march out and die if I order it."

"You've always had too much conscience," she observed. "You'd fight Ruval yourself if you could, wouldn't you?"

"It's not my fight. I'm insignificant. I'm only the High Prince. Pol's Sunrunner and *diarmadhi* both. I envy him, if you want the truth." He gave a rueful smile. "Not for the battle he must fight that I can't, but because I'm too old, I haven't his gifts, and I'm not even in the running to try."

"Ah, so you're ancient, decrepit, useless, and powerless," she mocked. "You'll excuse me if I don't agree."

"You can hardly do otherwise. You're six winters older than I am." He sank into a chair and frowned. "Damn it, where's Arlis?"

"Didn't sleep much, did you?"

"Enough."

"I'd take bets you won't be able to eat a bite."

"Fainting from hunger isn't in the plan for today."

She leaned forward eagerly. "Then you *have* plans. Tell me."

He sighed. "Tobin, you're my sister and I love you dearly. I honor your opinions and your wits, and I've relied on your counsel for years. Your marriage brought me my best friend. You've supported me, schemed for me, and given me absolute honesty all your life."

"And if I don't shut my mouth and get out of here, you'll have me forcibly removed." She came to him and took his face between her hands. "We're not as young as we used to be, I'll admit. But I think we've held up pretty well, all things considered. I love you, too, little brother. More than that, despite my irritating questions, I trust you." She kissed his brow tenderly. "You're my brother and my prince. So do what you must. Whatever it is, it will be the right thing."

He closed his eyes under the caress, wearier than he would have shown to anyone but her. "I'm glad *someone* thinks so."

"Those who know you could think nothing else."

Rohan looked up. "Oh, but you were right to begin with, you know. We could have avoided the whole sordid mess by killing them outright. I should have killed Masul days before I actually did. But I got forced into a position where I had to behave as a barbarian, not as a civilized prince. And now I've gotten Pol into the same fix."

"The circumstances are hardly civilized," she reminded him, fingers resting lightly on his shoulders. "What's civilized about sorcery?"

"But Pol still must choose between the two—prince or savage."

"He's your son. You and Sioned raised him. Lleyn and Chadric and Audrite fostered him. Urival and Morwenna trained him. You told me you're sure of him because you have to be. I tell you now, Rohan, that you're sure of him because of who he is. Your faith in him is your faith in yourself—and I've rarely seen you lacking in that. And if you *do* have doubts right now, please recall that the rest of us do not." She smiled down at him. "Do us the honor of believing us, please?"

He couldn't help smiling back. "Now I remember why I long ago forgave you for the torment you made of my childhood."

"Torment? Oh, you mean like this?"

Rohan yelped as she tweaked his ear. "Stop that! I

take it all back, you're as much of a monster now as you were then!"

"And *you've* gotten stuffy, pompous, and boring!" She attacked his ribs and in the next moment they were rolling on the floor, tickling each other and giggling like the children they had not been in forty years.

If Arlis was slack-jawed at seeing the royal siblings behave as if they had never left the schoolroom, Chay was not. He surveyed the battle and commented, "They must be mellowing—neither of them fights as dirty as they used to." Then he gestured to the squire to place the tray on a table and proceeded to help himself to Rohan's breakfast. "By the way," he went on as the pair got in a last few scores, "if anybody's interested, Miyon's packing up."

Both sat up at that, gasping for breath. "Who does he think he is?" Tobin demanded, while Rohan exclaimed, "Leave me a crumb or two, Chay!"

His sister stared at him. "Doesn't it worry you?"

"Not at all." He got to his feet, extending a hand to help her up. She took it, gathered her legs under her—and sat back down hard as he let her fingers slip from his. "Serves you right. You and those damned nails of yours." He rubbed his side.

"Never mind that," she snapped. "What are you going to do about Miyon?"

"Have Sioned ask him in her sweet inimitable way why he intends to miss the proceedings. If his answer amuses me enough, I might even let him leave." He claimed his breakfast tray and carried it to the bed. Seating himself, he began munching on a marsh apple.

"Rohan, you *know* he's behind much of this," Tobin insisted. "You can't just let him go!"

"Don't worry," Chay soothed. "I don't think any answer would be amusing enough. Unless he admits flat out that he's sure Ruval's going to lose."

"Exactly," said Rohan. "Because Pol said something else last night. You recall Meiglan's hysteria? It's a bit complicated, but she recognized Marron as having met with her father—who also foisted off Mireva on her as a second maidservant. I don't know if Miyon knows that his own daughter gave him to us, but I don't think he wants to wait around here in any case."

Tobin frowned worriedly. "If he *does* know, the girl's life is at risk."

"I don't think so," Rohan murmured. "Not when Pol hears."

Chay blinked. "He can't possibly want to marry her!"

"What can we do to stop him?" Tobin fretted.

"Plenty! She's the bastard of a lying, scheming, power-hungry—"

"So," Rohan said very quietly, "is Pol."

***

Sioned had spent a weary dawn sitting on the edge of Princess Milar's fountain in the early sunshine. As she had suspected, *faradh'im* from Dorval to Goddess Keep itself had heard Ruval's starlit claim and challenge. And their reactions distilled to a single truth: *If this man wins, there will be war.*

At least they all realized it. There was unity among Sunrunners such as there had not been since Andrade's death. And how it would gall Andry to know that they rallied in support of Pol, not him.

She splashed water on her face to banish fatigue, plunged her hands over and over into the coolness. Pol had told them last night that he would ride to Rivenrock at sunset to face the challenge. She had plenty of time between now and then to—to do what? Nothing. If it had been necessary to construct the Sunrunner half of the starfire dome, she would have drilled Maarken and Hollis all day in the technique. But Rohan's neutralization of Mireva had canceled the need. Pol had spent part of yesterday reading the Star Scroll and would return to it today. If he asked, she would help. But if he did not ask, she would not offer. Rohan was right; he must do this on his own. It was his testing ground as a prince, as a Sunrunner, as a man.

She ranged out on sunlight once more, out to Rivenrock whence the challenge had come. Measures of flower-strewn Desert stretched below her, the very trail she had ridden thirty years ago this spring. She lingered over the exact spot where she had first seen Rohan, and again saw herself: the untried Sunrunner who had been ordered to marry a prince glimpsed in Fire and Water. The sight of her vision-made-flesh riding toward her across the sere and forbidding landscape had taken her breath away. He could still do that to her sometimes. She could still feel the first rush of joyful, bemused excitement at his presence. With him she had gone places she had never dreamed of going. *It's a long journey we've had, my love,* she thought. *We've walked beside each other almost every step of the way.*

Rivenrock Canyon was empty as far as she could tell. But Ruval would be holed up in a cave to escape the day's heat—and prying eyes. Another memory touched her, of the first time she had ever been inside a dragon cave. It had been at the last Hatching Hunt, after she and Rohan had kept Maarken and his twin brother Jahni from a scorching by a terrified little hatchling. Shell shards and slender broken bones had littered the sand within; she wished Ruval a pleasant day amid the remains of a hundred generations of dragons.

She scanned the cliffs carefully for signs of treachery: piles of loose stone that could fall at a sorcerer's thought; a pit dug out and covered by cloth, then camouflaged with plants and sand; rope stretched between rocks that would be nearly invisible by night. There was nothing, and that worried her. Everything she knew and everything she intuited about Ianthe's eldest son pointed to cunning. But then she realized that it was not only as Ianthe's son, Roelstra's grandson, that he would be fighting. His claim was based on his lineage, but his challenge had been to sorcery. And by its arts he would battle Pol until one of them lay dead on the sand among the sunbaked flowers.

Returning to the gardens, she dipped her hands yet again into the cool water, indulging a last memory. It had been here that she had seen Pol for the first time. Vision in Fire and Water of a tiny, perfect son, so obviously Rohan's with his golden hair and finely carved features that her heart had sideslipped in her chest. She had seen herself holding him, nursing him, a welt burned into her shoulder caused by her own Fire. The qualms of last night returned full force. Was it only chance that the scar was not on her shoulder but on her cheek? Or had she truly made some error in bringing that vision to pass, a mistake born of impatience and too-powerful emotion that would be paid for, not only in the mark on her face but in danger to Pol?

During the long days of watching Ianthe from Stronghold, she had seen the three other children several times.

If she had been ruthless enough that night, if she had not concentrated so wholly on Pol, would Ruval, Marron, and Segev have died then? Was the difference in her scars the visible token of a fatal flaw in what she had done?

In such thoughts lay madness. Sioned rose from the fountain and dried her hands on her trousers. What was done was done, and could not be undone. But it terrified her that Pol might suffer for whatever mistake she had made.

She left the gardens for the main courtyard, where horses were being saddled by orange-clad Cunaxans. It was one of Sioned's curses as a public person that her firegold hair was instantly recognizable; she had never been able to mingle anonymously in any crowd, no matter how plainly she was dressed. When Miyon's guards saw her, they stopped working, stopped talking, and practically stopped breathing.

"Good morning," she said to their commander. "I see you're going out on patrol."

"Good morning, your grace. We—ah, that is, I—"

Sioned gave him her blandest smile. "It *is* a patrol you're going on, you know."

"Yes, your grace," he replied helplessly.

She nodded and continued sympathetically, "The suspicion cast on your soldiers by recent events must have been most shocking. To find out that not one but two of the ancient race of sorcerers had infiltrated—somehow."

"A—shock, your grace."

"It must be equally a relief to know that your ranks are no longer fouled by their presence. I keep wondering how they got in, though. Granted, sorcery is a powerful tool, but someone must have proposed them to you— perhaps even insisted that you accept them on this important journey."

The man was almost writhing now, but had wits enough to slide past her implication. She expected nothing else; he would not hold so trusted a position in Miyon's guard if he was entirely stupid. But neither, she noted with interest, was he willing to take responsibility from his prince for the hiring of the two. He said, "It's a great relief, your grace, that we are no longer suspect."

"Of course. Still, it would be interesting to know how they managed it." She let him sweat out his reply for a moment, then continued, "Be sure to take time to refresh yourselves today. Like so much in the Desert, the heat can be deceptive."

"I thank your grace." He bowed. She smiled. She was not yet out of hearing range when he gave an explosive sigh of gratitude for his deliverance.

Miyon would not be so easily dealt with, she knew. If she was lucky, he would take a hint and stay at Stronghold without a direct order from the High Princess. She entered the foyer, hoping no argument would be necessary.

But it had already started without her, and in a manner Sioned never would have believed. Meiglan stood at the top of the steps—actively, stubbornly, and absolutely defying her father for the first time in her life.

"What do you mean, 'no'?" Miyon was demanding in tones of disbelief rather than anger.

"I'm sorry, Father, but I don't want to leave Stronghold."

"What you want is of less importance than the smallest grain of sand in the Desert! Your things are packed and ready!" He gestured to the servants who tottered slightly under the weight of caskets and satchels. "You're going to get on your horse and—"

"No, I am not."

Sioned blinked, almost as astonished as Miyon. But she was forced to grudging admiration of Meiglan's tactics; perhaps the girl wasn't entirely the fool she seemed. Or perhaps she was no fool at all. The timing and location of her defiance had been nicely planned. She had obviously come along meekly enough—until she had an audience. Sioned had always thought it bad taste and worse policy to conduct a private quarrel in public, though she knew people who argued anywhere they felt like it with what they considered a fine aristocratic disdain for anyone else's opinion. But Meiglan required witnesses— especially the emissary of another prince. Lord Barig stood on the landing in the upper hall, frankly staring as Miyon raised his voice.

"How *dare* you, you little slut!"

She didn't even flinch. Sioned's brows shot up. Perhaps association with women who said and did what they liked without fear of their men had put some backbone into the girl.

"Her grace the High Princess told me I may stay as long as I want," Meiglan said. "And I don't want to leave."

"*You* don't want—?" he echoed in shock.

"What's all the fuss?"

This, mildly and innocently, from Tallain, who arrived with Sionell down the second flight of stairs. Meiglan's face lit momentarily at this new source of strength and support, a light quickly hidden by downcast lashes. Sioned leaned against the newel post, folded her arms, grinned, and shamelessly settled in to watch Tallain do her work for her.

Miyon was grinding his teeth, but managed to be civil. "I have neglected my princedom too long this spring. It's time I left for Castle Pine."

"Left? But surely you must understand how much you're needed here, my lord!" Tallain looked and sounded sincerely troubled. Sioned bit her lip to keep from laughing. Rohan himself couldn't have done it so well. "Lord Barig is fortunately present to carry the truth to his cousin of Gilad, but you're the only other impartial prince at Stronghold and your value as a witness is inestimable."

"That's right," Sionell said, as if she'd just thought of it. "My lord is so very wise." She cast an adoring glance at Tallain, so overdone that it nearly destroyed Sioned's determination not to laugh. "You simply must stay, my lord. Your word will be essential at the *Rialla*—a formal inquiry is certain."

"So you see we really must stay, Father," Meiglan added.

"Yes, of course you must," Tallain said. "There will be questions asked that only you can answer, my lord."

Miyon swallowed with some difficulty. And Sioned was pleased to note that even Meiglan understood what questions Tallain referred to. She judged it time to intervene. Smoothing her expression, she started up the stairs.

"Ah, my lord," she said to Miyon, "I've just seen your guard off on patrol. It was very thoughtful of you to add to our safety by sending your own people."

He was trapped and he knew it. She had to admire his recovery as he said with adequate aplomb, "I considered that you and the High Prince have enough to do, and perhaps this person may get careless and be caught."

"We can only hope so," Sioned told him. "I want above all things to hear everything he has to say."

"It should be quite a story." Tallain sighed and shook his head.

Sioned conducted a little experiment. "Tell me, my lord, do you think Princess Chiana was under the influence of sorcery? Nothing else could explain the madness of the attack on Dragon's Rest."

"I think it likely," Miyon said, and in his eyes was a glimmer of hope. Sioned wondered if he really believed they would let him get away with that excuse. But she perceived that he would try it. Although admitting to beguilement would make him appear ridiculous in the eyes of other princes, it would give him a chance to keep his life. She would enjoy watching him squirm before Rohan condemned him to death.

"I think so, too," Tallain put in, aiding and abetting her shamelessly. "Lord Ostvel's report through the Sunrunner Donato regarding the shattering of the mirror—shocking. Sorcery is the only reasonable explanation. No one is so stupid as to believe that their graces of the Desert and Princemarch could be defeated."

Sioned saw Meiglan lower her lashes and turn white. So she could still feel fear—not of her father, but for her father. Amazing. But Sioned could not fault her for it, and, indeed, would have thought less of her had she greeted Miyon's approaching downfall with glee.

The tension following Tallain's last remarks was dissipated by Sionell. She took Meiglan's arm and said, "I was just going for a stroll in the gardens. Won't you come with me?"

"Thank you. I'd like that very much."

The retreat in good order from a victory was gracious, graceful, and sent furious color into Miyon's cheeks. Sioned smiled.

A little while later she had related the whole story to Rohan, Chay, and Tobin. "Cool as a cloud, not just standing up for herself but confident about it, without a trace of the hysterical child. I don't know how it happened, but I wouldn't have missed the sight of Miyon's face for all the gold at Skybowl!"

"You already own all the gold at Skybowl," Chay reminded her, grinning. "But I take your point. So he's staying. Good. Rohan, will you have him executed here or at the *Rialla*?"

"Oh, do wait!" Tobin said, a wicked gleam in her eyes. "I wouldn't want to miss hearing him try to explain in front of everyone how it was all due to sorcery."

"Speaking of which. . . ." Sioned hated to wreck the ease brought by laughter, but she had to. "Have any of you seen Pol this morning?"

"Maarken saw him on the way to your office," Chay said. "I assume he's studying the Star Scroll. And I'm told he now knows everything. You don't think he's fool enough to proclaim his ancestry as further proof of his right to Princemarch, do you?"

"I hope not." Tobin shook her head. "I'm beginning to think you were right all these years, Chay, and I was wrong. He ought to have grown up knowing, so it wouldn't be such a shock to him."

Her lord and husband clapped both hands to his heart. "Fetch a scribe! Find parchment and pen! This is historic— she's admitting to a mistake!"

Sioned met Rohan's gaze. *Our mistake*, they told each other silently.

Tobin saw and understood the look. "Stop that at once," she said severely. "We all did what we thought best."

"And now he's paying for it," Sioned murmured.

"I said to stop it and I meant it!" Tobin exclaimed.

Chay added lightly, "I'm sure you can find something better to occupy your minds than what might or should or could have been."

"Don't patronize me," Rohan snapped irritably.

Sioned recognized the warning signs and exchanged a glance with Tobin. But she had to agree with the silent message she received in reply. Leaving Rohan alone would be even worse than keeping him company. Truth be told, *none* of them wanted to be left alone to think too much. Pol would ride to Rivenrock at dusk. There was nothing anybody could do until then but wait. It was a thing at which they had all had a great deal of practice.

Not that that made it any easier.

***

As grateful as Meiglan obviously was for Sionell's support and the timely exit she provided, once they reached the grotto it was obvious that the girl wanted to be alone with her excitement. Sionell had certain things to discover first, and went about it as obliquely as she could manage.

"Be careful to stay in the shade—that pale hair of yours is no protection at all from the sun." She touched

Meiglan's untidy curls. "Was your mother's hair this color? You don't resemble your father at all."

"My mother was blonde—" Meiglan stopped, her dark fawn's eyes blinking up in confusion. Sionell waited, then smiled as the girl understood her real meaning. "No, I'm nothing like my father."

"I thought not. Why don't you stay here for a little while? Your maid needs the time to unpack your things."

Another meaning to that, as well; this time Meiglan caught at it eagerly. "I don't think she packed much. It was her suggestion that I stay here at Stronghold."

"I see. Well, I hope it's not too much work for her, taking care of you—now that Mireva is no longer available to help her."

Quicker and quicker, Sionell mused. Meiglan comprehended this game. As big eyes grew even bigger, it became an interesting choice between believing her sudden apprehension was real and suspecting it was not. Sionell had given her the opening. It remained to see what she did with it.

Innocent worry clouded Meiglan's face, as expected. But Sionell had not anticipated the narrowing of those eyes, the thoughtfulness of the voice, as if she puzzled this out aloud.

"Thanys—she did whatever Mireva told her. She was the senior of them, having been with me over two years, yet she—" Panic again, and honest concern for her servant. "Oh, my lady, do you think *she* could have been a victim of sorcery, too?"

"It's possible, I suppose." Sionell hid surprise—and admiration of the clever excuse, if cleverness it was. Goddess, she thought impatiently, when would this child reveal her true coloring?

"I shall have to question her very closely," Meiglan went on, seemingly oblivious to her companion's irritation. "Or should I ask someone else to do it? Tell me what to do, my lady."

"As you think best," Sionell replied, more sharply than she'd intended. "You are, after all, a lady who holds a manor in your own right. Your servants are your responsibility."

"But I don't know how!" the girl burst out. "I watched you at Tiglath—and the High Princess and the others here—you never have to give an order twice, sometimes you don't have to give them at all! I can't be like you, I don't know how to be a great lady or even a little one!"

"Yet you see and understand the way we do things. It's not difficult, Meiglan." Sionell gave a little shrug. This was no time for lessons in highborn ways. Was that why she wanted to stay here at Stronghold, to learn how to be a High Princess? *Stop it!*

"No one would ever obey me," Meiglan said sadly.

"Oh, I don't know. You did a good piece of work on your father today."

A tiny smile hovered around her mouth. "Yes—I did, didn't I?" In a rush, clasping a startled Sionell's hand, she went on, "I couldn't have, not without you and Lord Tallain and the High Princess—I was so frightened, I was sure he'd beat me right in front of all of you. But I stood up to him, didn't I? I said what I wanted—oh, Sionell, I was so angry! He used me against all of you, who've been so kind to me—he gave me all those jewels and pretty clothes and the *fenath*, and he was only trying to—"

"To *what*?" Sionell asked softly, and when the small hand tried to escape she held it fast. "How was he trying to use you, Meiglan?"

"I–I don't know—"

"Of course you do."

"No!"

"I knew it was Pol you saw that night at Tiglath. Or *claimed* to have seen."

"But I did—he as in my room, I saw him—"

"Did you?"

"Yes!" she wailed, struggling to free herself, tears welling in her soft eyes. "Please, you're hurting me—"

Sionell let go. Memory gave her the farcical little scene played out that night—for whose benefit? Hers? Meiglan's? Pol's? *Whose*, Goddess damn it to all Hells—

Meiglan was rubbing her wrist. It astonished Sionell that she had not fled. Surely she knew there would be more questions.

"My lady," the girl said with a pathetic dignity, "I can't make you believe me. I only know what I saw. And—and what I felt when we came here to Stronghold and it was *him*. I think my father used me as a d–diversion. So you would all look at me and s–suspect me. And so

Mireva could c–come along and be free to work—he used me to bring a sorcerer here to destroy you—"

Seeing that her moment of self-command had vanished and tears were imminent again, Sionell looked down into pleading eyes and knew she had to make a choice, one way or the other. She could believe Meiglan innocent or suspect that she was not. This had nothing to do with Pol or Miyon's plots or anything else. This was between the two of them. She had offered Meiglan friendship before; she could continue to do so and have it be the truth or a lie, or reject her outright, now.

No one could possibly be so innocent. No one could possibly be so guilty and gaze up at her with such guile-less liquid eyes.

***

As Sunrunners from Dorval to Kierst had heard Ruval's challenge on the last starlight, thus did they hear Pol's acceptance on noon sunlight.

Strong and sure, with a power previously felt only by those who had had contact with such masters as the late Lord Urival or those of Pol's own remarkable family, colors flowed along rivers of sun. Diamond-white, deep emerald, iridescent pearl, glowing golden topaz, the jewel tints of his mind were as a pattern in stained glass through which light streamed without shadow.

A few of those touched responded in words. Meath, who had been Pol's first teacher, paused in a meander through the ruins of a *faradhi* keep on Dorval where he had found the scrolls. Donato, who had accompanied Sioned to the Desert on Andrade's order thirty years ago, spoke from Pol's own Dragon's Rest. Several others who knew Pol or Sioned or both gave proud answer. One who would have could not; Alasen, playing with her children in the coolness of the bowl-shaped garden at Castle Crag, lacked the training to respond. But for the first time in her life she wished she did know how. She wanted to tell Pol how sure she was of his victory.

The rest received the communication in silence. Of these, the Sunrunners at Goddess Keep were the most troubled, just as they had been by the challenge of the previous night. For they, like Rohan, understood that it was not just Pol and his princedom at stake; it was all *faradh'im*. When they responded, it was to seek out Andry.

He confirmed their suspicions and soothed their worries. What he did not reveal was that while Pol did battle with Ruval, he had other plans for Mireva. Andry wanted to be here even less than Rohan and Pol wanted him here—but here he would stay until this was over. Nialdan and Oclel chafed at the delay, not understanding why he had not ridden out immediately after the High Prince's unfair decree. He knew they suspected he was hoping for a softening in Rohan's position; Andry didn't bother to tell them that until Ruval and Mireva were dead, he would stay if he had to learn shape-changing himself in order to do it.

Pol finished his work and rested in the shade on a bench circling a tree in the gardens. Instinct had guided him to choose sunlight rather than stars. *Diarmadhi* blood he might have, but he had been trained as a Sunrunner and thought of himself as such. Eventually he would get used to the idea that he possessed other powers—things he expected to use tonight—but for now he was strictly a Sunrunner. No one must ever know otherwise.

One of the few people who did know appeared quite suddenly from the grotto pathway. Pol straightened from his weary slump at the sight of Sionell. She saw him at the same instant and her step faltered. Emotions tangled in his throat: shame, regret, resentment, longing for the old Sionell with her ready smile—and for the old Pol, who had been so blithely innocent. He sat there staring at her, unsure of his reception at her hands for the first time in his life. Speech or silence, either might bridge the chasm between them or widen it.

She spared him the trouble of deciding. After another moment's hesitation she approached and said, "I understand Ruval has made challenge to you."

Pol nodded. "I've just finished accepting. On sunlight."

"Of course." Her eyes, a deeper and truer blue than his, were calm and quiet. "I would have liked to have heard it."

"Just arrogance and posturing," he replied, shrugging. "It's expected. I'll meet him tonight, at Rivenrock."

"Alone?" Her voice betrayed a hint of bleakness, of pity. Then she answered her own question. "No, plenty of witnesses, of course."

But still alone, her eyes said, and he wondered why he deserved her compassion. "I'd like you to be there, Ell."

"Invitation to an execution by sorcery," she mused. "A thing not to be missed, obviously."

The muscles of his arms, shoulders, and back tensed as if preparing for a battle of swords, not words. "If you'd rather not—"

"Oh, I'll be there. It ought to be very educational, even for those of us who know nothing of what Andry now calls magic." She paused, raking the dark red hair from her eyes. "You know, when I was little I wanted more than anything else to be one of you. To fly on sunlight the way dragons soar through the sky. . . ." Sionell clasped her hands behind her back; he wondered if it was to hide their trembling. "The art of being *faradhi* is one thing. The power of magic—I wouldn't have it now if someone offered it to me."

"Why?" he challenged. "Are you afraid of it?"

"Of what it does to people. Your mother and Morwenna and Maarken and Hollis—they have such joy in what they can do. Such delight in the chance to fly. Andry doesn't. He might have had, once. But not anymore. You can see it in his eyes. He's learned how to use his gifts to kill." The blue eyes became piercing. "What about you, Pol? How much joy will you take in your powers once you've used them to kill your own brother?"

"What else can I do? Why are you making this worse for me? To pay me back?"

"Do you think I'm like that?" she flared. "That I'd deliberately—" She stopped, calmed herself with visible effort, and finished, "I said it because I don't want to see you become like Andry. With no joy left in your eyes."

That stung. "Ell—"

"I owe my first loyalty to your father as my prince, but you'll be in his position one day—High Prince and Sunrunner both. I want to see you become what you *can* be, not what events bludgeon you into becoming." She looked as if she would have said more, but ended only with a little shrug.

"So your worry is for what kind of prince you'll have to deal with in the future," he said bitterly, and the hollow where certainty of her love had been ached anew. He was a political reality to her now, not a man. And it was his own fault; he had destroyed anything she might still feel for him.

A wiser part of him whispered that it was better so. Tallain deserved all of her heart. But it hurt; Goddess, how it hurt to know that his own words had cost him Sionell's caring, lost him that part of her he had always thought of as his alone.

He got to his feet, more drained now than even the strain of a powerful Sunrunning had made him. "Thank you for your honesty. What was it Mother told you when we were little? That a prince who reminds others of it isn't much of a prince? How much less a prince he is if others have to remind *him*! If you'll excuse me, I'll have preparations to make for my coming act of fratricide."

"Stop it, Pol!"

But he strode away from her, seeking the shaded silence of a little grove near the grotto from which she had come. She did not come after him. And perhaps that hurt most of all.

***

"So," Miyon drawled. "My little hothouse rose, so carefully nurtured, has grown thorns."

Meiglan froze. Miyon smiled down at her where she sat on a flat rock near the grotto pool. His quiet, silken approach had terrified her more than if he'd come here roaring out his rage. Good.

"You have few usable wits, but enough to understand that this has not endeared you to me. Had you thought about what will happen once you have no highborn allies to protect you?"

She looked sick, her skin turning slightly green.

"At Castle Pine there will be no one to rescue you when I whip the skin from your bones."

"I won't go. I'm staying here."

The defiance infuriated him, but he made himself laugh. "By the Goddess, it has a brain after all! Yes, you *will* stay here! Can you guess why?"

"Stay—?" she whispered. "You will let me stay?"

Miyon loomed over her, and menace replaced the laughter. "Until the *Rialla* at Dragon's Rest. After that, you will *stay* there. As Pol's wife."

Meiglan stared up at him dumbly. Breath rasped in her lungs and she trembled like a captive wild thing.

"He can't keep his eyes from you. It should be fairly easy for you to trap him into a formal Choice. Use these newfound wits of yours. Because only when you are his wife will you be safe."

Her mute anguish ignited his temper at last. Plucking her up by the shoulders, he shook her until her bones rattled. But she did not cry out, which angered him even more.

"Do you understand? Do you hear what I'm telling you, daughter of a whore? Your mother schemed to become a princess. You will be *High Princess* once that dragon-spawn who sired Pol is dead. It's the only way to save your own life."

"And yours," she breathed, and light came back into her eyes.

Miyon dropped her to the ground, where she crumpled like a rag doll. "I was afraid I'd have to use words of one syllable," he snapped. "You're quite right, my precious jewel. Rohan can scarcely execute the father of his son's wife."

"No." But it was not agreement with his analysis; rather, defiance.

"You will do it," he said. "Wed him and bed him and make him the perfect little princess. Goddess help him!" He managed a real laugh this time. "A mouse has more spirit, a plow-elk more intelligence! You have beauty and music, and that's all. No use to a prince. He'll rule alone. You'll never be any worth to him except in breeding his heirs and playing him to sleep with your lute."

She flinched, but there was something in her eyes—something. He must not lose his advantage of terror over her, lest she see his own fear. His life was in the hands of the daughter he despised. She held the whip now; he could not let her feel it in her fingers.

"No," she said again, this time with more voice in it. "I won't do this. Sionell will protect me—she's my friend, she said so just now—"

"Brave try," he sneered. "There's only one problem. You want Pol. Don't you, sweet little flower? Don't you!"

He had her now. It didn't much matter why she obeyed him—through fear of him or love of Pol—as long as she did obey. And she would, or lose the dragon's son forever. She bent her head to her knees and quivered, but the sound that came from her was not a moan. It was "Yes."

Satisfied, Miyon gazed down at her for a moment

more. Then he hauled her up by the shoulders again. "Future High Princesses do not bury their faces in the dirt," he mocked, "not even to their fathers."

She looked up at him, dark eyes sparking with some of the courage of that morning. He slapped her across the face, snapping her head to one side and nearly breaking her nose.

"Remember that," he growled, and released her. She staggered but managed to keep her feet. With a last contemptuous glance that hid his relief, Miyon turned on his heel and strode away.

***

Meiglan's ankle stabbed painfully as she limped to the pool. She knelt to wash her face, crying out softly when her scraped and bloody hands contacted the cold. The water she splashed on her face dripped dark. Her cheek was on fire, her nose not quite numb. With movements which after a time became automatic, she kept rinsing her face until the bleeding stopped.

For the second time that day she was startled by a voice behind her. But this one—soft, worried, weary—caught her heart. "My lady? Are you all right?"

Frantically she sluiced more water onto her burning face. Though there was no more blood, she could feel the bruises swelling her cheek and nose. Yet she could not avoid him. So she stood, trying not to favor her injured ankle, and met his gaze with what she hoped was pride enough.

His reaction was immediate and frightening. His eyes kindled with fury, lips thinned to a lethal slash, it was a face she had never seen him wear. "Your father?" he demanded.

She nodded helplessly. "I don't want to go back to Castle Pine! Ever!"

He came toward her, mist from the waterfall gathering in his hair. As he passed from shadow into a shaft of sunlight through the trees, the droplets shone like a crown of tiny rainbows. "Ah, Meggie," he whispered, brushing the curls from her brow. "You needn't be afraid of him ever again. I promise."

The sound of her childhood name was so piercing sweet that tears came to her eyes. And again she surprised herself, for she had not wept in front of her father, not even when he had slapped her. But now—now a sob strangled her breathing. It escaped as a soft moan and she turned away.

"You don't believe me?" he asked.

She made herself answer. "If you say it, then it must be true."

His hands rested on her shoulders, light and tender over the bruises her father had given her. "It helps me, knowing you trust me. That seems to be in rather short supply."

She risked a glance over her shoulder. His face was pensive, solemn. "How could anyone *not* trust you?"

Her honest amazement made him smile, and he turned her to face him. "You are the most wondrously innocent person I've ever met. There's no subterfuge in you, is there? None of that proud cleverness that surrounds me— that I flatter myself I possess."

She remembered her father's mockery, and flushed.

"That's the difference between me and my father," he went on, more to himself than to her. "He has a patience I envy but will never possess. It's the patience of cunning— but I'm not comfortable with it. I can't emulate him."

She struggled for understanding. "You have your own way of doing things, my lord."

He continued as if she hadn't spoken. "I think what it must be is that he feels things more deeply than I do. He takes them personally. Not in the sense of being offended, but—as if he's responsible even when he isn't. I don't have the courage to inflict that on myself. I don't know how he does it, quite frankly—or why. I don't have patience or strength to fight the way he does."

"But not everything that goes wrong is your responsibility," she ventured, trying to comprehend him. "Your way is better than his."

"Do you think so?" He was truly concerned with her reply. She gave it without hesitation.

"Yes, my lord. You are not your father. Your battles are not his."

"And there's a battle coming tonight for me that he can have no part in." Pol touched her hair again. "Meggie—afterward, if I survive this—"

"Of course you will survive! You must!" She could not

conceive of what might happen if he did not; the very idea terrified her.

A smile came to his face again, softening his expression. "Thank you. Whether you said that because you know it's what I needed to hear, or whether you truly believe it, thank you."

"I trust in you, my lord. You will win."

He must.

Pol leaned down and kissed her mouth: gently at first, quietly, but with a growing passion that not even an inexperienced virgin could mistake. As his lips traveled slowly down her throat, she gave a tiny, shivering sigh.

She was confused when he lifted his head and looked into her eyes again. Had she done something wrong? Was she supposed to say something, do something?

"So innocent," he whispered, "you *are* innocent, Meggie."

Her cheeks burned anew. Of course he was used to women who knew how to kiss a man. He was her first. It humiliated her that this was so obvious to him.

He was smiling at her now, a wistful smile that melted away all emotion but newly discovered love for him. He was powerful; he would protect her with his cleverness and his strength; she would be safe. The notion was as foreign to her as the love, as the sudden desire that trembled through her while looking up at the sweet curve of his mouth.

"May I watch tonight, my lord, when you take the battle to your enemy?" Surprise flickered over his face. "I want to see you win."

"You really do believe it, don't you?" he mused.

"Yes, my lord."

He smiled again. "Meggie, my name is Pol. Say it for me."

She did so, shyly. Feminine instinct roused for the first time in her life and she knew as she said his name that he would kiss her again.

Chapter Twenty-seven

Rivenrock Canyon: 35 Spring

Ruval pressed his back to the ragged wall of the cave, breathing hard. He had just used hated sunlight for the fifth time that day, trying to find Mireva. There had been nothing from her, not the slightest whisper. He had been about to search on the noonday sun when Pol's acceptance had come to him, a declamation powerful as a storm wind through pines. The satisfaction of having an affirmative answer at last had not survived his failure to find Mireva. Now it was getting on toward sunset. Soon the sky would blacken and the stars would pock the night. He must accept that he would face Pol alone.

Alone.

He whipped back rising panic with pride in his lineage, his powers, and his training. He would win. Mireva had chosen him as her instrument of vengeance against all Sunrunners. He would confirm Mireva's choice, avenge his mother, sit in his grandfather's place as prince at Castle Crag. Roelstra had failed, and Ianthe, to break Rohan's power. They had been cunning—but Ruval possessed knowledge they had not. He knew how to kill Pol, and in a way no one would ever suspect.

So he scoffed away trepidation and settled once more on a little shelf of stone at the cavern mouth, eating the last of his meager provisions as the shadows lengthened. He didn't much like the canyon, though it would be a magnificent arena for his victory. The shadows carved deep into the rock walls were black and silent, like eyes disguising secrets. The cave he rested in was littered with the leavings of countless dragon generations—skulls with staring sockets where eyes should have been, shattered shells half-blackened by fire. A stiff, leathery bit of wing had fluttered in the afternoon updraft that swept through the canyon, startling him into a cry that echoed from wall to wall outside. He set himself to planning the eradication of every dragon now living—he'd discovered they were fine sport, and old Prince Zehava had had the right idea about proving prowess by killing the great beasts. But, more than those things, he disliked the feeling he got in this place where dragons had been. It was their place, not his; he intended that every grain of sand in the Desert and every handspan of soil on the continent belong to him alone.

Just before the sun vanished, he sifted *dranath* into his wineskin and drank it down. The drug bolstered his courage, gave new strength to his blood. Very softly, Ruval began to laugh. The sensuous haze of the drug rippled through his body, and then the welcome sensation of power. He clenched sand in his fists, let it trickle through his fingers, admiring the sparkle of golden dust visible even in the dimness. This, too, was power. Ruval decided to let Rohan live for a time, to feel the agony of loss and failure Ianthe had known. Then he would die, and all his family with him. Princemarch, the Desert, the gold—everything would be Ruval's. *And* the title of High Prince.

With the first stars came the call of dragon horns. Ruval stood, brushed off his hands, and smiled. He needed no one. He was alone, but it was better so. Everyone would see that his were the greater powers, and bow to him as sorcerer and prince. It was the moment his mother had craved and been cheated of. He would kill Pol with her name on his lips.

***

The setting sun blooded the Desert, turning the swells and hollows of flower-strewn sand to waves in a dark crimson sea. Sioned rode with her husband behind their son, watching the light redden Pol's hair until it was almost the same firegold as her own. She could sense other presences behind her, riding by twos—Chay and Tobin; Maarken and Hollis; Tallain and Sionell; Walvis and Feylin. Miyon rode with Barig, Arlis with Morwenna. Rialt and Edrel brought up the rear. Ruala and Riyan were missing—she was still shaken and though he fiercely wanted to witness the battle, Pol had ordered him to stay with her. Andry and the Sunrunners Oclel and Nialdan had also stayed behind. Meiglan, like Pol, rode alone. She had been the subject of a heated discussion that afternoon between Sioned and Rohan.

"Well, he can't marry her." They had just seen the pair from their windows, strolling the gardens.

"Has it occurred to you that he may actually love her?"

"Impossible! She's not what he needs. Look at her, keeping him wandering around down there when he ought to be reviewing the Star Scroll—if she cared for him at all, she'd—"

"Sioned, it's in her eyes whenever she looks at him. And he looks at her—"

"Oh, yes, I've seen it," she said derisively. "He plays the big, strong, protective male with her. Goddess preserve me from imbecilic masculine fantasies! Pol doesn't need some delicate little flower who'd be crushed by the first stiff breeze. He needs a wife and a princess. And he knows what kind of woman he ought to Choose."

"You mean the kind of woman you think he ought to Choose."

"Why are you defending her?" she exclaimed. "Meiglan could never comprehend even the smallest part of Pol's work as a prince!"

"Did you ever think that perhaps he doesn't need what I did in a wife? I may have required a living flame—but not every man needs that kind of woman."

"You'll never convince me he needs some shatter-shelled little fool who never opens her mouth except to whimper!"

"From what you yourself said, it seems to me she did pretty well against her father this morning."

She scowled. "That has nothing to do with it. She's wrong for him."

"Pol's not five winters old anymore, Sioned. He's a grown man entitled to make his own decisions."

"And his own mistakes?" Sioned swung on him furiously. "I won't let him do something that would ruin his life!"

He replied with the deceptive mildness that would ordinarily have been warning enough. "My father would probably have considered *you* a mistake. But my life has hardly been ruined."

"I won't allow it, Rohan. He's not going to marry her."

At last his patience gave out. "If he does, you'll damned well have to get used to it! And don't make him choose between you," he finished. "You might not like the result."

Now she stared down at her gloved hands on the reins, ashamed and afraid. She knew there had been women in Pol's life—unimportant ones, known in pleasure but never in love. They didn't matter. But his Choice of a wife mattered desperately. She could have given him to Sionell, or someone like her. Had he Chosen a woman of strength and intelligence and ability, she could have let him go—not gladly, for no mother ever relinquishes an adored son without regret. Much as Tobin loved Hollis, she had privately confessed twinges of sadness at no longer being first in her son's heart. Sioned assured her that this was only natural. Now she was feeling the same things. But it would not have been so bad if only he had fixed on a woman worthy of him.

Meiglan was not. She was not worthy to take Sioned's place either as the most important woman in Pol's life or as the next High Princess. And Sioned was terribly afraid that the girl would indeed become those things.

She fretted at her emotions as she would at a sore tooth all during the ride—until she realized that this was exactly what she should not be doing. All her thoughts and energies must be directed toward what would happen at sunset. There would be time later to dissuade Pol from a disastrous marriage.

Sioned calmed herself just in time; the dragon horns sounded at the canyon mouth, startling her. She hadn't even noticed that they had arrived at Rivenrock. Quickly she scanned the area, looking once again for traps. There were none that she could see. She considered searching the area by the light of Sunrunner's Fire, but Rohan had been adamant: this battle must be Pol's from beginning to end. She accepted that. She had to.

Chay and Maarken rode forward to repeat the call of the horns. Pol sat his stallion like a statue as they passed him, barely nodded when they turned their horses smartly in unison and bowed to him. Chay came to a halt next to Rohan, and Sioned heard him murmur as he slung the horn over his shoulder, "Damned thing always leaves me winded. But, Goddess, the *sound* of it!"

He was sixty winters old and his dark hair had gone silvery, and a tight grin emphasized the lines scoring his face. But out of his eyes looked the fierce young warrior who had fought beside Prince Zehava and won his daughter, who had ridden with Rohan to defeat Roelstra's armies, who had been Battle Commander of the Desert for thirty-eight years. Sioned felt her spirits lift slightly. Power was in Sunrunner skills and sorcery, in gold and in cunning, but most of all it was in the quality of the people who had been given to her and Rohan and Pol.

A shadow appeared high on the canyon wall: tall, lean, the shape of a man blacker than the cavern he had emerged from. In his hand a sword gleamed like steel lightning. He paused, making sure he possessed the attention of all, then made his way lithely down the slippery stones.

Pol gestured with one hand, and Edrel sprang off his horse, running forward to hold the great stallion's reins while Pol dismounted. The others rode up to form a half-circle. Hollis' braids shone like plaited gold; Tallain's smooth shock of fair hair glinted like a mail battle coif; Meiglan's curls clouded pale and misty around her white face. But the tinge of red clung to Pol's hair, and as he approached his parents his eyes were entirely blue without a hint of green—and he looked like Rohan and Sioned both. Not like Ianthe at all.

And yet as he stood between their horses, looking up at them with calm and confidence, the clarity of innocence was gone. Replacing it were knowledge and purpose—grim things, both of them. Mourning, Sioned reached down to touch his cheek, the place where her own face wore a scar.

Rohan was the one who remembered the rules. "Insist on the traditions that will help you—and don't allow any of the rest." He gave Pol the wineskin strapped to his saddle. "*Dranath.*"

Pol nodded. He looked steadily up at Sioned, wanting to speak but just as obviously unable to find the right words. She summoned a smile and brushed back his hair—gesture from his boyhood, inappropriate to a man. She did it anyway. He caught her hand between his palms for a moment before pressing a kiss of loving homage to her fingertips.

He left them to speak soft words to Edrel. Then, after taking several steps toward the canyon, he paused once to look back over his shoulder. Not at Sioned or Rohan: at Meiglan.

The sudden glinting smile was for her, no one else. The look he received in reply was of such glowing translucence that it lit the sunset. *"You'll damned well have to get used to it!"* echoed Rohan's voice. Abruptly Sioned remembered Pol's description of a vision in Fire and Water near the old Sunrunner keep on Dorval. *"It was just my face, Mother—I was expecting to see someone else with me, the way you saw Father. But it was only me, wearing a prince's coronet. In a way, it was a little lonely."* And perhaps that was how he was meant to rule, even *wanted* to rule: alone. If so, Meiglan was the perfect Choice for him. She tightened her grip on the reins as Ruval's boots crunched through the rocky soil at the canyon mouth. Pol should not be thinking of Meiglan. He should be concentrating on the battle. Yet he loved her, and she him. Just as Miyon had planned.

Pol turned to face his half-brother with his perfect calm intact. What he had seen in Meiglan's face had evidently reinforced his confidence. Sioned had seen it, too: innocent faith, blind trust. No striving, no blaze of a brilliant mind, no real strength. Only love. Sioned hoped it would be enough.

"Why does it happen this way?"

Rohan's whispered bitterness startled her out of her own. His face was as composed as Pol's, but his eyes were open wounds. "What do you mean, beloved?" She made her voice gentle, forbidding fear to scrape the words raw.

"This," he repeated. "Always. One man battling another."

Himself against Roelstra, Maarken against Masul, Pol against Ruval. Whole princedoms distilled down to two men. "Better one battling one than thousands battling thousands," she answered softly. It was the High Princess speaking, not the woman who had watched husband and nephew and now son go forth to their small, private wars.

He glanced at her, murmured that she was right. But one look at his eyes and she knew she was wrong. There was another combatant here, one who could not join in the actual fight but who would nonetheless participate in every attack and counterthrust—even though the battle would be conducted with powers he did not possess. Rohan would feel it all, take it into himself as if this small war between two men was being fought inside his own flesh. His bones and his blood and his brain would become a battleground, for he was the kind of man and the kind of prince who pulled conflict into himself, who was willing to make his own being its focal point. He internalized war, as if he had swallowed fire.

Sioned ached for him, for the impulse that made him bring battle unto himself for resolution. It was the price of his vast patience. He waited for the fire to be brought to him, then absorbed its violence into himself. It was the measure of his vast strength that no war had yet broken him.

But Pol would never be that way. His battles would rage externally, treated as invading enemies who might storm his citadel of self but would never batter him down. He would not swallow the fire; he would *become* fire.

Shadows darkened the canyon and the first stars appeared in a deep blue sky. Pol walked forward, the colors of him so strong they were almost an aura around him. *Aleva*, the Star Scroll called it; the circle of fire proclaiming power.

But the same shone around Ruval's dark head. Amethyst and ruby and dark sultry garnet, they were opaque colors, lightless though not lifeless. As surely as Pol's bright pale colors accented by emerald shimmered just on the edge of her Sunrunner's vision, so did Ruval's darkness swirl in subtle patterns of force. Sioned reached one hand instinctively to her husband, felt his firm grip, and silently pleaded that he would not let go until it was over.

***

Pol had not seen the sunset scarlet of the Desert as Sioned had. Instead of blood, he was reminded of fire. In his imagination it rippled across the dunes, making the flowers and tall dry grasses separate small torches. When the sunlight vanished over the Vere Hills to the west, the flames did not die out; they only paled on their leap into the sky. The stars ignited one by one—the first ones far away in the near-blackness over the Long Sand—then spread like wildfire. Much as he loved the verdant valley of Dragon's Rest, he sometimes hungered for this desolate sweep of sand and sky, this land his ancestors had fought for and kept. He wondered if their spirits hovered about him on the slight breeze, watching as he approached his own battle for their Desert.

Ruval strode a few more paces toward him, then stopped. He wore a flowing russet mantle, clasped loosely around his narrow hips by a belt of heavy linked gold circles. His blue eyes had picked up the blackness of his high-collared tunic. Pol sized him up quietly—not for strength or speed or skill of the body, but for the qualities of mind and power. But those things were forgotten as Ruval lifted both tanned, long-fingered hands.

He wore Sunrunner's rings. Ten of them, set with jewels.

The blue-black eyes laughed as Pol stiffened in outrage, the mocking glint in them saying, *And who's to deny me, princeling?*

But for just an instant, there and gone so fast Pol barely knew it had happened, it was not Ruval he saw standing before him. It was Andry.

A casual flick of one finger, and flames blossomed from a boulder on Pol's left to light the space between them. He looked into his half-brother's eyes, searched his face for any hint of similarity between them—and thanked the Goddess that his father's blood was so strong in him that there was no resemblance at all. He felt no call of kinship, no pull of shared origin. He wondered briefly if echoes of his own face in Ruval's would have made this harder.

He conjured answering Fire on a large stone to his right. The area was well illuminated now, light seeping into the craggy stone face of the canyon mouth. How many days since he rode here with his oh-so-clever plan for Meiglan in mind? He felt a hundred years older now. Knowledge had changed him.

So had Mireva. He shied away from that memory, and the need for a cleansing image sent his thoughts to Meiglan. It was surprising to realize that she, too, had changed him with her trust and faith. She asked nothing, demanded nothing—because in her eyes he was already everything that could protect and cherish her, everything he had always wanted to be: a true prince and Sunrunner; powerful, strong, and wise. Always before when he had looked at a woman and wondered what it might be like to have her as his wife, he had considered the issue only in terms of himself. *His* wife, *his* Choice, *his* marriage—as if he was the only one involved. With Meiglan, the only way he could explain it to himself was that when he looked at her, he wanted to be *her* husband.

There was a serenity in that, unexpected and welcome, a sureness of heart that matched his faith in his power. Not arrogance, not vainglory, but simple awareness that whatever must be done, he had the strength to do it. So he faced Ruval with unfeigned serenity, waiting.

"The smart thing to do would be to kill me where I stand," Ruval said. "Or have one of them do it for you." He gestured toward their audience, standing nearby beside their horses, forming a rough semicircle.

Pol nodded agreement.

"But you're not smart, Pol. You're honorable." He sneered the word.

"I wouldn't want to disappoint anyone." Pol hesitated slightly. "You say Roelstra was your grandfather, Ianthe your mother. What proof can you offer?"

Ruval's face betrayed surprise. He had not been expecting a challenge of this nature at this late date. He took a small gold coin from one pocket, and tossed it at Pol. "You'll recognize my grandsire's face."

Holding it between thumb and forefinger, he asked in honest amazement, "Do you seriously expect me to compare profiles?"

The coin sprouted tiny, cold flames. In them Pol saw a roomful of gold lit by a single torch held high by a very beautiful, very pregnant woman. His heart stopped, then raced: Ianthe.

"A small trick," Ruval said negligently as the flames flickered out. "But I'm sure you're aware that such a memory could only be conjured by one who was there to see it. Who else would Princess Ianthe show her gold to but her eldest son? Gold your father provided in exchange for *dranath* to cure the Plague."

Pol struggled to recover from stunned astonishment. The display had been impressive, not only in its casual power but in its effect on him: his first and probably only sight of his mother. Pregnant. Carrying *him*. His fingers felt welded to the coin, even though the flames had held no heat.

"Satisfied?" Ruval demanded.

"I—" He cleared his throat. Ruval had made it all too easy to put the right tremor into his voice. "Is there anything that will content you other than this battle?"

His half-brother looked interested. "What did you have in mind?"

"Land. A castle. Perhaps Feruche, which your brother wanted enough to die for—"

"You're that frightened of me?" Ruval laughed. "Oh, I'll have Feruche, all right. And Dragon's Rest and everything else you own—especially Castle Crag."

"And if I refuse this battle?"

"Back down in front of all these people?"

"You have no army, now that Chiana is out of the way. You'd lose a war."

"Andry used the more benevolent *ros'salath* at Dragon's Rest. Make war, or even attempt to kill me here with treachery, and I'll show you its true power."

Pol bit his lip and was sincerely glad that his cousin was absent tonight. Evidently the Star Scroll had not taught him the fatal version. "I agreed to meet you here—I didn't accept formal challenge."

"I noticed that in your wording," Ruval commented. "Allow me to convince you. If you refuse, I'll reveal the Desert's most cherished secret."

The blood froze in his veins. "And that might be?"

"Gold." He waved to the canyon behind them. "Unlimited, secret gold. Dragon gold! I know about Skybowl. In the memory of that coin is the smelter there. Accept my challenge, Pol, or Miyon and Barig will soon know the truth—and you'd have to kill them to keep them from spreading the knowledge to every other princedom."

"It seems I have no choice." He hid his relief and tossed the coin back at Ruval with what he hoped was a good show of false bravado.

"None whatsoever," Ruval replied cheerfully.

Pol pulled his shoulders straight and asked, "Shall we settle on the rules for the *ricsina*?"

Ruval's brows arched. "So you *have* read the Star Scroll."

"Certainly. Haven't you?"

"As much as Mireva could steal, from Andry's copy. Where is he, by the way?"

"Does it matter?"

"I suppose not. But he would have enjoyed watching you blunder around with spells you don't understand. You're not his favorite person."

"Granted. Well, shall we begin?"

"All Elements," Ruval said briskly. "And the two of us only. No other people. I don't need anyone else." He smiled. "You can't win, you know. There are things about sorcery that can kill you if you use them incorrectly."

Pol glanced away. "Agreed," he whispered.

"I also claim no weapons, no physical touch."

He didn't bother to hide his chagrin; there were several knives about his person that would have been useful if that rule had not been invoked. "I didn't expect an honest battle from you. But you're the one who can't win. Princemarch is mine, and you're going to die."

"I'll write that on a slip of parchment and burn it in the oratory at Castle Crag in your memory," Ruval grinned.

Pol ignored the taunt. "What about *dranath*?"

"What about it?"

"Do you need it?"

"Do *you*?"

For answer, Pol unhooked his father's wineskin from his belt, unstoppered it, and deliberately upended it. The dark liquid charged with power-enhancing drug spilled onto the sand.

He heard a soft gasp behind him—his mother, probably. Perhaps it was a foolish gesture, but it was one he had to make. Ruval was responding quite nicely so far. Rejection of *dranath* would not only further encourage belief in his weakness and stupidity, but it would also signify something more important: he was Sunrunner, not sorcerer. The stray thought teased at him that Andry would approve. Grudgingly.

"That leaves only the shielding," he said.

"Impossible. Tradition calls for three on each side. I have no one but myself. I *need* no one but myself to kill you."

"My mother, the High Princess, constructed one before."

"She knows nothing," Ruval scoffed.

"Yet she managed it."

"No. I do *not* agree."

Pol made his shrug one of disappointment; he hadn't really expected to win that point. "Yet I expect you *will* agree to the use of the Unreal."

"Oh, so you think to terrify me with horrible visions?" Ruval's good humor returned. "By all means! It should be interesting. If we're agreed, then call forward witnesses. Your father, Miyon, and Barig will do."

Pol did so, as if submitting to Ruval's authority. When the three stood near him, he listed the conditions of battle in a slightly hoarse voice. Rohan's carefully composed expression was belied by the dark concern in his eyes; Miyon seethed with a silent, angry demand that Ruval emerge the victor; Barig simply stared, understanding perhaps four words in ten. But he hadn't the temerity to ask for a lengthy explanation.

"The conditions are acceptable to both of us," Pol said at last. "If any of them are broken, the violator's claim is forefeit. Punishment is your responsibility, as witnesses."

"Understood," Miyon snapped. "Get on with it."

Ruval grinned at him. "Why, your grace! So eager to see your guards recruit win? Or do you expect me to lose?"

The Cunaxan looked ready to strangle him. He turned on his heel and strode back to his horse.

Barig said nervously, "As my prince's cousin and representative, I'll keep a damned sharp eye on the proceedings."

Pol appreciated his situation—and his bluster that tried to hide almost total incomprehension. "We thank your lordship for the assurances."

"And trust in your perceptions," Ruval added mockingly.

Rohan said nothing until Barig had returned to the group. Then he murmured, "You'll die tonight, Ruval—one way or another."

"Have you the stomach to kill the son of the woman who bore your child?"

Pol tensed in spite of himself. Rohan only lifted one brow.

"I saw him that night," Ruval went on. "Just after he was born. My last brother in his cradle where he burned to death."

"Such touching family sentiment is rather unexpected," Pol made himself remark.

"When I've finished with you, I'll settle with your mother—who killed mine." He glared at Rohan. "*You* I'll leave alive long enough to watch the death of the *faradhi* bitch who also murdered your son."

"Had Ianthe raised him, he would not have *been* my son," Rohan replied.

Pol swallowed hard. There was the center of it, he thought. And he was passionately grateful for Sioned's courage. He no longer cared whether or not she had been the one to kill Ianthe. He'd have to live through this, if only to tell his mother how deeply he loved her.

Rohan left them. Pol turned to Ruval and drew in a deep breath. He reached into his pocket, fingering a little golden talisman, remembering the wise old Sunrunner who had given it to him. The Star Scroll had taught him many things today—most of which he hoped he wouldn't have to use. He must defeat Ruval as a Sunrunner, not a sorcerer. Not just for symbolism's sake, but for his own. He was the son of Rohan and Sioned, not the scion of *diarmadh'im*. Yet the techniques perfected by his ancestors chattered in his mind, as if words written on parchment were speaking to him. They advised this spell or that, debated the merits of each, proposed new variations to fit the circumstances. But in a worried undertone a woman warned of danger. Her voice was his mother's and Lady Andrade's and Tobin's, and nervous fancy told him that some part of it was Lady Merisel who had written the words of the Star Scroll. She had preserved perilous knowledge and then hidden it away. Why? The scholar's fatal reluctance to let any learning disappear? Or something else?

Likely he would soon use that learning to kill his own half-brother. He looked into Ruval's eyes, and it was no blood-bond or sentiment between siblings that revulsed him from the inevitable. It was a terrible, will-destroying sadness. His princedom, his place, even his life, had been won with other people's bloody deaths: Ianthe and Roelstra, the pretender Masul, Segev, Marron, and now Ruval. What made him worth so much killing?

But then he remembered Sorin, and the anger swelled in him. Those others had died mortal enemies; Sorin had been murdered defending him. For Sorin he would win this battle. For his mother, who had risked everything for him. And for his father.

He held Ruval's gaze with his own, seeing not his brother but the Enemy, all Enemies.

"We begin," he said.

Chapter Twenty-eight

Stronghold: 35 Spring

Andry stood on the top step, looking down into the cellars. He told himself he was not afraid of Mireva. He also knew this was at least a partial lie. It wasn't what she might do—Rohan's gambit with the steel wire had all but removed that fear. It was what he might learn from her.

Secrets more deadly than those of the Star Scroll. Ways of power that, once learned, could pollute everything he was. Truths that might mean his eventual defeat.

Knowledge of any kind being power, he finally descended the stairs into the cool dimness. In chambers to his left were the enormous cisterns that held Stronghold's water supply—nearly overflowing this year, ensuring plenty of water for years to come. The grotto spring provided the main supply, but Andry could remember times in his childhood when it had nearly dried up. Even if it turned to sand for several years, Stronghold would still be awash in water, kept fresh by the addition of herbs that also gave it a clean, distinctive taste. It was one of the small things he missed at Goddess Keep, the subtle tingle of this water on his tongue.

He paused in a doorway to view the massive cisterns for what he fully expected would be the last time, then continued through the maze of crates, excess furniture, rolled-up carpets, and other stored items to Mireva's cell. Along the way part of his mind busied itself with contingency plans: how many of Radzyn's people could be housed at Stronghold when—and if—the castle fell? How many could the cisterns keep alive, and for how long? If Stronghold was taken as well, was there a way to deprive the invaders of this precious bounty of water in the Desert?

He believed in his vision as if it was already historical

fact. He had thought that perhaps it would come to pass this spring. But Radzyn still stood. He would detour there on his way out of his uncle's princedom. He desperately needed to see it whole and proud on its seaside cliffs. One last time.

There was a cellar below this one, so protected from the blazing heat that ice could be made within it. He remembered sneaking in with Sorin when they were children, scraping enough dry frost for good approximations of snowballs. He remembered so much . . . playing at dragons, learning to ride, trying bows that drew too much weight for little boys, causing dreadful mischief and never being able to talk their way out of it, taking seriously old Myrdal's bedtime tales of secret passageways and turning half the castle inside out before Chay caught them, and Sorin being unable to talk them out of *that* one, too. . . .

He stood before the locked iron door of the cell, conjured a flame to the torch set in the wall, and prepared to face the woman ultimately responsible for his brother's death.

He had been careful and silent in his approach. But before his fingers even touched the lock, her voice came muffled and mocking from within: "What? Not out watching sorcery at work?"

He opened the door. She stood against the far wall, long white-streaked hair straggling about her shoulders, gray-green eyes glittering, wrists bloody testimony to her efforts at escaping her bonds.

"I see you've made yourself comfortable," he said, matching her jeering tone.

"Oh, quite,"

There were any number of things he might have said. Any number of ways he might have opened his conversation with her. But the words that came from him were blunt, direct with the force of his need.

"Tell me what you know. I need your knowledge."

Mireva laughed at him.

"Tell me."

"And why should I do that?"

"Because it's your last chance." He paused. "Do you know what Rohan plans for you?" It had been mentioned this afternoon, before he had told Rohan he would not be going to Rivenrock. He wholeheartedly approved the idea; it had an elegant simplicity and promised days of excruciating torment. Rohan could be admirably ruthless when it suited him.

She shrugged. "Does it matter? We both know I'm to die."

"There are ways and ways of dying. I'd kill you myself, right now—but I must admit that he has a more interesting way." He stood in the open doorway, letting his shadow fall across her. The sight pleased him. "Are you feeling the lack of *dranath* yet?" he asked with malicious gentleness.

A spasm went through her that tugged her wrists apart, renewing a sluggish flow of blood down her hands.

Andry nodded. "I thought you might. Tell me what I want to know, and I may decide to end your life quickly."

Her eyes closed for a moment. Then she gave a resigned little shrug. "Very well. But release my bonds."

He very nearly laughed. "Not even for what I could learn from you."

"Fool! This cell may be four stone walls, but the ground beyond is laced with iron ore! Can't you feel it, Sunrunner? Are your senses that weak? The door's made of iron—I couldn't get past it even without steel in my flesh! If I'm going to die, at least let it be with a shred of dignity! Don't kill me when I'm trussed like a pig for slaughter!"

Andry considered, then closed the door. "I'll loosen them," he said at last, conjuring a bit of Fire high on the wall to see by. "But the 'earring' stays."

"As you wish," she answered sullenly.

He untwisted the steel wire connecting her arms, making sure each swollen wrist was still encircled, careful that the bonds were not loose enough to slip over her hands. She was free, after a fashion; the blood-dark wires were only bracelets now. He was confident that before she could work them off or remove the steel from her earlobe, he could get out the door and slam its iron shut.

"Too gracious." She rubbed her wrists. "What do you want to know?"

"Start at the beginning. It won't make any sense otherwise."

Mireva settled onto the floor. Leaning her head back against the wall, her hands in plain view, she held his gaze with her own and began to speak.

Years ago, before Andry had been born, Mireva had

changed her youthful shape to that of an old hag and given Lady Palila the secret of *dranath*. Roelstra's mistress had used the drug as Mireva had hoped. A Sunrunner named Crigo had been addicted and thereby enslaved. It was a satisfying thing to watch for a sorcerer who had spent her life in hiding. Yet as things developed, Mireva began to dare a larger hope: that when one of Roelstra's daughters by Lallante married Rohan, Crigo could be used even more effectively against Andrade by being in Rohan's inner councils.

"Tell me more about *dranath*," Andry interrupted.

"Think it might be useful, do you?" she jeered. "You know that it augments power? Ever used it yourself, Sunrunner?"

"And risk addiction?" he snorted. It was none of her business that he had experimented with the drug. "Leave myself vulnerable to what Rohan wants to do with you?"

"It's worth it." She shrugged. "If you ever plan on slipping your beloved cousin a little, be aware that anyone with the gifts can resist direction if he becomes aware of it—and it's not difficult to detect it, believe me. But unless he suspects, he'll be open to any interesting little suggestions you wish to make."

"What about ungifteds?"

"Nothing to work with. Their minds are empty so far as *dranath* is concerned. All it does is addict them. It takes the Blood to be vulnerable that way—which is why Ianthe was able to beguile Rohan into lying with her."

"Oh," he said, bored, "the phantom son."

"No more than Ruval or Marron or Segev! He would have had Sunrunner sensitivities from his father and the full *diarmadhi* gift from his mother." Her gray-green eyes unfocused. "What I could have taught him. . . ." Then she met Andry's gaze again with another small shrug for lost opportunities. "But he died with her in the razing of Feruche."

"You can mourn him some other time," Andry said impatiently. "Go on with the story."

She settled with her back against the wall, seeming to enjoy this chance to lecture the Lord of Goddess Keep. "Lallante was a kinswoman of mine. We married her to Roelstra hoping for a son who would be *diarmadhi* and High Prince both—just as Andrade mated her sister to

Zehava and Sioned to Rohan, wanting the same thing for you *faradh'im*. But Lallante was terrified of her powers and wouldn't use them. When she rejected her heritage, we gave up hope."

"We?"

"My father, her father, and I. They died shortly after she did." Mireva's voice was bitter and brooding. "Died of the failure. It didn't take a Sunrunner that time. Lallante was one of our own, and she betrayed us." Mireva wrapped her arms around herself and stared at the stone floor. "There were others who worked with us. But ours was the purest line—a lineage more royal than yours, Sunrunner." She grinned suddenly. "Descended from none other than your precious Lord Rosseyn, ally of Merisel the Cursed."

"He was no sorcerer!" Andry exclaimed.

"No. But his woman was. And so were her children by him. You weakling Sunrunners—it takes two of you to produce gifted offspring. The talent recedes without careful mating. But the *diarmadhi* powers are present in the children even if only one parent is gifted."

He stared at her, fascinated. "Then all Lallante's daughters—"

"Are part of us. Only that whimpering fool Naydra survives. With her dies Lallante's line. Except for Ruval."

"And so?"

"Crigo's death, Ianthe's failure to win Rohan—Pandsala's similar failure—but then there were Ianthe's sons. Three fine, strong, powerful boys. One of Feruche's guards was *diarmadhi*, my watch there. He brought them to me. I knew what it was to hope again. . . ."

Mireva had taken the boys in, nurtured their gifts, taught them who they were and what they must do to reclaim their birthright. Segev, the youngest, had gone to Goddess Keep that spring of 719.

"You never knew," she purred as Andry stared in shock. "That he was a sorcerer, you guessed. That he was Ianthe's son—" She laughed. "You and Hollis even let him help you translate the Star Scroll. Now *that* was irony! Even though he failed to bring me the original or even a copy, I saw enough of it on starlight to know it wasn't the thing whispered of in legend."

"Ah, but it *is*." He got some of his own back as her eyes widened.

"Impossible! The spells are wrong, they're—"

"Written that way deliberately. They only work if you know the code Lady Merisel used."

Breath hissed between Mireva's teeth. "So! That filthy bitch—she was arrogant enough after all to preserve what she stole from us!"

"Tell me about her."

Mireva's face darkened with fury. "This paragon of all *faradh'im*—she was Gerik's wife, but she slept with anything and anyone. She spread stories of her beauty, but she was hideously ugly—when she left her keeps she cast a shape-changing spell to foster belief in her loveliness. She ruled Gerik and Rosseyn and every Sunrunner alive with an iron whip—and killed those who didn't obey her."

Andry almost smiled. The woman whose strength and beauty sang from the historical scrolls bore no resemblance to the one Mireva described.

"She used treachery and deceit to destroy us—nothing was too low for her. The only time she was utterly disobeyed was when she ordered all children killed at our citadel of Castle Crag. Two of them were Rosseyn's. No one knew about them. He reported that all had been murdered—when he had in truth taken them to safety." Mireva sprang to her feet and began to pace the narrow cell. "As for the adults—the men she didn't kill outright, she gelded. The women she rendered barren through drugs. The pregnant ones—she tore the babes from their mothers' bodies and had them spitted on Merida knives. Did you ever learn the secret of Merida glass knives? They were hollow, filled with poison. When stabbed into flesh, they broke and the poison seeped out. Merisel used those knives against *children*!"

Mireva was panting for breath as she leaned one shoulder to the wall, as if the force of her hate had exhausted her.

"So all this is your way of getting even," Andry prompted.

"Nothing could ever repay us for what we suffered. This is only a flicker of revenge on her descendants."

Every muscle in his body drew taut. "Pol?"

"And you!" she spat. "Proud of it, are you, Lord of Goddess Keep? To be the blood of that murderous abomination?"

"How do you know this?" he breathed.

"Don't you think we've kept track of all of you through the years? And haven't you made the connection yet between Lord Garic of Elktrap and Lord Gerik, Merisel's husband? Ruala is one of us!"

"But the names—"

"A blind," she sneered. "To make everyone think that their power comes from Merisel and Gerik, not Rosseyn. She's as much a full-blooded *diarmadhi* as I am, as Ruval is! As *Pol* is!"

This time he was physically staggered.

"I don't know how, so don't ask." Annoyed by her lack of knowledge, still she obviously enjoyed her triumph. "Sioned's line is obscure in many places. He must get it from her. She wears no Sunrunner's rings anymore, so there's no indication that way of her blood. But if you placed such a ring on Pol's hand, and our arts were practiced around him, his finger would burn like fire."

"Pol," he breathed. He could scarcely believe it. Then, shocked anew: "Rings?"

"Don't you know anything?" she shouted. "In a Sunrunner with the Old Blood, the rings burn in the presence of one of our spells!"

"Tell me the rest," Andry said with no voice at all.

She rubbed her wrists as she told him Chiana's part in the plot—ripe for suggestion and sorcery, Chiana hated Sunrunners and Rohan about equally. Andry regretted her essential innocence. Then Mireva began to describe the scene of Sorin's death with vicious glee.

"Stop," he whispered, in pain.

"Stop? You're the one who wanted to hear all of it—and so you shall! He had to die, just as Maarken and his children will have to die so there will be no one left to inherit the Desert. Oh, and Hollis, as well—for murdering Segev. You claimed Marron's life for killing your brother. Ruval will claim hers for the same reason."

"You'll have to kill me, too."

"Not for dynastic reasons. No, you and your little bastards will die because you're Sunrunners, and Merisel's get."

The father in him trembled for Andrev and Tobren and Chayly. But what he said was, "You've already acknowledged that you're the one who's going to die—one way or another. Who's going to perform these executions?"

"Ruval."

It was fairly easy to laugh. "He'll be ashes by midnight!"

"Perhaps. But if not him, then others. How many of us do you think there are?" she taunted. "Hundreds? Thousands? Remember that one *diarmadhi* parent guarantees that all the children will inherit power. You Sunrunners are few and weak compared to us! And how would you even find us? Merisel drove us into the Veresch—but we have moved into every other part of the continent by now. As Sioned's heritage proves, the unsuspected power she gave to Pol. How will you find us, Lord of Goddess Keep? How will you eliminate us?"

"I have a question for you," he said with a tiny smile. "*How will you stop me?*"

He already knew how he would do it. Those who had joined Chiana were still captive at Dragon's Rest. It would be simplicity itself to be rid of them—but not until they had revealed the locations of the others. Additionally, anyone who possessed power probably used it; rumor alone would lead him to *diarmadh'im* from Firon to Kierst-Isel to Dorval. He would find them, and they would die.

His only problem would be the highly placed ones. Sioned. Pol. Riyan. But they were all Sunrunners—of a sort. He would find some way of putting them under his watch, if not his control.

His smile widened. "*How will you stop me?*" he repeated.

Her steel-braceleted arms came up and fire gushed from her fingertips. She screamed with the agony of working with iron piercing her flesh. But flames shot from her hands and his cry echoed with hers as his clothing caught fire. He fell, writhing, and rolled across the stone floor to extinguish fire before it charred him to the bone.

The next instant the flames were gone.

So was Mireva.

***

Her brain told her she must seal Andry inside the cell, but there was no time and she could not make her swollen fingers work. Half-blind, she stumbled toward the stairs, groped her way up them. Surely there had not been so many on the way down—

She sobbed as she collided with a door. It had no lock, but in the dimness, with pain bleating along every nerve, locating the latch and shoving the door open was endless agony. She moaned with relief when she saw the hall stretch ahead of her, empty. No one had heard her shrieks or Andry's cries. But this was the inhabited part of the keep, and she must be careful.

Mireva breathed slowly and carefully, wishing for just the tiniest pinch of *dranath* to clear her head. But the memory of the sweet invincibility was almost enough. She grabbed a torch from its sconce and wedged it under the door. It wouldn't slow Andry down for long, but it was better than nothing.

Twisting her hair into a knot at her nape, she brushed off her clothing and walked down the hall as if she belonged there. She met no one until a footman came by, loaded down with Fironese crystal on a silver tray—for Pol's victory banquet, Mireva thought acidly. She purposely stumbled into the man's shoulder. He swore and almost lost his balance. Her hands were still clumsy, but she managed to grab one of the thin-stemmed goblets. The crystal broke very neatly against the wall and as the footman righted himself, catlike, without dropping his burden, Mireva slashed his throat.

The ensuing crash would bring people running. She must hurry. Racing down the main corridor, she climbed the servants' stairs as fast as she could, encountering only an incurious maid carrying an armful of sheets. As she ran, she tried to pick the wire from her ear, gave it up as being too tightly wound, and started on the steel circling her wrists. By the time she reached Ruala's chamber, the first bloodied wire had fallen to the floor.

There were no guards, not even a maid sitting in the shadowy bedroom. Ruala was asleep. As Mireva opened the curtains, the flinch brought by the rasp of steel rings on rods was forgotten in the blessed sight of new stars. She rummaged frantically through Ruala's dressing table. Scissors at last to hand, she snipped the other bracelet from her wrist. Quickly, she must work quickly. She could draw on Ruala's power once she was free of the steel and could work. She tried to still her tremors and leaned down to get a better look in the mirror as she worked on the wire in her earlobe.

"Put it down."

She spun, astonished to find Ruala standing beside the bed, ready to kill her with the elegant jeweled knife clutched in her fist. She held the blade by its handle, not its tip, ready to throw it; she probably didn't even know how. Thus she would have to come closer—close enough for Mireva to disarm her, with luck. While the wire was still twisted in her earlobe, she could not use sorcery with ease—and she was two and a half times Ruala's age.

"Why isn't your loving lord hovering over his precious darling?' Mireva asked sweetly.

"Put the scissors down," Ruala said, just as quietly as before.

Long black hair swirled about perfect shoulders; the dark green eyes were reminiscent of Mireva's own in some lights. The old woman saw herself as she had been over forty years ago: young, beautiful, with the promise of power in her eyes. "We're the same, you and I," she murmured.

"We're no more alike than Fire and Water. Now, put it down."

Mireva set the scissors on the dressing table behind her. "I know power when it's near me. You're *diarmadhi*, just like me." She could almost feel Andry pounding on the door down below. Time, time— "Do you think Andry will let you live, knowing what you are? Or do you suppose your brave lord will protect you? How can he, when Andry will be after his blood, too?"

Ruala smiled. "You know power, do you? We'll see." She started slowly for the door, never taking her eyes off Mireva. But when she reached her hand to the knob, Mireva made a supreme effort—and what Ruala touched was a thing slimy and foul, a writhing piece of corroded flesh that oozed acid. She screamed and jerked her fingers away.

Mireva could hardly see. The pain was unendurable, spreading along her limbs from a brain that seemed to be on fire. But the torture was worth it. Ruala, stunned and terrified for that brief instant of sorcery, was vulnerable. Mireva threw herself blindly forward. They sprawled together on the floor, locked as tightly as lovers. Mireva dimly heard the knife clatter away.

She wrestled herself atop Ruala, gasping as fingers dug

so deep into her lacerated wrists that she was sure the bones would shatter. Ruala was no fool; recovery from shock had been swift, and she knew exactly where to hurt Mireva the most. Mireva flung them over and hoped her pain-hazed sight could be trusted. The thud of the girl's head against the stout wooden bedframe proved her correct. Ruala wilted.

Gulping for air, Mireva pushed herself to her feet and went for the scissors again. Her hands shook so hard that she drew blood from the side of her neck—but the wire dropped to the dressing table. She was free.

The stars beckoned. She wove their light swiftly, craving *dranath*, and hurled herself down the silvery skeins toward Rivenrock.

It was as she had feared. Pol and Ruval were already battling, Air and Fire whirling around them, hideous visions conjured and countered in a maelstrom of power. The ungifted onlookers were masked in horror at what they saw. Those who were sensitive to the arts—Sioned and Morwenna, Tobin, Maarken, and Hollis—were on their knees in the sand, faces contorted with agony. No *perath* had been woven to shield them. This suited Mireva perfectly. She could enter the battle without hindrance and the Sunrunners would feel the deathblow as if it had been directed at them.

Pol backed away from Ruval's gambit—a blazing whirlwind that sprouted claws from which lightning spewed. The princeling looked frightened. Mireva laughed her satisfaction. It seemed Ruval was doing just fine without her. Still, she watched in wariness for Pol's reply, for all she knew about him warned of cleverness.

His right hand groped in a pocket of his trousers, emerged fisted around some small thing. He flung it into the air as one might release a hunting hawk—and from a tiny bright glitter it indeed grew wings. Swirling with Sunrunner's Fire, the thing became an immense golden dragon as tall as the canyon walls, wings aflame, eyes glowing white as if suffused with stars.

Mireva gasped out a curse and hastened her own work. For the trick to this illusion was that some of it was *not* illusion. Fire concealed the working until it was ready in all its awful details—so that the portions that were real could not be guessed from watching its construction. Any part of the conjured dragon might be made from that small glinting thing Pol had thrown into the air. She had taught Ruval the technique, shown him how stone gathered from the sands could form talons and teeth, or real fire could gush from mighty jaws. If Ruval could not discern fact from illusion, it would cost him his life.

It was almost as painful to work without *dranath* as it had been with iron poisoning her blood. She needed the drug, could feel its lack screaming shrilly inside her as she readied her weapon. But she did it: Pol's dragon turned to glass. It cracked and splintered to the sand, and as it did the real portion of it—the lashing tail concealing the little golden carving—crumbled.

Pol fell back stunned as his masterwork vanished. Real fear flashed into his eyes. Mireva sobbed for breath, silently screaming at Ruval to be quick in his answering illusion. She could not sustain this for long, not without the drug in her veins.

She whirled then to stare at Ruala. The young woman was still unconscious, but her power was accessible. Without *dranath* it would be difficult, but if she did not try, Ruval might be dead before the next star appeared. She broke the threads of light and grunted with effort as she hauled Ruala over to the windows. The spell was arduous under the best circumstances; Mireva felt her head was ready to explode with the strain. But she probed and pushed, groping for the hidden core—and found it.

Swiftly she rewove the starlight. It was easier now, sustained by Ruala's young strength that had never been taught how to resist this. She saw the sand and walls of Rivenrock much more clearly now, and the two combatants.

Now it was Ruval who fumbled with something in his hand. A new inferno appeared, a monster forming within it. When the thing leaped from its concealing blaze. Pol fell back involuntarily. Fully the size of the dragon, it was the entirety of what Mireva had used to terrify Ruala. Had she had strength, she would have laughed in delight; she had taught Ruval this beast herself, they had formed it together.

She was momentarily distracted by a quiver from Ruala's mind. She was beginning to wake up, as if sensing the use to which her powers were being put, outrage and sheer terror rousing her from unconsciousness. Mireva groaned with the pain of keeping her under control, and returned her attention to the monster Ruval had conjured.

It was horned and crested and covered in livid scales of every conceivable color, like a stained glass window gone berserk. The gaping eyes oozed yellowish matter down to an open maw filled with endless sharp teeth. These dripped blood onto forelegs as big around as a horse that ended in thick, slime-coated claws like steel spikes. It reared back on its hind legs and plummeted down, ready to clamp its jaws around Pol.

Mireva knew the teeth were not real, nor the claws. It was the pus leaking from the eyes that was dangerous. Formed of sand mixed with a paste Ruval had learned to make as one of his first lessons, hidden in a pocket until he needed it, when it touched Pol's skin it would sear him to the bone.

She saw him leap away from the hundreds of teeth. Now, it must be now. She could feel her strength waning, her control over the awakening Ruala fading, her heart beating with savage throbs, her brain on fire. A last effort, a gust of Air conjured at an impossible distance—and a spurt of poisonous yellow muck spattered toward Pol.

She did not see it hit him. She was wrenched back to Stronghold by an agony so horrible that the scream died before it left her throat. The cool starlight turned to needles of ice and fire stabbing into her eyes, matching the stabbing pain in her heart. Her fingers groped for the knife, felt the jewels on its hilt. Staggering around from the window, she expected to see Ruala's white face as she fell.

"That's for Sorin," Riyan told her before she died.

Chapter Twenty-nine

Rivenrock Canyon: 35 Spring

Instinct screamed at Pol to wince away, but instinct was hampered by his mind's cold calculations over what was real and what was not. Part of him was well and truly horrified by this hideous apparition. Curses and screams behind him told him he wasn't alone. But another part of him writhed in a frenzy of analysis. What of this was real, and what not? The yellowish ooze might be only a feint, something to distract him while the true attack was mounted. Instinct and intellect interlocked in near-paralysis—but then he saw Ruval's eyes flicker with sudden astonishment.

Ruval had not expected the gust of Air that flung the ooze onto Pol; therefore someone else had initiated it.

No one present would dare such a thing; therefore Mireva was free to work.

She had expended a vast amount of power in calling Air from a great distance—therefore this foul matter was real and to be avoided at all costs.

The reasoning took a split instant. Pol flung himself to one side, but not quickly enough. The filth splattered onto his tunic; a drop hit his face. He was about to wipe it away when his cheek tingled with sudden heat. Within moments the pain was excruciating. If he touched it with his fingers, the agony would spread. And if the pus had hit his eye—

Frantically, trying to avoid gaping jaws that might or might not be real, he pulled a knife from his boot to scrape off the sticky slime. He wished he could throw the contaminated blade into Ruval's heart—but rules were rules, and if he broke them his honor would be forfeit. Stupid and possibly suicidal to have such scruples—but he could do nothing else.

He used the knife like a razor against his cheek, nicking the skin, groaning at fresh fire as a hint of the poison mixed into his blood. It felt as if skin and flesh had blistered black and peeled away to the bone. The pain half-blinded him, found outlet in a cry of sheer rage against Mireva's treachery. The knife nestled with deadly familiarity in his fist. But he couldn't use it. Rohan and Sioned—and Lleyn and Chadric and Audrite and everyone who had had a hand in raising him—they had all done their work too well. Roelstra's grandson would have loosed the knife; the son of Rohan and Sioned could not.

But nothing prevented him from using the matter that clung to the blade. The gruesome monster loomed over him, slavering for his blood. Pol took a deep breath and decided on the basis of no evidence at all that the only thing real was the poisonous filth—and strode right through the illusory body toward Ruval. As quickly as he could, careful not to touch the ooze, he flicked it back at its maker.

Ruval dodged it, terror in his eyes, so desperate to avoid the yellow muck that he lost his balance and tumbled to the sand. Pol flung the knife away and used the moments of Ruval's panic to catch his breath. His cheek still burned, but it was a goad now, not a crippling wound.

"Give it up," he panted. "Your best has failed."

"Best? That was nothing!"

Sheer bravado. "Give it up!" Pol shouted furiously. "I don't want to kill you, damn it! Yield! Princemarch is mine! The Desert belongs to me by treaty made before we were born!"

" 'As long as the sands spawn fire,' " Ruval quoted mockingly. "I see no fire here, princeling, nor is anyone ever likely to!"

"No?" Pol asked softly. And smiled—because suddenly he knew what had to be done. The shift of facial muscles brought back pain in sickening waves. But he refused to feel it. He was tiring—it was harder to concentrate, harder to summon strength enough. He raised both arms slowly, his gaze never relinquished his half-brother's. Starlight caught the topaz-and-amethyst ring, glowed from the moonstone that had been Andrade's. Arms straight, fingers spread, he stood very still. His hands clenched slowly into fists. He called, and the Fire came.

It sprang to life in grass and flowers baked dry by the hot spring sun. It filled the mouth of Rivenrock Canyon, fountained up the sandstone watchspire, spread across the dunes. The sea of sand became a sea of Sunrunner's Fire until it seemed the sand itself caught and burned.

Ruval conjured Air to bend the flames back toward Pol. It only fanned them higher. So great was Pol's control, so sure was his power, that he appeared to glow in the perilous brightness.

"Illusion!" Ruval bellowed. "Unreal!"

Pol laughed. "Walk into the flames and see!"

"You'll die by your own Fire, Sunrunner!" Ruval leaped for Pol. The physical attack was so unexpected that Pol went down in a tangle of limbs, feeling his knee wrenched nearly apart with the awkwardness of his fall. A long tongue of flame reached out nearby, licking across a growth of gray-green cacti, close enough to singe the two men as they wrestled on the sand. Pol felt beringed fingers lock around his throat, cutting off precious gulps of searing air. His vision began to go black around a raging wildfire. He tore at Ruval's hands, then took a terrible chance and rolled them both toward the blaze.

Ruval scrambled away with a howl of pain. He dug his right arm into the sand to quench the flames that had caught on his shirt. Pol tried to gain his feet but his knee collapsed, sent him sprawling once more. They were encircled, caught in a tiny space of sand and rock as the inferno raged all around them.

Pol ripped off his shirt and wrapped it tightly around his knee, hoping the support would be enough. He swayed up on his good knee, glaring at Ruval. "Illusion?" he mocked, bruised neck muscles making his voice a rasp. Gathering himself to take advantage of the shock he was about to give, he forced a tiny smile to his lips. "Would you kill your own brother?"

The flames etched Ruval's suddenly white face in red and gold.

"My brothers are dead!"

"What, no loving welcome? I distinctly heard you swear revenge on the High Princess for ordering your youngest brother's death. I'm hurt, Ruval. Deeply wounded." He

summoned the words of the Star Scroll to mind. So
simple, really, when one didn't consider their implications or intellectualize over right, wrong, and justice.
Power was there to be used; why else possess it? His
father's policy of acting only when action was necessary
was a waste of resources. But then, Rohan had never
experienced this kind of power. "I am Ianthe's lastborn,
Ruval. Sunrunner and *diarmadh'im*. How else would I be
able to do this?"

The fire he called this time came from the stars, sweeping cold and white down Rivenrock Canyon. It mantled
his own body in brilliant silver—and struck Ruval down
in a flash of lightning.

What he had kindled exhilarated and terrified him.
The way power should, he thought remotely. He watched
with breathless fascination, caught between exultation
and fear, between the thundering heat of Sunrunner's
Fire and the chill silver silence of a blaze called down
from the stars. Having ignited flames across the Desert,
he did not have to work to sustain it as with his dragon
illusion. But neither did the sorcery require thought.
Each came naturally to him, destruction from two opposing forces that met and merged within him. He throbbed
with power and the terror of power, not knowing which
kind and source of power he feared most.

Ruval lay writhing on the rocky ground. His screams
split Pol's skull like spikes. *"Would you kill your own
brother?"* Pol could do it; he had only to twist starfire a
little more tightly around Ruval, and the man would die.
He would not even be breaking the Sunrunner's oath he
had never taken—never to kill using his gifts. For it was
not a *faradhi* skill he used.

"Would you kill your own brother?"

The grandson of Roelstra would have done it. The son
of Rohan and Sioned could not.

Pol let the Star Scroll spell fade. He felt no exalted
sense of his own goodness or righteousness or nobility.
All he felt was empty, and grindingly tired. And something of a fool for not silencing his scruples and killing
Ruval outright. He rubbed his torn knee, waiting while
Ruval caught his breath. When there was sense in the
man's eyes again, Pol said simply, "Yield."

Fright competed with fury in Ruval's eyes. Then his head bent. "Help me," he whispered.

Pol snorted. "Life you may have. But trust? Stand on your own or stay there, I don't give a damn which."

"Don't you know what that spell does to *diarmadh'im*? I can't feel my legs, damn you! Look at the Fire—if we don't move, we'll burn to death! Help me up!"

"Do it yourself or not at all," Pol replied stubbornly.

The attempt was made, and Ruval toppled over on the sand, facedown. Pol swore and approached cautiously. His knee stabbed with every slow, suspicious step, repeating the fever pulse of his cheek wound. Ruval was barely breathing. His distress looked genuine enough—but Pol did not get within reach.

"Get up!" he ordered sharply, and coughed with the harshness of fiery air in his throat. He tossed his head to clear the sweat-thick hair from his eyes.

Ruval tried once more, pushing himself up onto hands and knees, head hanging as he fought for breath. Pol took a wary half-step back. His knee went out from under him and he fell with a gasp of pain.

Ruval was on him. And the face grinning ferally down at Pol was blond, pale-eyed—his own.

"Say 'please,' little brother." Ruval tugged Pol's injured leg to an excruciatingly painful angle. There was no need for any other restraint; the grip at his knee immobilized Pol completely. He moaned with the agony as bones ground together and tendons stretched to their limits.

"I'll keep this shape just long enough to kill your father," Ruval informed him, laughing softly. "Or maybe I'll wait until tomorrow, let them believe you won, and tonight celebrate victory between Meiglan's thighs."

He *was* a fool for allowing Ruval to live. Too late to flay himself over it now. Pol ordered every muscle in his body to go limp. "Quick death—don't torment me—" He interrupted this craven speech with a hacking cough.

His own face laughed with Ruval's voice, his own eyes shone with Ruval's triumph. "I told you to say 'please!' "

"Just tell me—why this way—you're my brother—would have given you—"

"By the Nameless One, are you really that stupid?" Ruval stared at him, and Pol felt the grasp on his leg ease a little. "You have many things that belong to me,"

Ruval explained as if to a particularly slow-witted child. "Titles, honors, Princemarch—"

"Don't kill my father! Spare him—and Meiglan—" Time, he needed time. . . .

"It's a thought," Ruval admitted. "Worse than death to him, seeing me as High Prince. But she'd be happy to exchange a puling princeling for a real man. Yes, I might just let them live for a little while. If you beg nicely enough."

Steeling himself, Pol whispered, "Please."

Ruval grinned. "Again."

"Please!" It tasted of acid, but he said the word a second time.

"The sweetest thing an enemy can say!" Ruval reached up to brush the sweat from his brow, chuckling.

Pol twisted his body as fast as he could, slamming his good knee into Ruval's chest. The breath whooshed out of him and he pitched backward. Pol groaned and tried to stand, ungainly as a newborn foal. He couldn't. He crawled away from Ruval, staring at the flames encircling their narrow battleground. Hauling in a deep breath and telling himself that his knee must support him or he would indeed die in his own Fire, he lurched through the blaze and went sprawling.

He never knew how long he simply lay there, stunned. He wondered vaguely why no one had come to help him. Didn't they understand that it was all over? Where were his father, his mother, Meggie, Sionell? Why didn't they help him?

His hearing returned before his vision. Someone was screaming. He frowned, knowing something was wrong but unable to figure out what. Struggling to his good knee, he turned and beheld himself. The mirror was still ablaze, but the image was perfect. Two of him were outside the flames. Scant wonder no one had come to his aid. Which was really him?

It was a question that pierced him in unexpected ways. But he had no time for it now. Ruval was still alive. He glanced back to the half-circle of pain-ravaged Sunrunners and horrified nobles, finding his father's face with surprising difficulty. But Rohan was not looking at him. He stared up at the firelit sky. Pol turned, searching, at last feeling the subtle flicker that should have alerted him long before this.

Dragon.

A real one, the color of the body dark and indistinguishable but the underwings shining reddish-gold by the light of the flames. A sire, come down from the Veresch for mating, huge and magnificent and thundering out his rage—and flying straight for them across the fiery sands.

Another scream was nearly lost in the shrieks of panic-stricken horses. They had turned skittish when Fire came, but dragons were something else entirely. Frantic hoof-beats told of their headlong rush for safety. Pol could not look away from the dragon. It was as if the legends were true, and those eyes had speared him from a distance, immobilizing him.

A prickling at the edges of his senses warned him too late. Ruval was at work on the dragonsire. Pol cursed, torn out of his fascination, and wove his own colors into the light blazing from the sky and sand.

Starfire and groundfire, barely controllable as they raged through him, made the sear on his cheek a caress by contrast. He flung his thoughts toward the dragon. Ruval got there first by spells the Star Scroll never mentioned. But this was different from what he had done in early spring. The dragon did not fall helplessly from the sky. Pol saw the great wings fold slightly into a controlled dive, then spread to correct the angle of flight. The talons reached out—for him. He flattened himself to the ground and writhed into the sand for what little protection it could offer. He felt something in his knee tear completely apart and muffled his scream of agony in the sand.

The wind of the creature's passing brought a gust of heat from the canyon fire. But the talons missed him. He scrambled up onto his good knee and stared skyward, breathing heavily, astounded. No dragon would have been so clumsy in snatching prey—and no dragon would have attempted to make prey of a man. However imperfectly, Ruval must be in possession of the dragon, controlling its flight.

And that made Pol so angry that the Fire-gold night around him turned the crimson of blood.

The dragon cried out, talons ripping at the wind as he

fought for flight. His wings spread, folded, beat a desperate drunken rhythm to gain distance. But he could not break free. Compelled, faltering, he swept over the flames that singed his belly and came for Pol again, screaming.

Pol wasn't even afraid. He was too furious for that, or to feel the torture of his wounds. If Ruval could do this to a dragon, so could he. He had touched dragon colors before. He knew what the fierce, primal minds felt like. He marshaled his strength and a rage that should have crippled him. He lashed out toward the dragonsire that had missed him again and was wheeling upward on angry wings, bellowing his fury to the stars.

It was something like making the link that allowed him to speak with other Sunrunners—only there was nothing delicate or precise about the way his mind slammed into Ruval's and into the dragon's. It was questionable which of the three was the more enraged: Ruval at Pol's survival after the initial attack, Pol at Ruval's use of the dragon, or the dragon himself at these two puny beings who fought for control over him.

Hues no one had ever seen or named spun in an explosion of color that had the nearby Sunrunners screaming. Pol hung on. He and Ruval battled for the dragon as if it, too, was part of the victor's spoils. But as they fought, Ruval lost control of his shape-change, Pol's stolen features fading away to reveal his own

And suddenly, faced once again by the "true" Ruval and not himself, Pol realized that this was all wrong. He was forgetting everything taught him by his father's example of wise patience. He was fighting the enemy on the enemy's own terms. He was *becoming* his enemy: using power for its own sake. And worst of all, he was using the dragon as his tool.

The beast screamed again, circling erratically above the Fire-strewn Desert as if his wings were not entirely his to command. The night spun in conflicting, burning colors, as if three blazing whirlwinds fought above the dunes and filled Rivenrock Canyon with unbearable light. Two of these had nearly merged, were nearly one. Pol was still apart, and knew he was about to lose this battle for possession of the dragon.

Ruval hungered for possession—of land, wealth, power. All would never be enough; for a man like that, there was no such thing as "all." There was only "more." He was not even like their grandsire, who had only amused himself with power. Ruval was as Masul had been: an embittered outcast, dedicated to exacting grim payment for perceived wrongs done him. But the pretender had been only a man. Ruval was a sorcerer. If he won this battle, Pol's would be only the first death.

Andry would be next—the only other person who could oppose him on his terms. Goddess only knew what he would then do to Rohan and Sioned and those Pol loved—and Meggie—

He shifted his mental and emotional stance, deliberately stifling fear that could only distract and harm him. It was the calm his father had taught him to seek at the *Rialla*, a patience that allowed him to hear meanings within meanings. But now he listened to his own mind, his own heart.

Into the place where fury had been he summoned his lifelong awe at the sight of dragons. He called up childhood memories of standing on Stronghold's ramparts as dragons filled the sky with the wind of their wings. He remembered that first ride into the valley of Dragon's Rest, now his mother had "spoken" with the dragon she'd named Elisel. He filled himself with dragon wings and colors and voices, his soaring joy at watching them, his delight when they flew in to Dragon's Rest and partook of the feast he gladly offered. He gloried in their strength and beauty and freedom, and even as the dragonsire swept down in another attack, Pol was smiling. Perhaps it was true that a dragon-sense had been passed down from Zehava to Rohan to him, that his line truly deserved the title of *azhrei*; he only knew that he loved the dragons for reasons beyond himself. He belonged to them as surely as they belonged to Desert skies.

Suddenly it was as it had been in the spring—an incredible whirl of power and colors merging with his own. There were no words, only emotions. But this time he felt not a dragon's dying anguish but a dragon's rage. Dimly, as if from a great distance, he sensed Ruval's faltering control—and the roar of the dragon echoed in his own heart as together they broke free.

For a few moments more Pol *was* that dragon. The

flush of new strength through blood and muscle was his; the powerful beat of wings, the rush of hot wind as he skimmed the flames that climbed the walls of Rivenrock. And he knew, not in words or coherent thoughts but in sheer savage emotion, what the dragon was about to do.

The next instant he felt rocks digging fresh agony into his knees. Close enough to spray sand over him, almost to brush him with an outspread wingtip, the dragon swooped across the sand with talons outstretched. They dug into Ruval's mantle. There was a gush of blood and the sound of ribs cracking, and a single shriek. Pol tilted his head back, gasping for breath, transfixed as the dragon carried his prey up into the starry sky.

Days later, halfway across the Long Sand, they would find a charred heap of broken bones and Sunrunner rings and a half-melted gold coin bearing Roelstra's likeness.

***

Meiglan freed her arm from her father's grasp and ran headlong over the sand. She flung herself into Pol's startled embrace, still so torn between terror and joy that she didn't even know she was crying.

Rohan helped Sioned to her feet, ran his fingers anxiously over the crescent-shaped scar, livid against her white cheek. She gave a tiny smile to reassure him. Then she sank very calmly down onto the sand, whispering, "I–I feel a little faint."

Morwenna pushed herself up from her knees, swearing. Her head ached as if she'd been drinking strong wine since the New Year Holiday, her fingers felt scorched to the bone, and her body hurt so much she suspected the bones would come apart at the joints. "Damned undignified position," she muttered as she struggled to stand.

Chay had kept Tobin upright during the battle only through main strength; she was limp, her eyelids fluttering. He swung her up into his arms and rocked her, calling her name frantically until sense returned to her face.

Maarken and Hollis knelt huddled in each other's arms, stricken, trembling. At length the agony of the assault on their senses faded. Walvis and Feylin helped them up. Maarken looked around, whispered his gratitude, and clung to his wife with what remained of his strength.

Sionell turned from the sight of Pol and Meiglan's

embrace. Tallain, holding her, didn't notice. He was staring at the Desert. The sand was still ablaze.

Rialt, with the virtue of practicality, had the presence of mind to send Arlis and Edrel running off to see if they could collect a few horses. None of the Sunrunners would be able to walk the whole way back to Stronghold.

Barig cleared his throat ponderously and said to Miyon, "Was this legal according to the rules agreed on?"

The prince replied, "Don't be a fool. A dragon isn't a weapon or a person. His grace won fairly." Though it seared the skin of his lips to have to say it.

Rohan looked up from where he knelt with Sioned cradled in his arms. He called Sionell over to tend her, then went to where Meiglan was helping Pol to his feet. The girl saw him first; she caught her breath and straightened defensively. Rohan realized that she feared him, but her trust that Pol would protect her was greater. She proved it by holding him tighter and meeting Rohan's gaze with a kind of apprehensive defiance.

Pol looked at him then, his eyes dim with exhaustion. It was clear that until that moment, no one had existed for him but Meiglan. Rohan repressed a sigh and, in a mild voice that fooled neither himself nor his son, said, "Will you kindly do something about this?" He gestured to the flames that scoured Rivenrock. "I really can't have you turning my princedom into a blast furnace."

Pol gave him a shaky smile. "Sorry. But I don't know if I *can* stop it. Or even if I should," he added pensively.

"Won't—won't it burn itself out soon?" Meiglan ventured.

"I suppose so," Rohan said. "Come to think of it, it does make a rather nice statement. Although setting your own beacon-fire comes somewhat in advance of your right to do so, Pol. I'm not dead yet."

The young man looked stricken. "Father—I—"

Rohan was surprised, but knew he shouldn't have been. For Pol, humor wasn't the weapon against impossible tension that it had always been for him. So he made himself laugh.

Pol relaxed at once. He even rallied enough to say, "It won't burn as far as Remagev—I think!"

"It's dry a few measures out from here, if memory serves," Rohan told him. "Not even this winter's rains made anything grow. But if it *does* get to Remagev, *you'll* pay to rebuild it."

"If Walvis lets me live long enough!"

Meiglan listened to the exchange with wide, bewildered eyes. Rohan smiled to hide his resentment of her presence. Had she not been here, he might have said to his son what he needed so much to say. Instead, he was forced to keep those words to himself. There might be time later to say them—and there might not.

There was a brief silence while father and son watched each other. Pol was the one to look away. "Ah, good—Edrel's found a horse. I doubt Meggie or our Sunrunners would make it back to Stronghold on foot. How's Mother?"

"Sionell's taking care of her." When he heard the tender nickname, his objections to Meiglan—concealed even from Sioned—were resolutely locked away. Pol had made his Choice. They would all just have to get used to it.

"How're your legs? Aside from that, you don't seem too much the worse for your little demonstration," he went on as casually as he could.

Pol shrugged off his concern. "I—have a few resources."

Rohan understood. The Sunrunners had been devastated by the lash of battle; Pol's *diarmadhi* blood had in some ways protected him. "I wouldn't vouch for that knee, though," he remarked. "And you'll have a scar on your cheek as a more permanent souvenir."

Pol touched his face, startled. Rohan wondered when he would realize that its shape and placement were almost identical to the one on Sioned's cheek.

"Yes. Well. . . ." Rohan said, then decided to leave them to each other and return to his wife. He had never been one to struggle overlong against the obvious.

Pol looked down at Meiglan, who had undertaken to support him. He smiled at her; so little and delicate, and trying to lend him her strength.

"I was so frightened," she whispered.

"So was I," he admitted frankly.

"You? Never!"

He gave a rueful laugh. "Come, let's find you a horse. And me, too—I hope a limp isn't my other souvenir of tonight—oh!" He looked around distractedly. "Meggie, do you see it? A little gold carving of a dragon—"

"Stay here. I'll find it for you." He swayed when she left him, barely able to balance on one leg. At last she returned with the piece. "Is this it?"

"Yes." He fingered it, held it up to the light. "Lord Urival gave me this a long time ago. It used to decorate the top of a water clock that belonged to my father."

"Yes, my lord?" Meiglan's face was all confused attention to his every word as she got her shoulder beneath his arm again.

But he could scarcely explain to her why Urival had salvaged it from the shattered remains of that elegant timepiece after Masul and Pandsala and Segev had died. Pol was now the last of Ianthe's sons. Hollis had killed Segev; Andry, Marron. Had it been Pol or the dragon who had killed Ruval? Urival had given him the little golden dragon the day of his death. "Talisman," he'd said with a grim smile. *Talisman and reminder.*

Pol placed the carving in her palm. "Your first dragon, my lady."

She stared at it, then at him. "First, my lord?"

"My name is Pol. You'd better get used to saying it."

***

Six of the nineteen horses were found, one of them lame. All the Sunrunners stated emphatically that they were perfectly capable of using their own legs. A blatant lie; they were in such obvious need that not even Miyon made grumbling noises about the long walk. Rohan, who lifted Sioned into the saddle, told her to be quiet and be grateful. After a few measures she overruled her husband, slid from the saddle, and offered the mare to Meiglan. It was a gesture whose meaning was lost on all but a few.

Maarken, too, had recovered, and after giving over his horse to Feylin, roused himself to use the light of the newly risen moons to communicate with his brother at Stronghold. Andry's colors were strangely darkened, and he neither asked about events nor offered any comment. He merely agreed to have more horses sent at once, and withdrew into himself.

Maarken suspected that sight of Stronghold would reveal other momentous events. He gnawed on possibilities until Nialdan and several grooms rode up with fresh horses on lead reins. Beckoning the Sunrunner aside, he asked about Andry.

There wasn't a coin's weight of dissembling in Nialdan's entire soul. When he answered that all was well, Maarken knew he was lying. But the man was so obviously distressed that Maarken didn't press it.

When they finally reached Stronghold, Andry, Riyan, and Ruala were waiting on the main steps. All three looked sick with exhaustion. Maarken was so intent on trying to read his brother's face that for a few moments he saw nothing else. Hollis gripped his arm and whispered his name. Flung across the bottom steps was a dark, limp shape. Mireva. Dead.

Rohan dismounted and walked slowly to the corpse. With the toe of one boot he nudged it onto its back. When he turned to summon Pol with a glance, Maarken had the impression that his uncle's bones had turned to steel, his flesh to stone.

Pol stared down into Mireva's dead eyes. Then he backed away a pace or two, and with a brief gesture called Fire.

They all stood for a time watching the flames. Rohan was the first to climb the steps and enter his castle. The others followed. The corpse of the sorceress was left to burn in silence.

Chapter Thirty

Princemarch: Autumn, 728

The seas foamed blood-red, the tide thick with bloating bodies, each wave capturing yet another corpse from the shore. The castle was in flames. When night fell, the burning stones that had been Radzyn Keep would signal the carnage for a hundred measures all around. Perhaps it would be seen all the way to Graypearl across the water.

Perhaps Graypearl burned, too.

The victors plucked their own dead from the waves—tall, broad, dark men, fierce even in death. The bodies were laid out carefully near a strange, flat ship, stripped, washed, anointed with oils from copper flasks. Gold beads threaded through long beards were polished one by one, and more added in token of this battle. Some of the dead from castle and port were given to the sea—victor's offering of vanquished. Hundreds of them.

The horses left behind in the frantic flight from Radzyn were not the best, but they were still better than any belonging to the invaders. Saddles and bridles were studded with silver and decorated with thin, fluttering strips of beaten tin; this brave show did not hide the heaviness of their thick-haired, short-legged breed and its total unsuitability to the Long Sand. So that was why they had attacked Radzyn, he thought. Anguish stabbed his heart as he watched tack transferred to his father's beloved horses. At least the finest, strongest stock had been freed, driven into the Desert where they could later be recaptured. But it hurt even more to see foals slaughtered so that the mares would be unencumbered by nursing.

Prisoners were marched in chains to the death ship. Their captors had no interest in questioning them; they were shoved on board and made to kneel. The dead were then placed slowly, reverently, all with their heads toward the sea. Torches were lit and flung on deck. By their light, as oil on naked flesh caught fire, he saw gold-beaded beards shrivel away to reveal, in the instants before flames charred flesh, ritual scars cut into jutting chins slack now in death.

The mightiest of the warriors put their shoulders to the task of pushing the ship out to catch the tide. Then all stood onshore to watch the flames. He knew the prisoners, the sacrifices, were screaming. He could see mouths agape, the swell and collapse of chests laboring for air enough to scream. But he could not hear them.

The port was afire, too. Three great conflagrations—castle, town, and death ship drifting out to sea—lit the dusk, rivaled the sunset blaze. Yes, they would see the glow all the way to Graypearl—if anyone was left at Graypearl to see it.

Radzyn's dead were left to rot on the beaches. He recognized some of them. There was a heart-stopping moment when he thought he saw his eldest brother's face, eyes staring sightlessly at the sky. But it wasn't Maarken. The blue eyes were Sorin's—and only then did he realize that this was but a dream. Sorin had died near Elktrap, far to the north.

Andry woke in a shaking sweat, gulping for air. The soft red-gold glow of a brazier was pale mimicry of the fires he had seen in his sleep. He watched the small, warm flames until his eyes burned, then turned over in bed and hugged the covers around his trembling body.

Andrade had had dreams, visions. So had Sioned. Andry believed in this one, this new aspect of the horrors he had seen years ago. Nine years ago today, in fact. Radzyn in flames, the hundreds of dead, the total destruction—these things were familiar. But now he could put faces and customs to the enemy. They were not sorcerers. They were only men. Merida, league of assassins, scarred on the chin—in token of the first murder, perhaps? He didn't know; it didn't matter. They had done—would do—this. Unless he could stop it somehow.

He calmed himself and sat up, swinging his legs over the edge of the bed. It was chilly in Princemarch, hinting at another long, rainy winter. He wrapped himself in his cloak and rose to pace the narrow room. Even his rings were cold on his fingers; he held his hands over the brazier to warm them.

The stones had a dark glitter, reflecting his thoughts. Ten rings indicating greater rank and power than any other Sunrunner—yet he was helpless to prevent the slaughter foreseen in his visions.

His fists clenched. He would not be helpless; he refused to be. He must strive and struggle, with no one to understand fully why he did what he did. They wouldn't believe him even if he explained. Why couldn't they trust in him?

In the aftermath of his victory over Ruval, Pol had done exactly as he pleased. He hadn't waited until the *Rialla* to marry Meiglan—but he had waited until Andry had left Stronghold, so that other Sunrunners and Rohan would be the ones to preside over the ceremony. As for Miyon, it was rumored that Rohan had given him one hellacious lecture in private, but had let him go free. Andry clenched his fists in his bitterness. The Cunaxan prince had given aid and opportunity to Ruval and his brother who had killed Sorin—and yet Rohan had let him go free.

Pol had also gotten his way over trade. Miyon could scarcely do otherwise than agree to everything proposed regarding Cunaxa, Tiglath, and Feruche, which was now officially Riyan's. As was Ruala. Their children would be sorcerers—and out of Andry's reach.

But there were plenty of others he could find and eliminate. That was why he was secretly in Princemarch.

Pol had even done the seemingly impossible: dragons had hatched in the caves at Rivenrock for the first time in twenty-seven years. Somehow, between the communication established with the dragonsire—whom Pol had named Azhdeen, "dragon brother," in a display of nauseating conceit—and the cleansing of the canyon with Sunrunner's Fire, the dragons had decided to use the caves there again. Feylin had been ecstatic, of course, when fully one hundred and eighty-nine hatchlings had flown from Rivenrock, Feruche, and elsewhere. The total dragon population was over three hundred and fifty. Along with Pol's princedom, dragons were secure. More accolades accrued to Pol's name, more respect for his gifts and his power.

Andry knew that none of it mattered. Not compared to what was to come.

Chiana had been excused her folly. She truly had been ensorcelled, unlike Miyon, who had merely claimed to be. Andry remembered watching her hysterical tears through Donato's unwilling eyes as she faced Ostvel at Dragon's Rest and bleated her innocence. Rohan had chosen not to punish her—but neither she nor Miyon would be able to spit without his being notified of it. Such was the power of the High Prince, Andry told himself acidly.

Geir of Waes had died, some said from one of his own archer's arrows. No one spared him another thought. But Chiana and Halian would not have the giving of Waes to another *athri*. Instead, it was to be organized as a free city, along the lines of Andrade's own ancestral holding of Catha Freehold. The latter had reverted to Syr at her father's death; Waes, having now no lord at all, would be chartered as a free city until and unless Rohan decided otherwise. Such was the power of the High Prince.

Thought of Syr brought a momentary softening to his face. Princess Gemma had that summer given Prince Tilal another son, and had asked Tobin's permission to Name the boy Sorin. He was a lively child, fair-haired and gray-eyed; Andry had made a special trip to High Kirat to see him after the *Rialla*. The detour had also afforded him means to pretend he was on his way back to Goddess Keep. He had sent the majority of his party there, and himself headed into the Veresch.

This was one of the few nights he hadn't slept out in the open. With gloves hiding his rings and armbands, and riding a rather undistinguished horse, he had gone mostly unnoticed. Strangers were always remarked on in the remoteness of the mountains, but as long as his hands were hidden and he made no verbal slips, who would know that it was the Lord of Goddess Keep who traveled by? And who would credit that a man of such exalted rank would be in the Veresch at all?

Nialdan and Valeda, his only companions, were similarly disguised. She had insisted that they find an inn that night, for Nialdan was sniffling in the first stages of a head cold. Andry was not fooled; she wanted to bed him in hopes of another child, even though Chayly wasn't even a year old yet. He had gently but firmly discouraged her at his door this evening—but now he wished he'd given in. It was cold and very dark and he was alone.

He found a few wood chips to stoke the brazier, and as he replaced its lid he stared at the pattern shining crimson and gold through the iron. Butterfly wings, like lace.

Alasen had been choosing lace veils when he'd found her at Castle Crag.

The day Mireva's corpse had burned to cinders on the steps of Stronghold, Andry used the sunshine streaming through the gardens to travel to Castle Crag. Alasen was alone. She knelt on the carpet of her bedchamber, sunlight glinting off gold and silver threads woven through some of the dozens of veils billowing around her. She lifted one to the sunshine, a fragile creation of blossompink and leaf-green, her face and her long hair shadowed by the trellis pattern as if she paused behind a garden's climbing roses.

But her eyes were anxious, as if this gentle occupation was an attempted distraction from worry. The veil drifted to her knees and she bit her lip. Andry knew why she sat in the sunshine, and in private; she waited for word of the previous night's battle. From Sioned, perhaps, or Maarken or Hollis. Certainly not from him.

He touched her as softly as possible. Still, her spine stiffened and her fingers clenched. She had no training in fending off his presence—yet the darkening of her colors in the sunlight told him she would have rejected him if she could.

Goddess greeting, my lady. Set your mind at rest—all is well. Ianthe's son is dead, and the sorceress who helped him. Pol is safely the victor.

Alasen leaned forward into the light, relieved, eager for details. She didn't know how to speak across the sunlight, but it was simplicity itself to discern her thoughts from her face.

The battle happened as planned—Sioned can tell you the rest, or you can wait until the official version at the Rialla. *I'm here now only to ease your worries—and to beg a favor. Alasen—I need your help. There are more of these* diarmadh'im *hiding in the Veresch. They are the enemies of every Sunrunner, of every prince and princedom. If any of us is to be safe, these people must be found and dealt with. I need you to tell me what's said in the precincts of Castle Crag—it was one of their fortresses long ago, there may still be many of them nearby. Perhaps even working in your keep, near your children day after day! I need rumors, legends, anything that might point to someone bearing the Old Blood. With Mireva and Ruval dead, they have no hope left for power—and yet often when there seems to be no hope people join together in one final—*

Her face had changed during this reasoned plea. She stared upward at the window with horror darkening her green eyes and her lips moving soundlessly on the word *No.* It struck him to the heart to know how much she feared him.

Alasen, please! You must help me! You, your children, Pol, everyone is at risk! No one would be safe! Get me the names. Help me to prevent them from slaughtering us— because they will, given half a chance. They killed Sorin— look how close they came to killing Pol!

She leaped to her feet and ran from the sunlight, leaving the soft lace on the floor.

At the *Rialla* late that summer, Ostvel had come to him privately, grim-faced. "You spoke to her because you thought she'd listen. And she heard, all right—a plan for wholesale murder!"

"I never said that. I want them found and taken care of."

"Killed is what you mean! You'd 'take care' of my son if you could!"

"You're imagining things. You've always hated me, Ostvel. And we both know why."

A long finger stabbed toward his face. "Hold your tongue and listen to me, boy. I know what you think of me and I know what you can do about it—precisely nothing. You'd get at me through Riyan if he didn't have the protection of his rank and Pol's friendship. But there are hundreds who don't have that direct protection. Even if you didn't intend to kill them all, don't you see the danger? How could you tell guilt of sorcery from vicious rumor or spiteful lies?"

Andry condescended to smile. "You're to be their protection, I take it."

"You can have that written in stone," Ostvel assured him.

"What makes you think you could stop me, whatever I decide to do?"

"Alasen."

He hid his fury as her very name was used against him. "You set too high a value on your wife's influence with me."

"We both know differently, don't we?"

"Get out!"

"Not until I've said two things more."

"Make them brief. You're boring me."

"They're so simple even you'll understand. Neither Alasen nor I nor anyone else with a conscience will be a party to such butchery." Ostvel's eyes were the cold silver-gray of steel. "And if you ever approach my wife again, for any reason, in any way, then Lord or no Lord of Goddess Keep, I'll take you apart with my bare hands."

But Ostvel himself had given Andry what he wanted. Each of those from Princemarch who had come south to join Chiana at Mireva's command had been questioned by Ostvel's order. Though little was learned beyond the fact that she had bade them fight, each interrogation had a name and a location attached. It had been so easy to set Nialdan to read and memorize those names on parchment by the light of moons or sun.

He chafed more warmth into his fingers and smiled down at the butterfly pattern of the brazier. Ostvel's protection was worthless. And even if Alasen found out about all this—he had lost her long ago. It didn't matter anymore.

Pol himself had dealt with the traitorous Lord Morlen. The execution had taken place before the *Rialla*—a stupid move in Andry's opinion. Morlen should have been killed in front of the other princes as a warning, the way Kiele and Lyell had died for similar treachery. But he ultimately approved Pol's foolishness; not only did the execution have less of an impact for being carried out with no royal witnesses, but the cost to Pol of having to commit legal murder with his own sword had been dear—or so rumor had it. His cousin was no warrior. He lacked Rohan's ruthless practicality. Andry had more than once heard the story of how his uncle had ordered the severed right hands of Merida enemies flung at the feet of their masters. Pol would never do anything of the sort. Pol was civilized.

He did not punish the others who had risen against him with more than a few confiscations of property as examples to others within the princedom. For his wisdom and his mercy he was lauded—publicly at least. And that had been the end of it insofar as Pol was concerned.

But Andry had the names, the places. He had already discovered the sorcerers within his own ranks. Torien, his Chief Steward, was distantly related to Ostvel's first wife, Camgiwen—from whom Riyan had received his other gifts. Andry's guess was correct; a simple sorcerer's spell worked by Andry himself in Torien's presence confirmed it. Throughout the summer the two of them tested others slowly, carefully, and without arousing suspicion. Those thirty-four whose reactions indicated *diarmadhi* blood were told that the specific spell caused their rings to burn—not a lie, but not the whole truth, either. None of them were banished; they were valuable. They would never rise to important positions, and certainly none but Torien would ever learn the craft of the *devr'im*.

Thus he had set his own house in order. He trusted Torien completely—the man's horror on learning what his reaction really meant had been proof enough of his loyalties, even if Andry had not been sure of him before. The others, equally ignorant of their mixed heritage, were not even watched for signs of treachery. But Andry had to know. Still, it wasn't his Sunrunners but those unknown hundreds in the Veresch who concerned him. Pol was criminally negligent in not seeking them out. He didn't know the favor Andry was doing him—and wouldn't have thanked him if he had.

But that didn't matter, either. Nothing mattered but the eradication of key *diarmadh'im*. Mireva was gone, and Ianthe's sons, but there must be others who were capable of mounting attacks that would be discovered too late.

And after his vision in dreams tonight, he knew why they must be found. The sorcerers had long used the Merida; it was written in Lady Merisel's scrolls, and Mireva had confirmed it. The men he had seen bore the telltale chin scar. If there were no sorcerers to command them, then perhaps that vision would not come to pass.

And yet—these new details, the encompassing new scene of tonight's dream. . . . Something Chay had said nagged at him in odd moments—an implication that by working so hard to prevent his visions, perhaps he was helping them to come true. Fulfilling their prophecy, endangering the whole continent. But his father was no Sunrunner. He saw only with his eyes, not his soul. Andry had to believe that his efforts would help turn aside the horror, or he would go mad.

Five days ago he had skirted the route that led to Dragon's Rest. Yesterday he had found and dealt with a man high on Ostvel's list of those who had led the rebellion against Pol. Mindful of Mireva's words about only one *diarmadhi* parent being necessary to produce gifted offspring, Andry had moved against the entire family. And in case someone missed the point, on the door of the remote woodland dwelling Nialdan had carved a sunburst radiating Sunrunner's Fire.

He couldn't deal with them all. He wished he could, but the hope was unrealistic. He could only remove as many as possible before the winter rains began and he must return to Goddess Keep. Next spring he would begin anew with those who had eluded him this time.

A scratch at his door tore him from contemplation and he whirled. "Who's there?" he snapped.

"It's only me," said Valeda in hesitant tones quite unlike her usual brisk confidence. "May I come in, please?"

He opened the door. She, too, was wrapped in her cloak. No nightdress swept below the voluminous gray folds, and she was barefoot. He arched a brow.

"I couldn't sleep," she said, shrugging. "Neither could you, by the looks of things."

"I dreamed again."

She nodded. Several times over the last few years she had been in his bed when the nightmares came. He never told her even the broadest outline of them. He had never told anyone about his visions except his brother, who was dead, and his father—who could never understand.

"And what's your excuse for being awake?" Andry went on with a slight smile. "Bedbugs?"

"Worse. My room is next to Nialdan's, and he snores like a dragon with a stuffy nose."

"You've never seen a dragon in your life, let alone heard one. And I doubt they snore. Anyway, it's hardly his fault he caught the sniffles."

"You're going to catch them too if you don't get back into bed where it's warm," she scolded.

"What about you? You're barefoot."

"Goddess, but you have a welcoming way with you."

When they lay together under the thin blanket and both their cloaks, Andry murmured, "I'm glad you're here."

"Compliments?" she riposted drowsily. "Whatever did I do to deserve this?"

"You're here, and you're warm." *And that's all*, he added silently.

The next noon he found the woman he sought. She was a few winters younger than Mireva and lived alone in a tiny cottage built half into a huge tree trunk. She answered readily enough to the name on Ostvel's list, a name that appeared several times in connection with those who had assembled at Mireva's order. But she professed to be only a lonely widow who lived simply in the forest, making the occasional sack of taze to sell or trade, working the occasional harmless cure for sick animals or a lover's woes.

Andry was scrupulous about making absolutely certain of *diarmadhi* heritage in these encounters. Most of the others had made it easy for him by attempting spells in their own defense. But few had ever studied the Star Scroll, and thus they were no threat. He admired this one's stubbornness, believed not a word of her protestations, and adhered to his self-imposed dictates about being sure.

There was a small, deep pond conveniently nearby. He had Nialdan throw her into it. A Sunrunner would have reacted with equal violence, would also have thrashed about and screamed for help. But a Sunrunner would have grown sick and disoriented, and drowned very quickly. This woman did not. She swallowed a lot of water and put up a good show, but finally swam to the pond's edge. Nialdan dispatched her with a single cut of his sword. While Valeda set about burning the corpse,

Andry watched as Nialdan carved a sunburst into the fallen tree.

"Mark of the Goddess and her Sunrunners," Nialdan said with satisfaction.

"People cannot fear what they understand." He heard his father's words and in his mind replied, *Exactly.* Leaving that proud sunburst behind would trumpet mysterious *faradhi* power through the forest silence. Perhaps it would become a sign of good luck—people would move into the abandoned dwellings and consider themselves protected against harm by the carving on their new doors. The notion amused him.

Occasionally he had twinges of conscience. Not at what he was doing; he believed in his actions with all his soul. But every so often he trembled slightly at what Alasen would think if she knew. Surely she would find out once rumors spread of unexplained disappearances and symbols left behind.

Too, perhaps Ostvel had been right, and innocents would die along with the guilty. But whenever he thought such things, he remembered scarred faces and the bloodreddened sea, and Radzyn in flames. If a few died by mistake in the eradication of sorcerers who could command an army of Merida to such destruction, that was an acceptable price. Alasen's hatred was more difficult for him to bear. But one day she would understand. He would save her—and all the rest of them—from what his visions had shown him. She would understand and forgive.

Let Pol mate with his pale, pretty Meiglan and rule Princemarch for as long as he could. Let Rohan and Sioned and all of them live in contented ignorance as long as they could. Andry knew what was to come—and whatever he must do to prevent it, this he would do and gladly.

He had been chosen by the Goddess to receive this vision of the future. She had also given him the power to prevent it.

Andry ducked under the low doorway into the dimness of the cottage. All was sparse and simple within—chair, table, and bed, a few plates, cups, and bowls on a shelf, and a small dead hearth with a copper pot and an iron kettle. The place smelled wonderful—drying herbs hung from the rafters, their tingly scents offset by the moist richness of the living tree that formed the back of the dwelling. Nothing out of the ordinary, nothing to indicate the woman had been other than what she claimed.

But from dim recesses came the wink of half-hidden silver. Andry approached cautiously. A fine old tapestry patterned in flowers and herbs was draped over something nearly his own height, a frame peeking from its folds.

Andry tugged the material away and caught his breath. A mirror—oval, surmounted by a triple pointed arch, beveled at the outer edges, without a speck or a ripple in the glass—but without reflection. His own face should have looked out at him. But there was only the silver-gray mist.

There had been no mirrors in the other *diarmadhi* dwellings. Mireva had used one to control Chiana—and to make her shatter it, to Andry's vexation. Nothing in the Star Scroll made mention of their use in sorcery except that order to destroy them. Mirror spells must be the province of the very powerful. And here was a beautiful mirror for his experimentation—if only he could discover its secret.

He inspected the frame, awed by its workmanship. He might have expected stars or some similar motif; instead, winding up each side were *dranath* leaves carved in silver. Hints of ancient enamel work lingered in flakes of blue and green and orange. Here and there were dents, scuff marks, and other minor damage sustained during the mirror's long service, but the whole was polished with loving care. He contemplated the serene, featureless glass for long moments. Was there a word or an act that would bring the mirror to life? Did he dare try to find out?

"I wonder what Andrade would have made of you," he murmured, as if the mirror might answer him. How might it work? Sunrunners used light—sun, moons, Fire. Sorcerers favored starlight but did not disdain other sources. He decided to chance it and conjured up a fingerflame. The mirror seemed to tremble fractionally. Encouraged, he thought the little Fire brighter, and again there was a subtle quiver, half-sensed, half-seen. But the gray haze remained. There was no image.

He glanced over his shoulder and called, "Valeda! Come in here and take a look at this!"

A wisp of—something—brushed past his mind. When he turned back to the mirror, the grayish haze was gone. Valeda had not come into the dwelling, but she was clearly reflected in the mirror. And around her body was the cool, bright spectra of her colors. The same hues he touched when he spoke with her on sunlight, or when they made love.

Andry backed up a cautious pace, frowning. At that instant Valeda stepped through the doorway and said his name. The image changed, became him.

"Andry?" She came forward. "What is it?"

"Hush!" For a few moments he stared in rapt fascination at the *aleva* surrounding his own image—fiercer colors than Valeda's, more varied. To the mirror he said, "Nialdan," and he was replaced by the tall, burly Sunrunner with his familiar pattern of blue and orange and white. "Rohan," and the mirror showed him the High Prince. To his astonishment, Rohan possessed an *aleva*—faint but noticeable, attesting to his halfling Sunrunner gift. Tobin, Chay, Maarken, and Hollis all appeared in succession at the command of their names; all but his father had the telltale aura of color, and even he was surrounded by the same hint as Rohan.

At last, agonizingly, Andry spoke his twin brother's name. But the mirror went blank. No one not alive could be reflected in this mirror.

Valeda gripped his arm. "Andry," she began—and his image instantly showed again in the mirror, startling them both.

As casually as he could, he said, "An interesting trick, but to what purpose?"

"I don't much care," she replied nervously. "Let's get out of here."

"We're taking the mirror with us."

"How? It's as tall as I am, and bound to be heavy."

He considered, and was forced to admit she was right. "Then we'll hide it, and send someone later to retrieve it."

"Why? It's of no real use."

"Why are you so afraid of it?"

"I'm not afraid—at least, no more than any Sunrunner confronted with one of the tools of sorcery."

"I wonder what it would show for someone who also has *diarmadhi* blood," he mused, then said, "Riyan."

The mirror went black.

"Riyan," he said again.

Nothing. Andry thought this over, then shrugged. "Chiana," he said, and the Princess of Meadowlord appeared—without an aura of color, for she was not even a halfling *faradhi*. As with the other images, Chiana looked oddly lifeless; the mirror presented unmoving portraits, not views of people such as might be conjured by a skilled Sunrunner in Fire.

"There really doesn't seem to be much use for it," Andry remarked, disappointed. "If it was really useful, it'd show me what these people are doing right now."

"You play with that awful thing as you wish," Valeda snapped. "I'm not coming near it again." And she strode out.

He was too intrigued by the mirror to care what she thought. On a whim he spoke the name of Goddess Keep. But evidently the mirror showed only people; gray mist clouded its surface again. He attempted a variation, wondering if the mirror would accept a more complex command, if it could reveal the living present and not just static portraits. "Princess Alasen at this moment."

Nothing.

Andry shrugged. It had been worth a try. So was something else. "Rohan on the day he married Sioned." Still nothing. A request to see them ten years in the future yielded only silvery blankness.

So. Portraits only of living persons, not future or present or past. What a waste of silver, glass, and sorcery, he thought in disgust. Still, despite the mirror's limited value, he wanted it. Extinguishing the fingerflame, he covered the mirror once more with the tapestry and considered the best method of concealment until he could send someone to fetch it. He decided to wrap it well and bury it beneath a tree outside.

Nialdan filled the doorway, blocking out most of the sunlight, as Andry was pulling the blanket and sheet from the narrow cot in the corner. "My Lord? We can leave anytime you choose."

"Help me with this, would you? Did Valeda tell you about the mirror?"

The big Sunrunner nodded without a trace of curiosity or unease. "What do you want done with it?"

"Dig a hole outside big enough to rest it in. We'll send someone for it this spring. It should be safe enough until then, don't you think?"

"Of course, my Lord." Nialdan gathered up the blanket and cloaked the mirror in its folds.

Andry gave thanks for a subordinate who never questioned and tugged the two pillows from their coverings, intending to rip up the cloth into ties to secure the sheet and blanket around the mirror.

There was something else here besides the pillow.

He nearly yelped with delight as a thin parchment came loose, much-creased and yellowed with age. His fingers shook as he picked it up. Complex formulas or notes on sorceries or some such would have been welcome. A blank page he could have dealt with; there were recipes in the Star Scroll for making ink appear where there seemed to be none. Instead, he squinted his way through a dauntingly ungrammatical letter from someone who signed himself "yor luving grandson."

Andry gave a rueful chuckle. So much for his hopes of a momentous discovery: a mirror of scant use and a barely literate note. He tore the pillow cases into strips and helped Nialdan tie them around the mirror.

"I won't need help carting this out," the Sunrunner said. "It's very light. The digging shouldn't take more than three winks of a maiden's eyelash."

Andry poked a finger into the bulging muscle of Nialdan's arm. "For you, of course. Whatever would I do without you, you bloody great tree?"

Nialdan grinned and left with the mirror firmly embraced. Andry lingered a while, wishing the woman had possessed something of real import. Still, he was lucky to have the mirror. He must remember to tell those he sent out in future to search for others. Who knew, one of them might—

In the gloom he almost missed it. There, on the shelf with the plates, was another glint of silver. *Probably nothing more interesting than a spoon*, he told himself, *which means I'll make a fool of myself again!* But he investigated anyway.

Nothing more extraordinary than a narrow circle of polished metal rested in his hand. But rolled within it was another sheet of parchment, sealed and ready to send. He inspected the clasp and saw a pattern of mountains and stars etched into the silver. This time his excitement was justified. Breaking the seal, he smoothed the parchment onto the table and conjured a fingerflame over his shoulder to read by. The translation didn't take very long. He was used to the ancient words.

Mireva received exactly what she deserved. You in your wisdom long understood this, and though I have doubted, I see now how right you always were. Our path lies in becoming Sunrunners and princes, not in killing them. Urival and Camigwen were the first of many who lived and worked at Goddess Keep. It is a satisfaction that her son now enjoys fine holdings and a place of trust with the High Prince. We may take the greatest pride in the fact that the next High Prince is one of our blood—and it will surprise even you to know that my researches have finally revealed exactly how this came to be. Mireva thought it must come through Sioned. But it is not so. His power comes from the strongest line among us. I have studied his aleva in secrecy—never satisfied with Mireva's explanation. I was frustrated by the fact that he has never used his gifts from us—his colors were all Sunrunner up until late spring of this year. But though diluted from purity by two generations—the mating with ungifted Roelstra and the faradhi *taint of Rohan, I have discerned our own beloved Lallante in him. He is her grandson—the boy born to Ianthe who did not die at Feruche.*

Andry was so stunned that his knees gave way, and he only realized it when he landed hard on the rough planks of the floor.

Ianthe's other sons never would have served; much as all of us value pure line of descent from our ancient forebears, the combination of our blood and the Sunrunners' has made Pol more powerful than any of our own people could ever be. Bitter this might be to admit; but we saw it in Urival and to a lesser extent in Camigwen and now her son Riyan. Thus it is with Pol—but his line being stronger than that which produced these others, it is only to be expected that his powers are the greater. He will be a High Prince of inestimable gifts. Under his rule, we will be safe—for he is one of us and knows it.

Andry turned the sheet over with hands that shook so hard he could barely grip the parchment. There was only a little more.

In the spring, subject to your approval, I will present myself at Dragon's Rest and learn all I can of Pol. Should he show willingness, I will reveal myself and teach him those things he needs to know about the battles you have foreseen. By the Nameless One, what a warrior he will make! I will come to you, if I may, and school myself in the details of history and defense, that Pol may be sword and shield. For he belongs not just to the Sunrunners or the common folk he rules, but to us as well.

The letter was signed by the woman Nialdan had just killed. There had been no salutation; Andry surmised that the silver circle around it was identification enough. He levered himself up off the floor. There was a bucket of clean water hanging from a nail near the hearth, and he dipped several cupfuls to flood his dry throat. Stronger drink would have been welcome, even tainted with *dranath* as it was bound to be, but he saw no wine bottles. He placed a chair at the table and sat down, still shaky but more ready now to think.

Forget for the moment whether or not this was true; should he keep it or destroy it? Would it be more valuable in his possession or was the knowledge alone enough? How could it be used? Was it really proof that Rohan and Sioned had lied all these years? Did Chay and Tobin know? Was there advantage in revealing Pol's ancestry? *Was this incredible thing true?*

The questions were coming too fast. He rubbed his temples and stared at the parchment. Keep it or destroy it?

But then he remembered its last few galling sentences about battle and Pol's prowess as a warrior. The words forming again in his mind brought him to two decisions: first, that the whole of it was true—his own visions had been too real, and this *diarmadhi* had evidently seen, too.

His second conclusion was that the letter must be destroyed. Proof though it was of Pol's heritage, the frank words about his strength and power were too dangerous. Additionally, if the letter existed, it might be seen by someone Andry might not wish to know its contents.

He conjured Fire in the hearth and burned the parchment to a crisp. When it was ash, he extinguished the flames with a thought. A pity he could not know to whom the letter had been addressed. He might have learned much before that person died.

Quelling all the insistent questions, he pocketed the silver circle and left the tree cottage. Nialdan was tamping down the last clods on top of the mirror. He replaced the shovel neatly beside the vegetable garden, kicked the soil from his boots, and gave a mighty sneeze. Andry laughed.

"Come, let's ride on and find you a hot bath somewhere. And remind me to buy you a pocket-cloth the size of a battle flag. You nearly bolted the horses with that last sneeze."

Nialdan shrugged good-naturedly and they mounted up. Andry fixed the location of the disturbed earth in his mind and glanced once more at the strange little cottage. With the next *diarmadhi*, he'd wait to inspect and question before ordering the execution.

Genealogy
(as of 719)

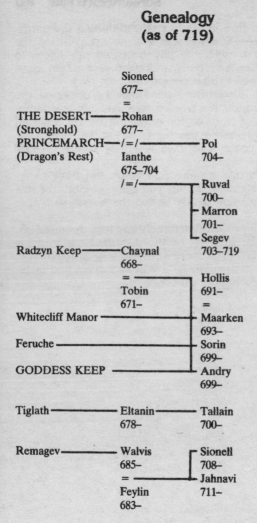

Sioned
677–
=
THE DESERT——Rohan
(Stronghold)   677–
PRINCEMARCH——/=/————— Pol
(Dragon's Rest) Ianthe   704–
                 675–704
                 /=/——————— Ruval
                                  700–
                                  Marron
                                  701–
                                  Segev
Radzyn Keep————Chaynal   703–719
                668–
                =   Hollis
                Tobin   691–
                671–   =
Whitecliff Manor —————   Maarken
                                  693–
Feruche ————————   Sorin
                                  699–
GODDESS KEEP ————   Andry
                                  699–

Tiglath————Eltanin————Tallain
            678–   700–

Remagev————Walvis————Sionell
            685–   708–
            =————————Jahnavi
            Feylin   711–
            683–

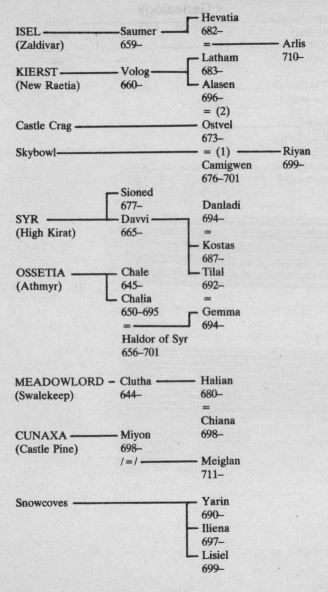

ISEL ——————— Saumer ———┌— Hevatia
(Zaldivar)   659–   682–
                              = ——————— Arlis
                                          710–
                          ┌— Latham
KIERST ——————— Volog ——┤   683–
(New Raetia)   660–   └— Alasen
                                  696–
                                  = (2)
Castle Crag ——————————————— Ostvel
                                  673–
Skybowl ————————————— = (1) ——————— Riyan
                              Camigwen   699–
                              676–701

                      ┌— Sioned
                      │   677–   Danladi
SYR ——————————┤   Davvi ——┤   694–
(High Kirat)   665–   =
                                      └— Kostas
                                          687–
OSSETIA ——————┌— Chale   Tilal
(Athmyr)   │   645–   692–
                  └— Chalia   =
                      650–695   ┌— Gemma
                      = —————————┘   694–
                      Haldor of Syr
                      656–701

MEADOWLORD – Clutha ————— Halian
(Swalekeep)   644–   680–
                                  =
                                  Chiana
CUNAXA ——————— Miyon   698–
(Castle Pine)   698–
                     /=/ ——————————— Meiglan
                                      711–

Snowcoves ————————————┌— Yarin
                          │   690–
                          ├— Iliena
                          │   697–
                          └— Lisiel
                              699–

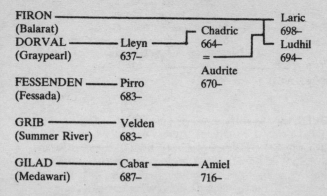

FIRON ——————————————————— Laric
(Balarat)   ┌ Chadric   698–
DORVAL ———— Lleyn ————┤ 664–   └ Ludhil
(Graypearl)   637–   └ =————   694–
                             Audrite
FESSENDEN ——— Pirro   670–
(Fessada)   683–

GRIB ————— Velden
(Summer River) 683–

GILAD ————— Cabar ————— Amiel
(Medawari)   687–   716–

Index of Characters

ABIDIAS (658–701). Lord of Tuath Castle. Died of Plague.
ADILIA (697–). Mother of Miyon's bastard daughter Meiglan.
AJIT (657–719). Prince of Firon. Killed by Pandsala.
ALASEN of Kierst (696–). Volog's daughter. m719 Ostvel.
ALLUN (685–). Lord of Lower Pyrme. m719 Kiera.
AMIEL of Gilad (716–). Son of Cabar and Kenza.
*ANDRADE of Catha Freehold (649–719). Lady of Goddess Keep 677–719. Twin sister of Milar. Killed by sorcery.
*ANDRY of Radzyn Keep (699–). Lord of Goddess Keep. Son of Chay and Tobin; Sorin's twin.
ANTALYA of Waes (679–701). m698 Eltanin. Mother of Tallain. Died of Plague.
ANTO. Guard at Dragon's Rest.
ARLIS of Kierst-Isel (710–). Son of Latham and Hevatia; heir to both princedoms.
*ARPALI (704–). At Tiglath.
ATHIL (680–703). Father of Ianthe's son Segev; killed by Ianthe.
AUDRITE of Sandeia (670–). m692 Chadric. Mother of Ludhil, Laric.

BARIG of Gilad. Cousin to Cabar.
BIRANI of Kierst (688–). m708 Obram of Isel.

CABAR (687–). Prince of Gilad. m705 Kenza. Father of Amiel.
*CAMIGWEN (676–701). m698 Ostvel. Mother of Riyan. Died of Plague.
CHADRIC of Dorval (664–). m692 Audrite. Father of Ludhil, Laric. Fostered at Stronghold 677; knighted 683.
CHALE (645–). Prince of Ossetia.
CHALIA of Ossetia (650–695). Chale's sister. m680 Haldor of Syr. Mother of Jastri, Gemma.

CHANDAR. Guard at Castle Crag.
CHAYNAL (668–). Lord of Radzyn Keep. m690 Tobin.
Father of Maarken, Jahni, Andry, Sorin. Battle Commander of the Desert 695–.
CHELAN (670–). Father of Ianthe's son Ruval.
CHIANA (698–). Roelstra's daughter by Palila. m719
Halian.
CIPRIS (687–708). Roelstra's daughter by Surya; killed by
Pandsala.
CLADON (681–). Lord of River Ussh. Father of Edrel.
CLUTHA (644–). Prince of Meadowlord.

DAMAYAN. Guard at Dragon's Rest.
DANLADI (694–). Roelstra's daughter by Aladra. m720
Kostas.
DAVVI of River Run (665–). Lord of River Run 680–705;
Prince of Syr 705–. Sioned's brother. m686 Wisla. Father
of Kostas, Tilal, Riaza.
*DENIKER (705–). *Devri.*
*DONATO (671–). Accompanied Sioned to Desert 698. At
Castle Crag.

EDREL of River Ussh (715–). Son of Cladon.
ELTANIN (678–). Lord of Tiglath. m698 Antalya. Father of
Tallain.
*EOLIE. At Graypearl.
EVAIS (674–). Father of Ianthe's son Marron.

FEYLIN (684–). m706 Walvis. Mother of Sionell, Jahnavi.

GARIC (642–). Lord of Elktrap Manor. Grandfather of
Ruala.
GEIR of Waes (707–). Son of Kiele and Lyell.
GEMMA of Syr (694–). Daughter of Haldor and Chalia.
Fostered at High Kirat 704–719. m719 Tilal.
GENNADI of Meadowlord (667–). Regent of Waes 719–.
Daughter of Clutha.
*GERIK. Ancient Sunrunner.
*GEVLIA (705–). Itinerant in Gilad.

HALDOR (656–701). Prince of Syr. m680 Chalia. Father of
Jastri, Gemma. Died of Plague.
HALIAN of Meadowlord (680–). Son of Clutha. m719 Chiana.

HEVATIA of Isel (682–). m707 Latham. Mother of Arlis.
*HOLLIS (691–). m719 Maarken.

IANTHE of Princemarch (676–704). Lady of Feruche 699–704.
Roelstra's daughter. Mother of Ruval, Marron, Segev,
Pol. Killed by Ostvel.
IAVOL. Steward at Castle Crag.
ILIENA of Snowcoves (697–). Sister of Lisiel, Yarin.
INOAT of Ossetia (644–719). Father of Jos. Killed by
Pandsala.

JAHNAVI of Remagev (711–). Son of Walvis and Feylin.
JAHNI of Radzyn Keep (693–701). Son of Chay and Tobin;
Maarken's twin. Died of Plague.
JELENA (689–701). Roelstra's daughter by Palila. Died of
Plague.
JOFRA. Guard at Castle Crag.
*JOLAN (702–). *Devri.*
JOS of Ossetia (709–719). Son of Inoat. Killed by Pandsala.

KABIL (692–). Lord of Tuath Castle. Grandfather of Rabisa.
KENZA (683–). m705 Cabar. Mother of Amiel.
KIELE (681–719). Roelstra's daughter by Karayan. m704
Lyell. Mother of Geir, Lyela. Executed.
*KLEVE (681–719). Itinerant Sunrunner killed by Masul.
KOLYA (696–). Lord of Kadar Water.
KOSTAS of River Run (687–). Davvi's son. Fostered at
Fessada 700; knighted 708.

LALLANTE of The Mountain (655–679). m673 Roelstra.
Mother of Naydra, Lenala, Pandsala, Ianthe.
LAMIA (683–701). Roelstra's daughter. Died of Plague.
LARIC of Dorval (698–). Prince of Firon 719–. Son of
Chadric and Audrite. Fostered at High Kirat 710; knighted
718.
LAROSHIN. Guards commander at Dragon's Rest.
LATHAM of Kierst (683–). Son of Volog. m707 Hevatia.
Father of Arlis.
LENALA of Princemarch (674–701). Roelstra's daughter.
Died of Plague.
LISIEL of Snowcoves (699–). Sister of Iliena, Yarin.
LLEYN (637–). Prince of Dorval. m660 Aliana of Adni
River. Father of Chadric.

LUDHIL of Dorval (694–). Son of Chadric and Audrite. Fostered at Fessada 705; knighted 714.

LYELA of Waes (709–). Daughter of Kiele and Lyell.

LYELL (683–719). Lord of Waes. m704 Kiele. Father of Geir, Lyela. Executed.

*MAARKEN of Radzyn Keep (693–). Lord of Whitecliff. Chay and Tobin's son; Jahni's twin. Fostered at Graypearl 702; knighted 712. At Goddess Keep 712–719. m719 Hollis.

MAETA (670–719). Commander of Stronghold guard. Myrdal's daughter. Killed at Castle Crag.

MARRON of Feruche (701–). Ianthe's son by Evais.

MASUL (698–719). Pretender to the throne of Princemarch. Killed by Rohan.

*MEATH (673–). Accompanied Sioned to Desert 698. At Graypearl 698–.

MEIGLAN of Gracine Manor (710–). Miyon's bastard daughter.

*MERISEL. Ancient Sunrunner.

MILAR of Catha Freehold (649–701). m670 Zehava. Andrade's twin. Mother of Tobin, Rohan. Died of Plague.

MIREVA (659–). *Diarmadhi*. Lallante's kinswoman.

MIYON (689–). Prince of Cunaxa. Father of Meiglan.

MORIA (684–). Roelstra's daughter.

MORLEN. Lord of Rezeld Manor.

*MORWENNA (684–). At Goddess Keep.

MOSWEN (692–). Roelstra's daughter.

MYRDAL (645–). Commander of Stronghold guard 675–703. Maeta's mother; Zehava's bastard cousin.

NARAT (667–). Lord of Port Adni. m705 Naydra.

NAYATI (684–717). Roelstra's daughter. Killed by Pandsala.

NAYDRA of Princemarch (673–). Roelstra's daughter. m705 Narat.

*NIALDAN (703–). *Devri*.

OBRAM of Isel (680–711). m708 Birani. Killed by Pandsala.

*OCLEL (705–). *Devri*.

OSTVEL (673–). Lord of Castle Crag. Second Steward of Goddess Keep 695–698; Chief Steward of Stronghold 698–705; Lord of Skybowl 705–719; Regent of Princemarch

719–. m (1) 698 Camigwen; (2) 719 Alasen. Father of Riyan.

*OTHANEL (706–). At Goddess Keep.

*PALEVNA (678–). Mother of Othanel. Accompanied Sioned to the Desert 698.

PALILA (669–698). Roelstra's mistress. Executed.

*PANDSALA of Princemarch (675–719). Roelstra's daughter. Regent of Princemarch 705–719. Killed by Segev.

PATWIN (691–). Lord of Catha Heights. m789 Rabia. Father of Izaea, Sangna, Aurar.

PAVLA (687–713). Roelstra's daughter. m713 Ajit. Killed by Pandsala.

PIMANTAL (657–). Prince of Fessenden.

POL of Princemarch (704–). Rohan's bastard son by Ianthe. Fostered at Graypearl 716–.

RABIA (693–715). Roelstra's daughter. m709 Patwin. Mother of Izaea, Sangna, Aurar. Killed by Pandsala.

RABISA of Tuath Castle (712–). Kabil's granddaughter and heiress.

RIALT (701–). Chamberlain at Dragon's Rest.

*RIYAN (699–). Lord of Skybowl. Son of Ostvel and Camigwen. Fostered at Swalekeep 711–713; Goddess Keep 713–717; Swalekeep 717–719; knighted 719.

ROELSTRA (653–704). High Prince 665–704. m673 Lallante. Father of Naydra, Lenala, Pandsala, Ianthe; Gevina, Rusalka, Alieta, Nayati; Kiele, Lamia; Moria, Cipris; Pavla, Jelena, Moswen, Rabia, Chiana; Danladi. Killed by Rohan.

ROHAN (677–). Prince of the Desert 698–; High Prince 705–. Fostered at Remagev 690; knighted 695. m698 Sioned. Father of Pol.

*ROSSEYN. Ancient Sunrunner.

RUALA of Elktrap Manor (700–). Granddaughter and heiress of Garic.

RUSALKA (680–712). Roelstra's daughter. Killed by Pandsala.

*RUSINA (708–). Devri.

RUVAL of Feruche (700–). Ianthe's son by Chelan.

SAUMER (659–). Prince of Isel. Father of Obram, Hevatia.

SEGEV of Feruche (703–719). Ianthe's son by Athil. Killed by Hollis.

*SIONED of River Run (677–). Sister of Davvi. m698 Rohan.
Princess of the Desert 698–; High Princess 705–.
SIONELL of Remagev (708–). Daughter of Walvis and Feylin.
SORIN of Radzyn Keep (699–). Lord of Feruche. Son of
Chay and Tobin; Andry's twin. Fostered at New Raetia
711; knighted 719.

TALLAIN of Tiglath (700–). Fostered at Stronghold 713–.
THACRI. Giladan master weaver.
THANYS (683–). *Diarmadhi* servant to Meiglan.
TIBAYAN (642–714). Lord of Lower Pyrme. Father of
Allun. Killed by Pandsala.
TIBALIA. Head of maidservants at Stronghold.
TILAL of River Run (692–). Davvi's son; Kostas' brother.
m719 Gemma. Fostered at Stronghold 702; knighted 712.
*TOBIN of the Desert (671–). m690 Chaynal. Mother of
Maarken, Jahni, Sorin, Andry.
*TORIEN (697–). *Devri*.

*URIVAL (653–). Chief Steward of Goddess Keep 681–.

*VALEDA (700–). *Devri*.
VAMANA (658–686). Roelstra's mistress.
*VAMANIS (700–). At Swalekeep.
VELDEN (683–). Prince of Grib. m708 Gaela.
VOLNAYA of Kierst (702–). Volog's younger son.
VOLOG (659–). Prince of Kierst. m689 Gyula. Father of
Latham, Birani, Alasen, Volnaya.

WALVIS (685–). Lord of Remagev. m706 Feylin. Fostered
at Stronghold 697; knighted 703. Father of Sionell, Jahnavi.
WISLA of River View (663–717). m686 Davvi. Mother of
Kostas, Tilal, Riaza.

YARIN of Snowcoves (690–). Brother of Iliena, Lisiel.

ZEHAVA (638–698). Prince of the Desert. m670 Milar.
Father of Tobin, Rohan. Killed by a dragon
ZEL. Guard at Dragon's Rest.

Genetics

The *faradhi* gene is recessive; the *diarmadhi* gene is dominant. Simply put, think of the Sunrunner gene as being like that for blue eyes, and the sorcerer gene as similar to that for dark hair; they have nothing to do with each other genetically, but the combination—used perceptively—can be startling.

ff: full Sunrunner. Almost all are unable to cross water without becoming violently ill. All are vulnerable to death by iron while working.

fx: "halfling gift." Possible seasickness; in particularly strong bloodlines, an itchy feeling around the edges of consciousness when spells are being worked. Cannot be trained as a Sunrunner.

Dxx: full sorcerer. No difficulty crossing water; not as susceptible to iron; vulnerable to mirror spells. Can be trained as a Sunrunner, as can all with the *diarmadhi* gene; also, all with this gene who wear *faradhi* rings feel them burn in the presence of a sorcerer's working, but if they themselves are doing the spell, the rings only tremble a little as if in protest.

Dff: full sorcerer and full Sunrunner. Most cannot cross water comfortably;

Dfx: full sorcerer; halfling Sunrunner. Same as above, but vulnerable to mirrors.

xx: no "magical" genes at all. Susceptible under influence of *dranath* to a powerful mind's suggestions, especially *diarmadh'im* using a mirror.

Offspring of *faradh'im*

ff = fx	ff; fx
ff = xx	fx
fx = xx	fx; xx
fx = fx	ff; fx; xx

Offspring of *diarmadh'im*

Dxx = Dff	Dfx
Dxx = Dfx	Dfx; Dxx
Dff = Dfx	Dff; Dfx
Dxx = xx	Dxx
Dff = xx	Dfx
Dfx = xx	Dfx; Dxx

Offspring of both

ff = Dxx	Dfx
ff = Dff	Dff
ff = Dfx	Dff; Dfx
fx = Dxx	Dfx; Dxx
fx = Dff	Dff; Dfx
fx = Dfx	Dff; Dfx; Dxx

Examples:

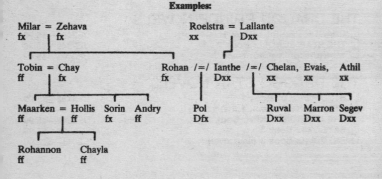

Milar = Zehava
fx   fx

Tobin = Chay
ff   fx

Maarken = Hollis   Sorin   Andry
ff   ff   fx   ff

Rohannon   Chayla
ff   ff

Roelstra = Lallante
xx   Dxx

Rohan /=/ Ianthe /=/ Chelan, Evais, Athil
fx   Dxx   xx   xx   xx

Pol   Ruval   Marron Segev
Dfx   Dxx   Dxx   Dxx

Melanie Rawn

EXILES

☐ **THE RUINS OF AMBRAI: Book 1**   UE2668—$5.99
☐ **THE RUINS OF AMBRAI: Book 1** (hardcover)   UE2619—$20.95
☐ **THE MAGEBORN TRAITOR: Book 2** (hardcover)   UE2730—$23.95

Three Mageborn sisters bound together by ties of their ancient Blood Line are forced to take their stands on opposing sides of a conflict between two powerful schools of magic. Together, the sisters will fight their own private war, and the victors will determine whether or not the Wild Magic and the Wraithenbeasts are once again loosed to wreak havoc upon their world.

THE DRAGON PRINCE NOVELS

☐ **DRAGON PRINCE : Book 1**   UE2450—$5.99
☐ **THE STAR SCROLL: Book 2**   UE2349—$5.99
☐ **SUNRUNNER'S FIRE: Book 3**   UE2403—$5.99

THE DRAGON STAR NOVELS

☐ **STRONGHOLD: Book 1**   UE2482—$5.99
☐ **STRONGHOLD: Book 1** (hardcover)   UE2440—$21.95
☐ **THE DRAGON TOKEN: Book 2**   UE2542—$5.99
☐ **SKYBOWL: Book 3**   UE2595—$5.99
☐ **SKYBOWL: Book 3** (hardcover)   UE2541—$22.00

Buy them at your local bookstore or use this convenient coupon for ordering.

PENGUIN USA P.O. Box 999—Dep. #17109, Bergenfield, New Jersey 07621

Please send me the DAW BOOKS I have checked above, for which I am enclosing $_____ (please add $2.00 to cover postage and handling). Send check or money order (no cash or C.O.D.'s) or charge by Mastercard or VISA (with a $15.00 minimum). Prices and numbers are subject to change without notice.

Card #_____ Exp. Date _____
Signature_____
Name_____
Address_____
City _____ State _____ Zip Code _____

For faster service when ordering by credit card call **1-800-253-6476**

Allow a minimum of 4-6 weeks for delivery. This offer is subject to change without notice.